Praise for the book

"I predict [The Almond Tree] will become one of the biggest best-sellers of the decade . . ."

". . . an epic drama of the proportions of *The Kite Runner*, but set in Palestine. A story that grabs you from the first page and makes your heart go out to the Palestinians without pointing fingers at anyone. This novel is not a political lecture, but a gripping and compassionate work of fiction."

Guillermo Fesser, Spanish TV and Radio Host, Huffington Post

"The story is spell-binding with universal appeal and has potential of becoming an international best-seller and can do for Palestinians what *The Kite Runner* did for Afghanis."

The Daily Star

"Arguably the most important book of the year."

Dream Crazy Book Reviews

"The prose is as evocative as it is powerful . . ."

The Hindu Business Line

". . . a moving and powerful novel based on historical events, which the writer weaves together harmoniously. . . . It is the type of story that will keep you wondering where reality ends and fiction starts."

Jamal Kanj, author of* Children of Catastrophe, *Gulf Daily News

"Corasanti's tale of resilience, hope, and forgiveness is a must-read . . ."

Washington Report on the Middle East

". . . a strong addition to coming-of-age fiction collections . . . highly recommended."

The Midwest Book Review

"Corasanti's accomplished debut novel offers a humanistic look into the Israeli-Palestinian conflict. . . . Sensitive, moving . . . a complex novel as necessary as ever."

Kirkus Reviews

". . . one of the most riveting books I have read. Corasanti takes a realistic premise and builds an interesting and highly believable story that only gets better as the pages fly by. . . . I highly recommend this book."

Charline Ratcliff / Rebecca's Reads

"Beautifully written."

". . . exhibits an inherent knowledge of life in the Occupied Palestinian Territories and Gaza."

"Corasanti's elaboration of history and fiction has created a touching narration which ensnares the reader from the first chapter."

Middle East Monitor

". . . told in a manner that strongly resembles the voice and narrative used by Khaled Hosseini in his popular novel, *The Kite Runner.*"

"A Palestinian tale told by a Jewish American."

The Times of Israel

"*The Almond Tree* has all the makings of a best-seller or a Hollywood film. It is a rags-to-riches (in this case tent-dweller to international award-winner) tale with love, suffering, death, and justice thrown into the mix."

***Selma Dabbagh, The Electronic Intifada, author of* Out of It**

". . . an engaging novel with an impressive degree of empathy and authenticity. It reads like a combination of *Mornings in Jenin* and *The Kite Runner.*"

***Pamela Olson, Mondoweiss, author of* Fast times in Palestine**

THE ALMOND TREE

Michelle Cohen Corasanti

To Sarah and Jon-Robert

"That which is hateful to you, do not unto another: This is the whole Torah. The rest is commentary—[and now] go study." Rabbi Hillel *(30 BC–10 AD), one of the greatest rabbis of the Talmudic era.*

To Joe who gave me the courage to embrace what I would have preferred to bury.

The seeds for this story were planted over twenty years ago. While still in high school, I went to live abroad in search of fun, adventure and parental freedom. Initially, I had wanted to go to Paris, but my parents rejected that idea and sent me, instead, to Israel for the summer with the rabbi's daughter. Uninformed of the situation there, at that time, I thought Palestinian was a synonym for Israeli. Seven years later, I returned to the US, more knowledgeable than I would have liked.

Idealistic, I wanted to help bring about peace in the Middle East. After a few years in graduate and law school in the states, I decided I just wanted to save myself. When I met my husband, I disclosed to him my experiences. He said I had a story. Unready, I buried it. But the past has a way of clawing its way out. I'd like to believe that I needed the perspective those twenty years gave me to write this story.

I'd like to thank my husband Joe for helping me with the research and writing of this book and my children, Jon-Robert and Sarah, for making me want to make this world a better place. I'd like to acknowledge my great editors who taught me how to put my story into words: diligent Mark Spencer, knowledgeable Masha Hamilton, capable Marcy Dermansky, my mother-in-law Connie who corrected every version, efficient Teresa Merritt and the talented Pamela Lane.

A special thanks to my editor Les Edgerton who really helped to make this book happen. My gratitude goes to Caitlin Dosch and Christopher Greco for their help with the science and maths problems. Much credit also goes to Nathan Stock from The Carter Center for his help and expertise, especially on Gaza. Finally, I'd like to thank the talented Shikha Sabharwal and my publisher Fingerprint!, my fabulous agent Kanishka, my great friend Abdullah Khan, and the brilliant Moe Diab.

PART ONE
1955

1

Mama always said Amal was mischievous. It was a joke we shared as a family—that my sister, just a few years old and shaky on her pudgy legs, had more energy for life than me and my younger brother Abbas combined. So when I went to check on her and she wasn't in her crib, I felt a fear in my heart that gripped me and would not let go.

It was summer and the whole house breathed slowly from the heat. I stood alone in her room, hoping the quiet would tell me where she'd stumbled off to. A white curtain caught a breeze. The window was open—wide open. I rushed to the ledge, praying that when I looked over she wouldn't be there, she wouldn't be hurt. I was afraid to look, but I did anyway because not knowing was worse. *Please God, please God, please God . . .*

There was nothing below but Mama's garden: colourful flowers moving in that same wind.

Downstairs, the air was filled with delicious smells, the big table laden with yummy foods. Baba and I loved sweets, so Mama was making a whole lot of them for our holiday party tonight.

'Where's Amal?' I stuck a date cookie in each of my pockets when her back was turned. One for me and the other for Abbas.

'Napping.' Mama poured the syrup onto the baklava.

'No, Mama, she's not in her crib.'

'Then where is she?' Mama put the hot pan in the sink and cooled it with water that turned to steam.

'Maybe she's hiding?'

Mama's black robes brushed across me as she rushed to the stairs. I followed closely, keeping quiet, ready to earn the treats in my pocket by finding her first.

'I need help.' Abbas stood at the top of the stairs with his shirt unbuttoned.

I gave him a dirty look. I had to make him understand that I was helping Mama with a serious problem.

Abbas and I followed Mama into her and Baba's room. Amal wasn't under their big bed. I pulled open the curtain that covered the place where they kept their clothes, expecting to find Amal crouching with a big smile, but she wasn't there. I could tell Mama was getting really scared. Her dark eyes flashed in a way that made me scared too.

'Don't worry Mama,' Abbas said. 'Ahmed and I will help you find her.'

Mama put her fingers to her lips to tell Abbas and me not to speak as we crossed the hall to our younger brothers' room. They were still sleeping, so she went in on tiptoes and motioned for us to stay outside. She knew how to be quieter than Abbas and me. But Amal was not there.

Abbas looked at me with scared eyes and I patted him on the back.

Downstairs, Mama called to Amal, over and over. She ransacked the living and dining rooms, ruining all the work she had put in for the holiday dinner with Uncle Kamal's family.

When Mama ran to the sunroom, Abbas and I followed. The door to the courtyard was open. Mama gasped.

From the big window we spotted Amal running down the meadow towards the field in her nightgown.

Mama was in the courtyard in seconds. She cut right through her garden, crushing her roses, the thorns tearing at her robe. Abbas and I were right behind her.

'Amal!' Mama screamed. 'Stop!' My sides hurt from running, but I kept going. Mama stopped so fast at 'the sign' that Abbas and I ran right into her. Amal was in *the field*. I couldn't breathe.

'Stop!' Mama screamed. 'Don't move!'

Amal was chasing a big red butterfly, her black curly hair bouncing. She turned and looked at us. 'I get it,' she chuckled, pointing at the butterfly.

'No, Amal!' Mama used her strictest voice. 'Don't move.'

Amal stood completely still and Mama blew air out of her mouth.

Abbas dropped to his knees, relieved. We were never, ever, supposed to go past the sign. That was the devil's field.

The pretty butterfly landed about four metres in front of Amal.

'No!' Mama screamed.

Abbas and I looked up.

Amal made mischievous eyes at Mama and then ran towards the butterfly.

The next part was like slow motion. Like someone threw her up in the air. Smoke and fire were under her and the smile flew away. The sound hit us—really hit us—and knocked us back. And when I looked to where she was, she was gone. Just gone. I couldn't hear anything.

And then the screams came. It was Mama's voice, then Baba's from somewhere far behind us. Then I realised that Amal wasn't gone. I could see something. I could see her arm. It was her arm, but her body wasn't attached to it anymore. I wiped my eyes. Amal was torn up like her doll after our watchdog ripped it apart. I opened my mouth and screamed so loud I felt like I was going to split in two.

Baba and Uncle Kamal ran up, panting, to the sign. Mama didn't look at them, but when they got there she began to whimper, 'My baby, my baby . . .'

Then Baba saw Amal, out there past the sign—the sign that said *Closed Area.* He lunged towards her, tears flooding down his face. But Uncle Kamal grabbed him hard with both hands. 'No . . .' He held on.

Baba tried to shake him off, but Uncle Kamal hung on. Fighting, Baba turned on his brother, screaming, 'I can't leave her!'

'It's too late.' Uncle Kamal's voice was strong.

I told Baba, 'I know where they buried the mines.'

He didn't look at me, but he said, 'Direct me in, Ahmed.'

'You're going to put your life in the hands of a child?' Uncle Kamal's face looked like he was biting into a lemon.

'He's no ordinary seven-year-old,' Baba said.

I took a step towards the men, leaving Abbas with Mama. They were both crying. 'They planted them with their hands and I made a map.'

'Go get it,' Baba said, followed by something else, but I couldn't understand him because he turned away towards the devil's field—and Amal.

So I ran as fast as I could, grabbed the map from its hiding place on the veranda, swung around for Baba's walking stick, and ran back to my family. Mama always said she didn't want me to run when I was holding Baba's stick because I could get hurt, but this was an emergency.

Baba took the stick and tapped the ground while I tried to get the wind back in me.

'Go straight from the sign,' I said. My tears blinded me, the salt stinging, but I wouldn't look away.

Baba tapped the ground in front of him before every single step and when he was about three metres out, he stopped. Amal's head was approximately a metre in front of him. Her curly hair was gone. White stuff stuck out in places where the skin was burned off. His arms weren't long enough to reach it, so he crouched and tried again. Mama gasped. I wished he'd use the stick, but I was afraid to say it to him, in case he didn't want to treat Amal that way.

'Come back,' Uncle Kamal pleaded. 'It's too dangerous.'

'The children,' Mama cried out. Baba almost fell over, but caught himself. 'They're alone in the house.'

'I'll go stay with them.' Uncle Kamal turned away and I was glad because he was making things even worse.

'Don't bring them here!' Baba called to him. 'They can't see Amal like this. And don't let Nadia come down here either.'

'Nadia!' Mama sounded like she had just heard the name of her eldest daughter for the first time. 'Nadia is at your house, Kamal, with your children.'

Uncle Kamal nodded and continued on.

Mama was on the ground next to Abbas. Tears streamed down her face. Like someone cursed and frozen in place, Abbas stared at what was left of Amal.

'Which way now, Ahmed?' Baba asked.

According to my map, there was a mine approximately two metres away from Amal's head. The sun was hot, but I felt cold. Please God, let my map be accurate. What I knew for sure was that there was no pattern because I always looked for patterns and these were random, so no one could figure them out without a map.

'Walk a metre to the left,' I said, 'and reach again.' Without even knowing it, I had been holding my breath. When Baba lifted Amal's head the air spilled out of me. He took off his kaffiyah and wrapped it around her little head, which was pretty much destroyed.

Baba reached for her arm, but it was too far away. It was hard to tell if her hand was still attached.

According to my map, there was another landmine between him and her arm, and it was up to me to direct him around it. He did exactly what I told him because he trusted me. I got him close and he gently grabbed her arm-bone and wrapped it in his kaffiyah. All that was left was her middle, and it was the furthest away.

'Don't step forward. There's a mine. Step to your left.'

Baba cuddled Amal close to his chest. Before he stepped, he tapped the ground. I guided him the whole way; it was at least twelve metres. Afterwards, I had to guide him back.

'From the sign, straight out, there aren't any mines,' I said. 'But there're two in between you and that straight line.'

I guided him forward, then sideways. Sweat dripped down my face, and when I wiped it with my hand, there was blood. I knew it was Amal's blood. I wiped it again and again, but it wouldn't come off.

Strands of Baba's black hair lifted off his face in a gust. His white kaffiyah, no longer covering it, was soaked with blood. Red blossomed down his white robe. He held Amal in his arms the way he did when she fell asleep on his lap and he carried her upstairs. Baba looked like an angel from a story bringing Amal back from the field. His broad shoulders were heaving, his eyelashes wet.

Mama was still on the ground, crying. Abbas held her, but had no more tears. He was like a little man, watching over her. 'Baba will put her back together,' he assured Mama. 'He can fix anything.'

'Baba will take care of her.' I put my hand on Abbas' shoulder.

Baba knelt next to Mama on the ground with his shoulders by his ears and rocked Amal gently. Mama leaned into him.

'Don't be scared,' Baba told Amal. 'God will protect you.' We remained like that, comforting Amal, for a long time.

'Curfew begins in five minutes,' a soldier announced through his megaphone from his military Jeep. 'Anyone found outside will be arrested or shot.'

Baba said it was too late to get a permit to bury Amal, so we brought her back home.

2

Abbas and I heard the cries before Baba. He was focused on inspecting our oranges. He was like that. His family had owned the groves for generations and he said it was in his blood.

'Baba.' I tugged on his robe and broke his trance. He dropped the oranges in his arms and ran towards the cries. Abbas and I followed closely.

'Abu Ahmed!' Mama's screams echoed off the trees. When I was born, they had changed their names to Abu Ahmed and Um Ahmed so as to include my name: that of their first son. It was the tradition of our people. Mama ran towards us with our baby sister Sara in her arms. 'Come home!' Mama gasped for air. 'They're at the house.'

I got really scared. For the last two years, when they thought Abbas and I were sleeping, my parents talked about them coming to take our land. The first time I heard them was the night Amal died. They fought because Mama wanted to bury Amal on our land so she could stay close to us and not be afraid, but Baba said no, that they'd come and take our land and then we'd either have to dig her up or leave her with them.

Baba took baby Sara from Mama's arms and we ran back to our house.

More than a dozen soldiers were fencing our land and home with barbed wire. My sister Nadia was kneeling under our olive tree holding my middle brothers Fadi and Hani while they cried. She was younger than me and Abbas, but older than the others. Mama always said she'd make a good mother because she was very nurturing.

'Can I help you?' Baba asked a soldier, between gulps of air.

'Mahmud Hamid?'

'That's me,' Baba said.

The soldier handed Baba a document.

Baba's face went white like milk. He started to shake his head. Soldiers with rifles, steel helmets, green military fatigues and heavy black boots surrounded him.

Mama pulled Abbas and me close, and I felt her heart beat through her robe.

'You have thirty minutes to pack your possessions,' the pimply-faced soldier said.

'Please,' Baba said. 'This is our home.'

'You heard me,' Pimply-face said. 'Now!'

'Stay here with the little ones,' Baba told Mama. She burst into tears.

'Keep it down,' Pimply-face said.

Abbas and I helped Baba carry out all one hundred and four of the portraits he had drawn over the last fifteen years; his art books of the great masters: Monet, Van Gogh, Picasso, Rembrandt; the money he kept in his pillow case; the oud his father made him; the silver tea set Mama's parents gave her; our dishes, cutlery, pots and pans; clothing and Mama's wedding dress.

'Time's up,' the soldier said. 'We're relocating you.'

'An adventure.' Baba's eyes were wet and shiny as he put his arm around Mama, who was still sobbing.

We loaded the wagon with our possessions. The soldiers opened a hole in the barbed-wire fence so we could get out, and Baba led the horse as we followed the soldiers up the hill. Villagers disappeared as we passed them. I looked back; they had completely fenced in our house and orange groves with barbed wire, and I could see them beyond at Uncle Kamal's, doing the same. They hammered in a sign: *Keep Out! Closed Area.* It was the same wording that was in front of the field of landmines where my little sister Amal had died.

I kept my arm around Abbas the whole time because he was crying hard, like Mama. I wept too. Baba didn't deserve that. He was a good person, worth ten of them. More: a hundred; a thousand. All of them.

They led us up the hill through thickets that cut into my legs until we finally arrived at a mud-brick hut that was smaller than our chicken coop. The garden in front was overrun with weeds, and that must have made Mama feel bad because she hated weeds. The shutters were dusty and closed. The soldier cut the lock with bolt cutters and pushed the tin door open. There was only one room, with a dirt floor. We unloaded our belongings and the soldiers left with our horse and cart.

Inside the house there were rush mats piled up in the corner. Goat skins were folded on top of them. There was a kettle in the hearth, dishes in the cabinet, clothes in the closet. Everything was covered in a thick coat of dust.

On the wall was a portrait of a husband and wife and their six children, smiling. They were in our courtyard in front of Mama's garden.

'You drew them,' I said to Baba.

'That was Abu Ali and his family,' he said.

'Where are they now?'

'With my mother and brothers and Mama's family,' he said. 'God willing, one day they'll come back, but, until then, we'll have to pack their belongings in our crate.'

'Who's this?' I pointed to the portrait of a boy my age with a thick red scar across his forehead.

'That's Ali,' Baba said. 'He loved horses. The first time he rode one, the horse bucked and Ali fell to the ground. He was unconscious for days, but when he woke, he went right back on that horse.'

Baba, Abbas and I organised our birthday portraits on the back wall in a bar graph. Across the top, Baba wrote the years, starting with 1948 until the present year, 1957. Mine was the only portrait in 1948. We continued with every year, adding the new children as they came. I was at the top followed by Abbas in 1949, Nadia in 1950, Fadi in 1951, Hani in 1953, Amal in 1954 and Sara in 1955. But there were only two portraits of Amal.

On the side walls, Baba, Abbas and I arranged the portraits of our family members who we knew were dead: Baba's father and grandparents. Next to those, we hung up our family in exile: Baba's mother embracing her ten children in front of the magnificent garden that Mama had built at Baba's family's house before they were married, when her parents were migrant workers in Baba's family's groves. When Baba came home from art school in Nazareth and saw Mama tending her garden, he had decided to marry her. Baba hung the portraits of himself and his brothers—watching their oranges loaded onto a ship at the port of Haifa, eating at a restaurant in Acre, in the market in Jerusalem, tasting the oranges of Jaffa, vacationing at a coastal resort in Gaza.

The front wall we reserved for immediate family. Baba had drawn many self-portraits while he was in art school in Nazareth. Plus there was: us having a picnic in our orange grove, my first day of school, Abbas and me at the village square looking into the box holes of the moving picture show while Abu Hussein turned the handle, and Mama in her garden—that one Baba had painted with water colours, unlike the others, which he had drawn with charcoal.

'Where are our bedrooms?' Abbas scanned the room.

'We're lucky to get a home with such a beautiful view,' Baba said. 'Ahmed, take him outside to see.' Baba handed me the telescope I'd made from two magnifying glasses and a cardboard tube. It was the same one I'd used to watch the soldiers plant the landmines in the devil's field. Behind the house, Abbas and I climbed a beautiful almond tree that overlooked the village.

Through my telescope, we took turns watching the new people, dressed in sleeveless shirts and shorts, already picking oranges from our trees. From our old bedroom window, Abbas and I had watched their land expand as they swallowed up our village. They brought in strange trees and planted them in the swamp. Right before our eyes, the trees grew fat from drinking the fetid juices. The swamp disappeared and in its place rich black topsoil appeared.

I saw their swimming pool. I moved my telescope to the left and could see across the Jordanian border. Thousands of tents with the letters UN littered the otherwise empty desert. I handed the telescope to Abbas so he could see too. One day I hoped to get a stronger lens so that I could see the refugees' faces. But I'd have to wait. For the past nine years, Baba had been unable to sell his oranges outside the village, so our market shrank from the entire Middle East and Europe to 5,024 now-poor villagers. We were once very rich, but not anymore. Baba would have to find a job, and those were hard to come by. I wondered if that would make him worry.

***

In the two years we had lived in our new house with the almond tree, Abbas and I had spent many hours in the tree watching the moshav. There we'd seen things we'd never seen before. Boys and girls, older and younger than me, held hands and formed circles and danced and sang together, their arms and legs naked. They had electricity and green lawns, and yards with swing sets and slides. And they had a swimming pool that boys and girls and men and women of all ages swam in, wearing what looked like their underwear.

Villagers complained because the new people diverted the water from our village by digging deeper wells. We weren't allowed to dig deeper wells like them. We were angry that while we had barely enough water to drink, the new people were swimming in it. But their swimming pool fascinated me. From our almond tree, I would watch the diver on the board and think how he had potential energy while he was on the platform and how that energy was converted to kinetic energy during the dive. I knew that the heat and wave energy of the swimming pool couldn't throw the diver back onto the board, and I tried to think what physical laws prevented it. The waves intrigued me in the same way that the children splashing among them fascinated Abbas.

I knew from a young age that I wasn't like the other boys in my village. Abbas was very social and had many friends. When they gathered at our house, they would speak of their hero Jamal Abdul Nasser, the President of Egypt, who had stood up to Israel in the 1956 Suez Canal Crisis and was championing Arab nationalism and the Palestinian cause. I idolised Albert Einstein.

As the Israelis controlled our curriculum, they always supplied us with ample books on the accomplishments of famous Jews. I read every book I could find on Einstein and after I fully understood the brilliance of his equation, $E=mc^2$, I was amazed at how it came to him. I wondered if he really did see a man falling from a building or if he had just imagined it while sitting in the patent office where he worked.

***

Today was the day I was going to measure how tall the almond tree was. The day before, I had planted a stick in the ground and cut it off at my eye level. Lying on the ground with my feet against the standing stick, I could see the treetop over the end of it. The stick and I made a right-angled triangle. I was the base, the stick was the perpendicular and the line of sight was the hypotenuse of the triangle. Before I could calculate the measurements, I heard footsteps.

'Son,' Baba called. 'Are you all right?'

I got up. Baba must be home from his job building houses for the Jewish settlers. None of the other fathers worked in construction, partly because they refused to build houses for the Jews on razed Palestinian villages and partly because of the Israelis' policy of 'Hebrew Labour': Jews only hired Jews. Many of the older boys at school said bad things about Baba working for the Jews.

'Join me in the courtyard. I heard a few good jokes at work today,' Baba said, before turning and walking back towards the front of the house.

I climbed back up the almond tree and looked at the barren land between our village and the moshav. Only five years earlier, it had been filled with olive trees. Now it was filled with landmines. Landmines like the one that killed my baby sister, Amal.

'Ahmed, come down,' Baba called.

I climbed down the branches.

He pulled a sugar doughnut out of the crumpled brown paper bag in his hand. 'Gadi from work gave it to me.' He smiled. 'I've saved it all day for you.' Red gel oozed from the side.

I squinted at it. 'Is that poison leaking out?'

'Why, because he's Jewish? Gadi's my friend. There are all kinds of Israelis.'

My stomach contracted. 'Everyone says the Israelis want to see us dead.'

'When I sprained my ankle at work, it was Gadi who drove me home. He lost a half-day's pay to help me.' He extended the doughnut towards my mouth. 'His wife made it.'

I crossed my arms. 'No thanks.'

Baba shrugged and took a bite. His eyes closed. He chewed slowly. Then he licked the particles of sugar that had gathered on his upper lip. Opening one eye just a little, he glanced down at me. Then he took another bite, savouring it in the same way.

My stomach growled and he laughed. Once again he offered it to me, saying, 'One cannot live on anger, my son.'

I opened my mouth and allowed him to feed it to me. It was delicious. An image of Amal rose, unbidden, in my mind, and suddenly I was overwhelmed with guilt at the flavour in my mouth. But . . . I kept eating.

3

A brass tray of coloured tea glasses scattered the sunlight that streamed through the open window like a prism. Blues, golds, greens and reds bounced onto a group of old men in battered cloaks and white kaffiyahs secured by black rope. The men of the Abu Ibrahim clan sat cross-legged on floor pillows placed carefully around the low table now holding their steaming drinks. They had once owned all the olive groves in our village. Every Saturday they met here, only occasionally exchanging a word or greeting across the crowded room. They came to listen to the 'Star of the East', Um Kalthoum, on the tea house's radio.

Abbas and I waited all week to hear her sing. Um Kalthoum was known for her contralto vocal range, her ability to produce approximately 14,000 vibrations per second with her vocal chords, her ability to sing every single Arabic scale, and the high importance she placed on interpreting the underlying meaning of her songs. Many of her songs lasted hours. Because of her great talent, men flocked to the only radio in the village to hear her.

Teacher Mohammad wiped the sweat that trickled down his nose and dangled there, about to drop onto the playing board. We both knew there was no way he could win, but he never quit and I admired that trait in him. The cluster of men gathered around the backgammon board teased, 'Well, Teacher

Mohammad, it appears that your student has beaten you again!' 'Concede already! Give someone else a chance to take on the village champion.'

'A man never quits until it is over.' Teacher Mohammad bore a chequer off.

I rolled a 6-6 and lifted my last chequer from the board. From the corner of my eye I saw Abbas watching me.

A smile blew across Baba's face and he quickly took a sip of his mint tea—he never liked to gloat. Abbas didn't care. He didn't try to conceal his smile.

Teacher Mohammad extended a sweaty hand to me. 'I knew I was in trouble when you started off with that 5-6.' His handshake was firm. After my initial high roll, I'd used the running strategy to beat him.

'My father taught me everything I know.' I looked at Baba.

'The teacher is important, but it's the speed at which your brain fires that makes you the champion at only eleven years of age.' Teacher Mohammad smiled.

'Almost twelve!' I said. 'Tomorrow.'

'Give him five minutes,' Baba said to the men who'd gathered around us in the hope of playing me. 'He hasn't even had his tea yet.'

Baba's words warmed my insides. I loved how proud he was of me.

'Great game, Ahmed.' Abbas patted me on the shoulder.

Men reclined on floor cushions, clustered around low trestle tables set up in lines down the length of the room on top of overlapping carpets. Um Kalthoum's voice overpowered the medley of voices from the men.

The attendant emerged from the back room with a pipe in each hand—long, coloured stems hanging over his arms, charcoal glowing on the tobacco—and set them in front of the remaining men of the Abu Ibrahim group. They thickened the air with sweet-smelling smoke, which mixed with the smoke from the oil lamps hanging from ceiling rafters. One of them told a story about how he had bent down and ripped his trousers open. Abbas and I laughed with them.

The Mukhtar entered, raising his arms at the door as if to embrace the entire tea house at once. Even though the military government wouldn't recognise the Mukhtar as our elected leader, he was, and men with disputes came to him. Every day he held court in the tea house. The Mukhtar was making his way to his spot in the back, but stopped to clap Baba on the back. 'May God bring peace upon you and your sons.' He bowed before us and shook Baba's hand.

'May God bring peace upon you as well,' Baba said. 'Have you heard that Ahmed is being promoted by three grades in the coming year?'

The Mukhtar smiled. 'He will bring great pride to our people one day.'

As men entered, they came over to Baba to greet him and introduce themselves to Abbas and me. When I first started coming with Baba, I felt strange because this was the domain of adult men who looked at me strangely. Only a few had wanted to play me at backgammon; but after I proved myself, I became a welcome and honoured guest. I earned my position. Now I was sort of a legend, the youngest backgammon champion in the history of my village.

When Abbas heard of my victories, he began to accompany us. He wanted to learn to play like me. While I played, he spent much of his time socialising with the men. Everyone always liked Abbas; even from an early age he had charisma.

On my right was a group of men in their twenties, dressed in Western clothes: trousers with zippers and button-down shirts.

They read newspapers, smoked cigarettes and drank Arabic coffee. Many of them were still single. Abbas and I would be with them one day.

One of them pushed his glasses up with his index finger. 'How am I supposed to get into medical school here?' he said.

'You'll figure out something,' the sandal-maker's son said.

'Easy for you to say,' the bespectacled man said. 'You have a trade to go into.'

'At least you're not the third son. I can't even marry,' another said. 'My father has no land to give me anymore. Where would my wife and I live? Both my brothers and their families already live with my parents and me in our one-room house. Now, Jerusalem . . .'

The radio's battery went flat right in the middle of Um Kalthoum's song, *Whom Should I Go To?* Villagers gasped and voices rose. The owner scurried to the large radio console. He turned the knobs, but there was no sound.

'Please, forgive me,' he said. 'The battery needs to be recharged. There's nothing I can do.'

Men started to get up to leave.

'Please, wait.' The owner made his way over to Baba. 'Would you mind playing a few songs?'

Baba bowed slightly. 'It would be my pleasure.'

'Gentlemen, please wait—Abu Ahmed has agreed to entertain us with his wonderful music.'

Men returned to their spots and Baba played his oud and sang the songs of Abdel Halim Hafez, Mohammad Abdel Wahab and Farid al-Atrash. Some sang along with him, others closed their eyes and listened, while still others smoked their water-pipes and sipped tea. Baba sang for over an hour before he put down his oud.

'Don't stop!' they cried.

Baba picked up his oud and started again. He hated to disappoint them, but as dinner approached, he had no choice.

'My wife will be upset if her dinner gets cold,' he said. 'Everyone, please join us tomorrow night after dinner to celebrate Ahmed's twelfth birthday.' As we left, villagers cried out thanks and shook Baba's hand.

Even this late in the day, the village square still bustled with activity. In the open-air market at the centre, pedlars lined the ground in front of them with clay pots filled with combs; mirrors; amulets to keep away evil spirits; buttons; threads; needles and pins; bolts of brightly coloured fabrics; stacks of new and second-hand clothes and shoes; piles of books and magazines; pots and pans; knives and scissors; field tools. Shepherds stood with sheep and goats. Cages held chickens. Apricots, oranges, apples, avocados and pomegranates lay on tarps next to potatoes, squash, aubergines and onions. There were pickled vegetables in glass jars; clay pots filled with olives, pistachios, and sunflower seeds. A man behind a big wooden camera, half hidden under black fabric, snapped a picture of a family in front of the mosque.

We passed a man selling the paraffin that we used to fuel our lanterns and to cook with, then the herbalist, whose fragrant wares disguised the petroleum smell of his neighbour's. There were dandelions for diabetes, constipation, liver and skin conditions; chamomile for indigestion and inflammatory disorders; thyme for respiratory problems and eucalyptus for coughs. Across the way, we could see women gathered at the communal ovens chatting while their dough baked.

We passed the now-vacant Khan, the two-room hostel where visitors once stayed when they came to sell their goods in our village, or for festivals, or during harvest season, or on their way to Amman, Beirut or Cairo. Baba told me that when it was open, travellers came on camels and horses, but that was before there were checkpoints and curfews.

The roar of military Jeeps speeding into our village silenced the chatter. Rocks flew through the air and pummelled them; engines screeched to a halt. My friend, Muhammad Ibn Abd, from my class, ran past us, through the square, with two steel-helmeted soldiers with face protectors and Uzis on his heels. They threw him down on a tarp of tomatoes and drove the stocks of their Uzis into his skull. Abbas and I tried to run to him, but Baba held us back.

'Don't get involved,' he said and pulled us towards our house. Abbas' fists were clenched. Anger bubbled inside of me too. Baba silenced us with a glance. *Not in front of the soldiers, or the other villagers.*

We made our way towards the hill where we lived, past clusters of homes like ours. I knew each of the clans that lived in these family groups, as the fathers would split their land among their sons, generation after generation, so the clan stayed together. My family's land was gone. Most of my father's brothers had been forced into refugee camps across the border in Jordan twelve years ago, on the day of my birth. Now, my brothers and cousins and I would have no orange groves, no houses of our own. As we passed the last of the mud-brick homes, my head pounded with rage.

'How could you stop me?' The words burst from my mouth as soon as we were alone.

Baba took a few more steps, then stopped. 'It would accomplish nothing but to get you into trouble.'

'We need to fight back. They won't stop on their own.'

'Ahmed's right,' Abbas chimed in.

Baba silenced us with his look.

We passed a pile of rubble where a house used to be. In its

place was a low tent. Three little children held onto their mother's robe while she cooked over an open fire. When I looked over at her, she lowered her head, lifted the pan, and ducked into the tent.

'For twelve years, I've watched many soldiers enter our village,' Baba said. 'Their hearts are as different from each other's as they are from ours. They are bad, good, scared, greedy, moral, immoral, kind, mean—they're human beings like us. Who knows what they might be if they were not soldiers? This is politics.'

I gritted my teeth together so hard my jaw hurt. Baba didn't see things the way Abbas and I did. Uncollected rubbish, donkey dung and flies littered the path. We paid taxes but received no services because they classified us as a village. They stole the majority of our land and left us with one half of a square kilometre for over six thousand Palestinians.

'People don't treat other human beings the way they treat us,' I said.

'Ahmed's right,' Abbas said.

'That's what saddens me.' Baba shook his head. 'Throughout history the conquerors have always treated the conquered this way. The bad ones need to believe we're inferior to justify the way they treat us. If they only could realise that we're all the same.'

I couldn't listen to him anymore and ran towards home, shouting, 'I hate them. I wish they'd just go back to where they came from and leave us alone!' Abbas followed on my heels.

Baba called after us, 'One day you'll understand. It's not as simple as you make it out to be. We must always remain decent.'

He had no idea what he was talking about.

The flower scent reached me about halfway up the hill. I was glad we lived only five minutes from the square. I wasn't like Abbas, outside playing games with friends and running all the time; I was a reader, a thinker, and this running fast made my lungs burn. Abbas could run all day and he'd never even perspire. I couldn't begin to compete with his athleticism.

Bougainvillea in shades of purple and fuchsia climbed the trellises that Baba, Abbas and I had made to run up the outside of the little house. Mama and Nadia were taking more trays of sweets to their storage place under the tarp near the almond tree. They had been baking all week.

'Go inside,' Baba said as he trudged up behind Abbas and me. 'They're starting curfew earlier today.'

***

Sleep could not find me. My anger made me invisible and when it visited the rest of my family, it overlooked me. So I was the only one who heard the noises outside. Footsteps. At first I thought it was the wind in the almond tree, but as they drew louder, closer, I knew it was not. No one was ever out after dark except soldiers. We could be shot if we left our homes for any reason. It must be soldiers. I lay very still listening for the pattern, trying to discern how many feet. It was one person, and not in the heavy boots of the soldiers. It must be a thief. Our home was so small that, in order for everyone to lie down, we had to place many things out of doors. The food for my birthday party was outside now. Someone was creeping up on it. I stepped over my family's sleeping bodies, afraid to be seen outside, but more afraid to let someone steal the food Mama and Nadia had worked so hard to prepare, and that Baba had saved all year to buy.

The chill caught me off guard and I wrapped my arms around my chest as I picked my way along, barefooted. There was no moon. I didn't see him. A sweaty hand clamped over my mouth. Cold metal pressed against the back of my neck—a gun barrel.

'Keep your voice down,' he said.

He spoke in my village's dialect.

'Tell me your full name,' he demanded in a whisper.

I closed my eyes and envisioned the tombstones in our village cemetery.

'Ahmed Mahmud Mohammad Othman Omar Ali Hussein Hamid,' I squeaked, wishing to sound manly, but sounding like a little girl.

'I'll cut your tongue out if I catch you lying.' He spun me around and jerked me backwards. 'What's a rich boy like you doing in my house?'

The scar on his forehead was unmistakable. Ali.

'The Israelis, they took our land.'

He shook me so violently I feared I might vomit.

'Where's your father?' He jerked me further backwards. I grabbed onto his arms with all my might and thought of my family asleep on their rush mats in our house, Ali's home.

'He's sleeping, doctor,' I said, adding the title as a show of respect so that he might not slit my throat there, next to the birthday pastries.

He thrust his face into mine. What if he asked what Baba does?

'Right this very minute, my comrades are burying arms throughout this village.'

'Please, doctor,' I said. 'I could pay attention much better if I were vertical.'

He slammed me backward before he yanked me upright. I looked at the open bag next to his foot. It was filled with weapons. I looked away, but it was too late.

'See this gun.' He shoved the pistol in my face. 'If anything happens to me or my weapons, my comrades will chop your family to pieces.'

I nodded, mute to this horrible vision.

'Where's the safest place to hide them?' He glanced towards the house. 'And remember, your family's lives depend on it. Don't even tell your father.'

'I would never,' I said. 'He doesn't understand. We have no choice. Hide them in the dirt behind the almond tree.'

He walked me over with the pistol against the back of my neck.

'There's no need for the gun.' I lifted my hands away from my sides. 'I'm quite willing to help. We all want freedom for ourselves and our brothers in the camps.'

'What's under the tarp?' he asked.

'Food for my celebration.'

'Celebration?'

'My twelfth birthday.' I could not feel the gun against my skin anymore.

'Have you a shovel?'

He followed me.

***

When we finished, Ali stepped into the trench and laid the bag of arms down the way a mother would place her baby in his bassinet. In silence we scooped dirt from the mound beside the trench until we covered the bag.

Ali grabbed a handful of date cookies from under the tarp and stuffed them into his pockets and mouth. 'Palestinians trained to use these weapons will come.' White particles sprayed from his mouth. 'You'll protect them until the time is right, or your family will be killed.'

'Of course.' I couldn't believe how lucky I was to become a hero of my people.

I started to return to my rush mat inside the house, but Ali grabbed my shoulder. 'If you tell anyone, I'll kill you all.'

I turned to face him. 'You don't understand. I want to help.'

'Israel has built a house of glass, and we'll shatter it.' He cut the air with his fist then handed me the shovel.

There was a skip in my step as I returned to my house. I lay again in the darkness next to Abbas, my body and mind charged with the thrill of what I'd participated in. Until it occurred to me—what if the Israelis found out? They'd imprison me. They'd bulldoze our house. My family would have to live in a tent. Or maybe they'd exile us. I wanted to talk to Baba or even Abbas, but I knew Ali and his comrades would kill us. I was caught between the devil and the fires of hell. I had to move the weapons. I'd tell Ali they weren't secure. I couldn't dig them up now. Where would I put them? During the day, someone could see me. I'd have to wait until curfew. The whole village would be at our house this evening. What if the soldiers came? What if my family noticed, or someone from the party? The village cemetery. New plots were dug there almost daily. I'd go after school to scout out a place.

4

I had to go outside and make sure nothing looked suspicious. I was getting up when Mama placed the cake on the dirt floor in front of me. She pushed me back down and kissed my cheeks.

'Why are your eyes so bloodshot?' she asked.

I shrugged.

My siblings gathered around me.

'I laboured with you for fifteen hours . . .' Mama began.

'Can you retell the story later?' I asked. *We could all soon be dead and she wants to tell the story of my birth?*

Mama pointed to the picture Baba drew of her, pregnant, lying in the dirt between our orange trees. Crates overflowing with oranges concealed her from all sides.

I wiped the sweat from my forehead.

'While I was birthing you, Israeli tanks entered our village and sprayed it with deadly fire.' Mama's eyes never left me. 'The Israelis separated the men and women. With guns pointed at their heads, the soldiers marched the men in the direction of Jordan. Women dug up jars of money, gathered their gold and clothes. With their bundle of valuables balanced on their heads, house-keys around their necks and children under their arms, the women also marched. By the time you emerged, the soldiers were gone.' Mama smiled at me. 'Because of you, we aren't refugees.'

She motioned to my sister Nadia. 'Bring the birthday king his coffee.'

I could hardly breathe.

Nadia placed the white cup filled with Arabic coffee in front of me. I gulped it down, leaving a small amount.

Mama watched me. 'You're going to choke.'

I handed her the cup. She turned it around three times, covered it with a saucer, flipped the two upside down and faced them towards me. The coffee grounds settled at the bottom. Carefully, Mama looked into the cup for the symbols that would tell my future.

Her face darkened, her body tensed. She grabbed the earthen pitcher and dumped well-water over the grounds. Baba laughed. Abbas covered his mouth with his hand.

'What is it?' I said.

'Nothing, my love. It's not a good day to read your future.'

A wave of fear hit me. Was it because of the weapons? Was I to die?

Mama would spend the day preparing more birthday sweets. I needed to make sure she couldn't see anything.

'I am in the mood for a date cookie.' I rose.

Mama pulled me back down. 'Nadia, fetch Ahmed a cookie.'

Suddenly I thought of all the cookies Ali had eaten.

'Never mind,' I said.

Mama squinted a bit, like she was trying to see through my odd behaviour. 'Are you sure?'

'I had a lot last night.'

Baba reached into his jacket pocket, pulled out a small brown bag and extended it to me. His face glowed. Our eyes met as I took the bag from him.

'It's the two magnifying glasses you wanted,' he said. 'For your telescope.'

'Where did you get the money?' I asked.

He smiled. 'I've been making payments since last year.'

I kissed his hand. He pulled me close and hugged me.

'What are you waiting for?' Abbas asked.

Baba handed me a book: *Einstein and Physics.*

I placed the 3 cm magnifying glass between my eyes and the opened book. With my other hand I held the 2.5 cm glass above the 3 cm one.

'Why are your hands shaking?' Mama asked.

'Emotion.' I moved the lens until the print came into sharp focus.

Abbas handed me a ruler.

'Three centimetres,' I said.

I felt like a tsetse fly under a microscope.

'Here.' Abbas passed me my homemade telescope and a knife.

I measured carefully and cut two slots into the cardboard tube, inserted the lenses and secured them with fabric. Through the telescope my book was huge. 'Twice the power.'

I hugged Baba again. What had I done?

The school bell sounded.

'I don't want to be late.' I'd sneak back to the almond tree before I left for school.

'I'll walk you,' Baba said. 'I've taken the day off to help Mama prepare.'

***

After school, I stopped by the cemetery, found the appropriate plot and went straight to my almond tree. The dirt looked the same.

'Come sit with me.' Baba appeared next to me. 'I heard a few new jokes.'

My heart was beating so fast I couldn't think straight. I held the telescope up. 'She's beckoning me.'

'How can I compete?' Baba said.

I climbed our almond tree. Abbas and I had named her Shahida, 'witness', because we spent so many hours in her watching the Arabs and Jews that she felt like a playmate deserving of a name. The olive tree on Shahida's left we called Amal, 'hope', and the one on her right was Sa'dah, 'happiness'.

Baba leaned against the mud-brick wall of our home to watch me. I aimed the lens of my new telescope at Moshav Dan's swimming pool.

'I wonder if Einstein made his own telescope. You'd do well to follow his example,' Baba said.

'Abu Ahmed!' Mama called. 'I need your help inside.'

Baba walked to the front of the house.

I aimed the lens of my telescope to the west of the village. Our hilltop home was the highest point in the village. All the remaining homes were one-room cubes, mud-brick with square flat roofs. The sweat dripped into my eyes. Would this day never end?

Baba reappeared. 'Dinner's ready.'

A book hit the almond tree and crashed to the ground. I jumped off the branch.

'I hate maths.' Abbas kicked up the dirt. 'I'll never be able to do it.'

'A man who needs fire will hold it in his hand,' Baba said.

'I've tried, but I keep getting burned.'

'Ahmed will help you.' Baba put his arm around me. 'God has blessed you with an extraordinary mathematical mind for a purpose.'

Abbas rolled his eyes. 'How can anyone forget?'

'Maybe if you spent less time with friends and more time with your books like Ahmed does you wouldn't have any trouble with maths.' Baba raised his eyebrows and patted Abbas on the head.

'Dinner.' Mama's voice was soft; she was just reminding Baba of what she had sent him to do.

'We'll be right there, Um Ahmed,' Baba said. 'Let's go, boys.' We walked towards the house, Baba in the middle, his arms around Abbas and me.

Inside, my little sister Sara ran to Baba, nearly toppling him over. Mama and Baba's eyes met and she smiled.

'Let Baba breathe,' Mama said.

'Here it is.' Baba pointed to this year's portrait of me, which hung in the birthday section of the wall.

'You look just like your father.' Mama grabbed my cheeks. 'Look at those emerald eyes, lush hair and thick black lashes.' Mama raised her eyebrows. 'You're my masterpiece.'

Abbas and my other siblings looked like Mama, with their skin the colour of burned cinnamon, black unruly hair and long arms.

'Take these.' Mama handed Nadia small dishes of hummus and tabboulie, which she placed on the dirt floor.

'Come, Mama prepared a feast,' Baba called to Abbas and me. He sat cross-legged next to the small dishes. 'I swear to you she is the best cook in all the land.'

He looked at Mama. The corners of her lips rose and she lowered her head.

Abbas and I sat next to each other as we did for every meal. The rest of our siblings joined us on the floor around the dishes.

'It's your favourite,' Mama said. '*Sheikh El Mahshi*.' I could not meet her gaze. 'No thanks.'

'Is something wrong?' She looked at Baba.

'I'm too excited about the party.'

Mama smiled at me.

'Those are yours,' Mama said to Baba. She pointed to a plate of miniature aubergines stuffed only with rice and pine nuts.

Baba was vegetarian; he would have no killing in his name, even of an animal for food.

***

Baba sat with his oud on the stone wall next to Abu Sayeed, the violinist.

I'd started to walk back to the almond tree, when I felt Baba's hand on my shoulder.

'Stand next to your portrait,' he said.

Abbas walked behind the house with a group of his friends. My stomach dropped. I stood beside Baba next to the easel that held my portrait.

Men lined up, arms on each other's shoulders, and began to dance the dabkeh in the middle of the courtyard. Others went behind the house. I could feel the wetness under my arms. The guests were dressed in their Friday best. The older people wore their traditional robes.

Children shouted, the babies yelled, and everyone laughed while Baba sang his heart out. Abu Sayeed tapped authoritatively on the side of the violin, tucked it carefully under his chin, and then waved his bow in the air in an elaborate flourish. He manoeuvred it like a magic wand. More and more children headed for the backyard.

'Let's go!' Abbas returned for me. I looked at Baba. He nodded. I ran past Abbas to the back of the house where a group of boys sat on the ground.

Abbas gave me a handful of sand. I placed it in a bucket of water. Everyone gathered around. After stirring the water, I pulled the sand out dry.

The audience clapped with enthusiasm. I noticed my brothers Fadi and Hani walk to the spot where the weapons were buried with sticks in their hands. They spent every day together looking for clues so that they could solve mysteries that didn't exist.

Sweat beaded up on my face. 'Join us, brothers.'

'We want more,' the children chanted.

'No thanks,' Fadi said.

'We're hot on the trail of something big.' Hani said the same thing every time Abbas and I asked him what he and Fadi were doing.

I rubbed the bristles of a hairbrush against a wool sweater while I watched them scrape at the dirt over the weapons. I moved the brush close to Abbas' head. His hair immediately stood on end, following the brush.

'By order of the military governor, tonight's curfew will begin in fifteen minutes. Anyone caught outside his or her home will be arrested or shot,' the amplified voice said in heavily accented Arabic.

Soldiers swarmed into my birthday party like locusts. They stared at Abbas' hair. Without explanation, curfew was starting an hour earlier tonight.

'Party's over,' a soldier said. 'Everyone go home.'

They waved their guns at us. I turned to look for Fadi and Hani.

'Move it,' the soldier said to me. I scurried to the front of the house, but soldiers remained at my almond tree. It was difficult to breathe. The guests dispersed. Baba offered the soldiers sweets.

'Don't look so upset,' Baba said. 'We had a great time. We'll do it again next year.'

'Hurry,' Mama called to my sisters. 'Help me with the mats.' Nadia and Sara placed ten rush mats on the dirt floor where we'd eaten dinner. The soldiers left and Mama blew out the lanterns.

I lay in the dark on my mat trying to banish the terrible thoughts by recollecting the next problem from the physics book I was reading. Even so, I kept listening for the sounds outside of soldiers uncovering the cache.

A rock being shot from a slingshot accelerates over a distance of 2 metres. At the end of this acceleration it leaves the slingshot with a speed of 200 metres per second. What would be the average acceleration imparted to the rock?

The rock was accelerated from rest. Its final speed is 200 m/s; it's accelerated over a known distance, 2 metres; $v^2=2ad$*;* $(200\ m/s)^2 = 2a(2\ m)$*; then* $a=40{,}000/4=10{,}000\ m/s^2$*.*

I was starting on another problem when I heard noises outside. I sat upright and squinted into the darkness, trying to decide what to do. Was it the freedom fighters? Or the soldiers?

5

Boom! Our tin door crashed to the ground. Mama screamed. Flashlights exploded into the room like firecrackers. My siblings fled to the southwest corner of our room. Mama picked up screaming seven-year-old Sara and followed. Baba pulled me back to the corner. We crouched together so closely we melded into one.

Seven machine-gun-bearing soldiers, their faces rigid and their chests heaving, blocked the door.

'What do you want?' Mama's voice trembled.

A sick feeling of horror gripped my heart in the harsh light that focused on us, trapped together in the corner. One soldier, with a neck sufficiently thick to support a donkey, stepped towards us, holding the butt of his machine-gun against his shoulder. With his finger on the trigger the soldier aimed directly at Baba.

'We captured your accomplice. He confessed everything. Get the weapons.'

'Please,' Baba stammered. 'I don't know what you're talking about.'

I tried to open my mouth to speak, but no sound emerged. My heart felt like it was about to break out of my chest.

'You dirty, lying piece of shit.' The soldier's body shook. 'I'll splatter you against the wall like a cockroach.'

My siblings clung to Baba. The soldier paced menacingly close as Baba pushed us back, behind him, and stretched out his arms to protect us. Mama moved in front of us with her arms out too, making a two-layer wall between us and them.

'We know nothing.' Mama's voice was so shaky and high-pitched she didn't sound like herself, but like a very old, insane woman in our village.

'Shut up!' the soldier snarled.

I couldn't catch my breath. I was going to faint.

'You think you can get away with helping a terrorist sneak arms into this country?' the soldier asked Baba in broken Arabic.

'I swear to God.' Baba's voice shook. 'I know nothing.'

'You're a stupid man if you thought we wouldn't find out.' The soldier grabbed Baba by his night robe, like he was a chicken, and yanked him to the centre of the room. His olive skin turned white in the Israelis' harsh lights.

'Leave him alone!' I screamed as I ran at the soldier.

He knocked me to the ground and kicked me with his steel-toed boot.

'Stay in the corner!' Baba spoke in a way I'd never heard him speak. With his eyes, Baba commanded me back to the corner. I felt compelled to obey.

'Did a terrorist come to your house last night?' The soldier lifted his arms in the air and drove the stock of his machine-gun into Baba's chiselled face. Blood spurted. He crumpled to the ground, gasping for air.

Mama mouthed a prayer.

'Don't hurt my Baba!' Abbas grabbed the soldier's thick arm.

The soldier swatted him away like a fly. Abbas slammed into the ground. Mama pulled him back to the corner.

As Baba lay in a foetal position, the soldier rammed his gun into his side.

'Stop it,' Mama said. 'You're killing him.'

'Shut up.' The soldier turned to look Mama in the eye. 'Or you'll be next.'

She covered her mouth with her hands.

'I'll give you one more chance, you terrorist. Your fate is in my hands.'

The soldier jabbed the butt of his gun into Baba again.

'You're hurting Baba!' Abbas lunged at the soldier again. Mama grabbed the back of his robe and covered his mouth.

In a low voice and with hesitation, a soldier said, 'That's enough, commander.'

'I'll tell you when it's enough.'

Baba was very still. I stared at his chest, hoping to see movement. The commander lifted his gun and drove it into Baba's limp back. The air stopped circulating. I froze.

I thought of Baba sitting in the courtyard, drinking tea and laughing with his friends. How foolish I'd been. I should've listened to him and not got involved in politics. Now, I had killed my father. A ferocious trembling gripped my body.

From outside someone called, 'Commander, we found guns and grenades buried in the back of the house.' Each word penetrated my heart like a bullet.

'Drag this piece of shit out of here. Throw him down the hill. Terrorists don't deserve to be carried.'

'Don't take Baba away!' Abbas grabbed at them while Mama held him around the neck.

Hani slipped past her and ran at the soldier. He grabbed Hani and pinned his little hands behind his back. A few of the other soldiers laughed.

'Your messiah has arrived,' a soldier said. 'Defender of his father's honour.'

Hani struggled, trying desperately to free himself from the

soldier's grip, but he couldn't break loose. Fadi grabbed Hani's legs and tried to pull him free.

Mama began to retch.

A soldier spat at her.

Baba lay on the ground, his lips parted innocently, his eyes closed as if he were asleep, except that blood poured out of his nose and under his head. My eyes never left him as two soldiers dragged his limp body out into the darkness.

'Stay stong, Baba!' Abbas screamed. 'Stay strong!'

Outside, I heard three gunshots fired at close range. My heart convulsed. I looked over at Mama. She had dropped to the ground, her arms around her knees, rocking back and forth. No one could save us. My muscles tensed. How could we go on?

My family's wails, as we huddled together, penetrated my bones. I willed myself dead in Baba's place and knew, as simply and certainly as a twelve-year-old boy knows anything, that I'd never be happy again.

6

The roar of tanks and military Jeeps grew louder as a wave of nausea rose into the back of my throat. I couldn't swallow the goats' cheese in my mouth. Mama sipped her tea next to the stove, unaware. Since they had taken Baba two weeks ago, her eyes had been empty; she seemed to slip further away from us each day.

Now, the military was coming to get me. My gut knotted.

I thought of Marwan Ibn Sayyid. He was twelve years old when he saw a soldier beating his father in the street. Marwan jumped on him. They held him in an adult prison with Israeli criminals for two years before his case even went to the military court. Marwan tried to kill himself twice in his cell. He was finally sentenced to six months and when he was released, he ran into the road waving a plastic gun at the soldiers. They killed him instantly.

Abbas sat next to me on the floor with our siblings around dishes of pita, zatar, olive oil, laban, and goats' cheese. They continued to eat, oblivious to my fate. The window beckoned, but I fought the urge to look out. I wanted to give my family these last moments of peace.

The screech of tyres at the bottom of the hill brought me back to reality. My family froze. How could I protect them? Abbas grabbed my hand.

I studied the room—perhaps for the last time. The rush mats and goatskin blankets stashed in the corner; the shelf bearing my chemistry, physics, maths and history books. Above them, Baba's beloved art books. The clay jugs of rice, lentils, beans and flour. Mama's silver teapot on the stove. Baba's portraits on the wall. And his beloved oud that was made for him by his father, untouched since he was taken.

Boots dug into the hill, crushing the terrain. 'Everyone out of the house!' The faceless voice of the army called through its megaphone from our yard.

Would they beat me in front of my family and neighbours? Would they make an example of me, something for everyone to think about as my blood dried on the cracked earth? Would this be the end of me? As fearful as I was, I almost welcomed it. It would finally be over.

Mama's eyes widened with terror. I opened the tin door that I'd just fixed. A dozen gas-masked soldiers stood in our yard like giant insects.

A soldier lifted his mask. 'Out! Now!' He was a chubby-cheeked teenager, a grotesque doll come to life. Another soldier aimed a rifle at the open doorway and fired a canister of teargas into the house. It missed me by a few centimetres and slammed into the back wall.

'Hurry!' Mama shouted as the burning gas hissed out.

My eyes were on fire. I dropped to the floor—smoke rises, stay near the ground—crawling towards Baba's oud while the others pushed outside.

I couldn't hold my breath any longer. Baba's oud was still out of reach.

'Ahmed, Sara!' Mama cried.

Sara? With my arm out in front of me, I searched as quickly as I could move through the smoke for Sara. She was nowhere. I couldn't leave without her, but I had to breathe soon. My fingers tangled with something—her long hair. Her face was warm and wet. I picked her up, still without taking a breath, my eyes streaming with tears and pain, my chest about to explode. Blindly, I pressed forward with her limp body in my arms. Outside, I devoured a mouthful of fresh air.

Smoke poured from the open door. We were barefoot and in our pyjamas. Nadia's eyes were reddened slits. Mama gasped. Sara's face was covered in blood that came from a huge gash on her forehead. She must have tripped during the chaos. I placed her small limp body on the ground, ignoring the pain from my eyes, and blew air into her mouth. Gently slapping her face, I pleaded, 'Wake up. Wake up, Sara.' Another breath. 'Breathe!'

Mama sobbed. Over and over again, I blew into Sara's mouth.

'Get water!' I screamed to anyone.

Mama was frantic. 'The jug was destroyed!' She looked at the soldiers, who did not seem to see us hovering around Sara, did not see the five-year-old turning blue right in front of them. Even the closest neighbour was too far.

Abbas grabbed Sara's hand, rubbing it briskly, as if to wake her up.

Mama leaned over my shoulder. 'Save her, Ahmed.'

Sara never moved. Her eyes never fluttered. I kept breathing into her mouth and tapping her face. Nothing worked. She was blue and still. My beautiful innocent little sister. I wanted to weep but my tears were all dried up. I felt black grief sweep over me like a heavy cloak, enveloping me in its heavy folds.

'Please, Ahmed,' Mama cried.

I lifted her to my shoulder and patted her back, bouncing her. Perhaps she had choked on something in the assault. I bounced and patted. 'Wake up, please wake up, Sara.' But nothing worked.

Mama finally said, 'She's gone, son.'

Wailing, Nadia pulled Sara from me and held her tightly.

'You killed my sister,' Abbas yelled. 'What do you want?'

They aimed their Uzis at our house.

'Is everyone out?' Mama's voice was panicked.

As the soldiers sprayed the house with bullets, my eyes combed the yard. Abbas. Nadia. Fadi. Hani. Sara's little body. They were all outside.

'Move away from the house!' the baby-faced soldier yelled. We were already outside; what more could they want?

The lack of bulldozers had thrown me off. The soldiers entered the house with sticks of dynamite. We stood outside while they laid the charges.

'My father's innocent,' I said.

The soldiers glared at me and I lowered my head. 'Of course he is,' Baby-Face taunted.

I wanted to tell them the truth. It was the middle of the night. I hadn't thought it through. I hadn't meant for any of this to happen.

'Say goodbye to your house, terrorists!' a soldier said.

My legs felt weak. 'Where will we live? Please,' I begged, a whining child, nothing like the man I wished I were.

'Shut up!' a soldier said.

Abbas stood next to me. 'Arrest me instead,' I begged. 'Don't punish these children.'

'We don't want you,' Baby-Face said.

Abbas stared at the soldiers with hatred in his eyes. Nadia clutched Sara's body tightly, as if she could protect her. I held onto Hani while he cried. Fadi picked up a stone, cocked his hand back. I grabbed his arm and pulled him into my embrace with Hani.

Vivid memories flashed through my mind. Mama's precious

silver teapot and tray—wedding presents from her parents. Baba's portraits—his dead father; his brother Kamal on a ladder picking oranges and placing them into crates we had woven from wet pomegranate branches. The portraits of Baba and his brothers—floating on the Dead Sea with the orange cart and the donkey parked on the shore, smiling on a beach in Haifa with the waves crashing behind them, the orange cart to the side. And Baba's most precious portrait, the one of his parents picnicking in front of a patch of sunflowers. Gone would be the portraits of Mama and Baba's exiled family members; my dead sisters Amal and Sara; and my imprisoned Baba. Gone, too, would be Mama's hand-embroidered Bedouin wedding dress that she'd always told me she was saving for my wife. Baba's oud. Most of all, Sara. A little girl who had never done anyone a bit of harm.

Mama collapsed at the soldier's feet and clutched his ankles. 'Please, we have no place left to go.'

Mama's desperation broke my heart. We had no place to go. What had I done? I let go of the boys for a moment and moved to her, trying to lift her by the arms. 'Mama, please, get up.' Her flesh was hot. 'You don't have to do this. We can find another place to live.' I gritted my teeth to keep from shouting. 'We don't have to beg.' I felt like a thick blanket was smothering me in a heavy darkness. There was no saviour. No uncle, brother, or father that would come and rescue us. It was up to me to protect my family.

Trembling, Mama turned her eyes to the sky.

Four soldiers emerged from our home.

'All set,' the last soldier said as they hurried from the house. The earth under my feet shuddered. Smoke and the shattered particles of what had been generations of portraits, the white robe Mama had made for my birthday, her roses, her mint and parsley, her tomato plants, our backgammon board, clothes, rush mats and jugs filled the air. Everyone coughed except the soldiers.

Flames shot up, charring the walls, which disintegrated into ash before our eyes. Our home was gone. In its place was glowing, red hot rubble. As the inferno died down, I could see that Amal and Sa'dah, our two olive trees, were on fire. Total despair weakened my knees. But then I noticed our almond tree, unharmed; only her flowers were gone.

The soldiers removed their gas masks. 'Terrorists don't deserve houses,' the baby-faced one spat.

***

For five hours I waited in my pyjamas in the hot sun in front of the military outpost to get a permit to bury Sara, but I couldn't get an appointment. What would we do with Sara's body? If we buried her without permission, the soldiers might dig her up.

Back at our almond tree, Nadia sat in the dirt and rocked Sara slowly. Mama held Hani and Fadi in her arms. Abbas and I began to scour the hot rubble with our bare hands for anything that might be salvaged.

That night, Nadia swaddled Sara in my kaffiyah. 'God forbid any bugs should get her.'

Mama and Nadia held Sara's dead body all night so that she wouldn't be alone. When Abbas finally fell asleep, he ground his teeth so hard, the front one cracked. I remained awake the entire night. When curfew ended, I ran to the outpost and waited six hours under the brutal sun before they granted me a permit to bury my sister.

***

Abbas and I went to the cemetery and dug a hole next to Amal's grave. The sun felt like fire on our backs, but we didn't stop until our hole was two metres deep. Abbas and I were so dry, we were no longer perspiring.

'The Israelis will pay for this,' Abbas kept muttering. 'They only understand violence. It's the only language they speak.' He stopped digging. 'An eye for an eye.'

Mama carried the tiny body to the grave. Nadia never let go of her hand. We kissed her cheeks. Fadi and Hani clenched their fists. Abbas' eyes were stone. Mama lowered Sara into the ground, but refused to let her go. Nadia cried.

'No,' Mama said. 'This is a mistake.'

Finally, I took Sara from her. In the hole, I laid her down. I bit my lip. When I climbed out, Abbas and I covered her with dirt. As I filled the grave I kept seeing Baba in the bottom of a hole like this one, being covered in dirt by some Israeli bulldozer. All hope was gone.

Where would we live? What would we do? We needed a home to protect us from the brutal summer heat and the torrential winter rains. We couldn't build. We didn't even have enough money to buy a tent.

7

Uncle Kamal bought us a tent from the village market. For the past two weeks we'd all slept outside, under Shahida, dressed in the ill-fitting clothes Mama made from rags that Uncle Kamal found for us. Abbas and I used rocks to knock cedar stakes into the ground under the almond tree and, when curfew began, the six of us squeezed in and lay crushed together, the little ones on top of the bigger ones. The high temperatures, body heat, sweat, lack of air and inability to move made sleep impossible.

***

The moment the curfew ended, I ran to the military's outpost again, determined to find out what had happened to Baba. For the past four weeks, I'd waited in line every day with hundreds of other villagers who sought permits to marry, or bury loved ones, or build a home; or to leave the village to go to the hospital, or work, or classes. A handful of villagers, like me, sought news of loved ones who had been arrested or taken from the village to unknown locations. Every evening I returned home not even knowing if Baba was alive. Today would be different, I told myself when I arrived.

Abu Yossef got in line behind me. 'You're not trying to get a permit to rebuild, are you?'

The heat was suffocating. The air was thick with the stink

from open sewage, donkey dung and uncollected rubbish.

'I know better than that,' I said.

He shook his head. 'Still haven't heard about your father?'

'He did nothing.'

'They say he was brutalised.'

I looked at the thirty people ahead of me. They presumably lived closer than I did. If there wasn't a curfew, I would've slept at the outpost. 'What are you here for?' I asked.

'Permission to buy apricots and oranges from my own trees, the ones my great grandfather planted and I kept alive in drought and war.'

'I hope my father's all right.' I looked at the ground.

'He'll be fine,' Abu Yossef said.

'He isn't strong.'

'Don't underestimate your father. He may be more of a fighter than you know.'

'Ahmed,' Abbas called, 'come here, I need to talk to you.'

'I'll hold your spot.' Abu Yossef gestured for me to go.

Sweat dripped off Abbas' eyebrows and chin. 'They arrested Uncle Kamal last night.'

'For what?'

'Aiding a terrorist.'

Did Ali go to his house as well? 'What terrorist?' I asked.

'Baba,' Abbas said. His eyes were bloodshot.

We were on our own.

***

Five minutes before the curfew, I returned to the tent exhausted, Baba's whereabouts still unknown. For the next six weeks, I continued to stand in line all day, every day, with no luck. I no longer went to school.

***

I was cooking rice and almonds on a fire that I had built near our almond tree when the barber's son appeared. We greeted each other quickly.

'My father was released yesterday,' he said. 'Do you know where your father is?'

'We haven't heard anything,' I said. 'It's been two months.'

'My father would like to see you.' He wouldn't meet my eyes. 'It's about your father.'

I feared I might be targeted if I was caught meeting with a released political prisoner. But this was about Baba. How could I not go?

***

The barber sat in the corner of his tent, a patch over his left eye. Cigarette burns covered his hands.

'I'm sorry, I can't get up.' The barber's voice shook when he spoke.

'You have news about my father?'

'He's at the Dror Detention Centre,' the barber said. 'In the Negev Desert.'

Joy surged through my veins. 'He's alive?'

'Barely.' The barber lowered his eyes. 'He wants you to visit him. You have to get him out.'

For the first time, I began to wonder what would've been worse: for Baba to have been killed, or to survive only to be subjected to long-term torture. If they didn't kill Baba, the snakes and scorpions in the desert might.

Every day I went to the military governor's outpost and begged for a permit to travel to the Dror Detention Centre. One month later, the military governor granted me permission. I knew I had to go and confess to Baba. I'd insist that we switch places. The thought of him in prison for my crime was too horrible.

With the little money Abbas and I made selling almonds

from our tree, I bought the six bus tickets I needed for my trip. Abbas didn't even bother to ask me if he could come. He knew we didn't have enough money.

8

I had only ever heard rumours of this place, so scorched that nothing could live. The Negev. Sand like ground glass blasted through the open window, pounding my flesh and eyes and settling in the dry corners of my mouth.

The bus finally stopped next to a tall barbed-wire pen with guard towers in each corner. I thought I wanted nothing more than to get off the sweltering, stinking bus, but when I saw what awaited me, I wondered if it wasn't the face of hell. On the barbed wire a sign with a black skull cautioned in Arabic and Hebrew: *Warning! Danger of Death.* The Hebrew was for show—there were no Jewish political prisoners detained here. My legs resisted after so long on the vinyl seat, but I forced them to hurry, my head down, past grim-faced guards standing lookout with rifles and German shepherds.

Maybe a thousand prisoners in black jumpsuits were working in this furnace of a yard. None raised his eyes when the bus arrived. I did; I had to look—could Baba be in there? What if I could not recognise him? I studied each man quickly, divining his height against a median, eliminating those more than two standard deviations from the mean—only those of average height could be my Baba. Some shovelled sand into large bags or dragged concrete blocks to a massive three-storey structure they were building, their black jumpsuits attracting the punishing sun. I looked for Baba on the scaffolding, mixing cement, lifting cinderblocks.

A gaunt, almost skeletal, prisoner dug his shovel into the sand pile, but when he tried to lift it, his body trembled, the sand spilled before his wheelbarrow and he collapsed. He lay there, ignored, like a crushed bird.

Next to the work area, inside the barbed wire, was another pen surrounding massive tents with no sides above wood-plank floors lined with mats.

I hurried to an area outside the gate where hundreds of other Palestinians sat on the ground and listened to a soldier call prisoners' names. There were women and children, old men, and other sons like me, alone. They were calling out the names of every prisoner, in order, while everyone waited. There was no shade. No water.

Two hours later the soldier called 'Mahmud Hamid.' Guards swarmed towards me as I entered the detention centre. One asked, 'Who are you coming to see?'

'My father, Mahmud Hamid.' I tried to stand taller than my twelve years on earth allowed. I tried to be a man, unafraid.

'He's yours,' the guard said to someone behind me in Hebrew. He motioned for me to walk through the metal detector.

An Uzi-bearing guard escorted me towards a door. Fear melted the muscles in my legs as my eyes adjusted to the dim light. Inside, guards groped naked men who stood against the wall.

'Strip,' my guard said.

My trembling body refused to obey.

'Strip.'

I willed my arms to move. Mechanically, I removed the shirt Mama had made for me the previous day from a used sheet. For hours, she had searched through the jars at the village square until she found matching buttons. The rest of the day she had spent stitching it together by hand, using dark thread to make each buttonhole. The guard extended his rubber-gloved hand, grabbed the shirt from me and tossed it on the dirty floor.

'Everything off.'

I slipped off my sandals, trousers and underwear, laid them next to my shirt and stood naked before the guard with my eyes glued to the floor.

'Against the wall.'

Trembling, I leaned forward.

'Shake your head.'

I shook my head.

The guard ran his gloved fingers through my hair as the smell of cigarettes on his breath soured my stomach. He thrust my head back and shone a light into my nose and mouth. I closed my eyes. After a metal probe was inserted into my nose and the crevices of my ears, I tasted blood. What was he looking for?

I wouldn't scream or whimper or beg. The gloved hands proceeded down my body to my buttocks and legs, which the guard kicked apart. I squeezed my eyes tighter and thought of Baba. Baba who was here because of me. I could endure anything to see him again. To tell him how sorry I was.

'Squat down.'

The guard pulled my buttocks apart and I gasped with pain as the instrument penetrated my rectum. I held my breath. When the instrument scraped my insides, my eyes watered. It was all I could do to keep from whimpering. The instrument snaked deeper inside me. My ears popped when the guard finally removed it.

Humiliated and naked, I stood before the guard, a person not that much older than me, while he examined every millimetre of my clothes.

'Get dressed.' He threw my clothes at my feet.

In the ten-by-ten-metre waiting room with the other visitors, no one made eye contact. We each knew what the other had gone through to get here, and we were ashamed. Veils covered the wrinkled faces of women as they squatted on the concrete floor. Leathery-skinned men in tattered robes and headdresses leaned against the walls. Parents attempted in vain to entertain their children, who cried and screamed and pushed each other. I stood in the corner and counted the people. Two hundred and twenty-four. I estimated that forty-four were under the age of five; sixty-eight were between six and eighteen; sixty were between nineteen and fifty-nine; and fifty-two were over sixty. The desert summer and number of people stole the air from the room.

Hours later, a guard led me to a glass booth with a telephone. Two guards assisted a shackled man dressed in a black jumpsuit into the room. My soul deflated. Baba hobbled towards me. When the soldiers burst into our family's home and beat him, a pit had formed in my stomach. Now that pit doubled in size.

His nose was thicker and tilted to the left. His left eyebrow and cheekbone were bigger than his right. I wanted to flee. I was going to pass out. But when Baba sat in the chair on the other side of the glass and picked up the phone, I did the same. He never lifted his eyes from the ground. Scabs covered his scalp. His once silky hair was gone.

'It doesn't hurt,' he said.

'How are you?' The lump in my throat made speech difficult. My eyes darted around the room at the other families gathered at glass windows.

'*Ilhamdillah*,' Baba replied in a low voice. Praise to Allah. What could I say?

'How's your mother?' Baba's head was still down.

'She wanted to come, but it was too expensive.'

'I'm glad she didn't have to see me like this.'

I rubbed my eyes.

'Did anyone find out what happened? I swear to you on Allah's life, I did nothing.' Baba's voice cracked and he took a deep breath. 'This is a big mistake.' He struggled to go on. 'But I'm afraid the Israelis will take their time uncovering the truth. My fellow inmate has been in here four years without being charged. You and your mother may need to provide for the family for a year or more. God willing, I'll be released sooner, but we need to prepare ourselves for the worst.' He laboured to breathe.

'A year?'

'They can detain me for a long time, even if I'm not guilty. They don't need to charge me with anything.'

The receiver slipped out of my sweaty hand. When I got it back to my ear, Baba said, 'I'm . . .'

On my left a woman began to wail while five young children clung to her legs. To the right of me, an elderly man held his hands over his face.

'This is all my fault,' I interrupted Baba, my voice barely a whisper.

Baba looked up for the first time. 'I don't understand.'

Haltingly, I began the story I had travelled so far to tell. The shame of it kept me from looking at him as I spoke.

Baba came close to the glass. My breath left me.

'Ahmed, my son, you're only twelve years old. Promise me you'll never tell another living soul that it was you, not me. Don't even tell your mother.'

Our eyes met for the first time since I began my confession. He was as white as a dove.

'Why should you be punished for my crime?'

'They'd imprison you.' Baba's facial muscles tightened. 'If

they didn't, others would have their young sons perpetrate these acts of liberation. They're not stupid. I'd be punished more if it was you in here.'

'But I should take responsibility.'

'It's my duty as a father to protect you.' He tapped his chest. Cigarette burns dotted his hands. 'A man is nothing unless he stands up for his family. Promise me that you'll make something of your life. Don't get sucked into this struggle. Make me proud. Don't let my imprisonment ruin your life. You need to find the best way to help your mother. She has no experience of being on her own. You're the man of the family now.'

'Please don't say such things. You'll be home soon.' I felt like I was falling down a well. There was nothing to grab hold of.

'No I won't.' He stared into my eyes. 'Promise me you'll take my role.'

'I don't know that I can.'

'When you have a son of your own, you'll realise what it means to love someone more than yourself.' Baba's voice cracked. 'I'd rather take a dagger to my chest than watch you suffer. Who knows what the soldiers would do to you?' He cleared his throat. 'Don't waste money visiting me. You'll need all you earn to support the family. Let everyone know my wishes. We can write. I'll be fine. Don't allow guilt to enter your heart, because it's a disease, like cancer, that'll eat away at you until there's nothing left.'

'What are we going to do without you?'

'Your mother and siblings will need you. Just promise me you'll make something of your life. I've so many things to tell you.' His voice choked. 'We only have a few moments left.' He spoke quickly. 'Go to my father's grave. Water the plants there every Friday.'

The phone went dead. I lifted my hand to the glass and so

did he. We looked at each other for a moment, until a guard came and yanked him up. Baba was so thin; it was like the man shook an empty uniform. He waved and the guard escorted him away. Without looking back, he disappeared through the door.

I stayed there, hoping something would happen. That the guard would return with him, tell me there was a mistake, that he was being released. Everyone around me was crying. The five wailing children on my left waved goodbye to their father. Their clothes were tattered, their stomachs distended.

I had promised Mama not to tell Baba about Sara or our house until he was released.

'There's nothing he can do about it while he's locked up.' She was adamant.

Now I realised that she was right; how could Baba stand to know that Sara was dead?

Courage, I realised, was not the absence of fear: it was the absence of selfishness; putting someone else's interest before one's own. I'd been wrong about Baba. He wasn't a coward. How would we survive without him?

9

After school Abbas and I made our way to the village square on an errand for Mama. We passed carts pulled by donkeys, and women with baskets on their heads, but when villagers saw us, they retreated, like they did when soldiers strutted through the village.

In the square, fresh apricots and apples gleamed in the sunlight. The sheep baaed and the lambs bleated. Two children peered into the moving-picture story box.

We turned towards the tea house and I thought of the day that I won the village backgammon championship. Baba had bought tea for everyone in the place—it took him a year to pay off his tab. The radio blared the latest news from Jordan, but I didn't tarry.

Inside the general store, Abbas and I scanned the wooden shelves behind the checkout counter. Arabic coffee, tea, tins of sardines, containers of olive oil. On the ground beneath the shelves sat large clay jugs marked bulgur wheat, semolina and rice. Three soldiers entered the store behind us.

'I'd like a sack of rice please, doctor,' I said; 'and charge it to my father's account.'

'His account's been cancelled,' the store owner said as he peered at the soldiers. Then he bent and whispered to Abbas and me, 'I'm so sorry.' I dared not argue with him, but how could I be the man of the house if I could not even get a little rice?

Abbas and I left the store empty-handed, knowing that we had eaten the very last of the rice the previous night. We had nothing else.

Fathers and sons were everywhere I went. In an attempt to keep from dwelling on thoughts about my own father, I played mathematical games. I estimated the number of villagers who came to the square daily. I thought of the factors that influenced the equation, like how many came to the mosque daily, the hours the tea house and store were open, the number of times people came to use the village well.

***

The tent, for me, symbolised ruin. It was constantly filled with flies, mosquitoes, ants and rats. The insects found our mouths as we slept. I opened the flap to crawl in, but before I could, Mama pushed out through it. She was holding a letter. 'What does this say?' She thrust it into my hand. Abbas, who was by my side, began to read along with me.

The words rose off the paper like waves of heat. I closed my eyes. This had to be a mistake. I reread it. For the first time in my life, I thanked God that Mama was illiterate. It was an Arabic form-letter with one handwritten sentence. *The prisoner Mahmud Hamid is sentenced to fourteen years.* I glanced at Abbas. He was white as labaneh.

I crumpled the paper and squeezed it in my left hand. The folded corner dug into my skin.

'Is it about your father?'

'Yes.'

'Was he hurt?'

'No.' I clutched the wadded-up letter to my chest.

'Does it say when he's coming home?'

'No.'

Abbas' and my eyes met. He knew not to speak.

'Is it about his sentence?'

My temples throbbed.

'It's about his sentence, isn't it?' When I didn't answer right away, she grabbed the letter, uncrumpled it and stared at it as if she were willing herself to read.

She looked directly at Abbas. 'Tell me what it says.'

He remained silent.

Fourteen years. That was 730 weeks rounded down. 5,113 days; 122,712 hours; 7,363,720 minutes; 441,824,200 seconds. Which figure sounded like the least amount of time? I took a long, deep breath and tried to steady my voice. 'Fourteen years.'

'Fourteen years?' she echoed. Her face was ashen.

'Yes.'

'How could he do this to us? Did he forget he had a family? All his preaching about not getting involved in politics, and he jeopardised our lives?'

'No, you don't understand.' The words stuck in my throat. 'They can sentence him even though he wasn't guilty.'

She took a deep breath. 'Did the weapons plant themselves?'

'They could have planted them,' Abbas said.

With the back of my hand, I wiped the sweat off my forehead. The images of Baba in the black prison jumpsuit, chained like an animal, filled my mind. I thought of him out in the pen forced to move sand under the scalding sun. What if he didn't survive? This wasn't like death, I tried to tell myself. It was only fourteen years. My mind began to conjure hideous scenarios: Baba hung upside down while they burned him with their cigarettes, shackled to a chair in their banana bend position until they crippled him. All the stories I knew to be true.

'You're right.' Mama shook her head. 'Your father would never do anything like that.' Then her legs gave out. Abbas and I caught her and helped her to sit down. Whimpering, she buried her wrinkled face in her hefty arms. Her pain scared me.

'What are we going to do? Tell me!'

'I'll support us,' I said.

'Doing what?' Her voice was muffled because her head was in her hands.

My heart felt heavier. 'I'll build houses for the Jews.' What else could I do? I was caught, again, between the devil and the hell fires.

'How can I let you do that?' she asked. 'You're only a child.'

'Good things make choosing difficult. Bad things leave no choice.' I repeated what Baba answered when I asked him why he went to work for the Jews. 'You'll see. I'll learn to take money from the lion's mouth.'

Mama's eyes watered. 'May Allah bless your every breath and footstep.'

'I'll work too,' Abbas said.

Mama shook her head. 'You're too young.'

'It'll be easier if we're together.' Abbas smiled at me.

'Tomorrow I'll start working,' I said with finality. I realised I hadn't yet told her about the rice: we wouldn't be eating tonight. Being a man was much harder than it looked.

'Me too,' Abbas said.

'You're only eleven,' Mama reminded him.

'Good things make choosing difficult, bad things leave no choice,' Abbas repeated with a little grin.

***

The next morning, Mama went outside the tent to boil water and found a sack of rice next to the tent. Abu Khalil, the owner of the general store, must have put himself at risk and brought it to us while we slept. Mama made us tea from well-water and the same tea leaves she'd been using for the last week. I grabbed the pitcher and poured cold water into our tea so that we wouldn't have to wait for it to cool down. Abbas and I gulped the tea and raced down the hill.

We were the only ones at the entrance to the village. I remembered Baba telling me that he'd started working for the Jews accidentally. He'd woken up early one morning to go and work at the moshav picking oranges. He'd been the first one waiting at the entrance when a truck of Jewish workers drove by. He'd put his arm out, thinking it was the moshav's truck. When it stopped, the driver told him that they were construction workers and that they could use a cheap, strong Arab labourer. He'd decided to try it out.

Abbas and I stepped into the middle of the road when we heard the engine. The truck came straight at us. I didn't care. I'd do whatever it took to make it stop. A few metres in front of me, the driver slammed on his brakes and the truck skidded to the side of the road. I ran to the driver's window while Abbas positioned himself in front with his arms out.

'Please hire us.' I'd rehearsed in my head all night what I'd say in Hebrew.

'You're children.' The driver looked us up and down.

'We're strong.'

'Move out of my way.' The driver beeped the horn.

'We'll work for free today. If we're not good, don't pay us. Please, give us a chance.'

'Free?' The driver raised his eyebrows. 'What's the catch?'

'My father can't work. We have a large family.' I took a deep breath. 'We need money.'

'If you're not good, you two will have to walk back.'

'You won't regret this.'

'I already do.' The driver motioned for us to get in the back with the other workers.

Abbas and I climbed into the cargo area. The olive-skinned labourers sat on the left, the light-skinned ones on the right.

'What do you think you're doing?' an olive-skinned worker asked in Hebrew with a heavy Arabic accent.

'We're going to work,' I said in Arabic.

'In this country, we speak Hebrew,' Olive-Skin said. 'Arabs and Arabic aren't welcome.'

Abbas opened his mouth to respond. He was not afraid to defend himself and others, which had led to more than a few fights at school. I squeezed his hand as tight as I could and stared into his eyes.

Abbas and I moved into the corner and the truck sped away from the village. All eyes glared at us as if we were vermin. The first second we were alone, I made Abbas promise not to respond, no matter what. I knew how difficult that would be for him, but he also knew that the welfare of our family depended on us. He gave me his word and I knew he wouldn't let me down.

10

During the break at work, the Ashkenazi Jews from Russia, Poland, Romania, Transylvania and Lithuania sat together under one clump of olive trees speaking in a language I didn't understand. We learned Hebrew in school, but this wasn't it. They mainly had light eyes, which turned to slits under the sun, while their fair skin turned bright red. They were our bosses. They gave directions from shady spots under the trees or inside the structures we built.

Under a different clump of olive trees sat the Jewish Sephardim from Iraq, Yemen, Algeria, Libya and Morocco. They drank tea and coffee and spoke to each other in Arabic. The Iraqi told the Yemenite that the Ashkenazim spoke in Yiddish. I guess Sephardim only spoke Arabic when they didn't want the Ashkenazim to understand them.

The Ashkenazim laughed at the Sephardim when they drank their steaming liquids. 'Aren't you hot enough?' The Russian pointed to their coffee. The Ashkenazim didn't understand heat.

Abbas and I worked through the break.

'Robot brothers!' Our main boss Yossi, a Polish Jew, motioned for us to come over. He'd given us the nickname after he saw we weren't stopping to rest.

Abbas looked at me, his eyes filled with distrust. 'It'll be fine,' I reassured him. Yossi met us halfway. Together we were so small that we could fit into his shadow.

'I changed my mind. You're worth a full Arab's wage. But know this: I can change it back if I see either of you slacking.'

I wondered what he meant by a full Arab's wage. We weren't even making a fraction of what Baba earned. 'We won't disappoint you,' I said.

Abbas and I filled wheelbarrow after wheelbarrow with cinderblocks from the truck on the road and wheeled them over to the construction site where we unloaded them. We worked together to move the wheelbarrow because we were half the size of the rest of the workers. My back ached. My clothes were soaked with sweat and covered with dirt. We built villas from the bottom up. In the week since Abbas and I started, we'd already built a first floor, and the second was two-thirds done.

The sun beat down. Abbas and I were loading the cinderblocks into the wheelbarrow when he pressed his hands on his back and groaned.

'Are you all right?' I could see the pain in his face. He looked like an old man, not an eleven-year-old boy.

'My back's stiff from bending.'

'Stand straight. I'll hand the blocks to you. Just load them into the wheelbarrow.' I bent and handed the blocks to Abbas. When the wheelbarrow was loaded, we took it to the mason. As we rolled it past the Sephardim, my eyes met the Iraqi's.

'What are you looking at?' the Iraqi asked me in Hebrew with a heavy Arabic accent. Too many years of coffee and tea had left their mark on his teeth. He thrust his arms at me from a dozen metres away, like he was going to wring my neck. I lowered my eyes and pushed the wheelbarrow forward.

'*Ben Zonah.*' Son of a whore. The Iraqi swore at me in Hebrew even though Israelis almost always swear in Arabic.

At lunchtime, we all grabbed our paper sacks from the back

of the truck and retreated to our usual places. Abbas and I ate alone.

The Iraqi and the Yemenite rolled their rice into balls with their fingers before eating. The Ashkenazim used forks, knives and spoons. Mama packed Abbas and me a piece of pita and a bag of rice and almonds.

'Here.' I handed Abbas the pita. He ripped it in half and gave me the larger portion. 'No, you take it.' I held it to him but he wouldn't take it. 'Please, Abbas. I'll throw it away if you don't take it.' I held it up as if to toss it; he grabbed it at the last moment. I took the smaller piece and placed the bag of rice on the ground between us, so we could scoop it up with pieces of the pita. When we finished eating, the Ashkenazim and the Sephardim threw their bags in with the rubbish. I folded ours and put it in my pocket, so Mama could use it the next day.

Before we left each day, Abbas and I always passed by the rubbish dump. Yesterday, we had found an old shirt and a radio battery. A couple of days before, we had found a plastic toy car. Even though we felt like scavengers harvesting olives after a locust swarm, that didn't stop us. We didn't care that the entire ride home the Jews laughed at us as we clutched their rubbish.

The Iraqi was the worst. I don't know why. When we stopped at his house to drop him off, there were at least fifteen children of all ages running around, dirty and unkempt. His wife emerged pregnant, with curlers in her hair and a missing front tooth. They lived in an Arab villa; once whitewashed, it was now the colour of mud. Laundry hung on lines, rubbish lay strewn across the yard, the gardens were overrun with weeds.

About the time the sun started to set on the western horizon, Yossi stopped on the road outside our village and Abbas and I jumped out. We walked painfully back to our tent. The tightness of the muscles in my back and neck made me stagger as if I were dragging shackles.

Mama made me write Baba a letter to tell him that Abbas and I had found work. She said it was important to let him think we were all right. Baba wrote back that he wished we could stay in school. With great sadness, I wrote to him that it was impossible.

11

The tar wouldn't come off my hands. Since water had failed, I was using sand, a trick Baba had taught me. I had begun to think I might be scrubbing off my skin, when I heard footsteps coming up the hill.

'Ahmed,' Teacher Mohammad called.

Ashamed, I hid my hands behind my back.

'Your absences from school are inexcusable.'

What did he want me to do?

He reached me and stood a metre away. 'Do not turn your back on your gifts. Let them be the lights that guide you through life. When obstacles get in your way, look to your lights.' He touched my chin to tilt my face towards him. 'You are destined for great things.'

I couldn't escape his eyes. 'There's no choice.'

'There's always a choice.'

'I have to work all day.' I turned from him just enough to evade his terrible compassionate stare.

I remembered the day I graduated from third grade. During the small ceremony in our classroom, Teacher Mohammad presented each student with a diploma. Afterwards, he called me back up.

'This certificate goes to the top student in the class.' He shook my hand and kissed me on each cheek. 'Keep your eyes on this boy. He's going to make our people proud.' Baba had made the V for victory with his index and middle fingers.

***

'I would like to tutor you,' Teacher Mohammad said. 'Every day after work. Let us start tonight. Have you had anything to eat yet?'

'Yes,' I lied. I was starving.

'Come to my house now. We still have two hours until curfew.'

The open blisters on my feet stung with every step I took towards his house. We sat at his kitchen table.

'Can I get you something to eat?' he asked.

'No thanks.' I didn't want to become a burden. My stomach growled and I squeezed it with my fist.

He wrote a maths problem on a slate and passed it to me. My hand was weak and burned from carrying hot tar up scaffolding, but I didn't care. If a person like Teacher Mohammad believed in me, I'd do whatever it took.

12

A shadow appeared over me. It had to be a soldier; no one visited us anymore. Abbas cowered next to me. Slowly, I turned.

'It's Uncle Kamal,' I said. He had been released. His cheeks were hollow and his shoulders slumped. He limped over.

'What happened?' Abbas shook his head.

'I fell.'

That's when I noticed his cane.

'Twisted my ankle.'

His wrists were bandaged.

Fadi and Hani sat in the dirt outside the tent comparing bullet casings.

'What are you doing here?' I asked. 'You could get sent back.'

'I had to see you.'

Neither Abbas nor I had ever spoken man to man with my uncle. At least three times a week, he'd come to play backgammon, or smoke water pipes with Baba. They'd talked of the days before the creation of the State of Israel when they'd travelled throughout Palestine.

Baba and Uncle Kamal had spoken of the coastal plains along the Mediterranean Sea with its sandy shoreline, bordered by stretches of fertile land. Mountain ranges. The hills of the Galilee with streams and ample rainfall that kept it green all year round. The rolling hills of the West Bank with its rocky hilltops and fertile valleys.

Abbas and I charted their travels on a map we drew that divided Palestine into districts: Acre, Haifa, Jaffa, Gaza, Tiberius, Baysan, Nazareth, Jenin, Nablus, Ramallah, Jerusalem, Hebron, Be'er Sheva, Tulkaram, Al-Ramla and Safed. Any time Baba and Uncle Kamal mentioned one of the over 600 Palestinian villages or numerous cities, we'd mark it on the map.

Jaffa, the bride of Palestine, occupied many of their talks. From these talks, Abbas and I learned how in the mid-nineteenth century Palestinians developed the Shamouti orange, also known as the Jaffa orange. Jaffa, a major port, was by 1870 already exporting thirty-eight million of those oranges through imperial and global distribution networks, along with other commodities. Baba even spoke about Tel Aviv, the city the Jews built in the sand dunes next to Jaffa. The only place Baba didn't speak highly of was the Negev desert, which unfortunately was still a desert.

The man who stood in front of us looked nothing like our Uncle Kamal, who used to love to laugh and speak of his great adventures. It was hard to see him this way. As the head of our household, I did what Baba would have done. 'We appreciate all you did for us.' I poured well-water into the pan and Abbas put it on to boil. 'But, you have a family of ten.'

'I want to help,' he said.

I tried to sound grown up. 'They'll send you back.'

Uncle Kamal's eyes darted around. He lowered his voice. 'What's happened to your father?'

'In his letters, he says he's fine. He said that one of the guards overheard him singing. They actually brought him an oud and he entertains them.'

The water began to boil and Abbas dumped the rice in.

'Yes, I'm sure it's so hard for the poor guards. How are you?'

'Abbas, take Fadi and Hani inside.' I motioned towards the tent and Abbas was immediately on it. We worked well as a team.

'May Allah have mercy on you, Uncle Kamal,' Hani said, before he disappeared inside.

Fadi remained outside staring at Uncle Kamal.

'Go!' Abbas pushed him in and then returned to my side.

'How are you boys?' Uncle Kamal asked.

'I'm fine,' Abbas and I answered in unison.

'This is so unfair,' he whispered. 'I fear for your father. The prison . . .'

I put my finger to my lips. What if, God forbid, Mama or my siblings heard? 'Let's talk later.'

'They have no regard for human rights,' he hunched over and whispered. 'What can I do?'

'You have your own family,' I said.

'You're in a tent, too,' Abbas added.

'They're not going to let your father go. Whose weapons were those? Did they plant them to get this hill? They have enough sniper towers.' Uncle Kamal shook his head.

I took the rice off the fire. 'Let's talk later.'

'They do whatever they want,' he said.

'Please. Not now.' I cocked my head in the direction of the tent in the most exaggerated way I could.

'Fourteen years.' He shook his head.

Mama came out of the tent with the wet rags she had been using on Nadia to bring her fever down. All night Nadia had been in and out of consciousness, burning up with fever. What if it spread to Fadi and Hani or, worse yet, Abbas or me? We couldn't afford to get sick.

Abbas handed Mama the pot of rice.

'Curfew's minutes away,' I said.

Uncle Kamal looked down at the ground. 'This must be awful for you.'

I stood, as if to shield myself from his sympathy. 'We're managing.'

'So what,' he asked, without looking up, 'did your father say they were doing to him?'

Why didn't he understand that I didn't want to talk about this? 'I need to check on my mother . . .'

'How did he look?'

Images of Baba shackled like an animal overwhelmed me. Uncle Kamal covered his eyes with his hands.

'I want to help.' His facial muscles tightened and his body shook. 'Please, excuse me. Honestly. I'm so upset. I'm sorry.' Tears formed in his eyes. He turned and made his way down the hill.

'We're fine,' I called to him. But we were not. How could I afford shoes for Hani? The cheap buckle on his already too-small sandal had broken and he'd been walking around barefoot for two weeks. No one had eaten until they were full since the house was destroyed; hunger tracked us constantly. There were afternoons when I thought of sneaking into Moshav Dan and stealing fruit. But then I thought of the barbed wire, the armed guards, the beatings. I was failing my family.

Every evening after dinner, I went to Teacher Mohammad's house. And for a short while, I'd climb out of my purgatory. The time with Teacher Mohammad was the most cherished part of my day. Somewhere inside of me, I knew that Teacher Mohammad held the key to Baba's wish.

When I was with him, I felt like I wasn't bearing my burden alone, that we were a team. When I was with him, I could see possibility. If Baba's imprisonment had been some sort of test of faith, my belief was in science to pull him through. When I'd return to the tent just before curfew, I'd continue studying by the moonlight and the lights from Moshav Dan. I was also tutoring Abbas, but he often felt too tired to study with me.

Before bed, I'd wash behind a sheet I'd hung from Shahida, the almond tree. I'd purchased a small tin tub, and during the day Mama would drag water up the hill. I'd be the last one each night to stand in it and pour water all over my body.

I knew the only way to improve our conditions was for me to work harder.

13

Bile rose up my oesophagus as I pushed a wheelbarrow filled with cinderblocks to the base of the house. Inside the structure, Abbas was hammering beams together. I had insisted he take that job. It was hard to work outside in the heat during the Ramadan fast. The sun was scorching, but I had the chills. My skin felt cold and damp.

No matter how thirsty I was, I wouldn't allow myself to take even a sip of water. According to the Imam, if I fasted for Ramadan, not only would Allah forgive all my past sins, he'd also answer my prayers. The sun pounded down on me. My threadbare clothing provided little protection.

I prayed that tonight would be the first sighting of the crescent moon, which would end this month-long fast. And then I began to regret it. This was the holiest month of the year; the month the Koran had been revealed. For the past twenty-nine days, all I'd eaten was a small portion of rice and water at the crack of dawn, and the rest of the day I fasted. By 6am we were on the job, and now the sky was beginning to darken.

The palms of my hands were raw where my blisters popped. The cinderblocks dug into my wounds and made them bleed, but I continued to load them onto the truck. Despite the hour, the air still felt like fire. I'd stopped perspiring. My vision had blurred. The day seemed never-ending. No matter what, I'd continue. I kept repeating the Imam's words, 'If you fast for the month, your sins will be pardoned.'

I unloaded the wheelbarrow as quickly as I could and only used the energy to lift my head when the barrow was empty. The air seemed full of fog, which was impossible.

Suddenly the Iraqi grabbed me by the shirt and cuffed me on the head. Instinctively, my arms shot up to protect my face. Stunned, I cowered.

'Avee!' the Russian said. 'Let him go.'

'He's too slow,' the Iraqi said. 'I need to keep him in line.'

The Russian took a couple of steps towards the Iraqi. 'Back off.'

'I'm warning you,' the Iraqi said. 'Don't disgrace me in front of the Arab. He'll never listen to me again if I don't keep him and his bastard brother in line.'

Thank God Abbas was out of earshot.

The Russian countered, 'Kindness creates loyalty.'

The Iraqi's face turned a dangerous colour of red. 'Let them take the rest of the day off.' The veins in his neck bulged. 'The house will build itself.'

The last thing I remember was vomiting on the side of the wheelbarrow and then everything went black. Cold water hit my head. A blurry face looked down at me. It was Abbas.

'Thank God.' Abbas' voice was choked. 'You fainted.'

'Did I drink any water?'

'No. Should I get you some?'

'Absolutely not.'

He extended his hands to me and pulled me up.

'The truck's here,' Abbas said.

Slowly I got up and brushed the dirt from my hair and clothes. He helped me to walk. We crammed into the back with the men. The stench of our sweat made me sick to my stomach.

***

We passed by children waiting at the entrance to our village. A truck from the moshav pulled up behind us and they ran to their fathers, hugging and kissing them, laughing and happy. I glanced at Abbas. Was that anger or sadness on his face?

On our walk up the hill, the aromas of grilled lamb, garlic and vegetable stew emanated from every house. Abbas walked with his head down. Everyone was preparing for the breakfast celebration.

'Do you think Mama has prepared a special meal?' he asked, with hope in his voice.

For his sake, I prayed she had. We'd been living on almond bread, almond butter, raw almonds, fire-roasted almonds, almonds and rice and almond soup. The almond tree was a blessing. But today was a holiday. Every year, on the holiday, we gathered together and ate *katayif* in honour of Amal. It was her favourite dessert. Would we still be able to do that this year?

'How was Baba able to support us?' Abbas asked.

'We lived mostly from money he saved when he owned the orange groves,' I said. 'And Baba made twice as much as Yossi is paying us together. We can't do the same work as an adult. And we have more expenses. Don't forget, everything we owned was destroyed.'

My hunger was greater than usual. My stomach convulsed as if it was attempting to eat away its own lining. With my hands, I pressed against it to dull the pain.

I began to calculate the number of almonds that grew on our tree every year. First I counted the number of branches in the tree.

'Ahmed,' Abbas said. 'Go and wash.'

'What about the muezzin's call to prayer?'

'You were passed out,' Abbas said. 'The crescent was spotted. Go ahead, you're the oldest.'

Mama handed me the pitcher and I poured the water over my hands before cleansing my mouth, face, arms and feet. Maybe I rushed my cleaning. The Imam said we needed to be purified for prayer. It was important for me to do everything right. Maybe this could help Baba. When Nadia finished cleansing herself, I washed my hands again.

'What are you doing?' Abbas asked.

'I missed a few spots.'

'Hurry up!' Abbas said. 'I'm starving.' I noticed the deep circles around his sunken eyes.

Abbas, Fadi, Hani and I lined up shoulder to shoulder outside our tent facing Mecca, Mama and Nadia behind us. We all stood erect, with our heads down and hands at our sides.

'*Allahu Akbar*,' we began. God is great.

With my eyes closed, I pretended I was eating the stews, sautéed vegetables and halal meats we always ate to break the fast. Visions of dishes appeared. Crispy hot falafel. Sweet baklava.

All we had was a bowl of rice apiece. After the meal, Abbas and I sat in the corner and read the Koran by lantern light. Our clothes were too worn out to wear into the mosque. Secretly, I prayed the Palestinian Freedom Fighters would capture an Israeli and Baba would be released in a prisoner exchange.

That night in the dark, I listened to Mama sobbing. She must have thought I was asleep. My stomach convulsed with hunger. Then it occurred to me. I could make weapons to hunt animals.

***

On Friday afternoons, we didn't have work because it was the Jews' day of rest, so Abbas and I headed out to what remained of our village's grazing pasture to set traps and try to catch rabbits and birds. We walked carefully, searching for bedding and feeding areas as well as waterholes. Luck was with us, and we happened upon a rabbit hole.

We lay on the ground, each of us on one side of the hole, and placed over it the noosing wand I'd built from a pole and piece of wire I'd found in the garbage at work. With the wire slip noose over the hole, we waited for a rabbit to emerge.

As we lay on the ground, I saw a herd of sheep coming in my direction. I could just see them over the tall grasses without moving from my position. Their short feet kicked up dust, their cries of *baa baa baa* were like the resonance of a musical instrument, and their progression was by sideways leaps and playful butting.

From their midst, a shepherdess appeared. She was a delicate girl with black curly hair that reached the small of her back, and green twinkling eyes. She was so petite, how could she possibly handle the entire herd alone? With her stick, she sharply tapped each sheep that tried to stray. Our eyes met. She was the most beautiful thing I'd ever seen. I smiled at her and she smiled back and, before I knew it, she and the sheep had passed by.

***

On Saturday morning I hurried back to the rabbit hole with a spear, a plank, forked sticks and a wire noose. I told Abbas he didn't need to come, that I could easily set the traps myself. Secretly, I hoped to see the shepherdess. On either side of the rabbit's run, I set up forked sticks, laid a cross-piece with a wire noose hanging from it across them and waited.

The wind carried a girl's voice to me, shouting, 'Help me!'

With my spear and plank in hand, I ran to the voice. The shepherdess was up against a tree, a raggedy jackal advancing towards her. I ran in front of her, waving my arms at the creature, but it didn't run away. That's when I saw the froth at its mouth. It continued to come at us, trance-like.

I ran at the jackal and drove my spear into its neck. With my other hand, I cracked it over the head with a plank. It fell to the ground and began convulsing. I clubbed it again and again until it wasn't moving anymore.

Perhaps I was in shock. I just stood over the thing, not believing what I'd done without thought, without fear. The shepherdess ran over and threw her arms around me. She must have realised her madness because, within a second, she released me and stepped back.

'Were you bitten?' I asked in an attempt to break the awkward silence.

'No, thanks to you.' Her face flushed.

'What about your sheep?'

'Not that I know of,' she said. 'The jackals always run away. This one was different.' She smiled and began to tap her sheep. Within seconds she was gone.

A rustling in the brush behind me startled me—what if there were more jackals? I swung around, but there was nothing. My trap! Caught in my noose was a big white rabbit. I picked it up by the ears and brought it home. Maybe my luck was changing.

***

The next day, the Jews declared the area where I'd encountered the shepherdess 'closed' and barred us from entering. The news about my killing the rabid jackal circulated throughout the village. When I passed villagers, they congratulated me with their eyes. Abbas asked me to repeat the details of the story numerous times. My siblings considered me a hero, but I felt empty. I didn't feel there was anything heroic about killing. The animal was sick. I'd done it in self-defence and for survival, but that didn't make me feel proud. The only person I confided my feelings to was Baba. He wrote back that he would have felt the same way.

14

The flatbed truck pulled up by our construction site to deliver trees. 'Where are you two going?' the Yemenite asked.

'To buy a sapling,' I said.

Abbas shook his head. 'What?'

'From the Jewish National Fund?' The Yemenite's voice was suspicious.

The driver showed me the different trees that were available that day: cypresses, pines, almonds, figs, carobs and olive trees. Abbas stood a metre behind me.

'I'll take that one.' I pointed to an olive sapling.

The driver scrunched his brow. I paid him my day's wage for the sapling and some mineral dust.

'Are you crazy?' Abbas' facial muscles were taut.

'We're going to plant it in Baba's honour.'

'A tree from the Jewish National Fund? They stole our land and forbade us to benefit from it. They don't need our money. They control over ninety per cent of the land.'

I shrugged. 'Where else could I buy this?'

***

That evening after work, Abbas and I gathered our family around the almond tree and I held up the olive sapling. 'Every year we'll plant an olive tree in Baba's honour until he's released,' I said.

Abbas and I dug an area sufficient for the sapling's size with the shovels I had used with Ali, and to bury Sara, and we planted the sapling. Together, Abbas and I spread well-rotted donkey manure that Mama had prepared over the area. When we finished, Mama spread the mineral dust.

Mama and my siblings sat in a circle around the tree and I read the relevant part of Baba's letter:

Your idea to plant the olive tree in my honour brought tears to my eyes. I don't care if you purchase the sapling from the Jewish National Fund. I pray our people and the Jewish Israelis will one day work together to build up the country, rather than destroy it.

I put the letter down. My eyes met Fadi's.

'You're both crazy.' He tried to get up but Mama held him down.

'Think of your favourite memory of Baba,' I said.

'No one could build things like Baba,' Abbas said. 'Remember the cart?' Abbas and I had helped Baba make it from wood. It was my idea to make the wheels from tin cans. When he pulled us through the centre of the village in it, everyone stared.

'What about the rocket launcher?' Fadi said. Baba had made the launcher from scrap pipes and an empty water bottle. The rocket could reach the top branches of the almond tree.

'And the skipping rope?' Nadia said. Baba had collected scraps of rope from work.

'Don't forget those bows and arrows,' Abbas said. 'And the cardboard bull's-eye.' Baba, Abbas and I had broken off branches from the almond tree to make the arrows. We'd painted a black dot with circles around it for the bull's-eye and had hung it from the tree. Abbas and I had spent hours trying to hit that centre dot.

'Nothing beats that backgammon board,' I said. 'Remember

how he painted the rocks for pieces.' Baba had spent hours playing with me until I became unbeatable.

'Let's go to the cemetery, to grandfather's grave,' I said. Every Friday before Baba had gone to the mosque, he'd stopped at the cemetery to water the flowers he'd planted at his father's grave. When Baba went to prison, I took over the job.

'Then, let's go to the mosque,' Mama said. 'Your father always went on Fridays.' It was important to Mama, I told myself.

In the mosque, Abbas, Fadi, Hani and I stood on the rugs that were laid on the glazed tile floor with all the fathers and sons. Mama and Nadia stood at the back with the women. Uncle Kamal was there with his sons. I couldn't help feeling everyone's pity and it saddened me. I looked at the mihrab that pointed to Mecca. I remembered when Baba showed me where Mohammad Pasha, a governor during the Ottoman rule, had inscribed on it his name along with the date 1663. Abbas' cheeks were wet with tears. It was so painful for me to watch all the other fathers and sons, to see Uncle Kamal, and to know that Baba was in prison and Sara and Amal were dead.

We sat on the prayer mats and the imam began his sermon from behind the white marble minbar about the importance of father–son relationships and how children were young for such a short time; how fathers should take the time to enjoy their children. I saw the barber with his son in the corner and I was reminded that Baba, too, would return. The limestone blocks and cross-vaulted ceiling of the mosque, which I had always looked at in awe, now shrunk me. Because of me, Baba couldn't enjoy its beauty with us.

As we returned to the tent we passed the square foundation of mud-brick that once was our home. I could remember each portrait Baba had drawn—especially the one of Baba holding me the day I was born. He looked like the happiest man alive. If only he'd known then the suffering I'd bring upon us all.

We sat around the fire and I told my siblings about Baba's orange groves and how he'd taken charity to the villagers, and made music at everyone's happy occasions. I wanted my siblings to know that they had a father; to know what he was like; to remember him. It was easier for Abbas and me—we'd spent more time with him—but Hani was so young.

***

Time moved forward, further from the days when my family was happy and complete. When the winter rain pounded our tent, I closed my eyes and thought of my cousin Ibrahim's wedding. I remembered Baba eating the sweet baklava and dancing dabkeh with the other men. I thought of all the weddings at which Baba had played his oud and I wished he could play me one of his happy melodies. Baba loved the rain. 'It's good for the land,' he'd say. 'The trees need it.' Even five years after our land was gone, he still rejoiced when it rained.

Now the water leaked into our tent, cold and damp. The ground under us became mud. I pretended we were back in our house listening to the patter of the winter rain on the roof from under our goatskin blankets. But I still felt the cold in my bones.

***

'Don't you bathe?' the Iraqi asked Abbas and me.

'They're stained,' I said, looking at my trousers. Even though Mama and Nadia washed our clothes daily on the washboard, they could never get out the stains.

'Your feet are a muddy mess,' the Yemenite said. 'What are you wearing?'

Abbas and I tucked our feet under us and hid the shoes Mama had made us from an old tyre.

That night, Abbas and I brought home one of the big cardboard boxes that the Jews' refrigerators came in and covered it in plastic. Mama slept in it outside the tent and awoke dry. Every day we brought home another box until each of my family members had their own.

Each time Abbas and I brought home the Jews' trash, we endured torment. I didn't know how much more Abbas could take before he snapped.

15

The January cold bore into my bones. Mama had knitted me a sweater, but the constant rain soaked it through. Abbas and I were tying in the last bit of rebar in preparation for pouring the fifth floor of an apartment building. Fortunately, the concrete moulds on the floor above protected us from deluge for the moment.

'Abbas?' I looked over. My little brother's teeth were chattering, his fingers trembling. If only I could get him a proper coat. 'Call for the cement dispenser.' I wanted to finish prepping the floor.

He glanced at me then turned towards the scaffolding. He walked hunched over, like he was trying to conserve his body heat by reducing his size. Once on the scaffolding, he motioned for the crane to bring the dispenser.

'Son of a dog!' the Iraqi shouted. He squeezed the trowel in his hand so hard his fist turned white. Earlier, he had spat on my foot. His phlegm was warm and sticky. When I bent down to wipe it off, he said, 'Your time's up!'

Yossi explained to Abbas and me that today was the first anniversary of the death of the Iraqi's son and that we should ignore him because he wasn't in his right mind.

I heard the trowel drop and turned to see the Iraqi run at Abbas. Jumping to my feet, I flew across the concrete moulds, but I was too late. The Iraqi pushed Abbas off the scaffold. He fell backwards. His arms and legs flailed. A primal scream pierced the air. Then, a horrible thud.

'Abbas!' Within seconds, I was on the ground floor running to him. His body was splayed in the mud. Blood pooled under his head. Rain pelted him.

'Abbas!' I bent next to his head, panicked. 'Get up!'

Yossi lifted his limp arm. I threw myself at Yossi and knocked him backward. 'Leave him alone.' Tears mixed with rain as I pinned my boss to the ground.

Yossi didn't fight back. 'His pulse,' he said.

The other labourers pulled me off him and held me back. It was my little brother. My best friend. My responsibility. My failure if he was dead. The rain blurred my vision.

Yossi felt Abbas' wrist. 'He's alive.' The Israelis went into action. 'Get the plank! I'll drive him. No time for an ambulance.'

'Stay strong, Abbas. Stay strong,' I shouted over and over again.

Abbas didn't respond.

'You're going to be fine, Abbas,' I said.

The labourers released me.

The Lithuanian and the Russian placed the plank on the ground next to him. Together, we slid it under Abbas' body and lifted him into the back of Yossi's pickup truck. I jumped in next to him, leaning over his head to protect him from the rain, holding on to the side of the truck for my life as Yossi sped on the dirt, then paved roads at a terrible pace. The scenario in the building played over in my mind. I would have set myself on fire if I could have prevented this from happening.

Yossi made the truck fly, but still the ride seemed never-ending. My body rocked forward and backwards as if it were part of the truck. We passed by cranes, buildings partially finished and new homes. Near them were older homes built from mud-bricks and local stone. I maintained my position over Abbas. But, despite my efforts to protect him from the rain, he still got wet.

'I'm right here,' I said. 'I won't let anything else happen to you.'

***

We pulled into the emergency room drive. Yossi ran inside and returned with a swarm of people dressed in blue pushing a stretcher. They transferred Abbas and rushed him inside. I stayed by his side until they wheeled him through swinging doors. When I tried to enter, a nurse held me back.

'We need some information.'

'I'm coming, Abbas,' I said. 'Please,' I told the nurse. 'My brother's only twelve.'

'Let him through,' Yossi said. 'His brother needs him.' The nurse started to follow me, asking about Abbas' medical history and insurance. 'Is he allergic to anything? Has he ever had anaesthetics?' I broke into a run, searching the corridors until I caught sight of him.

'Where are you taking him?' I asked the moon-faced man who pushed his stretcher.

'Surgery.' Moon-face did not stop. 'To your left is the waiting room. Get your parents. When the surgery's finished, the doctor will come to talk to them.'

I caught up and clutched Abbas' hand. 'I can't leave him alone.'

'It's not allowed,' he said. 'Go get your parents.'

A nurse came out of nowhere. 'Come, sit down. They're doing everything they can. Let them get started.' I squeezed Abbas' limp hand and whispered, 'Stay strong, Abbas. Stay strong.' They wheeled him into surgery.

The nurse guided me to a waiting area filled with people on plastic chairs. A young couple cried in the corner. The woman's face was pressed against the man's chest, which muffled her wails. A woman with a face full of creases and a humped back stood in the doorway, her mouth gaping like she was in a trance. An emotionless man with stooped shoulders paced back and forth across the room in five strides. Children pushed each other, bored. I found an empty chair in the corner. Yossi sat next to me.

'You don't have to wait with me,' I said, a little ashamed that I had jumped on him.

'I need to see how he is. I'm so sorry.' He shook his head. 'Avee wasn't himself today.'

'Who?'

'The Israeli from Iraq.'

'My brother didn't kill his son.'

'I'm not trying to justify what he did. Avee's a prisoner of his own hatred.' He raised his eyebrows. 'People have to learn.'

I would teach Avee a lesson he'd never forget. I would hurt him the way he'd hurt Abbas. My fists clenched at my sides as I imagined how he'd suffer for what he'd done. Then I saw the worried man pacing, and thought of Baba, shackled like an animal. I thought of Mama and my brothers and Nadia, my only remaining sister, alone while I rotted in prison. I thought of the promise I made to Baba. No, I told myself. I couldn't let my family down. I must rise above.

16

'Where are your parents?' the doctor asked when he finally emerged from surgery.

'They couldn't make it,' I said. 'I'm representing them.'

His mouth opened, but he seemed to rethink and paused. 'Is there some way I could call them?'

I couldn't hide the worry in my voice. 'No, just please tell me how he is.'

The doctor was tall and light-skinned. He spoke like the Russian. A paper mask hung from his left ear.

'All right, I'm Dr Cohen. Your brother's in a coma right now. We have to wait and see if he regains consciousness.'

'If ?' I asked.

'The longer the coma lasts, the worse the chances. I fused two broken vertebrae to healthy ones and removed his spleen, which had ruptured. There was a fair amount of internal bleeding, but I think we stopped it. You can see him now. He's in the recovery room.' The doctor pointed me in its direction.

Abbas was in the third bed from the door. In the first bed was a child Hani's size wrapped in white gauze. A veiled woman sat next to the bed. In the second bed was a boy about Abbas' age with bandaged stumps where his legs should've been. A man and a veiled woman sat by his bed. This must be the Arab ward.

Abbas' body looked smaller in the big hospital bed. Monitors and tubes were everywhere. Bending over the rails on the sides of his bed, my toes barely able to touch the floor, I whispered in his ear, 'I'm here for you, Abbas. I'm here for you.' I held his hand with the cannula taped to it. It was cold. Careful not to touch any of the tubes, I pulled the blanket over his shoulders. His eyes were closed, his lips parted. If only I'd run faster, got up quicker, gone to call for the cement dispenser myself.

His skin was dark against the white sheets. 'Is that better?' I asked, not expecting an answer, but hoping somewhere inside he could hear me, know I was there. I fought the urge to gently shake him, to try to wake him.

Memories flooded back: how Abbas grabbed on to my leg on my first day of school and wouldn't let go. Baba had to pry him loose. 'Don't worry, you'll be going to school soon enough,' Baba had told him.

I recalled how Abbas and I had climbed up into the almond tree and watched the Israelis from the moshav farm the land. The engine of the tractor roared as it cut the field into perfect rows. The plough turned over rich black earth. After the first rains, we'd watch the Israelis plant the land. With my telescope, we'd observe the first shoots sprout and then turn into squash, beans and aubergines. In July they'd harvested from first light straight through to dusk dressed in bright colours and sleeveless tops. The hardest part for us was watching them harvest our Shamouti oranges. Those were our favourites, thick-skinned, seedless and juicy. When the wind was strong, the scent of their blossoms in the spring and their fruit in the summer still reached us.

I thought of how Abbas had jumped up and down smiling, his fingers forming the V for victory the first time he played backgammon at the tea house and won. Baba had beamed. Baba.

How could I ever tell him about this? No, I decided. I wouldn't tell Baba. At least not until we knew what was going to happen to Abbas. There was nothing Baba could do for him. How would I tell Mama?

With the chair pulled as close as possible to Abbas' bed, I leaned against the cold rails, so he could feel me breathing.

'Abbas, I know it feels good to rest here where it's warm and dry. You've been working so hard. But now it's time to go home. Please, Abbas, open your eyes. Mama's waiting for us.' I squeezed his finger and blew air on his face. Nothing. 'Do you hear me? You're sleeping. Things are hard right now, but it'll get better. Soon Fadi will be working too.'

I opened the bag the nurse had given me with Abbas' sandals and bloodied clothes in it. I took his left sandal out, uncovered his left foot, slid it on and tied it. I noticed the veiled lady on my right look at me. I did the same with his other foot. I wanted to make sure he could get up and leave when he awoke.

Yossi entered the room. His presence upset me. I wanted to be alone with my brother.

'You gave us quite a scare today,' Yossi said to Abbas.

What if Yossi's presence scared Abbas?

'Let's go out into the hall,' I said. 'I don't want Abbas to hear us.' We walked into the corridor together.

'Let me take you home,' he said. 'Your parents will be worried.'

I leaned against the wall. 'I need to be here,' I said. 'Abbas will be scared if he wakes up alone.'

'He isn't going to wake up today. I'll bring you back in the morning, as soon as your curfew ends.'

'No, I can't leave him.'

'Your parents will be worried.'

'Give me a moment.'

I walked back and sat in the chair next to Abbas' bed. 'Remember that time Mohammad and I wanted to go to the village square and you wanted to come?' I whispered into his ear. 'I hid your shoes so Mama wouldn't make me take you.' I closed my eyes. 'And remember that red spinning-top Baba made for you? You couldn't find it anywhere. I stole it.' I opened my eyes and stared at his chest as it rose and fell. 'And when you struggled with your maths problems, I should've taken the time to explain to you how to solve them instead of just solving them for you. I'm sorry. But those mistakes are small compared to others I've made.'

I forced the words out of my throat. 'You're in a hospital bed instead of in school because of me. If I hadn't got out of bed that night, you'd be climbing up the almond tree, spying on the Jews or practising hitting targets with the bow and arrows.'

Abbas, who was always moving, lay still. What if he never woke up? 'I didn't want this for you. Believe me, I'd gladly switch places with you. I wish we could go back to the days when we raced around in the toy cars Baba built for us. If you die or don't wake up, we won't recover. We'll all die with you.' I leaned over his bed rail and kissed him on both cheeks. 'First thing in the morning, I'll be back.' I squeezed his left hand as I studied him—the scar that cut through his eyebrow, from when I'd tripped him on the school step. I couldn't bring him home. I couldn't leave him here. I had no good options.

I walked into the corridor. Yossi was waiting outside the door.

'I'll get permits for you and your parents,' he said.

'It's just my mother and me.'

I looked back at Abbas' door as Yossi guided me to his truck.

17

The rain pounded me as I slogged through my worry and the mud. The footpath sucked at my sandals, testing the straps with each step. When I arrived at the tent, I could see the sheet hanging from the almond tree. Behind it, Fadi was showering in the rainwater. I stuck my head inside.

'Where were you?' Mama was frantic. 'Where's the rice?'

She'd asked me to buy rice with my pay. I sat down facing out, removed my sandals and held my feet out in the rain. When they were clean, I crawled in and sat across from her.

'Where's Abbas?' Mama was hard at work, knitting hats. 'I finished his. Now I'm working on yours.' She held up Abbas' hat. 'These will keep your ears warm at work.'

Nadia fed rice to Hani in the corner.

'Is he taking a shower?' Mama asked.

Our eyes met.

She put down the knitting. 'Did something happen?'

I lowered my gaze.

'Please, Ahmed, tell me.'

Nadia turned.

'There was an accident at work.'

She grabbed my arms. 'Tell me.'

'He fell.' I swallowed. 'From the scaffolding.'

She swallowed hard. 'Is he dead?'

I thought of Abbas splayed on the ground, a pool of blood under his head.

Mama's hands gripped harder into my arms.

Words couldn't capture the regret I felt. This wasn't supposed to happen.

'Coma,' I whispered and stared at my hands. 'He's alive. They just aren't sure if he'll wake up.' I looked up at her.

Her hands went to her head. Her mouth was open like she was screaming, but no sound emerged. 'I must go to him,' she finally said.

'My boss will drive us there tomorrow.'

'He'll get better if I go,' she said with absolute certainty. It was as if her saying that made it true.

'The doctors aren't sure.'

'Your brother will surprise them all. You need to work.'

'I have to be with Abbas.'

Her shift from fear and dread to conviction was absolute. 'We can't live if you don't work. And now we'll have Abbas' bills.'

'You can't go alone with Yossi.'

'I'll go with Um Sayyid. Her husband's in a coma as well. Her son takes her every day.' And Mama picked up her knitting.

The world should have stopped, but it kept going.

***

As soon as the curfew was over, I walked Mama to Um Sayyid's tent. She was sat in the back of a donkey cart outside the tent, whilst her son, Sayyid, sat in the front, holding the reins.

'Um Sayyid!' I waved my arms in the air.

She looked over.

'How are you?' she asked Mama.

'Abbas is in the hospital. Can I ride with you?'

'My cart is your cart,' she said.

I took Mama's hand and helped her climb into the back next to Um Sayyid. They faced out with their legs dangling.

***

Yossi was waiting for me at the entrance to the village.

'Where's your mother?' he asked.

'She's going to visit Abbas.'

Yossi handed me Mama's permit to go to the hospital. Sayyid pulled his donkey cart next to us and I handed Mama the permit.

***

That day at work, the Iraqi wasn't there. The Russian came over as soon as I arrived.

'How's Abbas?'

'He's in a coma.' I lowered my face and rushed to the cinder-block pile. I filled wheelbarrow after wheelbarrow with cinder-blocks and placed them in the large container for the crane to take up to the fifth floor. The rain had washed Abbas' blood away.

At lunch, I ate my pita and almonds alone. I started to calculate how heavy was the house we'd built the previous month. The weight of the house was a good indicator of the energy used in its construction. I'd need to analyse the heavy and energy-intensive building materials.

I knew cement was a processed form of limestone and ash. To make concrete, the limestone had to be heated in a fossil-fuelled furnace, which released CO2. For every 1,000 kg of cement produced, 900 kg of CO2 was emitted.

Steel, which we used for many things, from rods to reinforce the concrete foundations to the support beams for the floors and roofs, was produced from ore. To produce one ton of steel alone from ore took about 3,000 kWh of energy. Then, I analysed the rest of the heavy building materials. From my calculations, I estimated the house weighed 100 tons.

Before the lunch break was over, I returned to the wheelbarrow. I worked harder than I ever had in my life. I lifted for myself, Abbas and Baba, moved cinderblocks, mixed mortar, lifted beams. The whole time, I calculated how many cinderblocks we'd need to build the rest of the apartment building, the number of blocks in each area and how much cement I'd need to make a small house for my family. In the house, there was a room for each child, new sinks, white bath tubs, running water and electricity.

My back ached and it was as though I were slogging through deep water. Every movement took more energy than before my little brother had been broken like so many twigs. My ears stayed warm though, because Mama had given me his hat to wear to work.

***

When I returned to the tent, Mama was waiting. 'The swelling needs to go down,' she said. 'He might be paralysed, if he wakes up at all.'

Nadia looked at me with mournful eyes as she cuddled Hani.

I went out and climbed Shahida, my almond tree. Desperate to talk to someone, I turned to her. 'I'll do anything. I'll give you my eyes, my arms, my legs, if you make Abbas well.' I pleaded with the almond tree as if she had the power to heal him. 'I'll work harder than anyone has ever worked. I'll make something of my life.' A wind came and shook the leaves on the tree. 'Please don't let him die. Abbas is so good. He didn't even take breaks at work. He should've been at school. I sent him to call the cement dispenser because I could tie the rebar faster. He wasn't as quick as me. I'm sorry. Forgive me. I should've gone myself.'

All night, I remained awake estimating distances, weights, anything. At least Yossi had obtained a permit for Mama to travel to see Abbas until he was out of hospital.

Day and night blurred into one another. In my head, I

worked through logic problems in maths, devised ways to make a thermoelectric battery, an electric motor, a wireless radio. I calculated the speed of a missile fired from an aeroplane, the force of a bullet fired from a machine-gun.

Mama prayed all night.

After her third day at the hospital, Mama returned home smiling. 'Abbas woke up.' Three words never brought such happiness. 'His eyes fluttered and he stared at me. Get materials for another tent; Abbas will need to be alone with me.'

I practically ran to the village square.

***

A week later, Mama brought Abbas home. Fadi, Hani and I waited at the bottom of the hill. Abbas lay on the wooden cart with Mama and Um Sayyid on either side of him. Sayyid pulled the donkey's reins and the cart stopped. I realised that just because he was awake, didn't mean he was well.

Bringing Abbas home wasn't a good idea. There were no doctors or nurses in our village. If there was an emergency, we'd need a permit from the military to transport him back to the hospital. And even if we were lucky enough to get a permit, we might not be able to get through the roadblocks. But what choice did we have? We couldn't afford to pay for him to remain in the hospital any longer.

'We're here,' Mama said.

Abbas opened his eyes.

I jumped on the back of the cart, crouched down and kissed his cheeks and forehead. 'Thank God,' I said.

'My back is killing me.' Abbas squeezed his eyes shut. His speech was slow and slurred.

The sound of his voice made my hand go to my mouth.

'May Allah improve your health and speed your recovery,' Hani said.

Fadi clenched his jaw. Fadi, Hani and I moved Abbas onto the plank the villagers used to carry corpses to their graves. He moaned in pain as we lifted him onto our shoulders, carried him up the hill and placed him in his new tent. Mama knelt next to him.

Abbas was incapable of any physical activity. Mama cared for him as though he were a newborn. She bathed him with a sponge and spoon-fed him rice. We had less money than ever. I was hungry all the time. Fadi, who was now ten years old, dropped out of school to help me work. At night, when I returned from Teacher Mohammad's, I tried to tutor Fadi, but he was too tired and Abbas was too sick.

Every day Mama moved Abbas' limbs into different positions. She had him sit and gave him rocks to lift. She and I got on either side of him at night and lifted him to his feet. At first we were holding him up. Then Mama made him start putting one foot in front of the other as he leaned heavily on us. Over the next few weeks, he began to walk. He complained bitterly of the pain, but Mama was relentless. At first he could only take a few steps, but every day Mama pushed him more and more. Abbas walked bent over like he was carrying an enormous burden. Permanent dark circles formed around his eyes. His hands trembled, but he was improving.

Still, I couldn't sleep listening to him suffer and cry out.

18

I splashed water on my face, rinsing the cement dust from my eyes.

'The moshav is building a slaughterhouse,' Mama said as she appeared from the tent.

I turned and noticed the wisps of grey hair where it had once been black. 'Where?'

'In the area where you used to hunt rabbits.'

'But the moshav's in the south,' I said, drying my hands. 'Why would they build in the north?'

Mama shrugged. 'They're taking more from our east, too. They need more pasture for a cattle race. Look for work there.'

Abbas called out from his tent. 'They steal our land and we're helping them.'

***

Fadi and I found employment at the slaughterhouse construction site. I was sixteen and Fadi thirteen. Although the slaughterhouse was built on our village's land, the barbed-wire fence they'd built around us required that we go to the one small gate, our only way out, and wait with the other workers for the guards to walk us over. Every week the number of villagers who sought employment from the Israelis grew; there just wasn't enough land left inside the fence to farm, and what was there had been overused.

The slaughterhouse and its accompanying maze of concrete-walled factories were up and running in a year. We were offered the jobs the Jews were unwilling to do and were happy to have the work.

While we waited to be walked over to our jobs, I'd listen to the cattle. Their constant mooing could be heard throughout the village. Mama often missed the muezzin's call to prayer because of the volume. I watched the Israelis, mounted on horses, galloping along the alley between the two pens with long whips they never hesitated to crack as they drove the animals to their deaths.

Inside the slaughterhouse, I'd wait for them to kill the first cow of the day so that I could begin my work. They forced each cow into a small pen, alone. Three Israelis tied a rope around the cow's legs and forced it, thrashing, to the ground. Once it was down, one man stood on its legs while others—including one man holding its head in place with a sharp metal pole—restrained it. Another wrapped a chain around one of the cow's hind legs. The kosher butcher, the shoket, entered and said a prayer before he slit the cow's jugular vein and carotid artery.

After the shoket cut the cow's throat, they hoisted it in the air by its shackled leg to bleed out. The cow struggled in this position, bellowing, for many minutes as buckets of blood gushed out. My job was to shovel the blood through holes in the floor which drained to holding tanks below. By the end of the day, I was standing in blood up to my ankles, despite the drain.

While I shovelled the blood, I watched the headmen behead the cows—it always took three strokes. Then others ripped off the cows' skin, rolled it up and took it away. Those were the good jobs. The Israeli jobs.

Our villagers dragged the meat into the chilling room to hang. The cows' blood and guts which I helped push through the holes in the floor were used in the pickling, canning and packing rooms where Fadi and the other children worked because of their small fingers. There was also a building where grease was piped and made into lard soap. The heads and feet were turned into glue, and the bones into fertiliser. Nothing went to waste.

The animals shrieked and kicked and struggled. Now I understood why Baba and Albert Einstein were vegetarians. After our experiences in the slaughterhouse, no one in my family ever ate meat again.

Moshav Dan had good reason not to want the slaughterhouse right next door. In the summer, the place filled with steaming blood and an overpowering stench. In the winter, the blood and guts froze my hands and feet. I'd go to work shivering and return with my teeth chattering. Hour after hour, day after day, I waded through guts from six in the morning until five in the evening with a thirty-minute break for lunch.

The chimneys from the slaughterhouse and accompanying factories spread thick, oily, black smoke throughout our village. Because we had no sewage system, the filth, grease and chemicals from the slaughterhouse soaked into our soil. Bubbles of carbonic acid rose to the surface, while grease and filth caked the land. Every now and then the land would catch fire and the whole village would run and put it out with buckets of well-water.

19

The cardboard boxes were long gone and the rain leaked in through our tent and dripped onto my face. The rugs under us were wet and muddy. The cold was relentless. Four years had passed, and we were still living in a tent. It was larger than our original one, but still untenable.

'Someone help me,' Abbas groaned. 'I can't get up.'

'You're just stiff.' Mama went and helped him up. 'It's the rain.'

'We need a house,' I said.

'We're still paying off Abbas' bills,' Mama said. 'And we don't have a permit.'

'They'll never give us a permit with Baba in prison,' I said. 'Look at Abbas. What choice do we have?'

***

For two months, Fadi and I made mud bricks after work, on Friday evenings and on Saturdays. Hani helped us after school. We built a one-room house next to our tent. Mama and Nadia lined the floor with the rugs we had used in the tent. We didn't fill it with all of our belongings; we knew what we'd done was illegal, so we left some of our valued possessions in the tent. That way we wouldn't have everything at risk in either place.

The first night we slept in our new home, I listened to the rain patter on our roof from underneath a blanket on a rush mat. I awoke in the morning dry and well-rested.

'I slept for a couple of hours,' Abbas said. Usually his pain was so severe he couldn't sleep for more than twenty minutes at a time. I was proud that my brothers and I were able to work together to alleviate his suffering. Things were going to change.

***

But the next evening when Fadi and I returned from work, we saw smoke rising from the direction of our home. Running up the hill, we found Hani crying, Abbas cursing the Jews, and Mama and Nadia shovelling dirt onto the last flames of what had been our new house. When Mama saw us, she dropped to her knees and began praying. She called on Allah, Mohammad and anyone else she felt could help us. Our house was now a pile of rubble.

'The Israeli settlers heard we built,' Mama said. 'The soldiers came to inspect.'

Nadia shook her head. Her eyes were red and swollen. 'When we couldn't produce a permit, the soldiers drenched our home in paraffin and set it on fire.'

'We tried to save the mats, the blankets, anything.' Mama shook her head. 'It was too late.'

'The flames were shooting from the house.' Nadia raised her hands. They were wrapped in rags. 'Thank God Abbas and Hani were in the tent, and not in the house, when the soldiers came. The flames grew so quickly, though, they soon caught the tent.'

Mama saw the shock on my face. 'We barely had time to move Abbas,' she said. 'We used up the jug of water we had. There was no time to run to the well.'

Fadi grabbed a large rock and rushed down the hill. I wanted to go after him, but I couldn't leave Nadia and Mama alone before the fire was completely extinguished.

When it was finally out, I hurried down to the village square. We needed to make a new tent. While I was haggling over the price of the cloth, I saw two soldiers wearing helmets and face shields dragging my handcuffed little brother towards their Jeep. I dropped the fabric and ran to him.

'What happened?' I asked Fadi in Arabic.

'They destroyed our home,' he said. 'I had no choice, brother.' The faces of the eighteen- or nineteen-year-old soldiers who were dragging him away were childlike, but not as childlike as his: he was twelve years old.

One of them smacked him across the face. 'Did I give you permission to speak?' He shook Fadi.

Anger grew inside me, but I remained still. 'Where are you taking him?' I kept my voice calm.

'The same place we take all the stone throwers we catch,' he said. 'To prison.'

The other soldier shoved Fadi face down onto the floor in the back of the military Jeep, got in and drove his black military boots into Fadi's arms, handcuffed behind his back. I winced, feeling his pain.

'I'll get you out,'

I screamed to Fadi as they drove away. 'Don't be afraid.' There were only fifteen minutes until curfew. I couldn't help Fadi, so I spent all of my wages on cloth for the new tent, cedar stakes and ropes, and went back to the almond tree. My family were gathered on the ground under her.

I had grown numb to delivering bad news. 'Fadi was taken away,' I said.

Mama looked at me with disbelief. 'Why?'

'He threw a stone,' I said. 'At the soldiers.'

Mama extended her arms with her palms facing the sky. 'Allah, please, show us your mercy.' Her faith, in the harsh light of reality, was difficult to fathom.

Abbas' whole body shook with rage. 'These Jews only understand violence.'

Nadia wrapped her arms around Hani as they cried.

'Mama,' I said. 'You'll have to go to the military outpost tomorrow. I have to work. If I miss even one day, I'll lose my job.'

Mama went to the military outpost every day for the next week without success. Then a letter from Baba arrived. Fadi was imprisoned with him at the Dror Detention Centre. The Israelis demanded the equivalent of three weeks of my wages to release Fadi. I wrote to Baba that I'd be at the prison as soon as I raised the money.

***

Four weeks later, I took the bus to retrieve Fadi. I couldn't see Baba because visiting day was only the first Tuesday of every month and that was three weeks away. Mama wanted her child back as soon as possible.

The Fadi that emerged from the prison wasn't the same boy who had entered. The skin around his eyes was yellow, the way a bruise looks before it goes away. Red scars were visible around his wrists. He seemed calmer, though not in a good way, as if the soldiers had broken his spirit.

'I saw Baba,' Fadi mumbled on the bus back. 'I'll never do anything like this again.'

I leaned over and hugged him. 'We all make mistakes.'

'Baba is so strong,' he said with a certain amount of wonder.

I knew exactly what he meant.

20

As the sun dropped low in the sky, the guards led us back into the village. Teacher Mohammad, stood by the gate, began to walk towards us. Did something happen to Mama? Or Baba? Maybe it was Abbas. Why didn't one of my family members come? What if my family was dead? The workers around me were talking, but all I could hear was Teacher Mohammad's approaching footsteps growing louder and louder.

'The Israelis are holding a maths competition for students in their last year of school,' he said. 'You could win a scholarship to the Hebrew University.'

For a moment, I felt exhilarated. And then, just as fast, I remembered. 'I don't have time.'

'You cannot throw away your gift,' he said. 'I know it seems like there is no way out right now, but you can choose a better path.'

If only I could believe him, but he was suggesting the impossible. What could I do except what I was doing already? Abbas' injury had happened five years ago, but I was still paying off his medical bills. Abbas was improving, but he couldn't work. The only jobs available to us involved physical labour, which Abbas would never be able to do. He was in constant pain. His friends would come to the tent to visit him or he'd meet them at their homes or at the tea house, but, other than that, he wasn't able to do much. 'My brothers don't make enough without me.'

'If you win, I'll find jobs for your brothers in my cousin's moving company.'

'I need to support them.'

'If you graduate from college, you'll be able to earn more money. Let's just see if you win.'

'No, I can't.'

The smile left him. 'I am not your father, Ahmed, but I can't believe this is what he wants for a son with gifts such as yours.'

I wrote to Baba about the competition and my decision not to participate. Almost immediately he sent me a response.

To my dearest Ahmed,

You must participate in the competition and do the best you can. I'll love you whether you win or lose, but I'll be disappointed if you don't try. I know the family will initially suffer, but in the long run it will be better if you graduate from college. You'll be able to secure a better and more interesting job. When you do what you love, the money will come.

Love,

Baba

The moment I told Teacher Mohammad about my decision to compete, tears came to his eyes and he hugged me.

***

When Teacher Mohammad and I got off the bus at the central station, there were no soldiers waiting, no searches or demands for travel papers. From the bus we had seen Tel Aviv, a city so modern and clean it was hard to imagine it existed in the same country as my village. The city of Herzliya, although smaller, was filled with lively cafés, music and freedom.

'The military government doesn't rule here,' Teacher Mohammad said.

An Israeli driver pulled up alongside us in his Mercedes. 'Do you need a taxi?'

'To Herzliya High School.' Teacher Mohammad motioned for me to get into the back seat.

'Is it cool enough back there? Do you want the air conditioner turned up?'

I looked around. Who was he talking to?

'Thank you,' Teacher Mohammad said. 'We are accustomed to the heat.'

I couldn't drink it all in fast enough. We drove past castle-like whitewashed homes with flowering red, purple and pink bougainvillea growing up their walls and bursts of colour in elaborate gardens. Mama would've loved to see those gardens. Mercedes and BMWs were parked in almost every driveway.

'Is this what paradise looks like?' I asked.

Teacher Mohammad patted my knee. 'We can only hope.'

Waves crashed onto sandy beaches as the taxi approached the white stone school covered in red bougainvillea, and I thought of Baba and his brother swimming in that ocean. Inside the school, we passed a gym, theatre, cafeteria, library, art studio, music room with a piano, and enormous classrooms.

'How can I compete?' I thought of our village school that was so small we attended in shifts, shared books, worked at broken tables, read from cracked blackboards, and rationed chalk.

Teacher Mohammad walked with determination. 'Genius is born, not taught.'

'Surely preparation plays a part.' I wanted to return to the village immediately.

'Many great men can attribute their success to the fact that they didn't have the advantages other men had.'

The auditorium, where the written part of the competition

would be held, was the size of my whole school. Heads turned. A multitude of eyes scrutinised me. My weather-beaten clothes hung from me, while the Israeli contestants wore dresses, or suits and ties. I didn't belong here and wondered again why I had allowed myself to be talked into coming.

The registrar examined me through reading glasses perched on the tip of her beak-shaped nose. 'I need your ID.'

I held my card in my calloused hand. Although the word ARAB was clearly written on it, the registrar didn't need to see it to know. My people were homogeneous.

'You're the only Arab here.' She directed me to a chair close to her. Did she think I'd cheat, or was she afraid I'd murder someone? The boy on my left chewed on the edge of his eraser. The girl behind me sounded like she couldn't catch her breath. I counted 523 students. Nervous energy filled the room. The proctor passed out the papers.

'You have two hours to complete this test,' he said.

***

Forty minutes later, as the other contestants' heads were still down, their pencils and erasers moving furiously, I turned in my completed test.

'The questions were too easy,' I said to Teacher Mohammad, who had waited outside the auditorium. 'Something's wrong.'

'It's your genius that gives you the ability to reduce the complicated to the simple.' He patted me on the shoulder and, for a moment, I smiled.

***

Mama was waiting for me outside the tent with her arms folded across her chest. 'Where were you?'

I hadn't told her because she wouldn't have approved. 'A maths competition.' I forced a smile, hoping it would be contagious. 'I'm trying to win a scholarship to the university.'

She didn't smile back. Holding my breath, I waited for her response. 'Don't even think about it.' Anger gurgled in her voice. I couldn't remember the last time she'd sounded so angry. 'He who aims too high will get a sore neck.'

'It's important to me.'

'We. Are. Not. Rich.' She articulated each word individually. 'We have expenses. Who knows if Abbas will ever be able to work again? I can't send Nadia to work. Who'd want to marry her?'

'Teacher Mohammad promised to help.'

Mama's face turned the colour of blood. I'd never be able to convince her. But Baba was right. I had a much better chance of success if I went to the university. I let it drop for now. I probably wouldn't win anyway. The Israelis would never allow the son of an Arab prisoner to win.

I wrote to Baba about how I finished the test first and how I feared that maybe I had done something wrong. Baba wrote back that the smart mind moves fast, like a bullet.

21

Teacher Mohammad handed me the letter. Clutching it tightly, I slipped my dirty index finger into the corner above the sealed flap, ripped along the top seam and extracted the parchment paper.

Dear Mr Hamid,

On behalf of the Faculty of Mathematics at the Hebrew University we are pleased to inform you that you are one of the ten finalists. You are invited to participate in a live mathematics competition. It will be held on 5th November, 1965 at 5pm in the Golda Meir Auditorium at the Herzliya High School.

Sincerely,
Professor Yitzhak Schulman

'Well?' Teacher Mohammad was excited and anxious.

My heart beat behind my eyes and in my ears. The world seemed to stop. I'd write to Baba immediately.

'Success is not about never falling, but about rising every time you fall.' Teacher Mohammad's eyes glazed over. He was consoling me.

'I qualified.'

He broke into a full smile. 'You cannot go back and make a new start, but you can start now and make a new ending.'

I wrote to Baba as soon as I returned to the tent. He was

thrilled. Whatever happened, he wrote back, he was behind me one hundred per cent.

The night before the competition, I couldn't sleep. Cold rain pummelled our tent, leaked in through the holes and wet my blanket. The wind blew with enough force to lift it off the ground. I went to work exhausted.

By the evening, I could hardly keep my eyes open—until Teacher Mohammad and I arrived at the school. A parade of luxury vehicles pulled up at the front door and the prodigies disembarked, dressed as if they were being judged on appearance.

Wearing my bloodstained work clothes—a shirt and drawstring trousers—I stood out like a donkey at the starting gate of a thoroughbred race. I wanted to disappear, but then I thought of Baba moving sand in the Negev heat, and I knew I'd stay.

The ten contestants sat in the middle of the expansive wooden stage in chairs arranged like a horseshoe around the blackboard. I was a lowly Palestinian sitting among the brightest Israelis in the country. None of them spoke to me.

The heavy red velour curtain parted and revealed the spectators. Their curious eyes moved from contestant to contestant, as if intelligence was something that could be determined from a seat in the audience. I felt they were staring at me. I wished I had a change of clothing. Mama would be upset if she knew I was up here covered in blood and sweat from work. Of course, she didn't want me here at all. Maybe she was right.

'Hello, I'm Professor Yitzhak Schulman, the head of the maths department at the Hebrew University. Welcome to our first state-wide maths competition.'

Applause.

'On stage are ten winners. Each has shown tremendous ability.'

Professor Schulman explained the rules. Each student would have a three-minute turn to solve each problem. If a contestant made a mistake, that contestant would leave the stage. The last five contestants would win scholarships to the Hebrew University of Jerusalem and compete for various monetary stipends. First place, of course, would be the largest.

Contestant number one rocked back and forth. His kepah, which was attached to his wiry black hair with a bobby pin, bounced with every movement.

The examiner approached the microphone. 'Let C be the unit circle $x^2+y=1$. A point p is chosen randomly on the circumference of C and another point q is chosen randomly from the interior of C. These points are chosen independently and uniformly over their domains. Let R be the rectangle with sides parallel to the x and y axes with diagonal pq. What is the probability that no point of R lies outside of C?'

By the time contestant number one picked up the chalk and began to write, I'd already solved the problem on the imaginary blackboard in my head. I could win. It didn't matter that I didn't have the opportunities others had. I possessed the gift. But what if the Israelis gave me impossible-to-solve problems? Who'd defend me?

'The probability is $4\pi^2$.'

'That's correct,' the announcer said.

The room erupted into applause.

When contestant number two stood, her left shoulder was higher than her right.

'Find, with explanation, the maximum value of $f(x)=x^3-3x$ on the set of all real numbers x satisfying $x4+36\leq 13x^2$.'

Sweat beaded up on her forehead as she stared at the empty board. The sound of the bell resonated off the walls. The audience gasped. Contestant number two lowered her head and exited the stage.

I was contestant number three.

The blood pounded through my veins as I walked to the blackboard. The eyes of everyone mocked me. I picked up the chalk.

'Let k be the smallest positive integer with the following property: there are distinct integers m1, m2, m3, m4, m5 such that the polynomial p(x)=(x-m1)(x-m2)(x-m3)(x-m4)(x-m5) has exact k coefficients. Find, with proof, a set of integers m1, m2, m3, m4, m5 for which this minimum k is achieved.'

'The minimum is k=3, and is attained for {m1, m2, m3, m4, m5}={-2, -1, 0, 1, 2},' I said as I wrote. Putting the chalk down, I turned and looked directly at the audience. The Israelis in the centre of the front row stared with their mouths open.

The announcer looked at me, as if in shock. 'That is correct.'

Round after round, I managed to remain focused, solving every problem I was given. My heart nearly stopped when the sixth competitor slipped up. I had won a scholarship. Now, I was competing for the best monetary package. Ten rounds later, it was only contestant number eight and me.

Contestant number eight went to the board.

'An arrow, thrown at random, hits a square target. Assuming that any two parts of the target of equal area are equally likely to be hit, find the probability that the point hit is nearer to the centre than to any edge. Express your answer in the form $(a\sqrt{b}+c)/d$, where a, b, c, d are positive integers.'

Contestant number eight closed his eyes, rocked back and forth, and only stopped to blot his palms on his black slacks. He began to write.

The bell sounded. The room went silent. Contestant number eight wasn't escorted off the stage because if I didn't solve my problem correctly, the contest would continue.

Teacher Mohammad sat on the edge of his chair and gripped the arms.

'Factor this polynomial: 7x3y3+21x2y2-10x3y2-30x2y.'

I took a deep breath and began to write on the board, stating the answer out loud as I did so. 'x2y(7y-10)(xy+3).'

When I finished, I looked over at the examiner. His mouth was open.

'That's correct,' the announcer stated.

Teacher Mohammad's fists went up in the air. Contestant number eight approached me and extended his hand.

'Sharpest mind I've ever encountered,' he said.

My lips trembled and my eyes welled up. Suddenly, we weren't a Palestinian and an Israeli; we were two mathematicians. Contestant number eight patted me on the shoulder. 'My name's Zoher. I look forward to seeing you at the university.' My emotions caught in my throat, and I could only nod.

The announcer hung a medal around my neck while a photographer from the *Yediot Ahronot* snapped my picture. My stomach churned. Other contestants came and shook my hand. I was caught in a spider web of emotions. The room filled with extraordinary energy. The Israelis, the people who were holding Baba in prison, were applauding me.

The next day, a big picture of me with the medal around my neck appeared on the front page of the Israeli newspaper. The caption read, 'Arab Boy Calculates His Way to Victory'. I sent the article to Baba. He sent me back a caricature of himself in which a huge smile covered three-quarters of his face.

The night before I was scheduled to leave for the university, sleep wouldn't come. I knew that the stipend I'd won was only meant to subsidise my living expenses, but what about my family? Could I leave them alone? For the last six years I'd been the man. Could they support themselves without me? I'd be gone for at least three years.

The morning I was to leave to begin my studies, Mama sat

at the entrance to the tent. 'I won't permit you to live among the Israelis.' She wagged her finger at me. 'They could kill you.'

'They're not all bad,' I said. 'Look how Yossi helped.'

'*Helped*? After they failed to kill me.' Abbas shook his head. 'I gave them a chance. I won't give them another.'

My siblings sat around the tent, gloomy and with tearful eyes.

'I'm going to study science and maths,' I said for the hundredth time.

'Man doesn't need to know more than is necessary for his daily living.' Mama's arms were clasped in front of her chest.

'I already know too much to ever be content working in the slaughterhouse, Mama. I want to discover the unknown. I want to make my living from science and maths.'

She rolled her eyes as if I were the stupidest person in the world. 'If you leave us now, don't ever come back.'

'My studies are the answer to our problems. If I make it I'll be able to provide for the whole family.'

'You know nothing of this world!' The words burst from her mouth. 'Your dreams are just dreams! The Israelis rule and they'll never see you as anything more than the enemy; a Palestinian. It's time you opened your eyes and learned the ways of the world.'

'One day I'll make it up to you.' I looked down at the ground.

'We'll never have enough money,' she said. 'Don't do this to us.'

'I have to go.'

'Please—' she started and then she was crying. Mama lowered herself to the ground and covered her face.

'Here.' I handed her the majority of my stipend. 'Buy a goat and a chicken. Plant vegetables. There isn't much land, but at least that way I know you'll have food.'

'Do you have money for yourself ?' she asked.

'If things become too difficult, I'll stop my studies and

return. Please, just allow me one month.' I held my breath and waited for her response.

Finally, she nodded. I wrapped my arms around her and she whispered into my ear, 'Stay away from the Israelis.'

I waved goodbye.

'You're putting your life in danger,' Abbas said.

'It's a risk I'm willing to take.'

As I walked to the bus stop, the breeze on my back pushed me to go. I knew from whence the wind came.

Thank you, Baba.

PART TWO
1966

22

The symmetrical arrangement of the buildings calmed me. I walked along the concrete pavement of the third row, past eleven buildings until I reached building twelve of the Shikouney Elef Dormitory.

I tugged at my homemade trousers, trying to get them to cover my ankles, but there was no way. Mama had made them for me three years before when I was a full head shorter. But these clothes that had started as used sheets, and the few things I had stuffed into a crumpled bag under my arm, were all I had.

The aroma of tomato sauce wafting from the first room on the left welcomed me. It was a communal kitchen and a girl in a tight scarlet top and jeans, with oven gloves on her hands, was lifting a pan of vegetable stew. Her shoulder-length hair bounced as she spun around. 'Hello,' she said to me in Arabic.

I couldn't find my voice so I nodded.

'Excuse me.' She carried the pan past me into the corridor.

Hebrew voices came from the hallway. What were they doing in our building? They must be soldiers. I wanted to hide. But where? The window had bars. The kitchen door opened outwards. There was nowhere. The last thing I wanted was trouble. I thought I'd prepared myself for a life surrounded by Jews, but now that the reality confronted me, I realised how mistaken I was.

My stomach sank as they entered the room—but they weren't in uniform.

'*Shalom. Mah neshmah*?' How's everything? Zoher greeted me in Hebrew, extending his hand.

I hardly recognised him dressed in jeans and a white T-shirt.

'*Tov, todah*.' Fine, thank you, I replied in Hebrew, almost forgetting to breathe. Another young man stood in the doorway.

'He's the maths whizz I told you about,' Zoher said to him.

'I'm Rafael, like the angel, but everyone calls me Rafi.' The blotchy-skinned man extended his hand. 'Be proud. Few people impress Zoher.'

I shook his hand.

'We're starting a study group,' Zoher said. 'My brother survived the programme and I inherited his notes. Care to join forces?'

What did they want to do? Make me fail? Hurt me? Maybe Zoher was angry that I beat him. This had to be a setup. I had never heard of an Israeli inviting a Palestinian to participate in any group. I didn't want to provoke them. Zoher did have a sharp mathematical mind, and the notes. Did I have a choice?

I forced a smile. 'Why not?'

'This Sunday at 6pm,' Zoher said. 'Room four.'

Rafi and Zoher would be living next door to me. Never did I imagine that I'd have to live in the same building as Jews. What if my roommate was one? I'd have to sleep with my eyes open.

'Where is the bathroom?' I asked.

'Behind you,' Rafi said.

I waved goodbye and entered the toilets. There were three permanent stalls, three gleaming white sinks and three rectangular mirrors in which I could see my reflection. How could I live like this when my family stood outside in a tin tub and washed with water they carried all the way from the village square? Baba's face stared back at me from the mirror.

I thought of how he'd handle the situation. When I asked him how he managed to sound so cheerful in his letters, he told me he wouldn't allow anyone to break his spirit. He wrote that when he was with people, he always tried to find common interests. If Baba could gain the respect of the prison guards with his singing, drawing and playing, I'd try to do the same with my abilities. Yes, I told myself, maybe it was a good idea to join their study group.

I left the toilets and walked down the brightly lit hallway. This is what electricity was like. With my key, I opened the door to my new room. I'd be living with only one roommate in a room three times the size of the tent my entire family shared. I was going to sleep in a real bed, while they slept on mats on the ground. I had my own desk, a sink in the room and my own closet.

'Welcome. I'm Jameel,' a young man with symmetrical chiselled features said in Arabic. He sat in the middle of the room. An older version of Jameel and a woman who must have been his mother sat across from him. Laid out before them on a white tablecloth was the vegetable stew along with tabboulie, hummus, baba ghanouj and pita.

What was going on? Three girls, dressed like Jews, sat on the beds eating. Fairouz's voice played on the radio behind them.

'I'm Ahmed.'

'What planet do you come from, Ahmad?' Jameel pronounced Ahmed without the rural accent. The girls threw back their heads and laughed.

'Ignore him,' one of the girls said, and rose. 'He's the only son.' She cuffed him on the head.

'Ignore my sisters.' Jameel motioned to the food in front of him with his hand. 'Please.'

His mother immediately filled a plate with vegetable stew for me. I stared at it for a moment. How I wished I could save it for my family.

'Please, start,' Um Jameel said.

I sat next to Jameel and devoured the stew. Um Jameel's face brightened and she scooped more onto my plate. I devoured another plate. Again she gave me more.

'It's delicious.' I hadn't eaten such food since Baba went to prison six years earlier. Aware that many pairs of eyes were watching me, still I continued to eat.

Um Jameel smiled. 'Look how he appreciates my food.'

'Where's your suitcase?' Jameel leaned to look around me.

'I like to travel light.' In my bag were my only spare work trousers and shirt , the book Teacher Mohammad had given me, and nothing else.

Um Jameel packed up their things and they prepared to leave. 'I'll see you and Ahmed on the sixteenth.'

'No one goes home every other weekend.' Jameel's voice was soft but firm.

'Don't start that again. I'm not going to worry what kind of food you're eating or if you're dressed in clean clothes. If you don't show up, we'll come to you.'

Jameel's face turned crimson. 'I'll come.'

'You too, Ahmad.' Um Jameel pronounced my name correctly, not like we did in the village. 'He'll need help carrying the food.' Um Jameel motioned towards Jameel, but now spoke directly to me. 'And don't think I'd let you go hungry either.'

Jameel walked his family to the bus stop. After I put my one shirt and trousers in my closet, I looked into Jameel's closet. Jackets and button-down shirts and trousers of a multitude of colours hung neatly, each on its own hanger. On the shelves above the hanging bar were sweaters of varying thicknesses, T-shirts, and a stack of pyjamas. At the bottom was a pair of leather sandals, shiny black boots with a platform heel, and spotless white trainers. His family must be very rich.

Jameel returned to the room and closed the door.

'I don't think my mother's slept all week. Separation anxiety.' He shrugged his shoulders, walked to the radio and changed it to Western music. From his shirt pocket he pulled out a pack of Time cigarettes and held it out to me.

'Smoke?'

'No, never,' I said.

'Try it.' He pulled one out, lit it and handed it to me.

I reclined on my bed, feeling the softness. 'Maybe later. Go ahead.'

Jameel put the cigarette in his mouth and began to bob his head, sway his hips and bounce around the room like a Sufi mystic in ecstasy. He tapped his cigarette into the ashtray then collapsed onto his bed. Staring at the ceiling, he puffed lazily.

'Let's see the campus.'

'I need to get books.' Teacher Mohammad had advised me to take the books out from the library straight away because they were too expensive to buy.

We headed across lush green lawns. Jameel tapped me on the chest.

'Take a look at that piece of tasty lamb.'

I followed his eyes to an Israeli girl sitting on a bench in front of the library. Her shirt was unbuttoned so low I could see the top part of her breasts. Her legs were crossed and she was wearing shorts that were barely longer than underwear.

'I'd like to rest my head on those pillows.' Jameel bared his teeth, shook his head and growled like a dog in heat. 'How I'd like to ride my camel between those mountains.'

'Please.' I scanned the campus for guards. 'What if someone hears you?'

He laughed, slapped me on the back, and we continued on.

23

I entered my first class, Introduction to Calculus, and had to stop and take it all in: freshly painted walls, rows of desks, the professor's big desk with a leather chair on rollers, and gleaming blackboards that looked brand new. The room was filling quickly with students all chattering at once in Hebrew. I avoided eye contact and looked for a seat in the back.

I got the last open seat in the last row, thank Allah, since the only remaining seats were directly in front of the professor. Israelis were everywhere. The one on my right said '*yiksah*,' got up and took a seat in the front.

My eyes met the professor's, who stroked his overgrown beard and leaned on his desk. After a few minutes, he stood, adjusted his kepah. 'My name is Professor Mizrahi.' White strings hung out from under his shirt, indicating that he was religious. Those Jews believed that God had promised them the land of Israel.

Professor Mizrahi's accent as well as his name told me he was Sephardic. This was just my luck; my first professor would hate me. Sweat beaded up on my forehead.

'When I call your name, you'll sit in the seat I assign you, and that will be your seat for the semester.' Professor Mizrahi looked down at the chart in his hand. 'Aaron Levi, Boaz Cohen, Yossi Levine . . .' Professor Mizrahi called one Jew after another and filled the class from the back to the front. He pointed to the desk in front of his desk and called, 'Ahmad Hamid' with perfect pronunciation.

I felt like a specimen under a microscope, between two Sephardic Jews, the only non-Jewish Arab in the class. They would eat me alive.

'Let's begin.' Professor Mizrahi picked up the chalk and wrote on the board 3x-(x-7)=4x-5.

'Mr Hamid?' He pointed with the chalk towards me.

'x equals 6,' I said from my seat.

'What did you say?' Professor Mizrahi cocked his head.

My heart pounded like a fist on a door. 'x equals 6.'

Professor Mizrahi blinked and read the next problem.

'Mr Hamid, can you find the instantaneous speed or instantaneous rate of change of distance with respect to time at t=5 of an object which falls according to the formula $s=16t^2+96t$?'

'The limit is 256, and this is the instantaneous speed at the end of the five seconds of the fall.'

The ticking of the clock in the front of the class was deafening.

'Thank you, Mr Hamid,' he said. 'Quite impressive.'

***

I had maths and science classes from eight in the morning until four in the afternoon. On the way to the library to study, I made a detour to the botanical garden between the administration buildings in the north and the National Library in the south. The *Sequoia sempervirens* and the *Sequoiadendron* were so gigantic they rose above the surrounding buildings. How I wished I could bring Mama to see the garden. I imagined Baba drawing her picture in front of the trees.

In front of the library, I craned my neck to see the vast stained-glass windows, illuminated from within, as if knowledge and light were one. I pulled open the door as if it were a holy shrine and that same bright light poured over me.

'Bag on the table.' The armed guard's words hit me like a gust of cold air. I complied. He dumped out my notebook and pencil. 'Against the wall.' He pointed. 'Shoes off.'

My face felt warm. I didn't want to draw attention to the sandals Mama had made for me from a used bike tire, but I had no choice. Slowly, I untied the rubber strips. The guard stuck his pencil through the back loop of one, lifted it in the air and examined it from every angle.

'Over here,' he instructed. 'Legs spread, arms out.'

While the guard patted down my left leg, a Jew bearing an Uzi and a backpack entered the library. All Israeli soldiers and reservists were required to carry their loaded Uzis in Jerusalem.

'Motie, I thought you were in the North,' the guard called to the armed man while he patted down my right leg. 'Did you run away?'

'Transferred,' Motie replied. 'Lucky for me this city's loaded with Arabs. There can never be enough soldiers here. Bad enough I have to repeat the year, I didn't want to miss the first week as well.'

For a split second, I wished I were Jewish so I could enter the library without being hassled.

Four Israeli men, the kind that looked like they cracked walnuts with their bare hands, motioned for Motie to join them at a large table.

Empty tables were everywhere, but I wanted an individual desk. From the corner of my eye, I spotted one and tried to look nonchalant as I rushed to it and pulled out my syllabi.

Inappropriately loud voices caught my attention and I glanced over. My eyes met Motie's. I turned my head away, but it was too late. He saw me look at him.

My eyes refused to focus on my Introduction to Calculus syllabus. The throaty voices grew louder.

'You go over,' Motie said.

'You have the gun,' a deep voice said. Bursts of laughter rang out.

Eyes glued to the syllabus, I watched the paper grow damp under my fingertips.

A screech, like a chair being pushed out from the table. The sound of boots getting closer. Breathe, I reminded myself. I glanced up. He was coming for me, Uzi in hand.

'Excuse me. You're Motie Moaz, aren't you?' The librarian intercepted him.

'Yes.'

'You still owe books from last year.'

'I read slowly,' he smiled. This was a man who was used to getting his way.

But she was having none of it. 'Come with me. I'll give you the list.'

The boots were gone, for the moment. I needed to find W.L. Wilks' *Calculus* before Motie returned. 'Calculus' was written on the shelf behind his table. Should I wait until his friends left? What if they were there all night? What if other students checked the book out by then? Why didn't they give us the list of books we would need before classes started? I took a deep breath, walked all the way around the edge of the cavernous room, entered the stacks from the back and darted to the Calculus section.

The men's deep voices grew silent as I approached my destination. My eyes scoured the shelf. I grabbed it. Pages stuck together. Where was the table of contents? Two silhouettes whispering to each other appeared in my peripheral vision. Where was that table of contents? This was it. I closed the book.

Book under arm, head lowered, I started down the long,

narrow aisle. Before I could exit, Motie appeared like a roadblock. I spun to go the other way. Two Israelis stepped into the aisle and blocked my passage.

Why did I answer those questions in class? Motie jabbed me in the stomach with the barrel of his Uzi.

'Are you planting something back here?' He jabbed me again.

'A book. For class.' I couldn't breathe. 'Excuse me, I need to pass.'

The veins in his neck bulged.

'Excuse me. Please. Let me pass.'

'Come with me,' Motie said.

'Now?'

'If all goes well, there'll be no pain involved.' With the barrel of his Uzi, he motioned towards the table.

He guided me with the barrel jammed into my kidney. 'Sit there.' The barrel pointed to a seat. I sank into the chair. The barrel pushed a piece of paper towards me. 'Answer the first problem.'

I looked at the problem. If $c(a)=2000+8.6a+0.5a^2$, then $c^1(300)= ?$

'308.6.' My voice trembled.

He raised his left brow. 'What's your secret?'

'No secret.' I squeezed the words out. Motie pointed the barrel of his Uzi to the next problem.

'I suppose it doesn't matter as long as you deliver the answers to us.'

'How do you know he's giving you the right answers?' one of the brutes asked.

Motie ripped a sheet of paper out of his notebook. 'Do your homework at the same time.'

A grim bearded librarian walked towards us, arms folded across his chest. His face was familiar. Our eyes locked. He was contestant number six. This wasn't good.

'Is he giving you trouble?' the librarian asked Motie.

'Everything's fine, Daaveed,' Motie said. 'We're having our first group study, right Mohammad?'

'Yes,' I whispered.

'Speak up, Mohammad,' Motie said.

'Yes. This is a study group.' My voice was only slightly louder than my previous whisper.

Daaveed sneered at me before he walked away.

I looked at my 'study group'. Would Zoher and Rafi's Sunday-night group also be at gunpoint? I looked at the clock. It was only 4:45. How long would they keep me? Would I have time for my other homework? I'd stay up all night. I didn't need to sleep. Motie would get tired, wouldn't he?

Motie took a book from his backpack and tossed it on the table. 'Physics' was scribbled on it in Hebrew with a black marker. Beneath it were the words *Tues and Thurs 9am–10am Professor Sharon.* The blood throbbed in my veins. Wasn't one class together enough?

'*Nu*.' Come on. Motie tapped the next problem.

The library was crowded now. All the larger tables were occupied by students engrossed in their books. I looked at the clock. It was 4:46. At least he allowed me to do my own homework. Light streamed in through the window. Would this day never end?

If Baba were here, I thought, he'd want me to teach Motie how to solve the problems, not just tell him the answers. For the rest of the questions, I went through the steps of each problem. Towards the end of the assignment, Motie actually solved the problems himself and only requested that I verify his answers. By the end of the assignment, he spoke without the help of his Uzi.

'I need to eat, but I shall return.' Motie half smiled at me. 'This was helpful.'

Did he expect me to wait in the library for him? With eleven checked-out books in my arms, I went back to the dorms. Now, I hoped, I wouldn't have to go back to the library for a long time.

'Open the door,' I called to Jameel from the hallway. The books cut into my palms and forearms. The stack reached over my head. Jameel didn't respond. When I tried to pull the key out of my paper bag, I destabilised the books and they toppled to the ground. Desperately I examined each one. What if one was damaged? How would I pay for it? I'd given my stipend to Mama. I only had enough for the bus fare back to the village and six loaves of bread.

Heart pounding, I unlocked the door, brushed off each book and carefully placed them on my desk.

24

It was after one in the morning when I heard Jameel's key in the door.

'Did you open your own library?'

'Haven't you started preparing for class?' I asked.

'I'm honing my English for the Saturday-night school dances.' He smiled. 'You should see these American girls. Rarr.' He shook his head. 'Come out with me tomorrow night.'

How could I go? I was here to study. He had no idea of the sacrifices my family were forced to make because of me.

'You need to go shopping.' Jameel smoothed his lapels. 'I need to teach you how to dress.'

How could I justify buying a new pair of trousers when Mama didn't even have a winter sweater to protect her from the biting wind?

'You're welcome to borrow my things,' Jameel said. 'I know how cheap you are.' He laughed.

***

In the morning, I woke up dreading my physics class. Jameel told me that our teacher was well known for his sharp scientific mind and his dislike of Arabs. Physics had always been my favourite subject, but now I wished it weren't a mandatory course.

'You're wrapped tighter than a mummy,' Jameel said as we walked to class together. In a black turtle-neck and black trousers, with a leather briefcase over his shoulder, he looked like a professor. I felt people staring at me as I walked next to him dressed in the outfit Mama had made. Jameel and I entered the class and headed straight to the back of the room.

Unlike the other professors, who dressed casually in jeans and cotton T-shirts, Professor Sharon strutted into the classroom in a perfectly pressed pinstriped suit and bow tie. His thick glasses, burly beard and overgrown moustache clashed with the rest of his getup.

'Ahmed Hamid?' Professor Sharon said. His voice made my upper lip tremble.

'Present.'

'Where are you from, Mr Hamid?' Professor Sharon asked.

'El-Kouriyah Village.' I could hear the unsteadiness in my voice.

When Professor Sharon had finished the roll call, he looked directly at Jameel and me as if he were looking at a lesser species.

'We're living in hostile times.' Professor Sharon's voice was serious. 'Every Israeli citizen must be on alert. Come to me with any suspicions you might have. Nothing is too small.' Professor Sharon cleared his throat. 'If a high-powered assault rifle whose mass is five kilograms fires a fifteen-gram bullet with a muzzle velocity of 3×104 cm/sec, what is the recoil velocity, Mr Abu Hussein?'

All eyes went to Jameel.

'I'm not prepared.'

'This is basic. Are you trying to be an academic zero? You need to shake the sand out of your head. You and your kind are a waste of space.'

Professor Sharon's eyes met mine. 'Mr Hamid, can you tell us?'

'Minus ninety centimetres per second,' I said.

Professor Sharon shook his head. 'How did you arrive at that answer?'

'The momentum of the system after the rifle has fired must equal the momentum before the rifle went off. Originally, the momentum of the bullet and rifle was zero, since they were at rest. Using the conservation of momentum equation (m1+m2) v0=m1v1+m2v2,m1v1=-m2v2,v1=-m2v2, m1=(15 g) ×(3×104 cm/sec)=-90 cm/sec.'

'Is this a sizeable recoil velocity, Motie?' Professor Sharon asked.

'Yes,' Motie said.

'And what would happen if the rifle wasn't held firmly against the shoulder of the shooter?' Professor Sharon leaned against his desk.

'The shooter would receive a substantial kick,' Motie said.

'If the shooter held the rifle firmly against his body, what would happen?'

'The shooter's body as a whole would absorb the momentum.'

'Excellent work, Motie.' Professor Sharon looked back at me. 'If the shooter's mass is 100 kg, then the recoil velocity from the shot is what, Mr Hamid?'

'4.3 cm/sec,' I said.

'Explain?' Professor Sharon's tone said he expected me to fail.

'I used for m1 the mass of the rifle plus the mass of the shooter. If his mass is 100 kg, then the recoil velocity which is now the gun plus the shooter is v1=(15 g)×(3×104 cm/sec) 5×103 g+105 g=4.3 cm/sec.'

Professor Sharon looked back at Motie. 'How is the magnitude of this recoil?'

'Quite tolerable,' he said.

'Excellent work, Motie.' Professor Sharon smiled.

When the bell rang, Jameel was the first one out the door. I was hurrying after him when someone tapped me on the shoulder.

'Great job with the homework.' Motie raised his eyebrows. 'Let's go do Professor Sharon's. We work well together.'

If I lied and said I had a class or something, Motie would check. And if he caught me lying, who knows what he'd do to me. I'd talk to Jameel when I got back to the room.

As Motie and I walked into the library I wondered if this was how the condemned felt on their way to the gallows.

'Bag on the table,' the guard said. 'Everything out.'

'He's with me and we don't have a lot of time,' Motie said.

I followed him past the guard and into the library. Within thirty minutes, we finished our homework; as before, I explained how to do the problems. Motie suggested we do Professor Sharon's assignment together every week. I nodded. Why not? I had to do the work anyway.

***

Jameel sat on his bed smoking a cigarette.

'We Arabs invented the zero,' Jameel said. 'Mohammad Ibn Ahmad introduced it in 967 ad. The West didn't get it until the thirteenth century. We invented algebra. We taught the world to separate trigonometry from astronomy. We founded non-Euclidian geometry. The Europeans were living in caves when we invented physics and medicine. Did he forget we once ruled from Spain to China?' He breathed hard and shook his fist.

'We'll study together.'

'May Allah send darkness on Professor Sharon's soul!' Jameel almost spat the smoke from his cigarette.

***

Every day after Professor Sharon's class, Motie, Jameel and I went to the library together. When Motie was with us, Jameel and I weren't searched. I explained the homework to both of them and they got it. By the end of the month, they could do the work on their own even though we still sat together.

A few times Motie stopped by our room for help in a different class. One time he stopped by to bring us a Russian cake his mother had made. It was delicious and made me think of Baba's jam doughnut all those years ago.

A month later, Professor Sharon handed back everyone's homework except mine. 'Homework is an integral part of your grade.' His voice was stern. 'I won't tolerate anyone not doing their homework.' He stared at me. 'You, Mr Hamid, are trying to mock me.'

What was he talking about? I stared, unsure what to say.

'You didn't do yesterday's homework.'

'I handed it in yesterday.' I clasped my hands together to hide my trembling.

The veins in Professor Sharon's neck bulged. 'You're a liar, Mr Hamid!'

Motie spoke up. 'Professor Sharon.'

The professor turned in his direction. 'What?'

'Ahmed and I did our homework together yesterday.'

'Well, Mr Hamid forgot to hand it in.'

'No.' Motie shook his head. 'I watched him hand it in.'

'Well, I'll check again.'

The bell rang.

25

Jameel stared at his reflection in the mirror. In his black turtle-neck and bell-bottom jeans, he could have passed for a Jew.

'These dances are overflowing with gorgeous American girls. Come with me. I'll take my pick and throw you my leftovers.'

'I need to work some numbers.'

'All you do is study. Look how you dress. Why are you acting like such a martyr?' Jameel asked. 'In the name of God, please borrow my clothes. I'm embarrassed to be seen with you. You look like a refugee, not a student.'

Unable to concentrate after he left for the dance, I opened his closet, took off my homemade clothes, and pulled on a black turtle-neck and a pair of his bell-bottom jeans.

In the mirror, I studied myself. With my eyes closed, I imagined I was at the party. The band played. Boys and girls danced together like they did in the moshav.

The knock at the door startled me.

'Is anyone in there?' The knob turned and Zoher walked in. Why had I left it unlocked?

'Particle dynamics are causing me grief.' He sat on my bed and scanned me from top to bottom. 'Are you going out?'

'Yes.' The lie exited my mouth before I could stop myself. Now I was forced to go to the dance. How would I explain it to Jameel?

'Can you stop by my room tomorrow? I've got a question for you.'

'No problem.'

***

The dance was in the auditorium on the other side of campus, near the entrance. It would take at least half an hour to walk there.

As I passed the Israeli flag waving from a tall pole, and the luxurious Kiriyah dormitories, I cursed myself. Why couldn't I fit in here? Why had I helped Ali all those years ago? Why wasn't I born in the United States or Canada?

I thought back to Year 5, and how Teacher Fouad had lifted a copy of our mandatory Israeli history book high in the air. 'The Israelis require I teach from this.' He shook the book. 'In it, the Israelis have erased our history. They call pre-1948 Palestine *Eretz Yisrael*, the land of Israel, and us, the Arabs of the land of Israel. But despite their efforts, the history of our people can never be erased. We are Palestinians, and this is our land.'

We chanted '*Filistine*!' Palestine!

Teacher Fouad said that if there hadn't been a rise of anti-Semitism in Europe at the end of the nineteenth century, the Jews wouldn't have wanted their own homeland. And that Britain, after pitting the Jews and Arabs against each other, realised the no-win situation and handed the question of Palestine to the United Nations. Should anyone have been surprised when, in the wake of the Holocaust, the United Nations partitioned the majority of Palestine to the Jewish minority? I wished that my people had just accepted partition, but Palestine had been erased from the map before I was born.

Girls, dressed in miniskirts, hot pants and high heels shimmied and shook to an Israeli band playing Western music. Jameel hadn't exaggerated. He stood, looking conspicuous, in the centre of the darkened room talking to a petite girl with hair the colour of sunflower petals.

Jameel noticed me approaching. 'What in God's name . . . ?'

'Who are you talking to?' I interrupted.

'This is Deborah.'

Strobe lights brought to life the diamond-encrusted Star of David on her gold necklace. It sparkled like it had magical powers. The Sephardic Jews at work used to wear the stars so that they wouldn't be mistaken for Arabs.

'One minute please,' I said to her in Hebrew.

I yanked Jameel's arm and pulled him towards the door.

'Are you trying to dislocate my shoulder?'

Outside, I scanned the area. There was no one in earshot. 'Are you without a brain?'

He jerked his arm from my grasp. 'What's wrong?'

I addressed the heavens. 'This guy just doesn't get it.'

'Get what?'

'What planet are you from?' I wanted to shake him. 'She's Jewish and you're Palestinian.'

'Your point?'

'Don't make me think that your IQ is under 60.'

'I've dated Israeli Jewish girls. And anyway, she's American. She's waiting for me. I need to get back in.'

He walked towards the door as I stared in disbelief. At the entrance he turned. 'Glad to see you finally borrowed my clothes. You've never looked better.' He smiled. 'Come on.' He held the door open, but I went back to our room instead.

***

Zoher opened his door. A backgammon board was laid out on top of a plastic table. He noticed me looking at it.

'Do you play?' he asked.

'Used to.'

'I'm the state champion.'

'You haven't played all its citizens,' I said.

'Is that a challenge?' He smiled.

I didn't want to appear too cocky—that's poor strategy. 'It's been a long time.'

'Give me a chance.'

Before I could pretend to refuse again, he pulled the table up next to the bed and pushed a chair up to the other side. He sat on the bed and motioned for me to sit. His white button-down shirt was wrinkleless.

This was what I really enjoyed; one-on-one competition with a worthy adversary. Like the Israeli guys on campus often said: *bring it on.*

He rolled the die with his baby-skinned hands and then so did I, with my callused earth-stained ones. Zoher rolled a five and I, a six. I adopted the running game strategy. Quickly, I moved my stones from his home board to his outer board; I planned on leaving a few exposed so they could be used as stepping stones to establish a strong offensive.

This was Baba's game too; the war he loved to fight. We'd often played together. Zoher picked up the dice. A wide grin stretched across his face and a sheen of sweat covered his high forehead. He rolled the controversial five-three. I sat up straight, glanced into his coffee-coloured eyes and then away. He picked up his black stones, but didn't make the best of the five-three. I knew I had him. Baba had explained this move: that it left blots exposed and, if hit, gave the opponent the immediate advantage, the opportunity to make the three-point being lost. Zoher pulled a handkerchief from his pocket.

I began to move my stones without gaps directly in front of his to build a prime blocker. Once I had placed six no-gap stones in a row, his stones couldn't escape. When I got my stones into my home board, I began to bear off.

Perspiration stains appeared on Zoher's perfect shirt.

When I finished, his mouth gaped open. 'Great game,' he said. 'When can I have a rematch?'

'A week from today.'

He smiled. 'Next time.'

We shook hands and I went back to my room. Every Saturday evening, for the rest of the school year, Zoher and I met to play backgammon and he never once beat me.

26

Jameel and I were in our room packing books for our bi-weekly trip to Acre when I heard a knock on the door and Deborah walked in.

'Shalom,' Jameel greeted her. 'Ready to go?' A bag larger than a handbag hung from her right shoulder.

'I love Acre.' Her Hebrew was good, but her American accent was strong.

Jameel looked over at me and smiled. I glanced at her Star of David. Had he lost his mind? What if the soldiers saw us? What would everyone think?

'Ready?' he asked me in Hebrew.

'You're sitting next to her,' I said in Arabic. 'I'm going to pretend I don't know you.'

He replied in Arabic, 'Do what you have to do. Let's go.'

Deborah smiled at me and I forced my lips up.

At the central bus station, Deborah walked over to a market stall. Jameel shrugged. 'She wants nuts for the ride.'

'Even the Prophet won't be able to save you!'

'Give her a chance.'

Deborah returned with a bag of warm nuts and held it towards me.

'No thanks.'

Her blue eyes sparkled like the ocean in the sun. She was

definitely the prettiest girl I'd ever seen.

Jameel and Deborah sat in the middle of the bus together and I in the back, alone, doing my organic chemistry homework. When we arrived, I waited for them to walk ahead of me, and then I followed.

Deborah turned to me. 'Come on.' They stopped to wait. I feared Jameel's parents' reaction. I could only imagine what Mama would have done if I had brought home a girl who wore the Jewish Star of David. I could just see Mama coming out of our tent and spotting the star displayed on the girl's chest.

'I've brought a friend,' I'd say.

Mama would be frozen with her mouth agape, her eyes wide in terror. In a shrill shriek, she would recite from the Koran, call on Allah, the Prophet Mohammad and anyone else she could think of to save me.

Then Abbas would appear. 'You bring her here to fornicate in our tent?'

Mama would tell me, 'My heart goes out to you like fire and your heart goes out to me like stone.' And then it would go downhill from there.

Um Jameel greeted us with a smile, steaming tea and an array of appetisers in small dishes she'd placed on their kitchen table: tabboulie, hummus, olives, fried halloumi cheese, falafel, warm grape leaves, labneh, baba ghanouj, and loubia bi zeit.

'Welcome to our humble home,' she said in broken Hebrew. 'Please, I wish I'd made more.'

Deborah, Jameel and Um Jameel made their way to the table. I stood motionless.

'Come on,' Um Jameel called.

I followed them to the table.

Abu Jameel appeared with a platter of grilled meats on skewers: chicken, lamb and kafta from the outdoor grill. We stood. Jameel kissed his cheeks and I shook his hand.

'This is my friend Deborah,' Jameel said.

Abu Jameel shook Deborah's hand.

'Our home is yours,' he said.

After lunch, Deborah, Jameel and I headed for the Arab bazaar. The stalls were filled with chess sets made of inlaid wood, hookahs, embroidered textiles, amulets against the evil eye, Bedouin silver-coin necklaces, oriental rugs, Arab headdresses and robes, together with T-shirts, hats and towels with the word *Israel* written across them.

While drinking freshly squeezed orange juice from a cart in the road, I heard a man's voice call Jameel's name from one of the stalls. We walked past brightly coloured robes and gold and silver bracelets, past necklaces and rings, to the back of the store.

Jameel and the man hugged. The grey-bearded man with the red-checked headdress motioned for us to sit on the low cushioned divan. A woman arrived with an ornate brass tray with demitasses filled with black coffee, and we drank before we made our way through the market towards the oriental sweets.

I shuddered upon seeing the butcher with a piece of raw meat hanging from a single hook. I thought of the Jews' slaughterhouse. No wonder we couldn't compete: my people were nowhere near as efficient as the Jewish Israelis. The butcher probably slaughtered one cow a month.

Spice sellers weighed small bags filled with saffron, turmeric, cumin and cinnamon.

I spotted the large circular tray of kanafi in the window and knew we'd arrived at Jameel's favourite sweet shop. A man brought us three pieces, poured us three glasses of water from a pitcher, and we ate together; Jameel, the Jewish girl and I.

***

On our way back to Jameel's house, I saw a pack of soldiers

in the distance running towards us and I stood in front of Deborah until they ran past.

Jameel cuffed me on the head.

'Do you know what they would do to us if they noticed she was a Jew?' I tried not to raise my voice and attract notice. 'They could kill us. I'm speaking to you in plain Arabic. Do you understand me?'

'Maybe in the rural villages where you come from, but the city-dwellers are different. We live here in peace with the Jews.'

'You must be blind.'

Jameel and I had been bickering for five minutes when we noticed that Deborah had disappeared.

'Where is she?' Jameel's voice was panicked.

'We shouldn't have brought her.'

'We have to find her!'

'Do you know what they'll do to us if something happens to her?' I asked.

Jameel and I ran around the stalls of the bazaar calling Deborah's name. People were everywhere. Children in strollers, old men with canes. French, English, Arabic, Hebrew, Russian. But there was no Deborah, and we'd go to prison if something happened to her.

I peered into every store, and eventually found her in the musical instrument shop, sitting in a chair, strumming an oud. She was oblivious to our panic—was she toying with us? How could things be so different in America?

Jameel interrupted the owner as he showed her how to play the oud. 'Where were you?' He was out of breath.

'I've played the guitar for years. I wanted to try the oud. I heard it at a school concert and fell in love.' She turned to the owner. 'I'll take this one.' She paid him the equivalent of what it took me two months to earn at the slaughterhouse.

***

At the house that evening, Jameel, his parents and I sat around his coffee table and waited for Deborah to play her new oud.

She tried to strum it standing, but it was awkward.

'Ouds were meant to be played sitting down,' I said.

She sat in the chair across from me and tried again, but the oud rotated.

'I've got to get used to holding it.' She shook her head and looked at me. 'It wants to slide off my lap. It wants to point itself at the ceiling instead of the audience.'

'Put it against your chest, not your belly,' I said. 'It'll stop it from rotating on you.' It was so unfair. She couldn't even play her new expensive oud. She would probably get bored with it in a day and never use it again.

'Like this?' She had it on her lap.

'Yes, but hold the neck more vertically.'

She strummed and it stayed in place.

'It's hard for me to get used to a fretless instrument. I'm used to the guitar's frets stopping the strings in exactly the right place for the pitch.' She complained as if it was a big problem. She strummed it a few more times.

'Why don't you start with the Maqam Hijaz?' I said, softening a little. Perhaps she was sincere in her admiration of our music; perhaps she deserved a chance.

'The what?'

Of course, she didn't know. 'A maqam is a concept related to the Western ideas of "scale" and "mode".' I looked at her. 'The Maqam Hijaz has an EH, BH, and F number in the key signature, and the tonic is D.'

She played the notes.

She looked up at me with those pretty eyes. 'How was it?'

'Your plucking pattern is off.' I sounded like Baba. 'The plucking motion should come mainly from your wrist. Yours is coming from your forearm. Hold your pick like it's an extension of your hand.'

'Like this?' She strummed the chords.

'Keep your wrist at the smallest angle you can, without it being impossible to play.'

She took my advice and strummed the chords again.

'That's right,' I said. 'Don't allow your elbow and wrist to take over.'

She played the Maqam Hijaz perfectly. I smiled the way Baba always did when he was able to teach me a melody.

Everyone clapped when she finished.

'I wish I wasn't going home next week,' she said.

'Home?' Didn't all the Jews believe Israel was their home, the one God had promised them?

'Home; you know, California,' she said.

***

The day before Deborah left, she stopped by our room with a box.

'I thought we'd have a last dinner together, American style.' She smiled. 'Pizza, Coca-Cola and Sonny and Cher.'

She put the box on Jameel's desk and plugged her cassette player into the wall. Cher's voice singing 'I've got you babe' burst from the recorder. Deborah handed us each a slice of pizza. We had just begun to eat when I heard a knock on the door.

It was my brother Abbas. He looked into my room. His eyes locked onto Deborah's Star of David and the colour drained from his face. I pushed him outside and pulled the door partially closed. He put his hands over his ears.

Abbas had the ferocity of a lion. 'You're partying with our enemies.' He shook his fists, and took some deep breaths.

'That's my roommate Jameel. He's Palestinian like us.'

'And the blonde with the Star of David around her neck?' Abbas spit the words out. 'I suppose you expect me to believe she's Palestinian as well.' He placed a letter in my hand. 'It arrived yesterday.'

I didn't recognise the sender's name, 'Aboud Aziz', but I did recognise the sender's address. The Dror Detention Centre. I pulled the letter out of the open envelope.

Dear Ahmed,

You don't know me, but I'm in prison with your father. He's had a fall. Visiting days are the first Tuesday of every month from noon to 2pm.

Sincerely,

Aboud Aziz

I'd promised Baba that I wouldn't visit, but, in my heart, I knew I was looking for an excuse. What if Baba was being tortured and only pretended that he was fine?

'Should I go?' I asked Abbas.

'Do you still have a conscience?'

How could Baba, who was so apolitical, who loved to tell jokes, survive in prison? What if the other prisoners beat him for being too accommodating to the Israelis?

'He told me not to come,' I said. The pit in my stomach grew heavier when I realised it was the first Monday of the month. 'I'll leave tomorrow,' I said. After eighteen years, the need for Arab Israelis to obtain permission to travel had just ended.

'Mama sent this for him.' Abbas handed me a paper bag filled with almonds. 'I need to return.'

'Stay the night,' I said. 'Sleep in my bed.'

'Absolutely not. I refuse to fraternise with the enemy.'

'Wait.' I brought him to the kitchen to give him the stash of food I had saved for my family. 'Please stay.' I handed him the bag of frozen food and he was gone.

'What's going on?' Jameel asked when I returned.

'My father's had an accident. I need to visit him.'

'Who was that at the door?' He put the last bite of pizza crust in his mouth.

'My brother.'

'Aren't you going to invite him in?' He headed for the door.

'No,' I said, louder than I intended. 'He went home. My mother needs him.'

'Aren't you going?'

'Tomorrow.' Yes, I'd go tomorrow. Abbas had given me the money.

While Jameel slept, I washed my shirt and trousers in the sink and hung them outside on the line to dry. I wanted to borrow something from him, but I didn't want to draw attention to myself. With a damp rag, I wiped my sandals.

***

When I heard the muezzin's call to prayer, I showered and washed my hair with soap. At the front gate of the campus I caught the first of the five buses I'd need. I'd get the notes and homework assignments from Motie, Zoher, Rafi and Jameel when I returned.

As I rode, I wondered what would happen if the other inmates found out that Baba built houses for the Jews. Had anyone from our village been arrested recently? The Israelis would definitely want that spread around. Images of Baba being beaten by both the Palestinian inmates and the Israeli guards entered my mind, and my grip on the bag of almonds Mama had sent tightened.

The relentless sun on the suffocating bus left me dizzy and parched. It reminded me of that first journey, years earlier, as I was careening, unprepared, out of the innocence of childhood.

I studied maths, chemistry, physics; anything I could to occupy my mind. But, despite my efforts, by the time I arrived at the prison I was nervous and sick. Stumbling towards the pen, I wondered how badly Baba must be hurt that the other prisoner felt compelled to write. Would I even recognise him?

I forgot my discomfort when I heard a piercing cry coming from the pen. Instinctively, I rushed towards it. A guard rammed his Uzi into a prisoner's ribs as the prisoner lay curled in a foetal position in the dirt. Was that Baba? I didn't want to look, but the wailing forced me. The man stopped moving. Was he dead?

I ran to the entrance and waited impatiently while the guard called name after name. If he had died, would they even call his name? I thought of Baba's name being called every month and no one being there to visit him.

The sun was like a hot poker. Many people sat in the sand. An older man with a cane fainted and his family gathered around him and wet his head with water from a bottle. Why couldn't they build a little shade for us? They surely had the labour. Babies and children cried, and I continued to wait. My mouth was parched and my skin burned. Two hours later, the guard finally called Baba's name.

'Who are you here to see?' the guard at the door asked.

'Mahmud Hamid, my father,' I said, looking at the floor.

'Oh, you're Mahmud's son? Great voice. He's been teaching me how to play the oud.'

I looked into his face and handed him the bag of almonds. He looked into it. 'You can't bring anything in, but, if you want, I'll give it to him later.'

'Thanks,' I said.

'You're all set here,' the guard said. 'Unfortunately all visitors have to be searched.' He turned around. 'Yo Bo'az, this is

Mahmud Hamid's son; take care of him.' He turned back to me. 'Nice meeting you.'

'You, too,' I said and walked towards Bo'az.

I entered the room with scores of other men. Bo'az patted my body down with my clothes on and let me proceed.

Baba appeared in the window. His face looked like leather with deep crows' feet and vertical lines across his forehead. I felt weighed down. Were all his letters lies? Baba smiled and I saw a glimmer of the father I remembered.

'Did something happen to Mama or one of your siblings?'

'I heard about your fall.'

Baba shook his head. 'I tripped—had a slight concussion. I'm fine now.'

'I thought the worst.'

Baba smiled. 'I'm so proud of you. A college student. Did you have to miss classes to come here?'

'I can make them up. I'll come every month,' I said.

'Absolutely not. I don't want you missing a single class. In life, if one wants to achieve something great, he and his loved ones must make sacrifices.'

When it was time to leave, Baba looked into my eyes. 'You've made me so proud.' He put his hand to the window and I did the same. I watched as he was escorted through the door, and then I cried like a child.

27

Professor Sharon wasn't in class. Instead, a freckle-faced man with golden dreadlocked hair dressed in ripped jeans and an untucked shirt leaned against his desk. 'I'll be filling in for Professor Sharon during his military reserve duty.'

I prayed Professor Sharon's duty would last the twenty more days until the semester was over.

After class, while walking by the professor's office, I caught a glimpse of a clean-shaven soldier in uniform speaking with Professor Sharon's substitute and stopped dead still. I remembered Baba curled up in a foetal position while the soldier pounded his machine-gun into his ribs on the floor of our house. I thought of the sneering, ruthless commander, a soldier who looked very much like the soldier in Professor Sharon's office.

The world tilted, hard. The eyes, the nose, the lips—it was Professor Sharon, clean-shaven. I stared. When he noticed me, I dropped my eyes and stumbled away.

It was years ago, and the room had been dark, except for the harsh light directed upon my family. I couldn't be certain. I recalled again the hate-filled commander who had sneered, spat and thrust his machine-gun into Baba's flesh. That soldier was Professor Sharon. I shook my head. No, it wasn't. Could not have been.

Maybe.

***

Fifteen days later, I entered the classroom and froze mid-step. Leaning back in his chair with his hands clasped behind his head, Professor Sharon locked his eyes onto mine. If there hadn't been students pushing into the class, I'd have turned around and left. My heart pounded. There were only a few days left in the semester, I told myself.

Professor Sharon handed out a take-home practice exam, which, he informed us, we would correct together in class.

'I wanted to correct them myself.' Professor Sharon's voice was serious. 'But due to the increasing Arab hostility, I've moved your exam to the day after tomorrow.'

For the last few years there had been mounting tensions between Israel, Jordan, Syria and Egypt over water and land rights. A prolonged chain of border violence had ensued.

***

Jameel and I were sitting at our desks in my dorm room, inhaling the aroma of stewing vegetables drifting in from the nearby kitchen, when I heard Motie's signature knock, three rapid taps, on my door.

'Come in,' I called to him in Hebrew.

'Bring your practice exam to the kitchen,' he said. 'Let's get it out of the way. We need to start studying for the real thing.'

On the kitchen table were five plates and a large bowl of cooked white fluffy grains.

Rafi and Zoher were already sitting at the table.

'Ever had couscous?' Zoher asked.

I shook my head.

'We'll study Moroccan style.' Zoher scooped couscous onto everyone's plate and Rafi covered it with a ladleful of vegetable stew. 'My mother's couscous was the best in all Casablanca.'

As we ate, we solved the test questions together.

***

On the day of the exam I entered the large auditorium and sat in the back of the room. I was staring at my desktop in an attempt to clear my mind, when I heard an unfamiliar voice inform us that Professor Sharon would not be present. A weight lifted from my heart.

I turned over the exam, looked at the first question, then the second and third. Maybe there was a mistake. The Israeli to my left was checking the cover of the exam as well. This test was exactly the same as the review test.

***

The car park outside the halls was filled with activity. Parents loaded suitcases into their car boots. Students carrying shoulder bags and backpacks gathered at the bus stop, in the hallways and in the road. The school year was over.

***

My first thought when I heard the knock on my door the next morning was that it was a mistake. The halls were empty. Jameel had already left and I was about to go back to my village for the summer.

A Jewish Israeli student stood there with his hands on his hips. 'Professor Sharon wants you in his office. Now!'

A bolt of fear shot through me. I was unable to respond.

'What's wrong with you?' the student sneered.

My first instinct was to flee, to return to my village. Professor Sharon must have been waiting for the semester to end to confront me. But then I started to think. Maybe he wanted to congratulate me on my test score. I was sure I had got all of the questions right. If he knew something about Baba, why would he wait until the end of class?

I was still tempted just to finish packing my bag and go back to the village instead of meeting with him. But then I remembered my promise. This was not about Baba, I kept telling myself as I walked towards his office. He didn't even know who Baba was. With a trembling hand, I knocked on his door.

'Come in,' Professor Sharon called.

A picture of Einstein hung above his desk with the $E=mc^2$ equation underneath. How bad could he be if he admired Einstein?

'Did you think I wouldn't know?' Professor Sharon hulked over his desk with a menacing look on his face.

What was he talking about?

'You cheated on the exam.'

Had I heard him correctly? This wasn't about Baba.

'This was on the floor near your seat.' He waved what looked like my answer sheet from the review test in the air.

'My review test is in my room.'

'Go and get it. I've informed the head of the department. Unless you have an explanation, you'll be expelled. We have a zero-tolerance policy.' He shook his head. 'You're like your terrorist father.'

I didn't want to go down this road. I knew that anyone in Israel who was accused of supporting the PLO was deported or imprisoned or murdered. He had the power to decide my fate. Every millimetre of my body wanted to yell, *What we do is defend ourselves against Israeli terrorism.*

'Why don't you Palestinians just give up? No one likes you.'

'Should the Jews in the concentration camps have given up?'

'You have no idea what you're talking about.' Professor Sharon's face was blood red.

'Did Hitler and the Nazis like the Jews? Who liked the Jews?'

'Shut up!' His voice was not his own.

'No one liked the Jews, but you fought back, even when everyone around you was trying to exterminate you. We Palestinians are like you Jews.'

'There's no comparison!' He cut the air with his finger. 'Get out of here.'

I had allowed myself to lose control. What was I thinking, talking to him that way? He'd tell everyone about Baba. I opened the door and ran out.

I was searching frantically for my practice test, when I heard a knock. My muscles tightened. The door pushed open.

'Professor Sharon has become lazy,' Zoher said. 'I wonder what he was thinking.'

I continued my search without responding.

'Here's black paper and tape,' he said. 'Everyone's supposed to cover their windows.'

I had no idea what he was talking about. 'What?'

'To block out the light in case of war,' he said.

For the last few months, with the rising tensions, everyone had been talking about the possibility of a war, but I hadn't taken it seriously.

I sat on the edge of my bed and covered my eyes.

'What's wrong?'

'Professor Sharon accused me of cheating.'

'You're the smartest in the class.'

'Who's going to believe me, an Arab?'

'It does seem far-fetched.' His voice was calm.

Professor Sharon would tell everyone about Baba. I wanted to be gone before they found out.

'Please, I need to pack.' I threw my books into a paper bag and ran out of the door, leaving Zoher sitting on my bed. I needed to think, alone.

'Wait,' Zoher called, but I was already down the hall.

On the way back to my village, the military were everywhere. The police had blockaded the road between Tel Aviv and Jerusalem to stop vehicles and paint their car lights blue-black, so that if a war broke out, their enemies wouldn't see the lights. When I finally arrived in the village that evening, Mama was coming down the hill.

'Was there fighting in Jerusalem?' she asked.

I lowered my head. 'I was thrown out of the university.'

'Good. We need to buy rice, lentils and potatoes,' she said, 'and fill up our pitchers with water.'

I followed her down the dirt path that ran between the houses to the flat ground towards the village square. The square pulsated with nervous energy. Women scurried from place to place with baskets of purchases balanced on their heads. The queue to the shop reached the tea house.

'We need to stock up,' she said, without looking back at me. 'The goat, chicken and vegetables we have won't be enough, especially if we're stuck up there.'

I realised war really was coming.

The next morning, I went down to the square to wait for the Israeli employers, but not one of them showed. So I sat in the tea house with the other men and listened to broadcasts from Egypt.

'Go back to where you came from. You don't stand a chance,' said an Arab voice in accented Hebrew on the radio. I couldn't suppress my smile. This whole nightmare could soon be over and Baba released if the Arabs won.

We devoured the Israeli newspaper *Haaretz*. The first- page headline read *Arabs Threaten to Push Us to the Sea*. The weight I'd carried around for the last seven years suddenly lightened with hope.

***

On May the 16th, 1967, when Egypt expelled the United Nations Emergency Forces from the Sinai, we danced the dabkeh in the village square, in front of the tea house. The Mukhtar, twirling a string of beads, led me and the other men who linked arms while we stomped, kicked and jumped to the lively tempo. With each stomp, we emphasised our connection to the land.

An explosion—flames and smoke—blew through the square like a sudden wind of fire. I was blown backwards and hit my head on the corner of a table. Hot tea splashed into my eyes and burned my skin. Glasses shattered all around me. Abu Hassan fell on top of me and others were on top of him. The screaming was primal. I felt the back of my head. There wasn't any blood.

'Abdul Karim Alwali was hit.'

I pushed my way from under the other men, jumped to my feet and looked. Nothing was left of him but blood, chunks of flesh and fragments of bone. His brother Ziad, who had been on one side of him, was on the ground. There were cords of red flesh, like pieces of raw meat, attached to his forearms where his hands had been seconds before. Shrapnel was buried in his face through bullet-sized holes. His left eye was swollen shut and his screams were gut-wrenching.

The Mukhtar's pick-up truck ripped down the road and screeched to a halt in front of us. Villagers lifted Ziad into the back. His mother ran to the truck, took one look at her son, screamed and burst into tears. She climbed into the back next to him and the Mukhtar took off. Some of the children came from their houses with plastic containers and began to gather Abdul Karim's flesh.

Abbas was stuck in the tent. It was hard for him to come down the hill and impossible for him to run. There was no reason for him to see this, and I was grateful he was spared. I wondered what Rafi, Zoher and Motie were doing.

***

On May the 22nd, I was in the tea house when Egypt announced it was closing the Straits of Tiran to all ships flying

Israeli flags. We thrust our fists in the air and paraded around the village square chanting, 'In blood, in spirit, we will liberate Palestine.' Other villagers joined in as we made our way through the village.

***

On June the 5th at 7:45am the civil defence sirens sounded. My spirits soared. I raced down to the damaged tea house. We chanted while we pulsed the V for victory in the air. Tears welled up in my eyes. Palestine would return to Arab hands.

'Israeli bombers crossed into Egyptian airspace,' the voice of the Arabs reported from Cairo. 'Egyptian aircraft fire shot down three-quarters of the attacking Israeli jets.'

Transfixed by the radio, I drank cup after cup of coffee.

'The Egyptian air force launched a counter-attack against Israel. Israeli forces penetrated Sinai, but Egyptian troops engaged the enemy and have taken the offensive.' We pounded our fists on the tables. The Arabs were winning. Baba could be released. Victory was in our hands.

'Throughout Cairo, the citizens are celebrating. Hundreds of thousands of Egyptian citizens have taken to the streets, chanting "Down with Israel! We will win the war!" ' The radio delivered more good news. 'We have shot down eight enemy planes.' I prayed for survivors so that there could be a prisoner exchange.

'Our aeroplanes and missiles are at this moment shelling all Israel's towns and villages. We will avenge the dignity we lost in 1948.' I felt like my luck was finally changing. I went to share the good news with my family.

***

The sky filled with the noise of an approaching helicopter. It hovered over our village. Then a deafening explosion shook the earth. The helicopter had fired a rocket into the mosque. I stood frozen. The muezzin had called the villagers to prayer minutes before. I ran for the mosque.

Bodies littered the ground, bleeding from shrapnel wounds. Hands stuck out from the rubble. Shrapnel-laden bits of arms, legs, torsos and heads were splattered throughout the square. I spotted Um Tariq face down on the ground, quiet and motionless, while blood oozed out from under her skull into the dirt around her. Small bits of brain matter clung to her black hair. Her four children were pulling at her robe, screaming for her to get up. Why were they firing into unarmed villages?

Panicked villagers were screaming and running. They pushed and bumped into each other. The sound of the names of missing loved ones being called by terrified family members floated up. Thick smoke billowed, obstructing my vision and making my eyes water. With my head down, I dug through the rubble until my hands bled, and then I dug some more. Maybe there were people buried alive. Others dug nearby. The sky darkened. I could no longer see. I had to go back to my family. I found Mama and Nadia huddled together crying.

'The Israelis must pay for this,' Abbas told Fadi. He was so angry he shook.

All night Mama, Abbas, Nadia, Fadi, Hani and I clung to each other. We knew that any one of us could die at any minute.

Desperate to hear encouraging news, I went down to the tea house. By 11am, the radio announced that Jordanian forces had begun firing long-range artillery towards Israeli suburbs near Tel Aviv. Within an hour, the radio reported that Jordanian, Syrian and Iraqi fighter jets were slicing into Israeli airspace.

'The Zionist barracks in Palestine are about to be destroyed,' Egyptian radio declared.

Explosions and the welcome sound of fighter jets graced the air. Our Arab brothers were on their way. 'The Syrian Air Force has begun to bomb Israeli cities and destroy Israeli positions,' Damascus Radio announced.

'We're today living the holiest hours of our life; united with all the other armies of the Arab nation, we're fighting a war of heroism and honour against our common enemy,' Prime Minister Juna said on the radio. 'We have waited years for this battle to erase the stain of the past. Take up your weapons and take back your country stolen by the Jews.'

Suddenly I heard gunfire spraying outside the tea house. We ran out. Israeli soldiers were everywhere. A few barefoot Jordanian solders had entered with primitive guns. An Israeli tank fired a missile. The Jordanian soldiers ran in circles, their uniforms and flesh aflame. They dropped to the ground, rolling in the dirt to try to put out the fire, but the flames devoured them. Thirteen charred Jordanian corpses lay in the village square, their arms and legs in unnatural positions, their flesh, muscles and tissue burned off. All that was left of them was charred bones.

That night none of us could sleep. We listened to the explosions of mortars and rockets in the distance. After a few hours of shelling it was quiet again. Then, a mortar exploded near our tent and blazed the sky like lightning. Another mortar exploded close to us.

'Get out of the tent!' Mama screamed.

The back side of our tent was on fire. Pushing and shoving, my siblings fled into the night. We had no cover. Black smoke billowed. Mama's face bled. Blood was splattered across Nadia's face. Abbas held his left arm. Hani cried. I ran my hands over my face and they filled with warm blood. The shrapnel had sliced through the tent into our skin.

We gathered under the almond tree and once again watched as fire destroyed what little we had. The flames that shot from the tent illuminated Mama's anguished face. Helicopters above us drowned out my thoughts.

We slept in the open air. In the middle of the night, another ex- plosion lit up the sky. Planes fired missiles into our village. Flames shot up from homes. I dreamed that Professor Sharon called me to the board to solve a mathematical equation and I couldn't see the numbers. He grinned and the Israelis laughed and taunted me. In the distance the mortars and rockets continued to explode.

In the morning, I awoke to the high-pitched whistle of yet another missile. Nadia comforted Hani as he cried. I heard shots and screams and ran down the hill.

People wandered about dazed and crying. Everywhere, rubble smouldered. The smell of burned human flesh was overpowering. The road was covered in reddish brown where Palestinian blood had been spilled.

The only thing that remained from the mosque was the top spire of the minaret with its onion-shaped crown.

Chanting villagers packed the tea house.

'*Filistine! Filistine!*' Joining in with the others, I repeated the mantra over and over. My body swayed back and forth. Two Israeli tanks entered the village square.

'Go to Jordan or we'll kill you! You don't belong here!' the Israeli soldiers called from the first tank's loudspeaker. 'This time we'll leave no villagers alive!' The tanks started firing at the villagers. We scrambled through the back door. I ran up the road to the almond tree.

Mama was cooking a pot of rice over a small fire near Shahida. I decided not to tell her what the soldiers had told us. If they forced us to cross over the border, we would deal with it as it came. We had so little left, it wouldn't take long to pack it up.

‘I have to hear news.’ Abbas pulled himself over the ground. ‘Help me down there.’

‘It’s too dangerous.’ He’d never be able to get himself out of harm’s way, and there was nothing but harm in the village. I’d build him his own radio. I opened the plastic container I kept under the almond tree.

Separating the telephone wires, I wrapped one end around a branch, the second around a paperclip inserted into a piece of cardboard and the third around a piece of metal washer pipe, which I stuck into the ground. I threaded the end of a fourth wire through an empty toilet-paper tube and connected both ends of the wire to a paper clip.

I connected the earphone wire to the first paper clip by heating up the copper with a lighter, letting it cool and slipping it under the clip. I twisted a piece of wire into a V and mounted the dull end onto the paper clip. I pressed the pointed end into the copper, and connected the other earphone wire to the other paper clip. With the earphones on, I slowly moved the tip of the twisted wire across the surface of the copper until I heard Arabic. Abbas listened to the news all night.

***

At 6:30pm on June the 10th, Israeli radio informed us that the war was over. The United Nations had imposed a ceasefire. The Israelis had destroyed the Egyptian Air Force before it even took off on the first day. They had captured the West Bank, the Gaza Strip, the Egyptian Sinai Peninsula, the Syrian Golan Heights, East Jerusalem and the Old City with its holy sites. Villagers cried and hugged one another. I put my head on the table and hid my eyes. The Arab radio stations had all lied.

‘It started at 7:10 in the morning,’ the Israeli radio station Kol HaShalom reported. ‘Two hundred of our planes flew into Egypt so low that not even one of Egypt’s eighty-two radar sites detected them. Our pilots were so practised they were able to fly in complete radio silence.'

I put my hands over my ears, but I could still hear.

'We knew in advance about our Egyptian targets: the location of each Egyptian jet, together with the name and even the voice of the pilot. The Egyptians concentrated their planes by type: MiGs, Ilyushins, Topolors, each to its own base, which allowed us to prioritise our targets.

'The Egyptian jets were parked on open-air aprons. Almost all of their planes were on the ground, their pilots eating breakfast. The conditions for the attack could not have been better. Visibility was excellent. The wind-chill factor was close to zero. The Egyptian pilots didn't have time to reach their planes.'

It was so unfair.

'Not only did we destroy all of the Egyptian planes, we also destroyed their runways with Durandal bombs, which left craters five metres wide and one point six metres deep. The Egyptian planes were inextricably trapped, easy prey for the thirty-millimetre cannons and heat-seeking rockets that next raked them. By 8am our time, twenty-five sorties had been carried out. Four airfields in Sinai and two in Egypt had been knocked out. The main communication cable linking Egyptian forces with headquarters had been severed. In less than an hour, our air force destroyed 204 planes. Not only were our tanks, artillery and aircraft superior to those of the enemy; we knew how to use them more effectively.'

Israel decided to assimilate only East Jerusalem and the surrounding area, while it kept the West Bank and the Gaza Strip as zones of military occupation to leave open the option of one day returning them in exchange for peace.

Israel's territory grew by a factor of three, including about one million additional Palestinians placed under Israel's direct control. I felt like I'd been kicked in the stomach. Israel had showed the Arabs that it was able and willing to initiate strategic strikes that could change the regional balance. Now Israel had a bargaining chip. Land for peace. The war was over.

28

Fadi and I worked at the slaughterhouse all week to afford the materials for a new tent. Once it was completed, we all gathered inside to eat almonds and rice.

'Ahmed Hamid. Come outside,' a voice boomed through a megaphone. My family froze in place. The soldiers always called the villagers out before they blew up a house, but I'd never heard of them calling us by name. Whenever they hunted down someone specific, they always came at night, so they could take him when he was asleep. This must have something to do with Professor Sharon. What if Professor Sharon had told them to arrest me? I couldn't wait inside for them to come up and possibly harm my family, so I began to stand up. Mama grabbed my shoulders.

'No, please Ahmed, don't go,' she whispered in my ear, pulling me towards her.

Fadi, Nadia and Hani were like pillars of salt. Fadi held a folded piece of pita suspended over his plate. Abbas cursed louder than he probably realised, since he had earphones in and was listening to the news. Since I had built him the radio, he was always listening to it. Nadia hugged Hani.

'Ahmed Hamid, come outside!'

I prised myself from Mama's embrace. She covered her mouth with her hands. 'Ahmed!' she whispered with a desperation

I had never heard. I turned to look at her. Her arms extended towards me.

I raised my hand. 'It'll be all right.' I stepped out and closed the flap.

'Are you Ahmed Hamid?' The soldier used the megaphone even though I was standing right in front of him. 'Identify yourself.'

'Yes, I'm Ahmed Hamid.'

The soldier lifted the megaphone and spoke in the direction of the village this time. 'We have Ahmed Hamid. Bring him up.'

'What do you want with me?' I asked in Hebrew.

'Someone wants to see you.'

I could make out the shape of a civilian being escorted up the hill by soldiers. Among the green fatigues, metal helmets and M16s, I met Rafi's bloodshot eyes and went to him.

'Zoher's gone,' Rafi said. 'He was killed in the Sinai when his tank stalled.'

I shook my head. What was Rafi doing in my village with the military? Was he in with Professor Sharon on his scheme to expel me? After all the help I had given him. I had thought of him as a friend, as preposterous as it sounded now. Maybe Professor Sharon had told Rafi about Baba.

'His ashes were scattered at sea.'

Was Rafi here to blame me? Why else would Rafi travel five hours to enter a Palestinian village with a military escort?

I lowered my head. Did Rafi know about Baba?

'He figured out what happened. He went to the Dean. You have been exonerated.'

I looked up at him. Tears spilt from his eyes.

'Now, Professor Sharon's fate is in your hands.'

A million thoughts raced through my head. It was hard to believe Zoher had defended me against his own, and Rafi had driven all the way to my village to get me. It suddenly occurred to me, I'd never see Zoher again. I felt a void inside.

'Where's your house?' Rafi asked.

I pointed to the tent.

He seemed surprised. 'Trying to get in touch with your Bedouin roots?'

'No permit.'

The distant roar of helicopters grew louder. I shuddered and forced myself not to run back to my family to protect them.

Rafi turned to a nearby soldier, incredulous. 'Isn't the war over?'

'It's never over,' he said.

Rafi motioned with his head towards the bottom of the hill. 'Are you coming?'

'Ahmed!' Mama called as Abbas limped out from the tent behind her.

'I'm going back to the university,' I yelled, so that she'd hear my voice over the helicopter.

She was holding a jug in her hand. 'We need to talk.'

'Can it wait?'

Abbas' face lost its colour. He took the earphones out of his ears. 'You're leaving with them?'

Rafi was at the bottom of the hill. 'Are you coming?'

'Give me a minute.'

He looked up at the helicopter.

Mama threw the jug to the ground. It shattered. 'You're not going anywhere.' She crossed her arms over her chest.

I took a couple of steps towards her. 'I have to.'

'Don't do this to me,' she pleaded, on the verge of tears.

I knew this was an unwinnable argument. 'I'm doing this for us.'

'They're going to kill you.'

'Ahmed,' Rafi called. 'We need to go.'

'One second,' I shouted to Rafi in Hebrew.

Mama grabbed hold of my arms and shook me.

'Don't go with them,' Abbas said.

'It's only temporary.'

The helicopter hovered above us.

I started to walk away. 'I'm sorry.'

'Ahmed!' Mama called.

I turned to look at her. Her arms reached for me and I went to her. She hugged me tightly.

'What have we done to you to deserve this?' she whispered in my ear.

I tried to pull away, but she held me tighter.

'I'm doing this for us.'

'What?' she asked. 'Killing us?'

'Ahmed, it's getting dark,' Rafi said.

She wouldn't let go. 'I want you to be able to marry and have a family of your own.'

'I have to go.'

'Please don't leave me.'

I pulled away from her grasp and left. I had to go back to the university for Baba. I didn't care if everyone hated me because of what they thought he did. Zoher stood up for me, Rafi came to get me, and Baba believed in me. If I encountered hostility, I'd endure it. I couldn't wait to write to Baba. There was so much to say.

29

The Dean informed me that it was up to me if Professor Sharon would be fired. I asked him to grant me until the first Tuesday of the next month to decide and he agreed. On that day, I travelled to the Dror Detention Centre to discuss my situation with Baba.

A temporary pen made from barbed wire the size of a soccer field had been erected near the first one. Inside it, there were so many prisoners they barely had enough room to walk. It reminded me of a gigantic tin of sardines. There was no floor under the tent tops in the new pen, just soil. Guards were everywhere. Men, women, boys and girls crowded together waiting to hear the names of their loved ones.

Baba appeared. 'Tell the Dean that you don't want Professor Sharon fired as long as he hires you as his research assistant.'

I looked through the glass at him, still gripping the receiver. How could he suggest something like that? His eyes were heavy. I would do whatever he asked.

'What if he sabotages me?'

'Then the Dean should fire him. People hate out of fear and ignorance. If they could just get to know the people they hate, and focus on their common interests, they could overcome that hatred.'

'I think you might be too optimistic. Professor Sharon is evil.'

'Find out what's driving his hatred and try to understand it,' Baba said.

I thought of Einstein's words to Chaim Weizmann saying that if the Zionists were unable to build an honest cooperation and honest pacts with the Arabs then they had learned absolutely nothing during their two thousand years of suffering. Einstein had warned that if the Jews failed to assure that both sides lived in harmony, the struggle would haunt them for decades to come. He felt that the two great Semitic peoples could have a great common future. Maybe Baba was right.

***

'The Dean threatened to dismiss me if I don't employ you as my research assistant,' Professor Sharon said. 'Frankly, I was ready to leave. If it hadn't been for Zoher's father, I would've found employment elsewhere. Just so it's clear, I'm doing this for Zoher, not you.'

And I'd do this for Baba. 'Thank you for this opportunity. I can start tomorrow.'

'Yes, I know. The Dean has informed me that he wants you to start immediately. We don't need to see each other. I'm trying to improve silicon as a semi-conductor.' He smirked. 'Don't come back to me until you've figured out how.' He probably thought that he had given me an impossible assignment and, when I came back with nothing, he'd tell the Dean I was worthless. I'd show him how wrong he was. From his office, I went straight to the library.

30

Professor Sharon looked up from his reading.

'Good evening,' I said.

Upon seeing me, he immediately reached into his desk drawer, took something out and laid it on his lap. His eyes were black, like death. 'I told you not to bother me.'

'I had an idea.' I'd got the idea after reading two articles. The first was a lecture given by physicist Richard Feynman at Caltech in 1959 entitled 'There's Plenty of Room at the Bottom' in which he considered the possibility of direct manipulation of individual atoms. I believed his theory could help us in our research. The second was a 1965 article by Gordon F. Moore in *Electronics* magazine in which he predicted that the capacity for transistors in integrated circuits would double every two years.

'Unbelievable.' He slapped his hand on his desk. 'I'm going to tell the Dean this isn't working out.'

'I don't want to have to tell the Dean that you wouldn't listen to my idea.'

He tapped his fingers, like I was wasting his time. 'What's your stupid idea?'

'I know you want me to focus on improving silicon as a semi-conductor, but I think silicon has long-term limitations; problems with heat generation, defects and basic physics.' My voice shook.

He dismissed me with a wave of his hand. 'Silicon is the best choice.'

'Silicon technology enabled the development of revolutionary applications of the microchip in computing, communications, electronics and medicine.'

'I don't see your point.'

'Moore's Law.'

'What's Moore's Law?' He rolled his eyes.

'His first law says that the amount of space required to install a transistor on a chip shrinks by roughly half every eighteen months.'

'That's exactly why we need to improve silicon.'

'Moore's second law predicts that the cost of building a chip-manufacturing plant doubles roughly every thirty-six months. Eventually, when the chip gets to the nanoscale, not only will the prices skyrocket, but also, since properties change with size at the nanoscale, a new design methodology will be needed. When we shift from the microchip to the nanochip, all the basic principles involved in making chips will need to be rethought.'

'What are you saying?'

'The best alternative still needs to be invented.'

'Do you plan on revolutionising the chip single-handedly?'

'We shouldn't be approaching this from the top down, starting with bulk matter and cutting, grinding, melting and moulding or otherwise forcing it into useful forms. We should be trying to construct things from the bottom up by assembling the basic building blocks.'

'You're so ambitious, aren't you? Do you know what you look like to me, with your tattered clothes? You're a terrorist's son, Mr Hamid. You grew up in a tent without water or electricity and you want to revolutionise science. You dare to disagree with my approach?'

I looked him in the eye. 'You see a lot, Professor Sharon. I won't deny anything you said. But the fact that I grew up in a tent has nothing to do with the approach I'm advocating.'

'Goodbye, Mr Hamid.'

'You're not interested because I'm an Arab. You'd prefer a lesser approach to listening to me. Ignore me. Years from now, you'll see I was right and you could have been at the forefront. I could have helped you advance.'

'Really.'

'Understanding the nanoscale is important if we want to understand how matter is constructed and how the properties of materials reflect their components, their atomic composition, their shapes and their sizes. The unique properties of the nanoscale mean that nanodesign can produce striking results that can't be produced any other way. We need to understand the single atom's structure in order to best manipulate its properties, so that we can, at an atomic level, build materials by combining atoms.'

'What you're talking about would require tremendous ambition; a lifetime of devotion.'

'I know.'

'What if nothing comes of it?'

I repeated what Baba had always said to me. 'I know that only if one dares to fail can one achieve something great.'

'What are you proposing?'

'It's relatively easy to calculate general equations for how two isolated bodies move under each other's gravitational influence, but it's impossible if you add even one additional body to the system.'

'How do you propose we get around that?'

'We can plug in the numbers for positions, speeds and forces at one instant, and calculate how they'll have changed a very short time later. Then we could do it again with the new conditions, and so on. If we do it often enough for short enough time intervals, we can get a very accurate description of how the system behaves.'

'The smaller the time intervals, the more accurate the description. We'd have to do a lot of calculations.' He raised his eyebrows.

'Computers can do the number crunching,' I said.

'Are you a computer expert now?'

'On weekends and evenings I can help enter data into the key-punch machine and the card reader. We can use the computer to simulate chemical configurations in order to figure out what forces act between all the atoms in a particular combination. Once we know that, we can determine which combinations and arrangements will be stable, and what their properties will be.'

His features had softened enough that I could tell he had switched gears from hate to scientific curiosity. I had a chance.

'Why don't you work on your idea this summer? There's no need for us to interact. In September, I'll take a look at your results. If they don't look promising, you'll tell the Dean you don't want to work with me anymore. If they show promise, I'll keep you on all year.'

'I accept,' I said.

Professor Sharon smiled. I knew he hoped he'd found an easy way out of his promise to the Dean, but I would not embrace defeat so easily.

***

That summer, I practically lived in the computer lab, plugging in numbers, concentrating on the simplest forms. By early fall, patterns were emerging. I organised all my punch cards, wrote up the data for Professor Sharon and waited until his office was dark to slip the material under his door. I prayed that his love for science was greater than his hatred for my people.

The next day, I was in the computer lab running numbers when the professor appeared.

'I reviewed your initial calculations.' He picked up my latest punch cards and looked them over. 'How did you happen upon these results?' He sat down next to me and I showed him how I ran the numbers, changing the conditions ever so slightly and running the numbers again. 'I'll allow you to stay on with me a little longer and then I'll re-evaluate. Why don't you show me your progress at the end of each week?' His voice was indifferent, but I knew he now understood the potential of my research.

***

Jameel returned for the second year and we shared a room again. Rafi, who now lived alone, moved Zoher's old desk into our room, where he spent most of his free time. Motie married his high school sweetheart over the summer and moved into the dorm for married couples. But I saw little of them, since I spent most of my free time in the computer lab.

A few days after the students returned, Professor Sharon called me to his office. He was sitting behind his polished walnut desk surrounded by shelves of maths and science books. I looked up at the picture of Einstein. He passed me the only object on his desk: a gold-framed picture.

'My family,' he said.

'Oh.' Did he fear for their safety because they stole our land? Were they afraid we'd come back to get it? 'Do they live in Jerusalem?'

'They're dead.' He looked at me.

My mouth opened, but no words came out. Was he going to blame their deaths on me?

'The Nazis exterminated them.'

He handed me another picture. This one was not in a frame. Its edges were worn.

'That's me arriving at the Port of Haifa.' He removed his wire-rimmed glasses and wiped them with the handkerchief he pulled out of his brown tweed blazer with suede patches on the elbows.

The man in the photograph looked more dead than alive.

'I'm sorry.' Did he not understand that it was the Nazis, not my people, who had done that to his family? Did that justify what the Israelis were doing to us?

'No, you aren't.' He put his glasses back on. 'How could you possibly understand? Israel hasn't gassed innocent people and buried their bodies like trash.'

I'd promised myself and Baba that I wouldn't allow him to goad me into talking politics. But how could I stay quiet?

'Israel has brought great suffering to my people.' I averted my eyes, unable to look at him. *And my people weren't responsible for the gassing in World War II.*

'Suffering?' He shook his head. 'You don't know what that means. What did my parents do to the Nazis? Nothing. And what did they get? I remember my father in the cattle car clutching a bag with three gold necklaces, my grandmother's engagement ring and silver candlesticks. The only possessions we had left.' He stopped and took a breath before he continued. 'He was going to try to buy our freedom.'

I crossed my arms on my chest. But then I let them drop to my sides.

'As soon as we arrived at Auschwitz, the Nazis separated the men from the women.' He removed his glasses and, with his left thumb and pointer finger, squeezed the inside corner of his eyes. '*Bishanah habaah bieretz Yisrael* were my mother's last words. "Next year in the land of Israel".' He put his glasses back on.

I wanted to take Baba's advice. Before you judge a person, try to imagine how you would feel if the same things had happened to you.

'An SS soldier took one look at my little brother Avraham, who was only six, and pointed in the direction of death.' The professor made a fist with his left hand. 'My brother clung to my father's leg screaming, "Don't leave me alone!" '

'Your father's alive?' I asked. In the back of my mind I was still protesting. His family's suffering didn't give him the right to inflict suffering on others.

'My father whispered to me, "Do whatever it takes to survive. Fight for your life with everything you have and when you don't feel like fighting, think of me and fight some more." And then he ran to my brother.'

Did Professor Sharon think that justified what he did to me? No, I thought. That was the wrong question. Baba wanted me to try to put myself in Professor Sharon's place. 'Why didn't you go with them?'

His facial muscles tightened. 'I promised my father I'd fight with every breath I had.'

I knew something about promises. 'What happened to your mother and sister?'

'When the war ended, I asked everyone I saw if they had any news of my mother and sister, Leah, but no one did.' He stared out of the window onto the garden outside. 'Lists of survivors were passed around. I scoured each and every one. But there was no trace of them.' He shook his head. 'Then, one day, I saw someone I recognised from the cattle car. I begged her to tell me. I told her I couldn't stop searching until I found out.'

'Did she know?'

He nodded. 'She saw an SS guard send Leah to her death.' He stopped speaking while he loosened his tie. 'When my mother ran after her, a soldier shot her in the back of the head.'

Silence hung between us briefly. 'My people didn't commit those crimes.' My voice rose louder than I had intended. I looked down at the gleaming white linoleum floor.

'No, but you threaten my people.'

'We have nothing.'

Professor Sharon stood. 'Your people have a legitimate claim to this land.' I looked up at him, my mouth agape. 'Don't think I'm so stupid.' He walked to the window. 'There was no other choice. The Holocaust proved Jews could no longer exist as a minority within other nations. We needed a homeland of our own.'

'We didn't cause the Holocaust.' I took my time to enunciate each word.

'It's the right of a starving man to take some of the only available food, even if it means someone else will have less, as long as he leaves enough for the other man.'

'Why should someone be forced to share?'

'It's the moral obligation of the man who possesses the food.'

'Winners do whatever they want.'

'I fight for life and freedom, not for ancestral rights,' he said.

'What about God's promise to the Jews?' I said.

He slammed his fist on his desk. 'God doesn't exist.' Then he stared for a moment at something invisible to me. His voice was different now, softer. 'You have no idea how hard I've worked to get this far.' He held out his powerful hand. I stared at it. I wouldn't allow my hatred to prevent me from fulfilling my promise to Baba. I extended my hand and he embraced it, loosely.

'These are for you.' He handed me a pile of punch cards. 'You've stumbled onto something.'

I knew at that moment that if I held onto my grudges, I'd suffer. This was my opportunity and I needed to be behind it one hundred per cent. Every week, I slipped my results under Professor Sharon's office door. He began stopping by the computer lab to watch me run the simulations. Each week, the potential of my research grew. Soon Professor Sharon was showing up at the lab to run numbers himself. When the patterns became more apparent and our understanding of the atoms' behaviour more discernible, Professor Sharon was at the computer lab running simulations whenever I went in.

We began meeting in his office weekly, and as our results grew, we met almost daily. It got to the point that I was in his office so often Professor Sharon moved a desk in for me. Every moment I wasn't in class or doing homework I spent trying to figure out how different systems worked.

On October the 23rd, 1967, I'd just handed him the latest simulation when there was a knock on the door.

'It's open,' the professor called, without taking his eyes off my results.

Abbas stood in the doorway.

31

Even before Abbas spoke, I knew instantly something terrible had happened.

'May Allah protect Baba,' he whispered.

'Is he alive?'

'We need to go to the hospital immediately.'

Professor Sharon looked up. 'What's wrong?'

I turned to him. 'I must go to my father.'

'You can't go now. Our research is about to take off.'

'If this were your father, would you wait?'

Professor Sharon paused, and then shook his head. 'Go.' He placed his hand on my shoulder and gave my flesh a gentle squeeze. 'Go.'

Abbas stared at us wide-eyed and open-mouthed.

Professor Sharon held out his hand to Abbas. 'I'm Professor Sharon. Your brother's my research assistant.'

Turning his head to the side, Abbas slipped his hand into Professor Sharon's for the slightest moment.

Abbas and I walked down the corridor, exited the building and headed across the yard to the bus stop. Abbas' gait was that of a cripple.

'Who's your new best friend?' Abbas asked as soon as we were outside the building.

'My professor.'

'You were alone with him, working?' Abbas' voice was controlled but just barely. 'I thought there would be separate Arabic classes. You know, like how our schools are separate from theirs.' He laughed, but there was no humour in it. 'Now I find you alone with an Israeli.'

I was too surprised to speak.

'You're an Arab,' Abbas said. 'You're not Jewish. They only want Jews in this country. The sooner you understand that, the better your life will be. Don't fill your head with phony ideas like equality and friendship.'

'He wants to work with me.'

'They are our enemies. Don't you get it?'

'How's the new house?' I changed the subject.

'Zoher's father must have had serious guilt issues about his son's death.' Abbas said. 'Why else would a Jew bother to build a house for us?'

'Zoher was my friend. Like you, I suspected it couldn't be genuine, but he proved himself to me. Although he was estranged from his father, the man still chose to do this for us in his son's name.' I spoke calmly, like Baba would have spoken to him. 'His father didn't have to build us a home, but he did.'

'It probably took him two seconds to get the permit,' Abbas said. 'After all, he's Jewish. He has his own construction company. I'm sure it didn't cost him much.'

'There are three bedrooms, a real bathroom and a large kitchen. He installed a wood-burning stove, glass windows and a front and a back door. It's a fine home,' I argued.

We walked in silence for a few minutes, my pace slow to match his. Finally, I put my hand on his shoulder. 'I'm glad you came.'

The words he didn't say weighed heavily on me. I swallowed hard, unsure of how to lessen the tension. 'How are you?' I asked when we reached the bus stop.

'Baba's in the hospital and I don't know what happened to him. I'm an eighteen-year-old cripple. Amal and Sara are dead. My brother sided with their murderers. How do you think I am?' His bulging eyes locked onto mine. 'I'm glad he let you go.'

'He's not such a bad guy.'

'May God forgive your stupidity.' He stepped away from me. 'You've been seduced by the devil.'

'Where will hating them get us?'

He thrust his hands, palms up, towards me. 'You need to listen to Dr Habash.'

I scanned the area around us. If any Israeli heard that Abbas supported Dr Habash, he could be imprisoned, exiled or killed. It was against the law to support a party that was opposed to Israel being Jewish.

'Careful,' I said.

'You don't want me to admit that I think we should have a secular, democratic, non-denominational state?'

'He advocates violence.'

'How else will we liberate Palestine? Should we just ask them to make this country secular?'

'Only forgiveness will set you free.' I repeated Baba's words. 'What's better? To forgive and forget, or to resent and remember?'

'You betray Baba and me and our dead siblings when you befriend our persecutors. They must pay for what they've done to us. A day doesn't go by when I'm not in pain. I can't work. Baba's still in prison. I pray that the day will come when we crush them like garlic.'

'If we avenge their actions, we'll be even with them, but if we forgive them we'll be ahead.' I quoted Baba again.

'I hate them.'

'Hatred is self-punishment. Do you think they're feeling bad because you hate them?'

'If I let go of my hatred, will they release Baba, relieve my pain and bring back Amal and Sara?'

'Will holding onto it accomplish those things?'

He squinted at me, his eyes fierce. 'I don't know who you are anymore.'

I sighed. He had no real memory of Baba. Talking to him about the Israelis was like trying to blow into a torn bagpipe. Doubts as to whether he and I could ever recover the closeness we once shared pressed on me. Wasn't there any balance in the world?

On the ride to the hospital in Be'er Sheva, Abbas barely spoke to me. I started thinking about Professor Sharon and my new approach to our research. I analysed the data in my head, trying to find a way to improve the predictability.

Sirens blared as we approached the hospital. The smell of death was in the air. Entering, I was filled with dread.

The guard at the door asked for our ID cards and we complied.

'Who are you here to see?' he asked.

'Our father, Mahmud Hamid,' I said.

The guard scanned through his papers and then his eyebrows rose.

'The convict?' the guard said.

'Yes,' I said.

The guard pulled the walkie-talkie from his hip strap and called for a military escort to the prisoners' ward. Two soldiers, wearing helmets with face shields, with Uzis in hand, grenades, billy-clubs and handcuffs in their holsters, appeared and escorted us to a room.

'Strip,' the soldier commanded.

I took off my trousers.

Abbas' eyes opened wide like he'd just witnessed a murder. 'What are you doing?'

'Undress.'

'Never.'

'I'll tell Baba you came.'

'I have so many things I want to tell him.'

He struggled to pull his robe over his head, but he couldn't lift his arms high enough. Mama always undressed him. The soldiers stared at us as I pulled Abbas' robe over his head. Abbas and I stood side by side in our underwear.

'Everything off !' the soldier commanded.

Abbas looked down at the ground and slipped off his underwear. He cursed under his breath.

'Shut up!' The soldier raised his Uzi over his head.

'Please!' I pleaded. 'He's recovering from a broken back.' I looked at my brother and begged him in Arabic, 'In the name of God, Abbas, stop muttering!'

He ceased.

The guards escorted us to the basement. Two more guards sat outside the door and three stood inside. Baba was shackled to a gurney in the corner.

Too choked with emotion to speak, I took one of his hands. Abbas took the other.

'You're so big,' Baba said to Abbas. 'It's been seven years.'

Fear filled Abbas' eyes as he stared at Baba.

'Don't worry,' Baba said. 'I'll be all right.' He looked like a tired old man lying there handcuffed to the gurney. I looked on his chart. He had three broken ribs and a severe concussion.

'Who did this to you?' Abbas asked through gritted teeth.

'There's a new commander.' Baba shook his head. 'He's filled with hatred. He snapped. The other guards felt horrible.'

Abbas' face was blood red.

'The other guards pulled him off me. I'm resilient.' Baba tried to smile, but he didn't quite pull it off.

Baba told us about the portraits he'd been drawing and the music he'd started composing. He asked about Mama and the rest of the family. He assured us that he was fine and somehow managed to cheer me up.

A bell rang and the visitors started to say their goodbyes.

'We'll return,' I said.

'No,' Baba said. 'You need to focus on your studies and save money. Your letters are enough.'

'Time to go.' The guard pointed his Uzi in the direction of the door. Abbas and I left with our heads down.

***

The bus dropped me off at the front gate of the darkened Givat Ram campus. Abbas would barely speak to me. Professor Sharon's office light was on. Maybe he was still working. I entered the building and was heading down the darkened corridor when I heard raised voices coming from his office.

'They're not even human.' I immediately recognised the woman's voice. It was Aliyah, or at least that was what she had changed her name to when she immigrated to Israel from South Africa. She was Professor Sharon's wife.

Aliyah obviously disapproved of her husband working with an Arab. A few weeks earlier, Professor Sharon had been home sick with the flu. He'd requested that I bring the latest data to his house, an old Arab villa near the central bus station. Through the latched chain, I had passed her the data.

'Let him in,' he'd called from somewhere inside.

'What will the neighbours think?' She'd slammed the door. Screaming had come from inside. A minute later Professor Sharon had appeared and let me in. Aliyah remained upstairs.

***

'This boy's a genius,' Professor Sharon's voice said. 'There's merit to his idea.'

Professor Sharon had other problems in his marriage. I'd overheard him tell others that Aliyah complained constantly—he worked too much; he didn't make enough money; all he was interested in was science; he didn't want to do anything with her. He claimed she had entitlement issues—she'd never worked a day in her life and spent all day shopping. She wanted him to go into industry because there wasn't enough money in academia. I even heard him say once that he wished he'd never married her.

'Building from the bottom up?' Aliyah spoke as if she were an expert in that area. 'That's ridiculous.'

'You didn't even graduate from high school. He's right. Small is the new big. That's where science is headed.'

'How can you work with him?' Disgust oozed from her voice. 'That position should go to a Jew.'

'I'm putting the advancement of humanity first.'

I couldn't believe it. Professor Sharon defended my idea.

'Where's your terrorist assistant anyway?'

I wanted to run back to my room, but my legs wouldn't move. When else would I ever get a chance to hear Professor Sharon defend me, even if it was only to upset his wife?

'Ahmed's dad is in the hospital,' Professor Sharon said.

'They want to exterminate us.'

'We have a bargaining chip. Land for peace. What are we going to do with the West Bank and Gaza? There are a million Arabs there. With their rate of procreation, they'll one day outnumber us.'

'Arabs aren't human. They're all terrorists. It's in their blood.'

'You sound like a Nazi. I know that, in the long run, if we work together, we'll all win.'

'Those cockroaches won't be happy until they have all of Israel back.'

A chair scraped the floor harshly. I rushed outside.

***

The next morning I arrived early. Professor Sharon was already in his office. I spotted a suitcase in the corner and a pillow and blanket on his office couch. From that day on we worked around the clock together. I grew accustomed to him, eager for our nightly meetings to discuss the results of the day. I looked forward to the cup of coffee that we drank together every morning. He'd given me the opportunity of a lifetime, or I had given it to him. Or maybe we gave it to each other.

32

1969 began with a miracle. The librarian announced it was snowing and we all rushed outside. I stood in my short-sleeve shirt and matching trousers in awe, as I watched the perfect snowflakes fall from the sky, the first I'd ever seen.

When I returned to my room, I couldn't bend my fingers. My teeth chattered. I lit the paraffin heater that we were issued for cold nights and placed it in the middle of the room. Wrapped in the university's blanket I continued to study. Jameel came in wearing a winter coat, gloves, hat and scarf. He had a large shopping bag in his hand.

'You need to go shopping,' he said.

'The snow won't last.'

'There's always the cold winter rain.' Jameel shook his head. 'You need to spend a little of your money. I can't believe the way you live.'

After Jameel went to sleep, I stayed up with my books. It was past midnight when I smelled smoke. I went out into the hallway, my blanket still wrapped around my shoulders.

Flames from a paraffin heater in the hall climbed up the door of room five, where two Israelis lived. Their room must have overheated and they had placed the heater out in the hallway too close to their door.

'Fire!' I yelled as loud as I could. 'Yonatan, Shamouel. Climb out of your window!' With the blanket wrapped around my hand, I broke the glass to the fire extinguisher. Still screaming for them to wake up, I sprayed the flames. White foam covered the door and floor. Jameel appeared in his night robe, hair standing up. Other doors opened and Israelis poured out dressed in pyjamas, underwear, bathrobes. Some were barefoot; others wore slippers, army boots or sneakers. Jameel grabbed another fire extinguisher and helped me battle the flames. Others battled the fire with blankets.

The outer door to our building opened and Yonatan and Shamouel appeared. They'd climbed out of their window when they heard me screaming. White foam was everywhere and the hallway was thick with smoke. We opened the doors at either end and let cold air blow in. Jameel, the Israelis and I worked in the cold for hours cleaning up the foam. Shaking, I unhinged their door and refastened another from an empty room.

When I had finished, everyone applauded.

'You're a hero.' Yonatan patted me on the back. 'Everyone in the kitchen. Let's toast Ahmed.'

We gathered, Jews and Arabs, together in the kitchen and drank *sahlab* topped with cinnamon, shredded coconut and chopped pistachios.

***

I finished my BSc in Physics, Chemistry and Maths at the top of my class. Professor Sharon suggested I become his paid teaching assistant—in addition to our joint research. The way Mama did things, my salary was more than enough to feed and clothe my whole family.

Professor Sharon insisted that he be my master's degree advisor. Together we had published five articles in the prestigious *Journal of Physics*. Prior to our research, his results had only been published in the *Journal* three times in his whole career. Jameel and I continued to live together, as he was doing his master's in maths.

The same week I began working as Professor Sharon's teaching assistant, I fell in love.

'Amani,' she said when it was her turn to introduce herself to the class. My eyes met her honey-coloured ones, shaped like a doe's, and our gaze lingered. In all my time at the university, I hadn't seen an attractive Arab girl until Amani. The pretty ones married before the age of eighteen.

Professor Sharon also fell in love that semester. The Association for World Peace sent their journalist, Justice Levy, an American, to interview us both about our work together. Justice had wild red hair that she kept moving out of the way as she sat in Professor Sharon's office. Her eyes sparkled as she took in his shelves of books. Dressed in a long flowing skirt, tie-dyed T-shirt and a macramé vest, and with silver peace signs the size of a fist hanging from her neck and ears, she was the polar opposite of his ex-wife, Aliyah.

Throughout the interview, Professor Sharon never took his eyes off Justice. She praised him for embracing me as his research assistant. They began dating. Within weeks, he moved into her apartment. At least once a week, Justice would insist that he bring me over for dinner. My relationship with Amani, however, remained only in my imagination. A few weeks after I first laid eyes on her, I mentioned to Jameel that she was in my class. He told me she was from Acre.

'Why isn't she married?'

'She's had many proposals,' Jameel said. 'She refused them all. She waged a hunger strike when her father tried to force her to marry her cousin. You know she graduated top in her class?'

I wanted to ask a million questions, but that would have been inappropriate.

All week I waited for Tuesday and Thursday mornings from nine to ten so that we could exchange glances.

At the end of the first semester, I collected the final exams and went directly to my office. Professor Sharon arranged for me to have a room with a desk, a lamp and three plastic chairs to receive students. I fingered through the blue test booklets until I found Amani's. Her grade was sixty-four per cent. I was disappointed. I'd thought she'd be both beautiful and brilliant; but I knew, too, that I could help her.

After I handed back the tests, I announced that I'd be available in my office after class to help any students who wanted to take the *Moed Bet* exam, the second-chance exam offered to students seeking to improve their grade.

I was in my office reading a book on quantum mechanics when I heard a knock. 'Come in,' I called in Hebrew.

Amani appeared, dressed in bell-bottom jeans and a red T-shirt. Her long jet-black hair framed her porcelain face. I took a deep breath. She came with a friend, an obese girl with acne who was there to bear witness that nothing improper occurred.

'How can I help you?' I asked in Arabic, surprised by my coherent speech. It was a highly improper situation for an unmarried male to help an unmarried female. Good girls didn't talk to men who weren't their husbands; but we weren't in the village. The only rule I was sure of was that the door must remain open.

'Can you help me?' Amani asked.

'Are you willing to work?'

'I'll do whatever it takes.' She looked directly into my eyes as she spoke. 'Science is my life.'

'Why's that?'

'The laws of nature.' She smiled. 'They fascinate me.'

I motioned with my hand towards the two seats on the other

side of my desk. 'Please.' The two girls sat down. 'Did you bring your exam?'

Amani placed her black bag on my desk and extracted her exam paper. As she laid it in front of me, she tilted her head and pushed back her silky hair while her eyes remained locked into mine.

I tried not to look at her.

'Let's start with the first question. A 0.2 hp motor is used to lift a crate at the rate of 5.0 cm/s. How great a crate can it raise at this constant speed?' I cleared my throat. 'We assume the power output of the motor to be 0.25 hp=186.5 W. In 1.0 s, the crate mg is lifted a distance of 0.050 m.' I opened my mouth to conclude, when Amani interrupted.

'Therefore, work done in 1.0=(weight)(height change in 1.0 s)=(mg)(0.050 m). By definition, power=work/time, so that 185.5 W=(mg)(0.00 m)1.0 s. Using g=9.81 m/s2, we find that m=381 kg. The motor can lift a crate of about 0.38×103 kg at this constant speed.'

I stared at her.

She winked at me.

I glanced at the clock. I had to go and teach my Advanced Physics class in five minutes. I arranged to meet Amani again the following morning in my office, though I was beginning to suspect that she didn't really need the help. I wondered why she'd done so badly in her exam.

I felt empowered to stand in front of the class even though I was in Mama's homemade clothing. The power balance had changed. In my classes, I was the authority figure. With Amani especially, the teaching gave me confidence.

Both Israelis and Arabs told me I looked like the actor Omar Sharif. I saw his picture in an Israeli newspaper. Nasser's government had almost withdrawn his citizenship when his affair with Barbara Streisand, a vocal supporter of Israel, was made public in the Egyptian press. At times, I'd catch the Israeli girls looking at me, but I'd never felt confident until I'd begun teaching.

After coming to my office every morning for a week with her friend by her side, Amani arrived alone. When I opened the door for her to enter, she didn't come in.

'Silwah's sick today.' She smiled and raised her eyebrows.

I shrugged my shoulders. 'I'll leave the door open.'

With a grin on her face, she entered my office and sat in her chair. I sat down next to her. She turned her head towards me and our eyes met again. Neither of us acknowledged it, but I was sure we had fallen in love.

***

Amani passed *Moed Bet* with a perfect score. I would've liked to attribute her success to my tutoring, but I was beginning to suspect she had failed her first exam on purpose. Did she do it to get to know me better?

My younger sister Nadia had been wed the previous month to a widower named Ziad. He had seven young children. Mama was beside herself with glee. The groom's wife had just died and neither our family nor his could afford a wedding. Mama brought the marriage contract home for Nadia to sign.

Nadia first met her husband after they were married, when she moved into a room half the size of my student room in his parents' home with him and his seven children. I felt bad that Baba hadn't been there to see his daughter move into her husband's family's home and so I promised myself that I would wait for him to be released before I married. He was thrilled when I wrote to him about Amani. I told him that I wouldn't marry until he was released from prison. My mother was eager for me to start my family, but she also wanted Baba to be there. He wrote back that

I didn't have to wait, but I convinced him that it would be better for my studies if I graduated first and he agreed.

***

By the end of my master's degree, Professor Sharon and I were just beginning to get some insight into how to go about building materials from the bottom up. He suggested I do my dissertation on the subject, but I argued that it was still in its infancy. It did have great potential, but that could take decades and I needed something ripe, secure and quick, for Baba's sake.

'If you want to get the fruit, you have to go out on a limb.' He explained it was a long-term investment. 'We can do it if we work together.'

'But my family—'

'Do you want the safe and easy road, or the road that leads to greatness?'

'My father—'

'Does he want a son who settles for less than his ability or a son who reaches his full potential?'

What could I do but agree?

***

Professor Sharon and Justice had got married during the middle of my master's degree. Amani and I had formed a platonic relationship and continued to meet to discuss her physics homework. We didn't need to speak of the chemistry between us. I also knew nothing sexual would ever transpire, not so much as a kiss, until we were married. Everyone, however, knew we were a couple, because Amani continued to meet me in my office after she passed my class, semester after semester, for the next two and a half years. She was scheduled to finish her bachelor's degree the same year I'd be finishing the first year of my PhD. Every semester, she made the Dean's List and was at the top of her class.

Two weeks before Amani was to graduate and return to her village, she and I were sitting in my office. She was preparing for her final in astrophysics when I looked into her honey-coloured eyes. I longed to run my fingers through her silky black hair and unzip her cream-coloured dress, but I knew I couldn't even kiss her.

'Will you do me the incredible honour of becoming my wife?' I should've asked her father first, but those rules only applied in the village.

She smiled.

'My father's in prison.' I looked down at my desk, afraid to see her reaction. Every time the subject of Baba came up, I found a way to sidestep it. Our relationship was limited to her visits to my office. Anything else could have got her into trouble with her family.

'I didn't know,' she said.

'He'll be released at the end of the school year.' I didn't want to tell her how long he'd been incarcerated. 'I'd like to marry you then.'

'My father.' Her face looked like she had just drunk sour milk. 'He won't authorise me to marry unless it's done according to tradition.'

'Where should we hold the wedding?' I asked.

'Anywhere but Acre.' She smiled.

'Where shall we live?'

She shrugged.

'I love you.' I gazed into her eyes. I longed to touch her hand and hold it in mine.

Amani leaned forward and kissed me. Her kiss caught me off guard. I wanted her to touch me more; my whole body ached. I shut my eyes for a moment. She smelled like a fresh breeze.

'Amani,' I said, and held her face. She smiled and kissed me again. I knew there would only be that one opportunity to kiss her so I held her face as long as I could. Her eyelashes fluttered. We bent our heads together.

'Is Jameel in your room?' she asked.

Had I heard her correctly? We couldn't go any further. If anyone found out, not only would Amani's reputation be destroyed, but so would that of her family. No one would marry her unwed sisters; people would speak poorly about her parents. If Amani's family was conservative enough, she could even be beaten or killed. What was she thinking?

33

Abbas and I waited at the gate of the Dror Detention Centre. I thought about what would have happened if Jameel hadn't been in the room. No, I told myself, we would be married soon enough. Mama and Nadia were home preparing for Baba's coming-home party. Hani was nervous since he had no memory at all of Baba. Fadi wanted to come with us, but Israeli law allowed only two people to receive each prisoner, so that the prisoner's release wouldn't be construed as a celebration.

I wanted it to be Abbas who came with me. I hoped that Baba could change his thinking, convince him that violence wasn't the way. Abbas was obsessed with Dr George Habash and his Popular Front for the Liberation of Palestine.

At noon, five Israeli soldiers opened the gate and stood pointing their loaded Uzis at me, Abbas and the other Palestinians, dozens of them, who waited excitedly for the release of their loved ones.

As we stood in this awkward face-off, the force of the wind increased. Particles of sand started to vibrate, then saltate. The saltation of the sand particles induced a static electric field by friction. The saltating sand acquired a negative charge relative to the ground which loosened more sand particles. Before I knew it, the sandstorm overwhelmed us. I couldn't see in front of me. It was in my mouth, ears, eyes. Children screamed. Men wrapped their kaffiyahs around their faces. Women did the same with their veils. Abbas lifted his arms to protect his face too quickly and winced in pain. When it died down, I brushed the sand off my body and then tried to brush off Abbas' face so that he wouldn't have to lift his arms, but he told me to stop. The tension between us was palpable. I couldn't believe how much we'd grown apart. I desperately wished I could find common ground with him, but he sabotaged my every attempt. He couldn't get past the fact that I worked with Professor Sharon.

The prisoners sat on the ground in lines, covered in sand. A soldier began calling out numbers.

'One, two, three, four . . .' he counted, finally ending with the number 2,023.

When a prisoner heard his number, he spun around and faced the prison. I spotted Baba in the crowd.

The head soldier lined up the twenty-eight prisoners who were to be released. As Baba walked to the line, the other prisoners shook his hand and high-fived him. Nearby guards even called their goodbyes, wishing him luck. This struck Abbas like a whip each time. Two soldiers patted down each prisoner as they proceeded, single file, through the gate to where we waited. Armed guards walked alongside them.

The prisoners, dressed in black, were of all ages. Some appeared to be not more than twelve or thirteen years old; a few looked like they were in their seventies. Guards propped up five of the prisoners who couldn't seem to walk on their own. Baba ended up at the back of the line because of all the goodbyes—he even had guards at the gate patting him on the back.

Unable to wait, I ran to him. His two front teeth were missing and his face looked like a crumpled paper bag. Abbas and I kissed his right hand. Uncle Kamal waited around the corner in the car that he used as a taxi. Enough years had passed since Baba's arrest that the Israelis no longer targeted our friends and family.

Mama and Nadia had taped plastic flowers all over the car and packed it with date and almond cookies, pistachios and almonds, figs, apricots, oranges, grapes and bottles of water.

Baba sat next to Uncle Kamal, but kept looking back at me and saying, 'I can't believe that you're a university student.'

Abbas was bent over holding his ribs and staring out of the window. Neither Baba nor I knew what to say to comfort him.

***

The courtyard of my family's new house bubbled over with villagers when we arrived. I was happy Baba would never have to know of the infested tents where we had been forced to live for so many years. He barely made it out of the car before Mama, Nadia and Fadi hugged and kissed him. Tears welling up, he said 'If only Amal and Sara were still with us.'

Hani stood back a little. I introduced him to Baba, and Hani held out his hand. Baba clasped it in his. It was awkward but I hoped, with time, they would get used to each other. Family members and villagers engulfed Baba.

Abu Sayeed brought his violin and Mama presented Baba with a second-hand oud. Within minutes, as if fourteen long years hadn't passed, Baba and Abu Sayeed played together. Baba strummed and belted out songs. We laughed and danced until the wee hours of the morning.

The military rule over our village had ended in 1966 and we were no longer subject to curfews. Now, the military ruled the West Bank and Gaza. The tents across the border in the refugee camp in the West Bank were gradually being converted into a warren of concrete walls and corrugated tin roofs. We could hear bulldozers and gunfire during the day. The nights were quiet, as the people were locked down by the curfew.

The next day I took Baba around the back of the house to see the fourteen olive trees we had planted in his name. Amal and Sa'dah, the two original olive trees, had grown back tall and thick. They reminded me of my people. I'd spent many hours watching the Israelis as they harvested the olive trees confiscated from our village. They violently beat the trees with sticks to knock down their fruit. I'd marvelled that despite their exposure to beatings, arid landscape and fierce heat, the trees survived and bore new fruit year after year, century after century.

I knew that their strength lay in their roots, which were so deep that even if the trees were cut down, they survived and sent forth shoots to create new generations. I always believed that my people's strength, like the olive trees', lay in our roots.

Under the almond tree, I reiterated to Baba my desire to marry Amani. He gave me his blessing. That night, as Mama, my brothers and I sat outside drinking tea, I announced my intention.

'Finally!' Mama blurted out.

I would go to Amani's house and ask for her hand in marriage.

34

On the bus to Amani's home, I planned what I would say to her father and thought about our life together. We'd marry in my village. Our first son would be named Mahmud. I anticipated kissing her, touching her. I'd do a post-doctorate abroad after I finished my PhD, maybe in America. Maybe, after that, I'd become a professor in an American university. Amani wanted to go to America.

Once I'd knocked on the door, I worried about my breath. My throat was so dry. How could I ask for her hand with bad breath? A man opened the door.

'Good evening. My name is Ahmed Hamid.'

The man, who looked like he was in his late forties, had the same cheekbones and jaw-line as Amani. I waited, but her father remained silent. Why didn't he invite me in?

'I'm a PhD candidate in physics at the Hebrew University. I'd like to talk to you.'

Without emotion, he signalled for me to enter. Then he looked outside like he was checking if anyone had seen me come in. Once inside, I remained standing because her father didn't invite me to sit on the floor pillows. The smell of my breath made me sick.

'I met your daughter Amani at the university.' I couldn't believe her father didn't even offer me water. He glared at me.

The silence in the room was crushing. Each minute felt like a month.

'I'm from the Triangle.' I forgot everything I wanted to say. More awkward silence descended upon the room. Her father must have known what I wanted. Why else would I be here? I was a PhD candidate in physics. I'd earned the respect of both professors and students, Jews and Arabs.

Amani was already twenty-one years old. Most Arab girls from my country were not only married by that age, but had a number of children.

I thought of how Mama had jumped for joy when Ziad proposed to my sister Nadia, offering her nothing more than a room in his parents' home. Nadia and Ziad had two more children and Nadia was pregnant again. There were already eleven in the room.

Amani's father, with his hands on his hips, acted like I was wasting his time.

'I've come to request your daughter Amani's hand in marriage.'

'No.' His refusal was immediate.

I felt like I'd been slapped across the face. I stood, stunned, for a few moments. Never did I consider the possibility that her father would say no. Maybe he knew Baba had just been released from prison. Would the Israelis have told him? I tried to think of my next move.

'Why not?' I asked.

'She's married to my brother's son.'

A knife in my heart would've been kinder.

'Where is she?' I asked. 'I want to talk to her.'

'She lives with her husband now.'

I managed to say, 'Thank you. Thank you for your time, doctor,' as I walked out. Once on the street, I cursed my culture for taking from women the right to choose their own spouse. I'd thought Amani had been waiting for me to come and propose. How would I be able to tell Baba that I'd been rejected? Hadn't he suffered enough? What about me? How would I go on without her? Had she known her cousin was going to marry her? Was this the same one she'd waged the hunger strike over to get out of marrying him? Is that why she dated me? Was she trying to make herself undesirable to him? Had she wanted to sleep with me so that, if she was forced to marry him, he would return her to her family because she wasn't a virgin?

I headed to Jameel's house. He knew I'd planned to ask her to marry me. Why hadn't he mentioned her cousin?

Abu Jameel, with his perfectly groomed moustache and white robe, answered the door. 'What an honour,' he said. 'Come in, come in. Please make yourself at home. Um Jameel, bring us tea, we have a very special guest. Ahmed's here.'

Um Jameel entered with tea glasses and cookies. 'I'll fix a tray of my tastiest desserts in honour of your visit.' She smiled.

'Jameel told me that you're doing your PhD. I'm so happy the two of you can continue living together,' said Abu Jameel.

Um Jameel returned with still-warm date cookies and a platter of baklava. After an hour-long discussion about my academic success, physics, chemistry and the university, Jameel entered the living room.

He said, 'What a great honour. I want to show you something,' and led me to his bedroom.

I was relieved to be able to speak to him alone, even though it had felt good that Abu Jameel, the principal of the Arab high school in Acre, treated me with so much respect after Amani's father's rejection.

'You know about Amani, I take it?' Jameel said as soon as we entered his room.

'Did you?'

'It happened yesterday.'

Yesterday, as I'd celebrated with my family the idea that I was going to propose to Amani as if our marriage was a sure thing.

'Is he worthy of her?'

'He failed out of Haifa University. I bet Amani will have to support him.'

'And my friendship with her?'

'Gossip is like a desert storm.'

I stared miserably at the floor. 'Did she know she'd have to marry him?'

'I think she did.'

I struggled to breathe. She had only used me.

***

On the bus home, I thought of Amani and got angry. Suddenly I realised that my family was waiting for me to bring news of my bride.

When I arrived at the top of the hill, Mama and Nadia ran to me ululating. I could see Baba standing behind them, smiling. I put my head down. Mama and Nadia surrounded me, continuing to ululate. What would I tell them?

'Finally, something good,' Mama said.

Mama and a very pregnant Nadia with her two children and seven stepchildren followed me into the house, still trilling. The smell of almond cookies was in the air. They had probably baked all day to celebrate my engagement.

'Congratulations, son.' Baba reached out his arms to embrace me and then stopped. 'Give me a minute alone with Ahmed.' We walked together to the almond tree.

I stared at the ground.

Baba put his hand on my shoulder. 'What is it, son?'

'There's not going to be a wedding.'

‘It wasn’t meant to be.’ Baba embraced me.

I pushed him away. ‘What am I going to do?’

‘Success in life isn’t about the number of failures we think we have, but about how we react to those failures. This happened for a purpose. The one for you is still out there. All you need to do is find her.’ He patted me on the back. The weight of my crushed dreams bore down on me—Baba had to hold me up as we walked back inside. ‘Focus on your studies and be patient. Where you least expect it, you will find her.’

***

For the next three years, Professor Sharon served as my PhD advisor. My thesis on building a non-silicon material from the bottom up garnered international interest and I was awarded the Israel Prize for Physics. Professor Smart, a Nobel Prize winner from MIT, contacted Professor Sharon about possible collaboration and encouraged him to take his upcoming sabbatical at MIT. Professor Sharon told him that he wouldn’t go without me.

‘I can’t go,’ I said to Professor Sharon. ‘My family needs me.’

He looked across his desk at me. ‘I need you.’

‘I can’t abandon them,’ I said. Even though I was a full-time student, I was able to support them with the money I made as Professor Sharon’s research and teaching assistant. If I left, all they’d have to live on was Fadi’s measly job at the slaughterhouse. Professor Sharon knew my circumstances.

‘I’ve spoken with Professor Smart already.’ A smile crept onto his face. ‘You can work as our post-doc. We’ll pay you $10,000 a year. You know you could never make anywhere near that amount of money if you stayed here.’

I knew he was right. There were no academic positions available and every job in Israel suitable for my qualifications required military service.

'Let me think about it.' I'd go home for the weekend and speak to Baba. After our fourteen-year separation, I was hesitant to move that far away.

***

When I went home that weekend, I told Baba about the post-doc offer. He told me I had to go and wouldn't take no for an answer.

***

As soon as I finished my PhD, Professor Sharon, Justice and I boarded a plane to America. I planned to live as frugally as possible so that I could send home every extra penny I had. I watched the airport buildings whizz by from my window as we picked up speed. The momentum increased and, before I knew it, we had left the earth.

'Thank you, Professor Sharon,' I said.

'Call me Menachem,' he said and smiled.

PART THREE
1974

35

From the massive windows of Baker House, I could see the banks of the Charles River. Menachem and I strolled through the interconnecting buildings, columns and domes of the Massachusetts Institute of Technology. The open floor plan allowed us to pass from one building to the other without ever stepping outside—this was a feature I especially admired, because the New England cold was like nothing I'd ever experienced.

'I've got something for you in our office,' Menachem said. Justice was waiting for us. She dragged a present out from under his desk by its thick gold ribbon. I hadn't received a gift in sixteen years, since my twelfth birthday when Baba had given me the lens for my telescope.

'It's for agreeing to tutor Nora,' Justice said. 'A little something from Menachem and me.'

Nora was the president of Justice's peace group, Jews for Justice. She was one of the Jewish women Justice was taking to Gaza in August. Justice had asked if I'd tutor Nora in Arabic. Although I could never refuse her anything, I was afraid the tutoring would cut into my research time.

I slid the gold ribbon off my gift carefully, not wanting to rip the white wrapping paper with its gold peace signs. Inside was a tweed blazer with suede patches on the elbows, a black wool turtle-neck, black wool trousers and a long black wool winter coat. The tweed blazer was similar to the ones Menachem always wore; he had the same turtle-neck and coat as well.

'It's too much,' I said.

'It's not enough.' Justice opened her arms and embraced me. 'Put them on.'

I changed out of my jeans in the bathroom.

'Now you look like a post-doc at MIT,' Menachem said.

***

We were going to meet Justice's friend and my future pupil at Habibi's restaurant. Outside, the American flag waved in the cool autumn breeze. Normally, I dreaded walking outdoors because I was always cold, but with my new clothes, I was toasty and the breeze on my face felt refreshing.

The weather started getting cold in early November and Menachem must have noticed that I was often shivering. Even though I had enough money to buy a coat, I didn't. I saved everything I could for my family. No one wanted to hire Baba because of his prison record. His only source of income was from playing at weddings, but most of the time his playing was his wedding gift. Abbas couldn't work and Fadi made very little at the slaughterhouse.

Candlelight cast a glow over the mosaic tile and dark wood at Habibi's. I was dressed in my new outfit, and the music of Fairouz was emanating from hidden speakers, when the loveliest girl I'd ever seen entered the restaurant. Heads turned. Light seemed to radiate from her. Spun-gold curls cascaded down her back. Her skin was luminous, like the moon.

As the girl walked towards us, I felt the blood rush to my face. The room seemed to part like the Red Sea. We stood.

'This is Nora,' Justice said. I stared at the girl with the golden hair. Her dress reminded me of my people's traditional embroidered clothing.

Justice introduced Menachem and then said, 'And this is Ahmed, your new Arabic teacher.'

I couldn't believe I'd had to be convinced into tutoring her.

'*Tasharafna*.' Nice to meet you, Nora said in the sexiest Arabic I'd ever heard. '*Inta takoun moualami?*' Are you going to be my teacher?

For her, I'd make myself available day and night. I'd be her slave.

We sat and Justice raised her water glass.

'Let's make a toast,' she said. 'To new friends.'

We raised our glasses.

'To Jimmy Carter's victory,' Justice added. 'To peace in the Middle East.' We clinked glasses. Nora could have been a beauty queen, but instead, Justice informed us, she was a first-year law student at Harvard.

'Two days a week Nora volunteers in Dorchester, helping abused women get restraining orders. On weekends she works in a soup kitchen. Last summer, Nora taught English in a Palestinian refugee camp in Jordan,' Justice said.

Nora blushed and lowered her head. 'It was no big deal.'

'I've read about that camp,' Justice said. 'The conditions there are atrocious.' She shook her head and then looked over at me. 'Nora has led the most fascinating life.' Justice looked at Nora, clearly waiting, but Nora didn't speak. 'She's always been an activist. She and her parents went to South Africa to protest against apartheid. She's an inspiration.'

'I haven't done nearly enough,' Nora said.

'Did you know that Ahmed is a brilliant scientist?' Justice continued.

My eyes met Nora's, which were the colour of a spring sky after the rains. Her face was flushed and she lowered her eyes. Perhaps she was not just pretty and smart; perhaps she was a little modest, too. I smiled at the thought that she might have anything in common with the women from my village, where modesty was almost an art form.

Nora leaned towards me. I could smell fresh flowers. 'There's a lecture this week on campus on Mahmud Darwish's poetry,' she said softly. 'You might be interested.'

Before I could even think what to do, I heard myself asking her, 'Can I call you?'

'Give me a pen. I'll jot down my number.'

'Tell it to me. I'm good with numbers.'

The meal was over, but I had Nora's telephone number and she gave me another wondrous smile before she disappeared into the night. She was beautiful, compassionate, sweet. She was a law student at Harvard. She could have anything, live anywhere when she finished; why would she want to go to Gaza?

36

Her blonde hair made her an orange in a basket of apples. Nora was sitting in the front row wearing a red blouse studded with mirror work. She waved, motioning me over, her silver bracelets tinkling. Her smile sparkled.

'I've just started taking a course on Arab poets. Mahmud Darwish is so powerful.' She removed the notebook in the seat next to her and motioned for me to sit.

I had no idea who Mahmud Darwish was.

Professor Elsamooudi, a visiting professor from Birzet University, stepped up to the podium. The students applauded.

According to the flyer on my seat, Mahmud Darwish was born in Palestine, fled in 1948, and returned illegally a year later. He missed the day that Israel counted the Palestinians who remained in what became Israel, so they labelled him an internal refugee and gave him the status of 'present-absent alien'. After being imprisoned several times for travelling without a permit, and harassed for reciting his poetry, he finally left in 1970.

'Not even by erasing his village from the face of the earth could the Israelis smother his feelings of nostalgia for his homeland, Palestine,' Professor Elsamooudi said. 'Now I'll read Mahmud Darwish's poem "Identity Card". This poem became a rallying cry for the Palestinian people. The Israelis actually arrested Darwish for writing this poem.'

When Professor Elsamooudi finished reading the poem, I clapped with all my might. I couldn't believe how much the poem moved me. Mahmud Darwish had put my feelings into words. I didn't know it was possible. I looked over at Nora, grateful.

'He's so powerful.' She dabbed her eyes with a tissue. 'I'm embarrassed that I'm crying—the words were so potent.'

I had no idea words could have so much power and beauty. I wished my brother Abbas could read this. Maybe he could use poetry to channel his anger, instead of quoting Dr Habash. I wouldn't dare try to get him a copy of this poem though—it was surely illegal in Israel.

'"Identity" and "identity card" were highly charged words in the 1960s in the Arab world,' Professor Elsamooudi explained. 'And this was especially true for the Palestinians, who struggled to maintain their national identity. The Israelis still use the identity card system today.'

'*Ahmed!*' I heard my name in a loud whisper. I turned and saw Justice. Menachem sat next to her. I waved to them and they waved back.

After the lecture, Menachem, Justice, Nora and I went to a café called Casablanca. Justice and Nora spoke of the oppression in Israel and the Palestinians' resistance and what they could do to bring about peace. Menachem and I discussed ways to better control and manipulate atoms to suit our purposes. Our lives felt worlds apart, yet Justice and Menachem seemed so happy together. Perhaps they never talked.

Justice and Menachem left after our first pot of tea, but Nora and I stayed at the café until closing. I kept adding more hot water. By the end of the night my teabag no longer gave off taste.

Nora told me more about her incredible life; how she and her parents had once lived in a tent with nomadic Moors in the

Sahara desert for a month when she was twelve years old. Each time they moved, the women dismantled the tents, made from wooden poles, palm mats and heavy strips of cotton, and loaded the camel in less than an hour.

'Did you like living in a tent?' I asked.

'It was groovy,' Nora said. 'What an adventure.'

I didn't want to tell her about the flies and mosquitoes that found their way into our mouths as we slept or the torrential rains and scorching summers. Nora was sincere, but she had never known suffering: hers was the vision of a tourist, a visitor to the agony of others, then onto a plane or a Jeep for the next escapade. I felt that she had so much to learn; not only about Arabic, but also about life. I wanted to teach her.

Nora told me that I needed to laugh more and eat pizza. We agreed to meet the following Sunday.

That night I dreamed I was being driven on a bus through the desert towards the edge of the earth, when Nora arrived wearing a flowing white robe on a camel and whisked me away to a nearby oasis.

On the way to my office the next day, I noticed the colourful leaves falling, the birds chirping happy melodies, students laughing and talking in the halls, glad to be alive. Why hadn't I noticed this beauty before?

***

On Sunday we met for lessons and tea, and then again the following weekend. The days between were agony. We began to meet more often; Nora took me to more lectures. We took walks through Cambridge.

I waited for Nora at the shelter where she volunteered. I sat on a bench outside the old home that had been converted into a residence for women and children fleeing abusive husbands. She never spoke much about it, only to say that she was concerned for the children who were caught in the violence and slipped through the cracks in a system that could barely handle the mothers.

Behind me was a small garden with a play set and swings. Four kids were there, running around. As I waited for her to come out of the front door I heard a fight erupt in the playground: two boys were shouting at each other. One hit the other in the chest, and the injured one started to cry. I turned back around.

Then I heard her voice.

'You're safe.' I turned and Nora was on her knees, holding the boy who had been hit in one of her arms as he cried on her shoulder, and the other boy, the one who had done the hitting, in the other arm. I wondered why she didn't punish the hitting boy.

'I know it's scary to be here,' she said, quietly.

'I'm not scared, I hate him.' The hitting boy tried to pull away from Nora, but she held him gently.

'I hate you too. You're worthless.' The crying boy had regained his bravado.

'You know, it's okay to be scared. I'm scared lots of times.'

The hitting boy seemed incredulous, 'Why would you be scared?'

'Sometimes I miss my home, and my dad. Sometimes I don't know what's going to happen next. I worry about a lot of stuff.'

They both watched her. 'You know, it's okay to miss your dad. To miss your friends.'

The hitting boy seemed suddenly melancholy. 'I don't want to be here. I wanna go home.'

Nora sank down and sat cross-legged on the ground. Each of the boys sat on one of her knees, cuddled into a little pile of humanity. 'I understand. Sometimes we have to do things that are hard. But when you feel angry, I want you talk about it. Tell somebody. You won't be punished. It's not bad to feel that way, only let's not hit each other. Okay?'

They nodded.

'And if you stick together, it'll be easier—you won't have to be alone.' She stuck her hand between them. 'Pinky swear?'

Both boys giggled and reached in with their little fingers. A few seconds later and they were in the sandpit playing with big yellow lorries. I turned back before Nora saw me eavesdropping. She would be a wonderful mother someday.

I was in love and I knew it. But I also knew that our relationship was impossible. How could I be with a Jewish girl? Still, I couldn't stay away from her.

Whenever Harvard had a Middle Eastern-related event, we went—a dinner at Habibi's; a screening of a film about three Palestinian refugees who tried to make their way to Kuwait concealed in the steel tank of a lorry; a lecture by King Hussein of Jordan at the Kennedy School of Government; a talk on human rights violations in the West Bank and Gaza; a performance by a high school dabkeh dance group from Deisha Refugee Camp; an Arabic music night. Many times Justice and Menachem would join us, and at least once a week Nora and I ate dinner at their house. Nora brought pizza to my office. She invited me to a friend's barbeque, to the movie theatre to see *American Graffiti*, to a Bob Dylan concert at Boston Garden. When I'd told Nora that I didn't have any extra money to attend such things, that I had to support my family, she was so moved that tears filled her eyes. I'd thought my words might distance her, but they had the opposite effect. She insisted that she always received the tickets free of charge. I enjoyed it all. I began to understand that there is more knowledge in the world than just science.

***

Four months after we met, we were drinking tea at Algiers

Coffee House, one of our favourite spots. Nora sat across the table from me, holding my hand.

'I want to be more than friends,' she said. 'Let's go back to my room.' She smiled and raised her eyebrows.

Up until then, I'd held Nora's hand, but nothing more. I suppose I knew this day would come—perhaps some part of me wanted it to come—but I'd never give in to that desire. I knew what was expected of me. To marry a girl from our village; to have children: to return to the family. I would never marry Nora, and I respected her too much to continue down this path. Only, I could not bring myself to tell her the truth.

I stood up too quickly, spilling the tea. 'No,' I said. 'Impossible. I have work to do.'

Her eyes misted up.

***

I tried not to think of Nora as anything but my student, a friend; but every night I dreamed of her. In my heart raged a struggle. How could I agree to an arranged marriage? How could I be with anybody else? Nora was smart and lovely. She was learning Arabic. The more I got to know her, the more I realised that I wanted a marriage based on love. I wanted a wife I could be proud of. An accomplished wife. But I knew in my heart that it couldn't be Nora. How could I disappoint my parents?

Every time Nora invited me back to her dorm room, I found an excuse not to go. 'I've got too much work.' 'I think I'm coming down with the flu.' 'I have a headache.' That line made Nora laugh. 'Don't you know?' she said. 'That's the woman's line.' One evening, I was having dinner with her at Casablanca. Sitting next to the fireplace in the dimly lit room, candlelight flickering on her face, she suddenly stopped eating, put her pita on the table and sat up straight in her chair. I dipped my pita into the hummus and was about to take a bite when she spoke.

'I want to be with you, Ahmed,' she said.

My hand was suspended in mid-air. How could I tell her I didn't want her because she was Jewish? Working with a Jew was one thing, marrying one and having children together was another. In Israel, my children would be considered Jewish and have to serve in the Israeli army. The folded piece of pita in my hand started to drip. I put it in my mouth and chewed, trying to buy myself time. Swallowing, I cleared my throat. 'I promised my mother I'd marry someone from my village.'

'We can't continue like this,' she said. 'It hurts too much. Can't you tell your mother that you met someone?'

'She won't understand.'

'Why not?'

'She doesn't want me to be with a Western girl.'

'I love you.' She waited for a response. Tears pooled in the corners of her eyes. 'You think I'm a foolish girl; that I don't understand. But I do. I choose to believe in love.' She got up and hurried out of the door.

My heart ached as I let her go.

***

Nora stopped coming to her tutoring sessions. Every time the telephone in my office rang, I jumped, but it was never her. When Justice asked about her, I told her that she wasn't the one for me. I worked around the clock. As long as I kept busy, I felt in control. I didn't need her.

Menachem received a grant for $20,000 from the Institute for the Advancement of Nanotechnology, so we went to Habibi's to celebrate. We were discussing what he wanted to do with the money when I noticed Nora with Justice and the others from their peace activist group at a different table.

'I'm feeling sick,' I said.

Menachem looked over at Justice and Nora. 'This was

Justice's idea,' he said. 'She thinks you two are meant for each other.'

'It isn't feasible.' I grabbed the coat Justice had given me and walked to Harvard Yard in a snowstorm to find the bench Nora and I always shared. The snow was several feet high. It was freezing, but I still hadn't put on my coat. I sat on the bench and let the frigid air punish me.

The more distance I put between Nora and myself, the more I wanted her. I had to regain control. As I sat there in the storm, Nora appeared. I rose. Before I knew what to do, she embraced me, crying. She held on tightly.

'I can't stay away from you any longer,' she sobbed.

'Don't cry.'

'I'm so sorry. I didn't know what to do.' Her hair smelled of green apples and cinnamon. 'I love you.'

'Please, Nora, don't.'

'I'm not strong like you.'

'I'm weak,' I said. 'Don't you see that?'

'Don't you desire me at all?'

My arms remained at my sides. 'Of course I do.'

'Then what?'

'Obligation. My family.'

'Please don't tell me I'm not good enough.' Tears trickled down her face. 'Show them that you could love a Jewish girl. Lead by example.'

Nora kissed me on the lips and I returned the kiss. Just for a moment I allowed myself that—Nora's sweet lips, which were as soft and inviting as I knew they'd be—and then I pushed her away and walked her to her car. As she drove off, I began to think that maybe I could marry her. I'd ask Baba for his blessing.

With the money I had made, I'd had a telephone installed in my parent's house. I went to my office and called him.

'Baba,' I said, not bothering with the normal pleasantries. 'Please listen. I've met the girl I want to marry. She's so beautiful, smart, kind. She speaks Arabic and wants to become a human rights lawyer. There's only one thing.' I took a breath. 'She's Jewish.'

There was silence.

Finally, he said, 'The Jews aren't our enemies.' He spoke slowly, choosing his words. 'Before the idea of the creation of the Jewish state, Jews and Arabs lived in peace together. Does this girl make you happy? Does she love you? Do you love her? Do you have the same values and outlook on life?'

'Yes. Yes to everything,' I gushed.

'Then you have my blessing,' Baba said. 'You've suffered so much. You're a grown man. It's not right for me to tell you who to marry. That's your decision.'

Mama got on the line. 'In the name of God, are you trying to rip my heart out with your bare hands?'

'He's sided with the enemy!' Abbas screamed in the background.

I heard a struggle and it sounded like the receiver was dropped. 'Call back later,' Baba said. In the background I heard Abbas yelling, 'He has lost his mind!' There was a click and the line went dead.

***

I waited outside the law library for Nora to emerge. When she saw me it was as if thick cloud cover had parted and a sunbeam was reflecting off her face—only it was night. We walked together through Harvard Yard. The stars were shining. Snowflakes drifted from the sky and landed on her blue ski cap. It was a perfect night. I walked her back to her dorm.

'Can I come up?' I asked.

Her eyes widened. 'Of course.'

I followed her up the stairs to her room. She unlocked the door and, when we entered, I was taken aback. Nora's walls were covered with framed pictures from her travels.

There was a picture of Nora when she was eight or nine kneeling with dark straight-haired girls carrying poles on their shoulders with buckets hanging from both sides.

'Look at you!' I marvelled at the young Nora.

'That was in Laos. The stream wasn't safe, but it was all the village had. For three months a year that stream dried up. The children walked five miles every day to get the water and carry it back over the hills and a rickety bridge. My parents installed a pump in the centre of the village and paid for a new bridge to be built.'

There was a picture of Nora kneeling in a cabbage patch with three skinny black girls.

'That's Rwanda. Did you know that fourteen per cent of the world goes to bed hungry each night? My parents belonged to an organisation that went to different impoverished areas and gave the locals advice on growing vegetables.'

Why hadn't anyone come to my village? Why, now that we were alone in Nora's room, didn't she try to kiss me?

'Did you know that while nearly a hundred per cent of children in the US and Europe go to school, in poorer countries only forty-five per cent of girls and fifty-five per cent of boys go on to secondary school? 550 million women and 320 million men in this world are unable to read or write.'

I thought of Mama, who never had an opportunity to go to school. And of Amal and Sara, who died. And of Nadia, Abbas and Fadi, who dropped out. Only Hani had continued. He was scheduled to graduate from high school at the end of the year.

I turned Nora to me, pressed my fingers to her lips, and

looked into her eyes. 'Would you do me the honour of becoming my wife?'

'Ahmed.' She seemed stunned. 'Yes.'

I leaned in and, for the second time, we kissed. I wanted to kiss Nora forever. 'Come to my office. I must call my parents.'

'Call from here.'

'It's too expensive.'

'Call from here. Your family needs all the money you make. We can live off my trust fund. Please, don't argue with me. I won't have it any other way. I couldn't live with myself if I took any money away from them.' She handed me the receiver and I dialled the number.

'She said yes,' I told Baba. 'We're going to get married.'

'May God grant you many happy years together. May I talk to your fiancée?'

I handed the phone to Nora.

'I'll take good care of your son,' she said in Arabic, her smile as wide as the sea. Then she handed the phone back to me.

We sat on her bed together.

'I want to get married as soon as possible.'

'Me too.' She leaned over to kiss me.

'Wait.' I pulled back. 'We should wait until we're married.' I wanted to do that for Baba.

Nora laughed. 'You're serious?'

'I am.'

She stood and put her hands on her hips. 'Then let's get married immediately.'

'And your parents?' I know she'd said that her parents were liberals, but they were also Jews.

'My whole life they've drilled into my head that people are equal, that differences add to personal relationships. I'll let you see for yourself. You'll meet them. You'll love them.'

‘I want to marry you this summer in my village.’

‘I’m not waiting that long.’

‘My family has to be there.’

‘We’ll have the ceremony there,’ Nora said. ‘And we’ll sign the civil contract here. It’ll be easier like that. Israel doesn’t permit interfaith marriages anyway. Your parents don’t have to know. If you want, we can sign a Muslim contract there. You can start applying for citizenship sooner. I’ll set it up.’

I agreed; after all, I was a twenty-eight-year-old virgin. We didn’t make love that night, but I did kiss Nora one more time before leaving her room. We were engaged.

37

'Orange blossoms represent everlasting love,' Nora said when she answered her door with the flowers in her hair.

Then she handed me a box. 'New clothes for our new life.' I changed into the white cotton turtle-neck and trousers in the men's room at the courthouse.

'Ahmed,' the justice of the peace said. 'Please start.'

I looked down at the paper in my hand. 'You have taught me that love is an emotion we can't control.' I looked at Nora for a moment and she smiled. 'I never wanted to fall in love with you, but I had no choice. God made you especially for me.' She took my free hand and held it. I looked back at the paper. 'You have lit up my darkness. I couldn't imagine a life without you. You are my sunshine.' The paper fell to the floor as I took her hands in mine and gazed into her eyes. 'Our best days are in front of us. I look forward to creating a family and growing old together. I pledge to you my everlasting love.'

The registrar looked at her. 'Nora.'

She pulled her own paper from the folds of silken white robes that made her spun-gold hair look like moonlight. 'Let our marriage be the first step towards the weaving together of two people.' Nora stopped looking at the paper and shared her longing through her steady gaze at me. 'Our love confirmed what I already knew. Love transcends the barriers set up by humans. You are the only one for me.' She glanced at the paper. 'I believe that a great marriage doesn't come from merely finding the right person, but by also being the right person. I hope that at the end of your days, you're able to look back on this one with certainty as the day you loved me the least.' She put her paper on the justice of the peace's desk and took my hands. 'May my love liberate you. I pledge to you my everlasting love.'

The registrar handed Nora the two-spouted jug filled with water that she'd brought with us and she took a sip.

'This water symbolises the sanctity of your union.' He read the lines Nora had written and then handed me the jug. I drank from the other spout. 'Water is a basic element without which there is no life.' The justice of the peace put the jug on his desk and looked at me. 'Do you, Ahmed Hamid, take Nora Gold to be your lawful wedded wife?'

I took her hands in mine. 'I do.'

Tears glistened in Nora's eyes.

'Will you love, respect and honour her for as long as you both shall live?'

'I will.'

'Do you promise to love and cherish her in sickness and in health, for richer and poorer, for better, for worse and, forsaking all others, keep yourself only unto her, for as long as you both shall live?'

'I do.' I smiled at Nora, she squeezed my hand and we laughed a little.

'The wedding band, with no beginning and no end, signifies never-ending love.' He handed each of us the other's ring, first giving us the final words of the ceremony. 'Repeat after me,' he said. 'With this ring, I thee wed.'

With the simple gold bands on our fingers, the justice of the peace pronounced us husband and wife.

Later, in her dorm room, Nora walked to her bed and held out her hand. I moved towards her as if she had just hypnotised me. Our lips met. She slid off my new blazer and folded it over the tartan chair next to the bed. My shirt stayed on the floor, where it landed.

I feared that I wouldn't know what to do, but when she leaned towards me, I felt her warmth and began to relax. We kissed. Her tongue teased my lips apart. Nora guided me towards what I believed to be impossible pleasure. Raw adrenaline pumped through my veins.

My hands roamed around her waist and caressed the small of her back. She stepped away and unzipped her dress. I focused for a moment on her pink-painted toenails as she stepped out of the pool of white her dress had become. Even her toes were magnificent, I thought. I marvelled at the beauty before me as my eyes took in the lines and texture of her silken flesh, which was clad now in only a brilliant-white lacy undergarment that conformed perfectly to the round fullness of her breasts. That such an item of clothing existed was yet another marvel. Then that, too, slipped to the floor.

Nora reclined on her bed like a marble nude in Baba's art book. I approached hesitantly. Could we both fit? Would I crush her?

She smiled a mischievous smile and reached for the zipper of my trousers. She tugged, but it wouldn't budge. 'Help me,' she whispered.

A thread had got caught. I yanked it free.

'Take everything off, my husband.'

I felt the blood rise to my face. How could I get naked with her staring at me?

As if she could read my mind, Nora slid under the covers and flung them open for me to enter. I quickly slid down my trousers and underwear and jumped in next to her so hard that the mattress bounced. We laughed, and I was glad.

She rubbed her hands on my chest. 'What a handsome man my husband is.' Her Arabic was like music.

I took a deep breath. 'Not nearly as beautiful as you, my wife.'

I glanced at Nora's sparkling eyes. She threaded her white fingers through my black hair. I was going to make love to her. Before her there had been no other woman in the entire universe. In an almost ironic way, this Jewish girl reminded me of my home. Holding Nora in my arms, I was overcome with feelings of completeness, security and love. Never in my wildest dreams had I ever thought that a Jewish woman would bring out those feelings in me.

When we were done, we lay panting, trying to catch our breath, with the blankets on the floor and my modesty dispersed. I started to laugh and couldn't stop.

38

We found an apartment in Somerville and I carried Nora over the threshold, which almost killed me—we'd rented on the third floor of a building with no lift. Nora insisted she pay the rent from her trust fund. I knew it was unmanly to allow my wife to pay, but my family meant so much to me that I preferred to swallow my pride.

Our main room was only eight by ten feet, but it was ours. On the left was our kitchenette with avocado-coloured appliances and windows on either side. The wall-to-wall, burned-orange shag carpet continued into the bathroom and stopped at an orange-and-green flowered shower curtain.

'I love it!' Nora seemed genuinely thrilled. 'Our very own apartment.'

I felt like my life was finally beginning.

With the money from Nora's trust fund, we bought a mattress, an avocado bedspread with big orange flowers, two card tables, two folding chairs, an orange Formica kitchen table, a black vinyl loveseat, a beaded curtain that Nora wanted to hang over the opening to the bedroom nook, an orange mood lamp, and an orange poster with a peace sign in the middle bearing the words, 'Make love, not war'. We put the loveseat against the wall next to the kitchenette and the mattress in the small nook. The two card tables and folding chairs went in the middle of the main room and the Formica table in front of the kitchenette, for cooking purposes.

Just like in her dorm room, Nora covered the walls with her framed pictures—the same way Baba did with his portraits. Mixed among the pictures, she also hung souvenirs from her travels—a *retablo* made by the Ayacucho of Peru, which was a painted wooden box framing a papier mâché Palm Sunday gathering scene; a Masai Kudu horn; a Zulu beaded belt; and a bow and arrow from the Bushmen of the Kalahari.

On the windowsill in our bedroom, I placed the two-spouted jug. Next to it, I set the silver spoon with our names engraved on it that Menachem and Justice had given us.

'So you'll never go hungry,' Justice had said.

On the wall over the loveseat, I hung the two portraits Baba had given me as a going-away present. The first was of us all together before Amal and Sara were killed. He drew both of them as they had looked the last time he had seen them. Right next to that portrait, I hung the drawing he did the week before I left, of the remaining members of my family. Seeing them next to each other saddened me, so I moved the recent portrait next to our bed.

This was the first home I could call my own, and I loved it—Nora's eclectic taste, the pictures of her, my beautiful bride, the crafts and the glowing mood lamp.

***

'We're getting close,' Nora said, bouncing a little and squeezing my hand. The taxi drove down block after block of manicured tree-lined streets with houses the size of castles. Ferraris, Lamborghinis and Rolls Royces were parked in the driveways. Finally, the driver turned into one. The iron gate opened and we proceeded along Nora's family's winding driveway.

'I didn't know you were so rich.'

'It's not important to me,' Nora apologised. 'My father inherited most of it. My parents use the house to host charity events.' The topic clearly made her uncomfortable. 'You wouldn't believe the kinds of fundraisers they throw.' The breach between our backgrounds widened. I was even more nervous than earlier.

Nora rang the bell next to her mammoth front door.

A man appeared. 'Your mother is in the loggia,' he said with a Spanish accent.

Nora seemed compelled to explain away each revelation of their immense wealth. 'My parents like to employ as many people as possible.' Nora gestured to an African woman dressed in a bright red, yellow and orange kaftan who was arranging flowers. 'All of them are heads of families.'

Nora and I were in a thirty-five-foot-high rotunda gallery with a sweeping staircase. She led me down the wide hallway. Before we arrived at the loggia, whatever that was, we walked past a living room with an oversized fireplace, a dining room, a cherry-panelled library with a marble fireplace, and what Nora called the 'preschool rooms'.

My palms were sweaty.

'All the workers bring their preschool children with them to work,' Nora explained. Her parents hired three teachers. They had three rooms: babies, toddlers, and preschoolers. They provided them with three meals a day, clothing and beds for naptime.

Outside, there was a pool surrounded by gardens.

'Mom!' Nora called. A woman, obviously her mother, was sitting on the terracotta patio under a yellow umbrella. Papers were scattered everywhere. Her mother put down her pen.

'What a surprise!' She stood up. 'Is everything all right?'

'Better than all right.' Nora smiled. 'This is Ahmed.'

'Your Arabic teacher?'

'The one and only.'

Nora's mother held out her hand. 'So nice to meet you.' She was dressed in a brightly coloured peasant blouse and skirt, which looked like the one Nora had bought in Ghana. Around her neck was a peace symbol. 'Nora can't say enough nice things about you.'

'Where's Daddy?' Nora bubbled, bouncing on her tiptoes.

'He should be home any minute.'

'I'll wait for him.' She grabbed my hand. Her mother tilted her head.

'For what?' she asked.

'We're married,' Nora gushed. 'I'm so happy. Aren't you just so happy for me?'

Nora's mother stared at us for a second before she dropped back into her chair. 'You're what?' She looked like she'd had a stroke. I had told Nora that we should tell her parents, but she had been convinced they'd be happy for us. She wanted to surprise them.

Nora ran over and hugged her mother, but her mother didn't hug back.

Her father appeared and she rushed to throw her arms around him. 'I'm married!'

Her father looked over at me. Perhaps he assumed I was a servant, carrying Nora's bags to the pool.

'To whom?' he asked.

'Ahmed, of course.' Nora did a little jump in the air. 'We wanted to surprise you.'

Nora's parents looked at each other. Her mother looked ill.

'What?' Her father was almost shouting.

'We love each other.' Nora's smile faded. 'Aren't you happy for us?'

Her parents looked at each other again. 'Could you excuse

us for a moment?' Nora's father took her mother's hand and led her into the house.

'I don't know what's wrong with them.' Nora chewed on her nails and began to pace. She tried to hide her face from me, but I saw the tears. 'This isn't like them.'

I looked at the swimming pool. How I wished she'd prepared them, as I had with mine. Nora seemed so worldly, but in many ways she was a naïve child. She couldn't understand the depth of hatred—or the platitudes under which it hid. I put my arm around her shoulders.

***

We all sat in the living room. Nora's father set his glass of scotch on a coaster on the marble coffee table. 'Did you have to get married?'

'Yes, we did,' Nora said. She wasn't at all giddy like she had been when we arrived.

'When are you due?' her mother asked. 'You know you have options.' Her father put his arm around her mother, protectively.

'I'm not pregnant,' Nora said.

'Then why did you rush into this?' Her father sat on the edge of the sofa. 'You haven't even finished school.'

'We want to be together. We're in love.' Nora's bluntness shocked me.

'You could have lived together,' her mother said. 'Why did you get married?'

My face immediately felt warm. 'That is not my custom,' I said. 'I have great respect for your daughter.'

'We can get it annulled.' Nora's father took a slug of his Scotch. 'No one will ever have to know.'

'Never!' Nora stood up. 'Let's go, Ahmed.' She took my hand, and we were heading for the door when she stopped and turned around. 'You're just hypocrites. Frauds,' Nora said. 'And to think, I actually believed in your commitment. You don't like him because he's Palestinian. Admit it.'

Nora's father held his palms up in surrender. 'You're right. It's just too much.'

'Don't call me until you're willing to accept him.' We left their house.

Months went by and her parents never called. They didn't cut off Nora's trust fund though, so she continued in school and still planned to go on her summer trip to Gaza after we were married in my village. We were still able to send my entire pay cheque home to my family.

'I don't need them at my wedding.' Nora took her underwear drawer and emptied it into the suitcase.

The phone rang and I picked it up. 'Are you really going through with it?' Abbas asked.

'With what?'

'Marrying the Jew?' Anger gurgled in his voice.

'She's not like you think,' I said. 'She's a human rights activist.'

'Of course,' Abbas said. 'They all are. If you marry her, you'll be dead to me.'

'Meet her first,' I said. 'You'll change your mind.'

Nora motioned for me to hand her the phone, but I waved her away. She didn't know how to handle Abbas.

'Her or me,' he said. 'Don't bring her here.' There was a loud noise and then the phone went dead.

I would talk with him tomorrow when we arrived.

39

Four Uzi-bearing soldiers tracked Nora and me through their riflescopes.

'You're way too obvious,' Nora said when we reached the tarmac.

'Keep your voice down,' I whispered in her ear. Why did she draw attention to us? She could be so provocative, my impetuous wife. These were Israeli soldiers.

We boarded the bus to the terminal with the other passengers. Two soldiers attached themselves to us. I could feel their breath on the back of my neck. Nora turned to them. 'You really should stop smoking.' She pretended to smile and turned back.

What was she thinking? Nora they wouldn't hurt, but they could lock me up indefinitely.

The soldiers followed us inside and flanked us while we waited in line, then followed us to the passport booth.

The uniformed man looked through our passports without making eye contact. On his desk was a small Israeli flag. He stared at my picture for too long. On either side of us, Jewish people passed through. I was the only Palestinian on the flight.

Nora turned to the soldiers. 'We've chosen the slow line.'

Three more soldiers appeared and motioned me towards them.

'I'll be right back,' I said to Nora.

'I'll go with you.' She took a step towards me.

'That won't be necessary, Miss,' a soldier said.

'I insist.' Nora took my hand.

We collected our bags and were taken to a side table. 'Please open your bags,' the soldier said. He took his time taking out each and every article: Nora's underwear, her toothbrush, a box of condoms.

She stared at the soldier without flinching. He took out my *Atomic Physics* magazine and flipped through the pages. 'Are you planning on building a bomb?'

'He's doing his post doctorate in physics at MIT,' Nora said, proudly.

The soldier put the magazine back in my bag. 'Thank you for your cooperation.' He pushed our bags towards us, across the table. Maybe I was the naïve one. I couldn't believe the way Nora had provoked the soldier, and he never even reacted.

Fadi drove us home in a junky little Nissan with plastic flowers taped to it. We passed electric wires, new developments, traffic, modern foreign cars, billboards of scantily clad women in bathing suits, signs in Hebrew and English, and military vehicles pushing through the traffic. Nora had to go to the toilet, so we stopped at a petrol station. As soon as she was out of earshot, Fadi leaned over to me. 'Abbas is gone,' he said.

'Where'd he go?'

'He left a note.' Fadi handed me the paper.

Ahmed,

You've left me no choice. I'm leaving the country to help our people. Don't try to look for me because we are no longer brothers. You're dead to me.

Abbas

I heard the car door open and Nora got into the back seat. I felt like I'd been kicked in the face with steel-toed boots.

Nora was chatty the whole way. Luckily Fadi answered her. I could barely concentrate.

'That's our village,' he said.

'Quite the hill.' Nora leaned in and craned her head between the front bucket seats.

'Most Arab villages are built on hills,' he said.

'Better views?'

'Of the enemy.' Fadi shrugged. 'Many people have tried to conquer us—the Romans, the Turks, the British, to name a few—but in the end, we sent them all home.' He pulled into our village and proceeded slowly up the road.

Everything was the same: the clusters of mud-brick one-room houses, the dirt paths, the barefoot children playing in the streets, women washing their laundry on washboards in metal tubs, laundry hanging on lines, goats and chickens running around.

'Each family builds its own house,' Fadi said. 'There's a special mould we use to make the bricks.'

Everywhere I looked I saw flies, poverty and crumbling homes. The stench of open sewage and donkey dung was more pungent than I remembered.

As the car approached our house, Fadi blared the horn. People emerged from their homes to see us—everyone knew I was returning with my bride. Mama ran over crying. She hugged me tight and whispered in my ear, 'You have to bring him back. Don't marry her. He'll never come back.'

Nora still hadn't got out of the car. She let me go to Nadia, who hugged me. 'He's gone,' she whispered. Scattered behind Nadia were her husband, three children and seven stepchildren. I felt Nora grab my hand and I turned, forcing a smile.

Baba looked content, sitting on the stone wall strumming his oud and belting out a welcome home song accompanied by

Abu Sayyid on violin. The village dabkeh group, dressed in their matching black satin trousers and white satin blouses with red cummerbunds, stamped their feet and jumped in the air. Villagers gathered around the table of sweets, others danced.

Dressed in a black robe with red geometric embroidery on the front panel, Mama had refused to look at Nora.

'Mama? This is Nora.'

Mama looked her directly in the eyes. 'Can't you find someone Jewish?'

'That's enough, Mama.' I turned towards Nora and said in English, 'She's a bit blunt. Once she gets to know you things will change.'

Nora smiled. 'No harm done,' she said.

Baba finished his song, came over, hugged me and, without hesitation, also embraced Nora. 'Welcome! Welcome, daughter. We're so happy to have you in the family. The song we just played, I wrote for you and Ahmed.'

Nadia's children and stepchildren surrounded Nora. They hugged and kissed her checks and stroked her hair. Nora got down on her knees and gave them lollipops. She was laughing and smiling. I had a sick feeling in my gut.

After the introductions were made and the greetings finished, Mama went inside.

'Where's Abbas?' Nora said.

'He's not here right now,' I said.

Nora and I followed Nadia to the courtyard. The children held Nora's hands and danced in a circle.

'Attention! Attention! Honourable guests.' Baba used his hands to make a megaphone. 'You are all invited to my son Ahmed's wedding on Friday. Please help me welcome his lovely fiancée Nora into our family and share in our joy.' The women ululated and Nora smiled.

Nora stayed in a room in my parents' home and I slept at Uncle Kamal's.

***

After breakfast, Nora and I climbed up the almond tree that I had told her so much about. She wanted to look through the telescope I'd made long ago. She pointed it at Moshav Dan.

'You guys are crammed into land caked in filth and grease,' she said. 'Carbonic acid is bubbling from your ground while the moshav has abundant fertile land, and they've surrounded you on three sides so that your village can't expand. How many people are crammed in here?'

'Over 10,000,' I said.

'How much land do you have left?'

'I'm not sure.' I swallowed.

'Don't lie to me,' she said.

'About .02 of a square kilometre.'

'They're doing the same thing in the occupied territories,' Nora said. 'They're confiscating the fertile land on the perimeter and building settlements on it that strangle the Arab villages.'

Why did Abbas have to leave like that? If he'd only taken the time to meet Nora, he would have loved her.

She pointed the telescope at the slaughterhouse. 'Look at that black smoke blowing into your village. I'm covered in soot.' She aimed the telescope at the cattle race. 'Those poor animals. I can hear their cries from here.'

'Why don't we go inside?' I said. 'I'm hungry.'

'After that huge breakfast you had?' She moved the telescope in the direction of the West Bank.

Sweat beaded on my forehead. 'Please Nora, I'm really thirsty.'

'Go ahead,' she said without putting the telescope down. 'There are soldiers everywhere. They have the people lined up at a checkpoint. Do they keep all the Palestinians in pens here?'

Shots were fired in the camp and there was smoke.

Nora immediately looked there with the telescope.

'We'd better get down,' I said. 'People will be coming over to meet you.'

I took the telescope from her and we climbed down.

***

Family and friends flocked to the house. Nora was polite and respectful and liked by everyone. When she complimented Um Osammah on her necklace, she took it off and insisted Nora have it. Nadia's brood drew Nora pictures, Baba painted a portrait of her and hung it on the wall, and Mama avoided her.

***

'This is for you.' Nora handed Mama a box.

Mama took it and eyed it suspiciously. 'What is this?'

'A present for you,' Nora said.

I had no idea what it was. Mama opened it and pulled out a dress embroidered with gardens of geometric flowers. It looked so youthful next to Mama, whose face was a tapestry of wrinkles. She held the dress out, staring as if her eyes couldn't believe its beauty.

'This is the pattern of my people,' she said matter-of-factly. 'How did you find it?'

'I described where you were from to a Palestinian seamstress I found, and she created this,' Nora said. 'I had it made especially for you.'

Mama's thank you was cold.

Nora turned towards Baba. 'And this is for you.' Nora handed Baba a wrapped present.

'Thank you, daughter.' Baba smiled.

It was an oversized art book in Arabic of the Masters—Monet, Van Gogh, Gauguin and Picasso. Baba carefully flipped through the pages then pulled the book close to his chest. 'A thousand thanks,' Baba said. 'This is my most treasured book.' He sat at the kitchen table and flipped through the pages, stopping at Van Gogh's 'Starry Night' to marvel at it.

Mama came in carrying a wedding dress. 'This is for you to wear. Don't get it dirty because it's only rented. And whatever you do, don't tell anyone you're Jewish.' It was a traditional wedding dress with several gold-embroidered layers, which were decorated and trimmed with an abundance of coins and jewellery.

***

After morning prayer, Nadia and some other women, except Mama, congregated in the back of the house behind the almond tree to begin food preparations. Women gathered around large shallow circular pans chopping parsley, cutting tomatoes, making date, cheese and nut fillings. Nadia prepared the dough, mixing, kneading and working it into circles of about thirty-six centimetres in diameter; others hovered around the five small fire pits cooking rice and goat yogurt, and worked the outdoor oven. Wood and manure heated the metal plate on which the flat rocks were placed to bake the bread. Nora sat among them kneading dough.

Under the almond tree were crates of tomatoes, cucumbers and oranges. Upon seeing me, the women began to ululate. Mama worked inside alone.

In front of the house, Fadi and Hani carried a velour loveseat to the far end of the courtyard next to where the band was setting up. The rest of the area was left open for dancing, except for the perimeter where white sheets were laid on the ground to serve as tables. At the bottom of the hill men lined long wooden benches along the side of the road. With everyone hard at work, Baba and I left for the tea house to drink coffee and play backgammon. It would be the only time we'd be alone together before I became a married man.

In the middle of the path, Baba stopped and looked around. 'Son, I'm worried. Your brother, Abbas; he's so filled with hatred, he can't be reasoned with.' Baba whispered the words in my ear. 'I'm afraid of what he might do.'

'This is all my fault,' I said. 'He thinks I've sided with the enemy. My marriage is what pushed him over the edge.'

'He's very confused. I don't believe he thinks that you've sided with the enemy; he believes you are the enemy. It's been hard for him to grow up in your shadow.'

'Mama is blaming Nora,' I said.

Baba shook his head, knowingly. 'I'll handle her.'

Hearing footsteps behind us, we continued on to the tea house.

In the evening, guests appeared bearing gifts of sheep, goats and wrapped presents. The greeter belted out thanks, while my cousin Tareq registered who gave what.

***

At Uncle Kamal's house, I stood naked in the middle of the room in a tin tub filled with soapy water. The men sang, clapped and danced around me as they poured cups and pitchers of soapy water over my head. Fadi lathered my face and shaved me, while my cousins washed me with sponges. Baba was outside greeting the guests—I was glad he would be there to welcome Menachem, Justice, Rafi and Motie. My heart felt heavy like a concrete brick.

When I was clean, the men dried me off and I dressed in a white robe. Mama entered holding a smoking incense burner, which filled the air with frankincense, and blessed me and my marriage. Baba must have talked to her.

'The horse has arrived,' Uncle Kamal announced, and the men followed me outside joyously clapping.

'Our groom has climbed onto the mare,' they chanted as I mounted the white horse, which was decorated with necklaces of fresh calla lilies. Baba, Fadi and Hani were directly behind me. We headed towards my family's house, the men chanting, 'A horse of Arab blood. The groom's face is as soft as a flower.' As I ascended the dirt path to my parents' home, men dressed in white, tan and grey robes with blazers and cummerbunds, and others in bell-bottoms and silk shirts, lined the road, sidestepping, clapping and chanting. I looked back and saw Mama and Nadia dressed in black robes with red geometrical shapes on the front panel. The women clapped and chanted behind the men. Children of all ages were running and laughing and holding hands with their friends. The boys were in their best clothes; white cotton tops and elastic-waisted trousers their mothers had made. The girls wore brightly coloured dresses of ruffles and lace.

When we arrived, the men surrounded me as I dismounted. Menachem and Justice waved to me from among the crowd. In the house, Nora sat on the loveseat, her face covered with a golden hand-embroidered veil that was trimmed with gold coins. Mama was on her left, Nadia on her right. Behind them was a sheet with plastic flowers sewn onto it. Baba handed me a sword and I walked to Nora. With its tip, I lifted her veil.

The women ululated so loudly I couldn't hear myself think.

'You look beautiful,' I whispered to her and she gazed at me, eyes wide with delight. Had I chosen her over my brother? From the corner of my eye, I saw Baba and Mama. Menachem was in the corner with Justice, Rafi, Motie and their wives. Nora and I headed out to the velour loveseat with the mahogany carved back in the courtyard. The guests followed us, clapping and singing in two groups. The first group chanted, 'Our bridegroom is the best of youth.' The second group responded, 'The best of youth is our bridegroom.'

Nora and I sat on the loveseat and the guests danced in front of us. Mama and Baba came over and kissed me on the cheeks. They took Nora by the hand and the three of them began to dance together. Menachem, Justice, Motie, Rafi and their wives were arm in arm with the villagers trying to learn the dabkeh. And it suddenly occurred to me that maybe peace was possible. I wished Abbas could see things through my eyes.

***

Baba played his oud and sang our praises to the beat of the violin, drum and tambourine. Our neighbours surrounded us as we sat on the loveseat at the end of the courtyard, side by side, like a king and queen. They danced in front of us. Mama, Justice and Nadia held hands and danced in a joyful circle. Despite the smiling faces and laughter, I knew Abbas' absence weighed heavy on my family.

All the villagers headed to the bottom of the hill. Nora was in a special plastic chair at the side of the road. The men formed a long oval in the road and danced around in front of Nora, jumping and twisting their hips, spinning in circles, clapping and singing. The women sat on the long benches on either side. Every time someone offered a gift, the announcer belted out a blessing of thanks. 'May Allah bless you and grant you peace!' 'May peace always be with you!' 'May the Divine pour his blessings on you!'

'Climb on,' Fadi said. I climbed on his shoulders, and he began to dance with me in the middle of the men.

'That's enough,' I said. 'I must be crushing you.'

'I can't stop.' It was like he was carrying the load for Abbas. He kept dancing and dancing, his lean twenty-four-year-old body stronger than I realised.

It wasn't until after midnight that Nora and I stood in front of the door to my parents' house. Everyone behind us, on the hill and road, was holding candles. Mama handed Nora a piece of dough.

'Stick it on the lintel.' Mama pointed to a spot next to the door.

Nora looked at me.

'Go ahead,' I said.

'It will bring you wealth and children,' Mama said.

The villagers began to sing:

We welcome you to enter your home
As roses and jasmine and flowers bloom
We pray for the Almighty
To defeat your enemies and bless you with many boys
Let everything we did for you become blessed
And arid land turn green at your feet
Had I not been shy before your kith and kin
I would kneel down and kiss the ground at your feet

Mama bent down and, with a needle and thread, loosely sewed the bottom of Nora's wedding dress to my robe. 'This is to protect you from the evil spirits,' she said and kissed me on the cheek; then she turned to Nora and did the same. Everyone was watching her. The women surrounded us ululating and clapping as Nora and I entered my parents' house attached by the thread.

***

The following day, Nora and I walked through the village and I introduced her to each of the places that had had an impact on my life, starting with the village square.

Nora stopped in the middle of the dusty road and turned to me. 'Where's Abbas, really?'

I couldn't look her in the eye. 'He's travelling.'

'Because it is so easy for a Palestinian to take off on a

sightseeing vacation through Israel, on his brother's wedding day, when he can barely walk?'

'This is really none of your concern, my wife.' I was uncomfortable, there in public, even though no one could hear our conversation.

'He left because of me. Because you married me, didn't he?'

'Did my mother say something to you?'

Nora seemed crestfallen. 'I was right.' She looked up into my face. 'You must go and look for him immediately.'

I started to walk her back towards my family's home. 'I can't; it's not that easy.'

She stopped. 'You must.'

I continued on, trudging up the hill. 'Where Abbas has gone, no one can follow. He is underground now.'

***

At the end of the week, I took the bus to Jerusalem. Menachem and I had been invited to give a series of lectures on our work for three days. Nora didn't want to leave the village. Justice was going to stay at my parents' house with her. They wanted to practise their Arabic before they left for Gaza at the end of the month. I tried to talk Nora into cancelling her trip, arguing that it was too dangerous there, that she should stay in the village instead, but she refused to listen.

'You know what the Israelis are doing to the Gazans. The world's forsaken them. I told you before we were married what I was going to do with my life.'

'You can help in other ways,' I said. 'Use your law degree. Raise funds. This isn't the way.'

'I couldn't live with myself if I didn't go there. I can't live safe in the US, living a life of privilege, while they suffer and die.'

What could I say? I'd gone into our marriage well aware of the person she was, but I'd always thought that I'd be able to reason with her. At least I had another three weeks to talk her out of going to Gaza. As soon as I returned from Jerusalem, I'd bring the topic up again.

40

As soon as I stepped into the central bus station in Jerusalem, I heard shouts. '*Pitzizah*!' Bomb!

People ran in all directions, fleeing from the threat of a blue backpack left on the bench for the bus to Haifa.

Fleeing people jumped, cowboy-style, over railings. A toddler in a pink dress and matching bonnet fell. Her mother yanked her up.

An older man with a cane was knocked down by the rush of the crowds. Out of nowhere, two soldiers appeared and lifted him to safety. Civilians evacuated. Soldiers poured in. I fled with the others to behind the taped-off area.

A team of soldiers blew up the backpack. Pieces of paper littered the air.

***

I was deep in an article in the *Journal of Physics* about the development of a new microscope that would probe the density of states of material using the tunnelling current. I needed to understand how the researchers at IBM were trying to develop this microscope that viewed surfaces at the atomic level. I looked at the clock in Menachem's office. It was only 10:00am. We didn't have to give our next lecture until noon. I had enough time to finish the article. The lecture we had given the evening before had been a great success.

'Need a refill?' Menachem held up the teapot.

'No, thanks. I still have some.'

The phone rang. Menachem answered, and I ignored it. Always too much work to do; not enough time.

'Yes,' Menachem said.

It was something in the way he said yes that made me look up. Menachem's hands started to shake. He almost dropped his full cup of tea, but caught it just in time. He looked at me, and I knew this call was different. Tears poured down his cheeks.

'I'm so sorry,' he said, and handed me the receiver.

I took the phone, worried something had happened to Abbas.

I held the receiver to my ear.

Justice couldn't get the words out. She was crying.

'Ahmed, I'm afraid I have the worst news imaginable for you.' Her voice cracked. 'We were protecting your family's house. The soldiers came. They said your brother was involved with a terrorist organisation. Their bulldozer crushed Nora. She died on the way to the hospital. I'm sorry. I'm so sorry.'

I hung up the phone. I could hear no more. I looked over at Menachem.

'Nothing in my life will ever be right again,' I said.

41

Later, I found out the details. Nora and Justice had positioned themselves between the bulldozer and my family's house. They wore fluorescent orange vests with reflective strips that clearly marked them as unarmed civilians; Justice had always kept them in her car. My family had begged Justice and Nora not to put themselves in harm's way, but they had insisted that the Israelis wouldn't hurt two American Jewish women. They had convinced my family that they'd be immune. Baba tried to talk them out of it, but they refused to listen.

Justice yelled to the bulldozer driver through her megaphone in Hebrew to stop. She was always prepared to protest against injustice. Nora was waving her arms in the air as high as she could. There was both an operator and a vehicle commander in the bulldozer. Nora and Justice maintained eye contact with the bulldozer driver the entire time. On-site there was also a commander of the operation watching from an armoured personnel carrier.

The bulldozer kept coming. It pushed the earth forward and Justice and Nora climbed on top of the mound. They were high enough to see directly into the cab. The bulldozer kept coming. Justice was able to jump out of the way. Nora lost her footing and was pulled under the blade. The bulldozer continued. My family and Justice pounded on the cab's windows. The bulldozer continued forward, until the blade ran completely over Nora and then it backed up. My family and Justice ran to her. Nora was still alive. She said something about a promise. I don't know what. Was it a promise to me? A promise to the Palestinian people she so desperately wanted to help? I never found out. Nora was pronounced dead in the ambulance. Nora saved my family's house. The demolition was cancelled.

Nora's parents flew in. They wanted to take Nora's body back to America, but I convinced them to bury Nora in my village, under the almond tree. Her death must have meaning. Crowds numbering in the thousands, Palestinians and Israelis together, marched through the village holding hands and yelling, '*Shalom Acshav*!' 'Peace Now!' Nora's body was too mangled to be carried on a board as we did with the other martyrs. We buried her in a pine coffin under the almond tree.

I was told that I repeated the details of what happened to everyone who asked—friends, family, students—telling of the bulldozer that crushed her small, perfect body. After Nora's funeral, I took to bed, never leaving my parents' house. I stayed in the bed that had belonged to Abbas, the only real bed, and it constantly reminded me that I had traded my brother for Nora and now had neither. At the foot of the bed, I placed the portrait that Baba had drawn of Nora and me sitting on the velour loveseat.

Food seemed without taste. Mama brought meals to me, preparing my favourite foods, but I had no stomach for it. Sometimes she would sit next to me, holding a date cookie or a piece of pita in front of my mouth, trying to cajole me into eating, like she had done with Abbas after his accident.

'Mama, please. Leave me. I'm not a baby.'

'A child is a child, even if he has built a city.' She squeezed my face gently, between her fingers and thumb. 'You can't join

Nora, my son. Your place is here. You must eat.' I would take a bite or two only to secure some quiet.

Even Baba could bring me no solace. I knew I'd failed Nora. I should have protected her—she was my wife. Yet she was Nora, who wanted no protecting. What could I have done?

Baba listened and said, 'Pound the water, and in the end it is still water.'

Nora's parents demanded an autopsy and an investigation, but no charges were brought. The Israeli government ruled her death accidental. Justice was there: she told everyone it was no accident. My family said the same thing. My wife was murdered in cold blood.

When we first arrived at my village, Nora made me promise I would one day write my story. I tried to tell her that no one would be interested, but she was so adamant. Was that the promise she had referred to?

I wanted to die too. Nothing mattered. But I knew I couldn't do that to Baba. He had suffered enough.

At the end of the month, Menachem appeared at our door. I told Baba to tell him I was sleeping, but instead Baba escorted him into the small bedroom.

'When Einstein's wife was dying, he wrote to a friend that intellectual work would lead him through all of life's troubles,' Menachem said. 'You'd do well to follow his advice.'

I slowly sat up in bed.

'Take it from me, the only way to overcome the complexities of human emotions is to delve into science and try to explain the unexplained,' he said.

Though I wanted to ignore him, I knew his words to be true. I couldn't ignore Einstein's example. He was a great scientist. The greatest.

'I'm not leaving here without you.' Menachem sat on the end of my bed as if he were prepared to take root there.

I packed my bag and we left that night.

42

Back in Somerville, I packed Nora's memories into boxes—the picture of her in South Africa waving a sign that read *Stop Apartheid Now!*; a seven-year-old Nora marching on Washington carrying a *We Shall Overcome!* sign with her parents; Nora in Los Angeles wearing the 'P' in the *PEACE NOW* that she and her friends had spelt out across their T-shirts.

I filled two boxes with pictures from the period before I knew her. Those belonged to her parents, so I mailed them to California. I kept the pictures of us together—signing the marriage contract in the justice of the peace's chambers; in her dorm room; on a bench in Harvard Yard; and all the pictures from our wedding in the village. Those pictures I placed in an envelope in my briefcase. That way, she'd always be near me. I also kept the spoon and the two-spouted jug.

On September the 17th, 1978, a year after Nora's death, Israel and Egypt signed the Camp David Accords. Several months later, I was watching news of the Arab League's summit meeting in Baghdad denouncing the Accords when I spotted Abbas. My brother was on the stairs outside the building. I couldn't believe my eyes. No one in my family had heard from him in over a year. Communication with any Arab outside of Israel was against the law and especially one who worked for Dr Habash. My family could be exiled, tortured or imprisoned for years. And even if we wanted to contact him, how would we find him? He was underground in the Arab world and we could never go there. But at least we knew he was in Baghdad, and still alive.

In February 1979, the Islamic Revolution in Iran occurred, and the Shah was ousted from power; then, on March the 26th, 1979, Israel and Egypt signed a peace treaty at the White House. I thought of Abbas, of the anger he'd feel knowing that Egypt had agreed to peace with Israel, especially since it had done so without solving the Palestinian problem as part of the deal. Nora would have been outraged. Even I felt that Egypt had betrayed my people.

Every morning I got up, went to the bathroom, brushed my teeth, showered, got dressed and walked out of the door. And then I worked. Work was the only thing that gave substance to my life. At first, my attempts to concentrate were fruitless. But I had known sorrow before. Work would be my only salvation. So I threw myself into my research, leaving no time to think about anything else.

I read every article I could find on quantum tunnelling. Menachem and I worked around the clock in an attempt to observe the spin excitations to determine the orientation and strength of the anisotropies of individual iron atoms on copper.

This tunnelling intrigued me. It was like throwing a baseball at a kilometre-high brick wall and, instead of bouncing back, the ball passed through to the other side of the wall.

Before we could apply our theory to anything, we had to figure out how things work at an atomic level. Once we figured out how to manipulate the atom, the possibilities would be incredible.

Grief came in waves, but, like a seasoned soldier, I was prepared. It always began with an empty feeling in my abdomen.

***

Menachem and Justice tried to make sure I ate. Justice would send a breakfast sandwich or muffins to the office. She packed lunches for Menachem and me. Menachem would heat up our meal. Usually Justice attempted to prepare Middle Eastern food—lima beans, lentils and rice, peas and rice—but her heart was much greater than her cooking.

I'd wondered how Menachem had managed to lose so much weight and keep it off after he married Justice. Now I knew.

In the afternoon, Menachem would make us mint tea, which we'd sip while we worked. I was ashamed to let them both take care of me, but I couldn't refuse their kindness. I couldn't look after myself, but Menachem was pleased with my work. We made tremendous progress. Nora, I knew, would be proud.

***

New York University offered us jobs. At last, I would be a professor.

'I'll only go if you go,' Menachem said.

I wasn't ready, but I knew I needed to make a change—leave the apartment that I had shared with Nora.

'You'd be a professor,' he said. 'We could apply for grants together.'

'What does Justice want?'

'Whatever is best for you,' he said.

Justice blamed herself for Nora's death. It wasn't her fault. I told her over and over, but she didn't see it that way. The professorship offered four times more money than what I received at MIT. Really, there was no choice to make. I'd send this money to my family. Fadi no longer worked because I'd hired Teacher Mohammad to tutor him: he was a student, full time. This year he was graduating from high school and showed a great interest in science. He wanted to study medicine in Italy and I wanted to make it happen. Hani was studying Middle Eastern Studies at the Hebrew University.

Two weeks later a man in a black pinstriped suit picked up Menachem, Justice and me outside New York University's Science Center in his shiny black Cadillac. He was the realtor the university had chosen to help me find an apartment. Justice and Menachem had already found theirs.

Despite the luxurious rentals available to faculty, I wanted to rent the cheapest place I could find. I didn't need much. I wanted to send home as much of my money as I could. I rented a small one-bedroom apartment like the one I'd lived in with Nora. The view out of the window was of a parking lot. NYU paid for movers to transport the black vinyl couch, Formica table, mattress, two card tables and two folding chairs, along with the rest of my possessions, to my new apartment. I moved into the office next to Menachem and we continued our work.

I was in New York, a city that Nora had loved. She would have taken me to readings and films, to museums and shows on Broadway. She would've attended protest marches, taken me to eat at restaurants, read books in Washington Square Park. She would've loved it, living in New York.

It didn't matter to me where I was.

43

Slaughtered Palestinian babies were in rubbish heaps alongside Israeli army equipment and empty bottles of whiskey. The buildings of the Palestinian refugee camp Shatilla had been dynamited to the ground. The TV camera zoomed in on the Israeli flare canisters still attached to their tiny parachutes that littered the area.

Corpses of Palestinian women were draped over a pile of debris. The camera focused in on a woman lying on her back, her dress torn open and a little girl pinned under her. The girl had long dark curly hair. Her eyes were open, but she was dead. Another child lay near her like a discarded doll, her white dress stained with blood and dirt.

Justice shrieked and Menachem and I stared at the TV unable to speak.

Two months earlier, 90,000 Israeli soldiers had invaded Lebanon to dislodge the six-thousand-member PLO. By August, Lebanon was devastated, its infrastructure destroyed. 175,000 civilians were killed, 40,000 injured, 400,000 left homeless.

'The Israelis have committed genocide,' Justice said. She burst into tears.

The US had brokered a ceasefire agreement. The PLO fighters had evacuated and Israel had agreed to guarantee the safety of the Palestinian civilians left behind in the camps, which included Sabra and Shatilla.

'Sharon's responsible,' Menachem said.

The Israelis, under the command of the Israeli Minister of Defence, Ariel Sharon, stood guard for three days over Sabra and Shatilla to make sure no Palestinians could escape while the Lebanese Phalange militia massacred thousands of Palestinian women and children. The Israelis were well aware of the Phalange's desire to rid Lebanon of the Palestinians.

All I could think of was Abbas. I didn't know where he was or if he was even alive. Once I got my American citizenship, I hired private investigators, but no one could dig up any information on him. I had a sick feeling that he was in Lebanon. He was a cripple. He would have been left behind with the women, children and elderly. Men like him had been lined up and shot, execution style.

That night I took a taxi back to my apartment. There, I sat on my black sofa surrounded by my things—volumes of science manuals; journals of physics; textbooks on quantum mechanics, nanotechnology and maths for physicists; the silver spoon; and the two-spouted jug.

While I waited for my parents to answer their phone, I decided I wouldn't mention to them my premonition that Abbas was dead. After all, it was just a feeling.

'I found you a wife,' Mama said. 'She's perfect for you.'

'I have a wife.' They must not have heard of the massacre, I told myself. I hoped they never did.

Baba got on the phone. 'Ahmed, please, for your mother's and my sake, think about it. Nora's gone. You don't have to stop loving her. Your heart is big enough to be shared. Please son, you still have your whole life in front of you. Don't squander it.'

What could I say? I owed my parents this. They expected grandchildren from me.

'The arranged marriage is the way in our culture,' Mama said.

'I don't live in the East anymore.' I flipped on the TV and muted the sound. Elderly men lay on top of each other, their limbs tangled and their bodies covered with flies. I tried to make out the faces. Could Abbas be there?

'It doesn't matter where you live,' Mama said. 'This is our tradition, passed down from generation to generation.'

'Baba chose you.' I turned off the TV. I didn't want to have anything to do with the Middle East.

'She's Mohammad Abu Mohammad's daughter, the village healer.'

'Mohammad, who was three years ahead of me in school?'

'He's respected throughout the village for his healing. People come from other villages to drink his potions and receive his blessings. He's agreed to give his daughter to you in marriage.'

'And her age?'

'She graduates from high school at the end of the year.'

'How would that look? I'm thirty-four years old.' This was absurd. What would we have in common? How could she compare to Nora, who was educated, from the West, had opinions of her own?

'Please, son,' Baba said. 'Do it for me.'

I thought of him beaten with a machine-gun. Kicked while he was unconscious. Wasting away in that hell of a prison. I would marry the girl for him. There was no choice. This would be the price I paid for absolution.

'Set it up,' I said. 'I'll marry her when she graduates from high school.'

With those words, I admitted to myself that Nora wasn't coming back.

'Thank you, son,' Mama said. 'You've made me very happy. Do you want me to send you her picture?'

'If you think she's acceptable, that's enough for me.'

At least now, when they heard about the massacre, my upcoming nuptials would comfort them.

44

Fadi, home on summer break from medical school in Italy, met me at the airport and drove me home in my parents' four-door Nissan. Mama, Baba, Hani, Nadia and Ziad and their children were waiting in the courtyard of my family's house. I always felt relief, coming home, to see the house still standing. And I felt proud that my family lived well with the money that I provided.

Baba was the first to hug me. Mama was next. The women started ululating.

'Come,' Baba said and he took me inside. Though they were unable to get a permit to enlarge the house, they'd managed to redecorate. The living room was furnished with a mahogany hand-carved sofa with red cushions, and matching chairs and ottomans. Mama had a new refrigerator, dishwasher, washer and dryer. The floors were marble, the sinks made from porcelain; the bathroom was as fine as any, with a new sink, shower and bathtub. Mama flushed the toilet. She was proud and happy.

We sat in the kitchen, at a dark wooden table with eleven small stools around it. My immediate family sat first.

When we finished eating, Mama and Baba took me to see Nora's grave beneath the almond tree. They'd built a bench under a trellised arch with bougainvillea densely entwined in it. White forget-me-nots were planted all around the grave and oversized sunflowers and roses of every colour.

Mama kissed my cheeks and I hugged Baba.

The next day, my parents and I walked over to Yasmine's family's home. It looked much like our old home, the one the Israelis had blown up. It was a small mud-brick structure with one window with shutters, a tin door and a small courtyard in front. Mohammad opened the door, welcoming us with a warm smile. Baba looked up at him with reverence in his eyes.

'Please come in.' My future wife's father was dressed in a long white robe and an Arab headdress. My bride's mother came out. A black veil covered her hair. She was as big as a tent in her long embroidered robe, with a callused, rough hand that she extended to me and a big, partially toothless smile. Black hair was growing on her face like a light beard. I began to question my consent to the arranged marriage. Why did I not ask for a picture?

'Welcome, welcome,' Mohammad said again, and he kissed me on both cheeks.

'Please come in,' my future mother-in-law said. 'Please sit.'

I suddenly felt sick to my stomach. What if my bride looked like her? Could I back out? What was wrong with me? Why should I care?

My parents and I entered their home and sat on the dirt floor. My future mother-in-law and a few of my future sisters-in-law, all of whom were veiled, placed small plates of food on the floor.

'What do you do?' Mohammad asked.

I knew that was only a formality. My future in-laws already knew all about me; otherwise, I wouldn't have been there. 'I'm a professor at New York University in the United States.'

'Where would my daughter live?'

'I've a one-bedroom apartment with a fully equipped bathroom, a kitchenette, a washer, dryer and a dishwasher.'

'How much do you have saved?'

I'd forgotten how blunt my people could be. I gave them a figure that temporarily silenced them.

'How often will she come home?'

'Every summer and every December for three weeks.' I told them everything that Mama had prepared me to say. I reminded myself that I was entering this marriage for my parents. 'I'd like to request your daughter's hand in marriage.'

Mohammad's body stiffened. He probably planned on asking a hundred more questions, but I didn't have the patience. I looked at Baba and smiled.

'I accept,' Mohammad said.

I let out a sigh of relief.

The women began with the ululations and the tea.

'Fetch your sister from your grandmother's house,' Mohammad said to my bride's brother.

Everything about my bride screamed ignorance. Her veil, her thick, unplucked eyebrows, her traditional robe. I immediately wanted to go back on my word. My bride, Yasmine, wasn't tall like Nora. Her facial features weren't delicate like Nora's; they were hidden in layers of baby fat. Her teeth were yellow and crooked and she was plump. Plumpness was a sign of beauty in my culture, but I had grown fond of a slimmer body. I couldn't see her hair because she was veiled, but I imagined it was black, like her eyebrows. And she was so young. How could I bring her to the States? How would she ever fit in at faculty parties? What would Menachem think?

Nora still had a hold on me.

Yasmine smiled at me with her eyes, and then lowered her head so as only to get a stolen glimpse of me. And with that one look, I understood that she was trying to convey both sexuality and submission. I wanted so badly to be attracted to her.

'This is your bride,' my future father-in-law said. I smiled, fighting back the image of Nora, her golden hair, and felt a pain in my heart.

'Isn't she pretty?' Mama asked me in front of everyone.

I forced a smile. 'Very much so.'

Yasmine and I signed the marriage contract and, just like that, I was legally married. Sadness descended upon me. We'd have the ceremony the next day.

We all sat on the floor, just as my family had done before I began sending extra money home. Yasmine and her mother laid out more little dishes of tabboulie and an array of salads; tomato, green bean, black-eyed pea and lima bean, baba ghanouj and hummus. They had probably been cooking since dawn for this occasion.

None of us ate much: Yasmine's family from sheer delight and I from the shock of finding myself suddenly remarried. I wished for Yasmine's sake, and for Mama and Baba's, that I could find a way to love her. I knew that the pleasure of pleasing Baba and Mama should have left no room in my mind for selfish distractions, but I couldn't help but wonder how on earth I was going to bring myself to spend the rest of my life married to this young girl, whose plumpness and dark hair would be a constant reminder of Nora's slim blondeness. I hated myself for my feelings.

***

The next morning, Mama came to get me for my ceremonial cleansing.

'It's time,' she said.

There was a loud ringing in my ears. Was that a warning? This marriage would satisfy Baba and Mama. That was all that mattered. It was my duty as their eldest son. I stood in a tub as my male family and friends danced around me, washing me and shaving my facial hair. My body was there, but my mind was elsewhere. I was thinking about the night I met Nora, how she had seemed to float across the room. What was I doing? What would she think about my remarriage? She wouldn't want me to marry Yasmine. She would tell me to educate her. I shook my head. This was my wedding day. I wouldn't permit myself to ruin it with thoughts of Nora. It wasn't fair to Yasmine. Instead, I began to think of the small fluctuations that altered the thermodynamic variables that might lead to marked changes in the structure, and compromise my work.

When I was pronounced clean, I dressed in a white robe and walked with the men to Yasmine's house. If she hadn't been wearing a wedding dress, I wouldn't have recognised her because her makeup was so thick and her hair so big.

***

After the ceremony, I took Yasmine, my bride, back to the room at my parents' home—the same room I had once shared with Nora. I was grateful that someone had removed our wedding portrait. The last thing I wanted was to see Nora staring down at me as I consummated my new marriage. All of the villagers waited outside for me to emerge with the bed sheet.

Without warning, memories of the first time Nora and I made love bombarded me. I remembered how she had stroked my hair and kissed me. She had whispered words in Arabic, urging me on. Nothing else in the world had existed. That night I had held her in my arms, wanting the moment to last forever. Her touch had felt electric to my body, her Arabic seduced me, her beauty captivated me and her body excited me. It had been my first time.

I looked over at my bride and saw that she was shaking. 'Don't be nervous,' I said. 'Everything's going to be fine.'

I took Yasmine's hand and guided her to the bed. This was for Baba.

'Take off your dress.'

She was plump, with a few rolls of fat, but not completely unattractive. With my eyes closed I pulled her close and kissed her, and then thought of the first time Nora had kissed me. I willed myself to erase those thoughts from my mind: this wasn't fair to Yasmine. And yet I couldn't help it. Knowing it was wrong, I pretended Yasmine was Nora when we made love.

Yasmine's crying brought me back to reality. She was a virgin and in pain. I opened my eyes and saw her young, round face. It was terribly awkward. This was my new life. Yasmine lay on the bed without movement, like dead meat. She knew none of the tricks of an experienced woman. She was so shy that when I told her to move her hips she reddened and cried.

***

That night I dreamed I was a bird that had fallen into a trap, been put in a cage, and was trying to escape. I felt so sorry for Yasmine. She deserved a husband who loved her.

During the days that followed, I passed the time with the men, and Yasmine stayed with the women. Meals were communal. At night, Yasmine and I would retire to our room. We would have sex, and then we would go to sleep like two strangers. In the morning we'd join my family for the Morning Prayer and then breakfast. We talked little, as we had little in common. She never spoke unless spoken to, and I rarely had anything to say.

Two weeks after our wedding, Yasmine and I boarded a plane for New York City.

45

For the majority of the flight, we sat in silence while Yasmine gripped the armrests as if she were about to be hurled out of the plane. Eight hours into the trip, she took the initiative and spoke.

'What's New York City like?'

'The opposite of the village.'

'Have you been to Times Square?'

I looked at Yasmine, surprised. 'What do you know of Times Square?'

She shrugged, embarrassed.

'Have you been to the Statue of Liberty?'

I shook my head. 'I don't have time for such activities, Yasmine. I'm too busy with work.'

'Do you have a lot of friends there?'

'My best friends, Menachem and his wife Justice, live there. Are you excited to live in New York? It sounds like you are.'

'I'm nervous. I'll miss my family terribly.' She started to cry.

I wanted to comfort her, but I didn't know how. We didn't speak again until we reached my apartment.

'This is it.' I opened the door.

I'd made no improvements in the years that I'd lived there. Justice had recommended that I buy new furniture for my bride, but I hadn't wanted to waste the money. I was her rich husband in New York and I didn't even have a proper bed. It was enough for me, and more than she'd ever had, I figured. Yasmine paused at the door and took in the mauve shag carpet, Formica table in front of the stove, oven, sink and refrigerator, and the black vinyl couch against the wall, facing the television: my only improvement.

Yasmine's mouth formed an O. 'It's wonderful,' she said, and I knew that she meant it. She was used to a dirt floor and an outhouse in the back. She lowered her eyes. 'I never in my life dreamed I'd be living like this.'

My stomach contracted. What had I got myself into?

I stopped working from my office at night—although I still worked just as much, I simply added a desk at home. Yasmine sat next to me, on the floor; like an obedient servant doing needlework or knitting blankets for babies that never came. We rarely exchanged words. She never left the apartment unless I accompanied her. She waited alone all day for my return and then followed me around as if she was desperate to have human contact.

'In the name of God,' I said. 'Take an English class. You need to leave this apartment. It's unhealthy. A wife has to shop for groceries on her own. I can't have this burden on me. I have work to do.'

Yasmine had a ready array of excuses: 'I'm scared'; 'I'm homesick'; 'I don't need English.'

I felt as if she expected me to entertain her. With every passing day, I respected her less. I began to wonder if she wore her veil to conceal her rock-headedness. Her whole life, her every thought was about me—and it was suffocating.

At night, she waited patiently in bed for me to plant my seed in her, but month after month her period continued to come. Making a baby had become a dreaded chore. I detested our sex life. I'd turn off the light and roll onto my side, begging to be excused of my responsibilities. 'I have a headache.' 'I have backache.' 'I have cramp in my leg.'

'Are you broken?' she finally asked.

I began to try to plant my seed again. All I needed was for her to tell her father I was failing in my duties as a husband and then the whole family would become involved.

The first time Yasmine told me of her belief that her father's prayers and potions would make her fertile, I stared at her in amazement. Could she really be that dumb?

'How can you accept such superstition?' My voice oozed disgust. 'We need to see a specialist.'

'My father is a specialist,' Yasmine argued.

'Your father is ignorant. He didn't even graduate from high school.' I hated myself for being cruel, but I didn't know how else to make my point.

'There is many a person who believes in the power and blessings of my father. He has cured many and I believe in his miracles.'

'Miracles don't exist.'

At these words, a familiar silence fell on the apartment.

'You aren't a believer.' Yasmine shook her head and covered her face with her hands. Not only did Yasmine believe in her father's prayers, but she prayed herself, and she instructed me on prayers that I, too, was supposed to say. I knew that Nora and I could have made marvellous babies.

'I believe in science.' My cheeks were on fire. I imagined that this must be what it would be like for a modern man to live in the pre-Islamic period, when they buried female babies alive.

'Science?' Yasmine took her hands from her face and looked pityingly at me.

'We need to see a fertility specialist.' I was agitated; nothing like the compassionate man I wished I was. 'You'll see; this doctor will help us.'

'Whatever you say,' Yasmine said.

I knew that she didn't believe in modern medicine, but she was glad, at least, to be the object of my attention. Never did we go out together during the day. I went to my office, she stayed home and cooked and cleaned.

I made an appointment with Dr David Levy, a fertility specialist in Manhattan.

Yasmine and I sat on Dr Levy's plush leather chairs opposite his mahogany desk. Diplomas covered his wall. An undergraduate degree from Yale, *summa cum laude*. A medical degree from Harvard, also *summa cum laude*. His board certification was as a specialist in reproductive endocrinology and infertility. There were multiple awards for research, teaching and patient care; his PhD was in early embryo development.

He entered the room with his slicked-back hair, firm handshake, and a voice for radio. 'I've reviewed your test results, Dr Hamid. Your sperm count is in the normal range.'

I tried to repress my smile. I looked over at Yasmine in her veil and her traditional black robe—she refused to wear the new modern clothes I'd bought her—and translated the doctor's revelation to her.

'What's sperm?' she asked.

'I need to examine your wife,' Dr Levy said.

I accompanied Yasmine to the examination room.

The nurse handed her a white robe. 'I'll be back in a minute,' she said.

The fluorescent light was not kind to Yasmine's plump body. She undressed carefully, making sure the whole time that her veil remained in place. Her panties were white and big, and her bra was full-coverage. Nora had never worn bras.

Yasmine put the robe on.

***

On the taxi ride home, Yasmine sat in an almost foetal position next to me.

'Your cervical mucus was normal,' I said, knowing that she wouldn't understand what that meant. How much more of this could I take? I wished she could take herself to the next appointment, where the doctor would test for blockages of her fallopian tubes, but Yasmine wouldn't leave the apartment without me. I hated myself for my feelings.

***

Dr Levy found no blockages in Yasmine's tubes. All of the tests came back normal, but, three months later, she still wasn't pregnant. Two rounds of intra-uterine insemination and still no results. The next step was in vitro fertilisation. The cost was 10,000 dollars, which my insurance didn't cover, so I decided we needed to take a break.

I didn't want to go back to my village, but Baba asked me to come for Fadi's wedding. He had graduated from medical school in Italy and passed the exam in Israel. As our village's first doctor, he set up his office in the square and proposed to Uncle Kamal's daughter Mayadah. Hani was in the last year of his PhD.

Baba was also sure that Yasmine's father could cure our infertility problem. He was a wise man but, in this, I knew he was wrong. Every time Mama called, her first question was always, 'Is Yasmine expecting yet?'

***

Yasmine's father was waiting for us at my parents' house and everyone insisted we go straight to his home. I couldn't believe what I had got myself into. Even before we entered his house, I could smell the frankincense; he lit more once we got inside. After preparing a tea, he turned and took our hands in his.

'Please grant them a child,' he chanted over and over again.

Yasmine joined in. 'Ahmed, you must join in as well,' she said.

'Please grant us a child.' I chanted along with them, hoping to get out of there quicker by playing along.

***

A month later we returned to New York. Yasmine's period was late, so I bought an over-the-counter pregnancy kit and explained it to her. When she came out of the bathroom, there were two pink lines. She was pregnant.

Pregnant.

I remembered something Albert Einstein said: 'Science without faith is blind.'

My wife smiled at me, and I returned it. We were having a baby.

***

Justice and Menachem had invited Yasmine and me for dinner countless times, but I always found an excuse. 'She's tired from the trip.' 'She has the flu.' 'She has a headache.'

It had been over a year since Yasmine's arrival when Justice walked into my office. I was grading papers. She sat in the chair on the other side of my desk and pushed her wild red hair out of her face.

I'd been avoiding her. I knew she wanted to meet my wife, but I wanted to postpone the inevitable for as long as I could.

'Is there a reason you don't want us to meet Yasmine?' She cocked her head to the side.

'She's not like Nora.'

'I wouldn't expect her to be.'

I was silent for a moment while I tried to organise my thoughts. 'She's young and inexperienced.' She looked like she could be my daughter. What would they ever talk about?

'You're our best friend.' Justice smiled. 'I'm sure we'll love her. Tonight, at our house for dinner.'

Justice got up and looked at me. 'And I won't take no for an answer.' Before I could respond, she was out of the door. I wanted to back out, but realised that I couldn't.

Upon arriving home, before I could even reach for my key, Yasmine swung the door open. She wore a black robe with red geometric embroidery on the front panel—just like Mama's. I wondered if she waited there listening for me to return. But she hadn't been idle; the aroma of fresh pita baking in the machine that I had bought her filled the air. The table was set with two plates and a mezze of little dishes: baba ghanouj, hummus, tabboulie, goats' cheese and falafel. Cooking on the stove was her musaka'a: an aubergine, tomato and chickpea stew.

'Could you change your clothes, please?' I asked. 'Menachem and Justice have invited us for dinner.' I would have called to tell her, but she never answered the phone.

'What about the food I've prepared?' She seemed crestfallen.

'Put it in the refrigerator.'

Tears formed in the corners of her eyes. She lowered her head, turned and walked towards the table. She was two months pregnant and very emotional.

'Wait a minute.' I called Justice, explained the situation and invited them over instead. 'Please Yasmine,' I tried my best to be polite, 'can you change into the Western clothes I bought you? And please, no veil.'

'What's wrong with what I have on?'

'We're in the West now. Please act accordingly.'

Yasmine put on a flowered peasant skirt and a loose blouse. She wanted to braid her hair, but I told her it made her look too young. She wore it down, and I was taken aback at how pretty she looked.

When Menachem and Justice arrived, Yasmine hid behind me like a child. Justice went right up to her as if they had been friends for years, handed her a bouquet of sunflowers, took her hand and led her to the couch. She babbled away, unaware that my wife barely spoke English.

'Beautiful wife.' Menachem inhaled. 'Is that fresh-baked bread?'

When Menachem and Justice used all of the pita to devour the mezze, Yasmine baked some more right in front of them. She always made everything from scratch, spending her days chopping parsley, mashing chickpeas and kneading dough.

'I must get the recipe for this bread,' Justice said.

Menachem took out the notepad he always carried with him in his jacket pocket and jotted something down. 'I'll get you the bread maker; maybe you can take some lessons from Yasmine.' I had to smile, understanding his enthusiasm for any culinary improvement.

When the mezze dishes were empty, Yasmine cleared the table. She then spooned her musaka'a into four plates and placed them in front of us. Justice took a bite, closed her eyes and savoured the taste. 'This is the best ratatouille I've ever had.'

I didn't know what ratatouille was, but I knew Justice had given a compliment. Yasmine blushed.

'Ahmed, I'm surprised you even leave the house,' Menachem said. 'What a talented wife.'

Little conversation was made, since the majority of the time was spent eating. Yasmine finished the dinner with her home-made baklava. Even I had never tasted anything as delicious.

'You must teach Justice how to make this,' Menachem said before he bit into his third piece.

'I'd love to learn,' Justice said. 'I could make it next week. I'm having my peace group over for dinner.'

'Wonderful wife,' Menachem whispered in my ear before he left, and I knew he meant it.

Justice followed up. Once a week, Yasmine taught her how to cook and Justice taught Yasmine how to dress, speak English and live more independently.

In March, Yasmine gave birth to our son, Mahmud Hamid. From the first moment I saw him, I understood the sacrifices Baba had made for me. Now I knew what it was to love someone more than myself. I would do anything to protect him from harm.

Yasmine wasn't smart in the ways of the world, but she was a natural mother. She bathed our son, breast-fed him, woke up with him in the middle of the night, sang to him when he cried and made up elaborate stories. And something about this change in Yasmine, the mother of my child, aroused in me a genuine passion for her. We were now united by a common bond. Yasmine's life was filled with our son and me. I began to see her through different eyes—I saw her the way Mama and Baba had when they urged me to marry her: as a simple girl from my village. She and I were cut from the same cloth.

PART FOUR
2009

46

The year 2009 did not start off well. For the last week, Israel had been waging war on Gaza. Yasmine and I had just returned home from a New Year's Day party, when I grabbed the TV remote off the coffee table and clicked the 'on' button, anxious to see the latest news. Yasmine snuggled next to me on the couch.

'Today an F-16 fighter jet dropped a 2000 lb bomb on the house of Dr Nizar Rayan,' the reporter said. 'He was a top Hamas leader who served as a liaison between the political leadership and its military wing. The bomb killed not only Dr Rayan, but also his four wives and eleven of his children, who ranged in age from one to twelve.'

The news showed footage of Dr Rayan before his extrajudicial assassination, and from the aftermath. The five-storey apart- ment building in which Dr Rayan and his family had lived was flattened. Yellow-vested men were evacuating the dead from the scene. Corpses, fire, smoke, the wounded, bloodied children; all were caught in the shaky camera footage. Many were scouring through the rubble looking for victims. Another explosion caused panic as the residents scurried for safety.

'According to sources, Dr Rayan had been an advocate of suicide bombing since 1994, when Jewish settler Baruch Goldstein entered a Hebron mosque during Ramadan and opened fire on unarmed Palestinian worshippers,' the reporter said. 'Goldstein managed to kill twenty-nine Palestinians and wound 125 before his ammunition ran out.

'In 2001, Dr Rayan backed his twenty-two-year-old son on a suicide bombing mission in which he died and killed two Israelis.'

The news played footage of Dr Rayan, a big bearded man surrounded by black balaclava-clad fighters with green headbands. They were fighters from the Al-Qassam Brigades.

I was about to turn the television off when I recognised a hunched and crippled man walk over to a bunch of microphones. It had been years since I'd seen Abbas, but his walk gave him away. He was now sixty-one years old, his hair was gone and his skin hung loose on his face like an oversized mask.

Abbas leaned forward and said, 'We will avenge the murder of our great leader, Dr Nizar Rayan.'

I sat straight up. 'That's my brother, Abbas.'

Yasmine leaned forward. 'All the investigators you hired, and now he turns up on TV ?'

Was he in the Al-Qassam Brigades? Had he been underground? He was a cripple; what could he possibly do for the military?

'Does your brother have a death wish?' Yasmine asked.

Why did he have to live in Gaza, the poorest, most dangerous place on earth? He should've never left our village. We may not have had equal rights, but we had better conditions than the people of Gaza.

'What do you think the Israelis will do to my family?' I pulled off my glasses and rubbed my eyes. 'Why did Abbas have to get involved in politics?' Gaza could never stand up to Israel, one of the strongest militaries in the world and the only nuclear superpower in the Middle East. 'I have to help my brother.'

'Now we know where he is,' Yasmine said. 'Let's try to contact him.'

In my study, Yasmine searched for Abbas' number on the internet. In Gaza, there were five Abbas Hamids and I contacted them all. None of these Abbases, however, knew how I could find him.

I contacted different government offices, including the President's. I left messages everywhere, begging Abbas to call me.

For the remainder of Israel's twenty-three-day war, I spent all my time watching the news on TV, the internet and reading it in the newspapers. I became more determined than ever to get Abbas out of Gaza after finding a YouTube clip that showed an expert on white phosphorus explaining how it had been used in Gaza by the Israelis.

The Israeli military had been air-blasting the white phosphorus shells, allegedly trying to create a smokescreen near the Jabaliyah camp, the most densely populated place on the planet. But the expert explained that the day on which they attempted this was so incredibly windy that a smokescreen couldn't be created. Instead, the flaming pellets rained down on this highly populated civilian area. This was particularly dangerous because phosphorus could be absorbed through the burn area, resulting in liver, heart and kidney damage and, in some cases, multiple organ failure. In addition, white phosphorus continues to burn unless deprived of oxygen, or until it is completely consumed.

How could I leave my brother in a place like that? What if the phosphorus burned him? The pain would be unbearable. I remembered the horrible burn my son Amir had suffered when a pot of scalding soup fell on his arm. How minor that would be compared to a white phosphorus burn. I thought about Abbas lying in a coma in the hospital bed all those years ago and how helpless I had felt.

I worked around the clock trying to contact Abbas, but with no success. Then, a week after the ceasefire, my luck changed. I received a mysterious phone call from a woman. 'If you want to see your brother Abbas, come to Gaza.'

I'd go to Gaza and try to save him.

'Are you all right?' Yasmine stood in the doorway of my study in her bathrobe. 'I heard the phone ring. Who was it?'

The tree outside our window reminded me of how Abbas and I used to climb the almond tree to watch the Jews through my telescope. 'I have to go to Gaza,' I said.

Yasmine's eyes widened. 'You can't be serious.'

'Abbas is in danger. I need to talk to him.'

'You'll be in danger.'

'He's my brother.'

'You can't go.' She took the time to articulate each word.

'This is my chance to atone.' I thought of Baba handcuffed to the gurney. Of Abbas, sprawled out on the ground, blood pooling under his head. 'I want to offer him the chance he never had.'

She crossed her arms. 'Why you? Why can't you pay someone to go?'

'It has to be me.'

'You have a wife; two sons; a career. Gaza is dangerous. What if Israel wages war on Gaza again while you're there? What about our families in Israel? What if they retaliate against them? Are you willing to risk everything for your brother?'

'Yes, I am.' Finally, I felt like I was doing what I needed to do.

Yasmine took a deep breath. She knew I'd made up my mind. 'I'm going with you.'

And I knew she had made up hers as well.

***

Fadi picked Yasmine and me up at the airport and drove us back to my parents' home. We didn't talk about Abbas in the car out of fear that it was bugged. After the first broadcast no one had known who Abbas was, but within days he had been identified as Abbas Hamid, a former Arab Israeli. It was then revealed that Abbas worked in intelligence for the Al-Qassam Brigades, and had been underground, along with the rest of the members, until the death of Dr Nizar Rayan.

Fadi kept looking in the rear-view mirror. Whenever we switched lanes, the military Jeep behind us did the same. It was practically riding our bumper. We drove through Tel Aviv; maybe Fadi thought he could lose the soldiers that way. I couldn't believe all the new glass and steel skyscrapers, condos and office buildings, and the new four-lane boulevards and expressways with landscaped avenues and highways. We drove by the sandy beach fringed by elegant cafés, bars and shops, and down palm- filled avenues. A lot of money had been invested in this city. We drove across the new superhighway, Kvish 6, with its elaborate bridges and tunnels. In record time, we were in the village with the Jeep still on our tail. It followed us up to the top of our hill.

Two soldiers were stationed outside our house. This time Fadi didn't blare the horn when we approached, and no family or friends waited outside to greet us.

'Baba.' I went to embrace him, but he didn't move from the loveseat in the living room, where his attention was glued to the TV news. He looked up with bloodshot eyes. Slowly, he rose and embraced us. It seemed he had aged a hundred years. 'What are we going to do?' he whispered in my ear.

'Yasmine and I are going to Gaza. We'll bring him back to

America with us,' I whispered back. We remained in the middle of the room, Yasmine next to me.

'It's too dangerous there,' Baba said into my ear. 'I can't let you go.'

'Good things make choosing difficult. Bad things leave no choice,' I whispered. 'How's Mama holding up?'

Baba shook his head. 'She's unbelievable.' He pulled me closer. 'She's actually proud of Abbas.'

How could she be proud of him for belonging to a party that believed violence was necessary for liberation? She had been so against my studies, and now this.

'Where is she?' She wasn't educated, I told myself.

Baba headed for the kitchen. Mama was in there, chopping parsley and humming a tune. Two soldiers watched her work through the window. Mama waved to them and laughed.

'Mama,' I called, 'what are you doing?'

'Your face looks like you just bit into a lemon.' She chuckled. 'When did you get here? Give me a hug.' She squeezed me, and then Yasmine. 'I'm so proud of your brother,' she whispered. 'Can you believe what he's accomplished? And to think, they almost killed him.'

Fadi walked in with his wife and two sons.

'How's Rome?' I asked Abdullah, Fadi's oldest. He was in his third year of medical school, studying in Italy at the same university that his father had attended.

He hugged me tightly. 'Thanks Uncle Ahmed,' he said. 'The car is awesome!'

'You're a Hamid!' I said. 'You need to travel in style. Do you like the apartment?'

'Thank you so much, again,' he said.

'How's Paris?' I asked Fadi's other son, Hamza.

'An artist's dream.'

'Been able to teach your grandfather anything?' I smiled over at Baba.

'He's long surpassed me,' Baba said.

Nadia, who lived down the street from my parents now, was in the States visiting Hani. I'd gladly offered to pay for her ten children and seven stepchildren to go to university. Only two of my nieces had married straight out of high school. Among the graduates were two heart surgeons, an orthopaedic surgeon, a radiologist, a mechanical engineer, an architect, a creative writing teacher, a human rights lawyer, an elementary school teacher, two nurses and a librarian. Of my remaining siblings, only Abbas and Nadia never finished school.

Hani had moved to California with his wife. They'd met at the Hebrew University. After he'd finished his doctorate in Middle Eastern Studies and she her BA in the same subject, they had gone to California, Hani having been appointed a professor of Middle Eastern Studies at UCLA.

In the morning, Yasmine and I drove to the American Embassy in Jerusalem to apply for permission from Israel to visit Gaza.

When it was our turn, the clerk was less than receptive. 'Don't you know it's a war zone there?' The woman looked at Yasmine and me as if I'd just revealed plans to kill ourselves.

'My brother's there,' I said. 'I need to see him.'

'I'll be frank with you,' she said. 'You're wasting your time. Israel doesn't grant permission.

'It's an emergency,' I said.

'Go back to America. That's my advice to you.' She looked past us. 'Next.' The line was long and she was the only one there.

'Can we submit our application, at least?' Yasmine asked.

'No can do,' she said. 'It's contrary to our government's travel advice.'

Disappointed, but still determined, Yasmine and I flew back to the States.

47

Yasmine placed a tray of kallaj on the table.

'I've never seen this one before.' Menachem transferred one to his plate.

'It's our special this week,' Justice said. 'We can't make them fast enough.'

Ten years earlier, Justice and Yasmine had opened a Middle Eastern bakery called 'Pastries for Peace'. Now, they had twenty-three throughout the United States. They donated all the proceeds to a programme they'd developed that granted micro-loans to Palestinian women interested in starting businesses.

I stared at Abbas in the portrait Baba had given me before I left for America: the one without my dead siblings.

'As you know, my younger brother, Abbas, is with Hamas,' I said. 'He's had a hard life. An Israeli pushed him off a scaffold when he was only eleven. He broke his back. He's been crippled ever since. My father was in prison. We lived in a tent. Can you help me?' It hadn't come out at all like I had practised it in my head.

Justice's eyes opened wider with every word, but Menachem's face remained the same.

I pushed my glasses up and pressed my fingers to my eyes. Yasmine passed the coffee, sat next to me and squeezed my other hand. I had to pull myself together. This was for Abbas. I was ready to beg if necessary.

Menachem was silent for a moment. Then he looked at me as if he appreciated what I had said. 'What can I do?'

I got up and went to the window. Thrusting my hands into my pockets, I turned to face him. 'Do you know anyone? Yasmine and I need to go to Gaza.'

'You could die there,' he said.

I shrugged.

I was sixty-two years old, but Abbas was still my little brother.

48

Six months later, Yasmine and I sat in the back seat of a taxi headed from Jerusalem to Gaza. We passed olive groves, almond trees and then the orange groves. When I saw the wheat fields, my stomach tightened.

We had spent the last three weeks trying to get through the gate into Gaza. Each day we wasted hours at the Erez Crossing trying to persuade the Israeli officials to allow us in. It didn't matter that Menachem had moved heaven and earth to get us permission from Israel. Every day we pleaded our case with the Israeli border officials, and every day they told us we needed a different piece of paper. Each morning we rose at five to begin our journey again with new papers.

I brought letters from Menachem and two Jewish Nobel Prize winners who worked with me at MIT. Yasmine and I both wrote personal letters accepting responsibility—we wouldn't hold the Israeli Government liable for what happened to us in Gaza, which we recognised was a war zone. None of it worked. Each day, the answer from the gatekeepers was the same: 'Come back tomorrow with a different piece of paper.'

Our Arab driver smoked incessantly with the windows rolled up, creating a toxic fog. Despite the closed windows, my thick sweater and heavy raincoat, it was freezing in the car. Yasmine was visibly shivering. I was used to winter weather, but this damp cold was completely different.

'Can you put the heat on?' I asked the driver.

'It's broken.' He turned and looked at me. 'They want a thousand shekels to fix it. Who has that kind of money?'

I reached into my pocket and counted out a thousand shekels. 'For you,' I said and handed him the money.

'What do you want?' He squinted at me. 'I've been to prison four times already. I'm not going again.'

'All we need you to do is get us to the Erez Crossing.'

'Why are you going to Gaza?'

'To see my brother.'

'Good luck.' He took a puff on his cigarette, then released the smoke over the back seat into my face. 'The Israelis will never let you in. When they left in 2005, they locked the people in Gaza and threw away the key. Do you know how many times I've driven people down to the Erez Crossing? Not one of them has ever got in. What makes you different?'

'We have the right papers,' Yasmine said. She always liked to be positive.

'Before Israel blockaded Gaza, Palestinian workers poured across the Erez Crossing to jobs here. Israel turned Gaza into a source of cheap labour. What choice did the Gazans have? They weren't allowed to develop their own economy.' He took a long drag of his cigarette. 'And once they were completely dependent, Israel goes and cuts them off.'

'I know,' I said. 'I understand.' I could barely breathe. The last thing I wanted to do was talk politics.

Yasmine and I got out of the taxi in front of a gleaming, shiny building. The Erez Crossing was a fortress. When it was finally our turn, we approached the Israeli soldier in the pillbox and handed him our papers. I was old enough to be his grandfather. He looked at our permits.

'Wait for me to call you.' He motioned for us to move aside.

'Over here,' a man called to Yasmine and me. He was huddled together with another man. 'Jake Crawford. I'm with CRS. And this is my colleague, Ron King.'

'Ahmed Hamid,' I said, 'and this is my wife Yasmine.'

The rain pounded us. The cold penetrated our bones.

'Don't look so glum,' Jake said. 'It could be worse. We could be at the Karni Crossing.'

'What happens there?' I asked.

'A huge traffic jam,' Jake said. 'Another colleague has been trying to get a truck filled with water through for months.'

'People are getting sick.' Ron shook his head. 'The water and sanitation systems are collapsing. Israel isn't allowing the parts needed to repair them to be brought in. The Gazans can't drink their water, and the Israelis won't let him in with clean water.'

'You should see all the trucks backed up there.' Jake sighed. 'Many of them have been trying to get into Gaza for months.

***

Hours passed before we were informed that our paperwork was ready. We handed it to the Israeli through a bank-teller window. We were searched and our bag was taken apart and every pocket and article inside scrutinised. The next stop was the gleaming stainless steel building that looked like a mix between a prison and an airline terminal. It must have cost a billion dollars with all its x-ray machines, video cameras, monitoring equipment and other devices. There were seven booths, but only one was manned. We passed through the maze of gates, holding areas and turnstiles. Getting into the Dror Detention Centre was nothing compared to this. Menachem's phone call to the Israeli Chief of Staff last night must have finally worked.

It was dark by the time we followed the signs to Gaza, through a long barren concrete tunnel which reminded me of the cattle race at the slaughterhouse. We had to carry our bags over approximately a mile of rock, dirt, dust and gravel that led to the Gaza side of the border. Desperate taxi drivers descended like crows on a carcass when we emerged.

'Let me take you!' they all screamed at the same time.

Soaking wet and shivering, we sat on the ripped upholstery of the back seat of a taxi.

A few barriers were set up in the road.

'A Hamas checkpoint,' the driver said. 'Just a formality.'

'Good evening,' the Hamas official said. We handed him our passports, he looked them over and gave them back. 'Welcome to Gaza.' He smiled.

It was too late to look for Abbas. We headed straight for the hotel.

We drove past unpainted cinderblock structures with giant gaping holes. Plastic covered most of the windows. Out in the rain, the streets were packed with wet people of all ages, dilapidated vehicles and donkey-pulled carts. Broken TVs, water heaters, cables and bent iron rods protruded from more piles of rubble. Apartment buildings rendered uninhabitable lined the narrow roads. Abandoned sniper towers were on every corner. Barefoot children sloshed in mud. Rubbish was piled everywhere. There were rows upon rows of tents. From what I could see, everyone in Gaza was in need. Yasmine's eyes were wide with horror.

'Why aren't there any trees?' I asked the driver. Baba had repeatedly told me of how the abundance of orange groves in Gaza infused the air with a sweet scent. Our oranges couldn't compete with the juicy, almost seedless oranges of Gaza. He'd described Gaza as a seaside resort where commerce thrived because of its strategic location.

'Israel uprooted the trees in this area,' the driver said. 'You can imagine what a threat to their security the trees must have posed: an orange must have dropped onto one of their tanks.'

We turned the corner into a neighbourhood full of concrete and stone apartment blocks and houses which, for the most part, were still intact, with the occasional building marred here and there by impossibly torqued beams. The driver turned again and drove down a paved road towards a white palace with arches.

The doorman greeted us with a warm welcome. This place had been built for visiting dignitaries and journalists, and exuded an air of privilege, even now. Inside were high vaulted ceilings and domes from which iron chandeliers hung. The lobby was white, clean and spacious, and I was grateful for the luxurious accommodation. Our room was filled with arches and black-and-white photos of Gaza in better times. From the window, Yasmine and I listened to the waves crash. A light sea breeze mingled with the hotel's sandalwood scent.

'Hear how angry those waves are,' Yasmine said. 'Even you wouldn't want to swim in them.'

I'd learned to swim in the Mediterranean, when I'd attended a physics conference in Barcelona; it was summer vacation and Yasmine and the boys had accompanied me. When the conference was over, we went to the Costa Brava and stayed in a hotel on the seashore. Mahmud was nine and Amir wasn't even eight. We used to get up early to swim on our own private beach.

'They're not like the waves in the Hamptons, that's for sure,' I said. My sons had taught me how to bodysurf there when we lived in New York City.

'This water's poisoned,' Yasmine said.

49

As we sat alone in the dining room, sipping fresh strawberry juice, a man in a pinstriped suit made his way to our table. 'Welcome. Welcome,' he said. 'I'm Sayeed El-Sayeed, the owner of the hotel.'

'Please'—I motioned to the chair across from me—'join us. I'm Ahmed Hamid and this is my wife Yasmine. You have a beautiful hotel.'

'I had great hopes for it.' He shook his head. 'I worked as an architect in Saudi Arabia for twenty years. With all the money I saved, I came back to Gaza and built the hotel.'

'Are you from Gaza?' I asked.

'No, Jaffa, but we fled here in 1948 before the war, when the Jews took our city.'

'Not a lot of tourists here these days.' I glanced around at the empty restaurant.

'Just you,' he said. 'At least, before, journalists and aid workers were allowed in.'

'Where do you get the fresh food and supplies?' I asked.

He gestured south. 'The tunnels. You know, the black market.'

'You have to get all your food from the tunnels?'

'No, no. The Israelis allow some basic food items in. I'm talking about the supplies needed to put together a hotel menu.'

'What are you going to do?' I asked.

He shook his head. 'Do you know anyone who's interested in purchasing a five-star hotel in a prison?'

50

I stared out of the taxi window.

'Where's the presidential building?' I asked the driver.

'It was there.' He pointed to the pile of concrete rubble. 'Now it's next to it.' He gestured to a partially destroyed building with plastic draped over the blown-out sections.

'We're looking for Abbas Hamid,' I said to the receptionist.

'Your name?' She had a patch over one eye. Two fingers were missing from her right hand. She looked grim in her black head-covering and black robe.

'Ahmed Hamid, his brother, and my wife, Yasmine Hamid.' I showed her our American passports.

She looked disdainfully at Yasmine in her bright yellow ruffle- collared raincoat that she had bought in Paris and her tight black trousers. Thanks to Pilates and power yoga, Yasmine remained fit. The woman flipped through her clipboard.

She lifted the receiver and dialled a number.

'Go outside,' she instructed. 'He's not here yet.'

Outside, it was damp, drizzly and cold. We didn't have our umbrellas. Across the street was a destroyed mosque. A group of girls approached, some in uniforms, others in crumpled and shabby clothes. Some had backpacks, while others carried bin bags. They giggled and whispered to each other when they passed us.

I spotted Abbas' crippled gait as he slowly approached with the help of a boy.

'Brother.' I went to him. 'Finally.' I hugged him, but he didn't hug me back.

He looked like he wanted to tell me to leave, but he glanced at the boy at his side and held his tongue.

'Is it safe for you to be out in the open?' I asked. I had read that the fighters from the Al-Qassam Brigades were all underground.

'I'm an old, crippled man,' he said. 'I, like Nizar, would like to die fighting for my country. He wasn't afraid to show his face. I refuse to hide any longer. Let the world watch the Israelis kill me.'

'Please don't put yourself in harm's way,' I said.

'Too late for that,' he said. 'I have a meeting now.'

'Where?' I asked.

He pointed to the partially destroyed building.

'Can you take some time off ?' I asked. 'I've travelled all this way to see you.'

'Excuse me if I don't drop everything to have tea with you, but I have a meeting to attend.' He looked at me with disgust. 'It's almost time for my grandson Majid's school to begin. Why don't you go with him? He can give you a tour on the way. When he's done, then we'll talk.'

'All day?' I asked.

'In Gaza, school's in shifts of four hours.' Abbas turned to the boy he was with. 'This is my brother, your Uncle Ahmed, from America.'

'I'm Yasmine, Ahmed's wife.' Yasmine smiled as she introduced herself.

Abbas acknowledged her with a nod and then turned to his grandson again. 'Show them around, let them meet some of your friends, then take them to school with you.' Before I could say anything else, Majid was helping Abbas up the stairs.

Yasmine and I waited until Majid returned. At least Abbas had agreed to see me after school.

'What grade are you in?' Yasmine asked as we walked together.

'Sixth.' He looked me directly in the eye. 'So you live in America?'

'We do.' I smiled.

He stopped, opened his backpack, pulled out an empty tear gas grenade and handed it to me. 'I believe it was a present from your country.' Majid smiled.

I took it from him. On the side of it was written *Produced in Saltsburg , Pennsylvania.*

'Tell your friends, thanks. We got their grenade.' He put it back into his backpack and pulled out another fragment. 'This came from a school. It's a fragment from a white phosphorus artillery shell.' Majid showed me the marking on his treasure. *Pine Bluff Arsenal.*

'Don't you have any books in there?' I asked.

'No, they got destroyed in the war,' Majid said.

I furrowed my brow. 'Then why are you carrying around a backpack?'

'We trade shells and fragments,' he said. 'My friend Bassam has this cool fragment from a 500 lb Mark 82 bomb I want.'

I thought of my brothers outside the tent comparing ammunition shells, which they had traded with each other the way my sons traded baseball cards.

Majid pointed to a group of tents next to the flattened school. 'That was my school last year.' A few grandparents or parents were talking to their children outside the tents, while others crawled in. 'Yo Fadi,' Majid called to a boy his size. The left sleeve of his worn blue sweatshirt hung empty. The boy came over and Majid put his arm around his shoulder. 'This is my aunt and uncle from America.'

'Nice to meet you.' Yasmine's voice was choked.

'A missile from an F-16 fighter plane blew off his arm,' Majid said matter-of-factly.

'If you give me a shekel I'll show you my stub,' Fadi said.

'No need.' I handed him a shekel from my pocket.

'Why didn't you tell me your uncle was so easy?' Fadi playfully cuffed Majid on the head with his good hand. 'I would've asked for more!' Majid and Fadi laughed, but then Majid coughed and tried to regain his serious demeanour. He glanced over at the tents, and spotted a little boy of six or seven.

'Amir!' Majid called. The boy came over. 'This is my uncle,' Majid said. 'He's from America.'

His left eye scanned Yasmine and me. The right one didn't move.

'Show them your eye,' Majid said.

The boy popped out his right eye. Yasmine gasped and the kids laughed. The empty socket was pink and fleshy.

'Are you crazy?' Fadi threw up his arm in the universal gesture of 'what the heck?' 'Why didn't you ask him for money first? You need to be a businessman like me.' Fadi tried to cuff Majid on the head again, but Majid dodged.

***

We arrived at a building that was badly damaged by shooting. Parts were burned out. Rain started to pound on its sheet-metal roof. This was the school.

Majid's classroom had no door or windows. Forty-six boys were packed into the room, sitting on the ground. It was dark and cold, but there were no light-bulbs in the sockets and there was no heat. A few of the boys had scars on their faces; most had dark circles under their eyes. On the cracked blackboard was a picture of a smiling young boy, who I realised must be a martyr. The boys chatted with each other.

A man in a wheelchair entered the classroom and greeted us. Majid went to him. 'This is my uncle and aunt. They want to join us today.' Majid turned to us. 'This is my teacher, Halim.'

'Please excuse us,' the teacher said. 'I'd offer you a seat, but we had to burn them for heat.'

'I'm a physics professor,' I said, awkwardly.

'We'll begin with science then.'

He handed me a sheet of paper dotted with jagged holes.

'What happened here?' I pointed to a hole.

'The eraser. We have to smuggle paper in through the tunnels. The quality is awful.'

I read the handwritten sheet.

	Heat Movement	
solid ↓ conduction	liquid and gases ↓ convection	space ↓ radiation

'Isn't this a bit easy for eleven-year-olds?' I looked at the teacher.

'The circumstances.' He lowered his voice.

How could that be? In Palestinian refugee communities, education was highly valued. Over the years, I'd encountered numerous Palestinian refugees doing their post-doctorates at top universities. 'Do they each have copies of this?' I said.

He shook his head. 'No. You know. The blockade.'

'Of course.' Yasmine and I stood next to him. I couldn't believe what I was seeing.

'Today we have guests,' the teacher said to the class. 'Majid's uncle and aunt. He's a professor of physics.'

The sound of jets flying over seemed to paralyse the class. One boy near us cringed visibly. When they were gone, the teacher asked, 'Who knows anything about heat movement?'

Hands shot into the air. He pointed to the small boy in front of me. 'Ahmad.'

'I-I-I do-o-n't kn-kn-kn-o-o-o-w,' he said.

When the science lesson was over, the teacher switched to maths. The children were still stuck on their two and three multiplication tables.

'Where's the restroom?' I asked. I had had too much strawberry juice at breakfast.

'The bucket's outside behind the sheet.' The teacher pointed.

Outside, I picked through the rubble and filled my trouser pockets with stones.

When I returned, the teacher was still trying to explain the maths lesson to blank faces.

'Do you mind if I try?' I asked.

Yasmine and I sat on the floor, surrounded by the kids. I laid two stones on the ground.

'One group of two is two.' I used a stone to write on the dirt floor 1×2=2. Next I laid two groups of two stones on the floor. 'Two groups of two are one, two, three, four.' I wrote 2×2=4 in the dirt. Next to them I placed three groups of two stones and continued through ten. Their eyes lit up. 'When you go home, I want you to use stones and the ground as paper and practise these tables.'

Yasmine taught them a couple of phrases in English, the way she had learned them, and had the children use them to make conversations. When our children were young, Yasmine had started taking courses at the university and hadn't stopped until she had her master's degree in elementary education. Although she chose to go into business with Justice, had I known how talented she was with a class, I might have encouraged her to become a teacher instead.

***

Majid left Yasmine and me outside Abbas' makeshift office. Abbas invited us to his house.

'Where are you parked?' I asked. It couldn't be too close because I'd seen him walk up.

'I live nearby.' His tone was cold. 'The doctor says I must walk or I'll be in a wheelchair.'

We walked slowly, Abbas' face contorted from the pain. He had borne the same expression fifty years ago whenever he walked. In silence we passed the crumbled charred remains of buildings. It began to pour cold rain. Children made their way through it to their four-hour shift at school. No one seemed to have proper coats or umbrellas, and no one seemed to mind.

My brother opened the tin door to his mud-brick house. 'I built it the way we did in the village,' he said. 'I've been teaching the families in tents how to do it.'

Two women sat on the floor holding crying babies, while three toddlers dressed in rags played catch with someone who looked from behind to be an older boy. He turned around and my breath caught. He wasn't a boy, he was a young man, and he looked exactly like me when I was his age. He even had my bushy hair, light beard and overall scruffy appearance. He kissed Abbas' hand.

'Oh God,' I said. 'I feel like I'm a teenager again.'

'Yes,' Abbas said. 'This is my youngest son, Khaled. He not only resembles you in appearance, he also has your gifts in maths and science. But he has different principles from you.'

'Are you my Uncle Ahmed?' Khaled asked. He seemed shocked.

Had Abbas spoken to him of me? I looked at Abbas, but his facial muscles were tight.

Abbas shook his head. 'How would you know who he is?'

Khaled swallowed. 'I read all his articles I could get my hands on. You know, he figured out how to compute the magnetic anisotropy of an atom.'

'Is that the work you did with the Israeli?' Abbas glared at me. He turned to Khaled. 'Did you know, your uncle spent the last forty years collaborating with an Israeli to achieve those results?'

Khaled lowered his head.

'What university do you attend?' I asked.

'I used to study physics at the Islamic University . . .'

Abbas interrupted. 'The Israelis blew up the science labs during their offensive, as well as the records department.'

'I read something about Hamas storing weapons there,' I said.

'You read Israeli propaganda. Did your colleague give you the article?'

'No, I read it in the newspaper,' I said.

'You should have read the United Nations fact-finding report,' Abbas said. 'These were civilian educational buildings and they didn't find any evidence of their use as a military facility that might have made it a legitimate target in the eyes of the Israelis.'

'Were you studying nanotechnology at the university?' I asked Khaled.

'I wish.' Khaled shook his head. 'They don't teach nanotechnology in Gaza.'

'Did you ever think of going abroad?' I said.

'MIT offered me a full scholarship, but the Israelis won't let me out,' Khaled said. 'I've applied for a visa many times.'

'How can they keep you from accepting your scholarship? You'd think they'd want an educated population; it is ignorance and superstition that promotes violence.'

Khaled opened his mouth to respond, but his father answered instead. 'No, it's poverty, tyranny and desperation—and denying children an education and a future promotes all of these things.'

'Maybe I could help,' I said. 'I have connections.' I would make it happen.

Khaled smiled, but his father stepped between us. 'Khaled doesn't want to stain his hands by collaborating with the enemy.' Abbas patted Khaled's shoulder.

I looked at Khaled. 'Let me at least look into your options.'

'There are over 800 students with scholarships abroad who can't get out,' Abbas said. 'Even your connections couldn't get Khaled out. The Israelis don't want educated Palestinians. It's part of their scholasticide policy. They want to make us desperate so that we have nothing to live for. They want to turn us into terrorists so that they don't have to make peace with us and return our land.'

I couldn't believe how paranoid Abbas was. I'd show him. I'd move heaven and earth to get Khaled a visa. I'd get all of them visas. After all, I had got into Gaza, hadn't I?

In searching for a way to change the subject, I noticed four framed pictures: a lovely kohl-eyed young woman, two young boys and a girl. I knew from the way the frames were decorated with plastic flowers that they were martyrs.

Abbas saw me looking at them. 'Those were my boys, Riyad and Zakariyah.'

They reminded me of Abbas and my brothers at that age.

'Riyad was seven. Zakariyah was only six.' Abbas pointed to the woman next to them. 'That was their mother, my wife, Malaikah. They were still living in Shatilla. Did you hear about the massacres at the Sabra and Shatilla refugee camps in Lebanon?'

'Yes, Abbas,' I said. 'When I first heard about it, I had a sick feeling that you were killed.'

'No, unfortunately I didn't die. My poor sons and wife did instead. May Allah have mercy on them.' He took a deep breath. 'I was forced to evacuate earlier that month.'

On the day my brother lost his wife, I had agreed to marry Yasmine. 'May their spirits remain in your life,' I said. 'May Allah shower blessings on their graves.'

'That was my granddaughter, Amal. She was hit by an Israeli missile walking home from school a few months after Israel told the world it had left Gaza. Khaled found what was left of her.'

Khaled turned his head and wiped his eyes, obviously embarrassed for us to see such a show of emotion.

A haggard-looking woman in a veil and tattered robe appeared with a tray and three glasses of tea. She squeezed Khaled's neck as she passed him and said, 'They were very close, Khaled and Amal; it has been very hard for him.'

'This is my wife, Mayada.' Abbas took a glass and thanked her. Yasmine and I followed suit.

Abbas introduced us to his daughters-in-law and grandchildren. His other two sons were out trying to find work. Mayada, his second wife, their three sons and eight grandchildren all lived together in his two-room house.

I'd bring them all back to America with me and transform their lives.

51

Abbas, Yasmine, Khaled and I got into Abbas' dilapidated little blue car with a yellow door. Yasmine and Khaled sat in the back seat. I didn't think it would run, but Abbas made it start.

'How have you been?' I asked.

'I'm busy now.' Abbas' voice was cold. 'I have important work to do for my people.'

Two toddlers were playing in mud and rubble. A woman emerged from a makeshift tent next to a collapsed house and waved for them to come inside.

'Are they paying you?' I asked.

'Why do you ask?' He took his eyes off the road and looked over at me.

I brushed the dust off my trousers. 'You're living in squalor.'

'I donate my money to the really needy.' Abbas shook his head. 'I couldn't enjoy it knowing others were suffering.'

Every building we drove past was either damaged or destroyed. I had seen areas of Gaza that were still intact—was Abbas deliberately trying to give me a false sense of reality?

'What have you been doing all these years?'

'I got a job working for Dr Habash's organisation.'

'Doing what?' He had no skills and could barely walk.

'Intelligence.' He smiled. 'I translated the Israeli newspapers and news to Arabic. Remember that radio you made me? I used it to listen to the Hebrew news.'

'I tried to find you.' The pollution made me sneeze. 'It was like you had disappeared from the face of the earth.'

Abbas drove slowly to avoid the giant potholes in the street. 'I was underground,' he said. 'The Mossad was after me. They had already killed a number of my colleagues.'

I couldn't believe he was bragging about his work for a known terrorist organisation in front of his son. I needed to come out with the reason for my visit. He and his family should not suffer another day here. I only hoped Abbas could see past his anger at me to do what was right. 'We've come to invite you back to the States with us. We can provide a better life for you and your family.' I glanced back at Khaled. He was sitting on the edge of the seat.

Yasmine remained quiet, her eyes on the posters of martyrs that lined the dismal streets.

'Yes, I'm sure you'd love me to abandon what I'm doing.' Abbas' voice was filled with bitterness. 'Defect to America, where I can have a fatal accident.'

'Abbas, you're my brother . . .'

'I've been following your career. I understand that you and the Israeli are still collaborating. Was he the one who made you come here?'

I was stunned. 'No one made me come. Hatred has blinded you to the good left in the world; I only want to share my good fortune with you and your family.'

'You never gave a damn about me or our people. You sided with the Israelis long ago.'

'I've taken care of our family single-handedly. Mama and Baba have a beautiful house, modern conveniences, and I put Fadi, his kids and Nadia's through school and graduate school. And now I am here for you and your family. I haven't sided with anyone.'

‘As Bishop Desmond Tutu said, ‘If you are neutral in situations of injustice, you have chosen the side of the oppressor.’

Abbas’ words hit me like a slap. If he could only understand. ‘I’ve tried to make peace in my own way.’

‘You’ve done what’s good for you. You’ve forgotten about your people. You’re a collaborator. Did you ever think that not all of us possess skills the Israelis can exploit?’

I didn’t mean to raise my voice, but it came out that way. ‘I don’t work for Israel; I never have. I’m an American. I work for science, for the world.’ He said nothing, so I turned the conversation back to him. ‘You’re risking your life.’

‘My people’s well-being is my life.’

‘Think of yourself, Abbas, your family,’ I said. ‘I can provide you with a nice life, a safe life, one without suffering. A future for your family. Your sons and grandchildren can get the education they deserve.’ He looked old enough to be my father. I had a few wrinkles on my face, but my body was firm and strong from years of running.

‘You’re different from me,’ Abbas said. ‘I want to do something for my people, but you know as well as I do that Israel wants a Jewish state for Jews only, across all of historic Palestine. And in your new country, the Jews determine Middle East policy. Israel knows it can do whatever it wants because Jews in America will support it.’

I rolled my eyes. ‘You are giving Jews in America too much credit. It’s also the Christian right. They believe Jews need to be here in order for the second coming of Jesus or something.’

‘So that’s why I should abandon my people and go to America, because everyone there wants to destroy us?’

‘Abbas, you’re not being rational,’ I said. ‘Hamas uses suicide bombers.’

‘Israel doesn’t have to use suicide bombers.’ Abbas’ facial

muscles tightened. 'It has tanks and planes. Suicide bombing is the weapon of the desperate. The Israelis have killed countless more of us than we have of them. They've been trying to eradicate us from Palestine since the 1940s.'

'I wouldn't go that far.' I focused on the dirt stain on the sleeve of my white linen shirt. 'Why focus on the past when we can focus on the future?'

'What future? Look around. Israel wants the same thing now as it did then,' Abbas said. 'Our land without us.'

'Listen, I'm no big fan of Israel, but I can't believe that. Israel wants security before it can make peace.'

'Peace brings security. Security doesn't bring peace.'

I thought of the Dalai Lama's words which hung in Justice's foyer. It went something like 'If you want to experience peace, provide it for another, and if you want to feel safe, cause another to feel safe.'

Abbas continued, 'Israel said it couldn't negotiate peace with us until it had security. We've stopped our attacks: where are the talks? Where there's oppression, there will be resistance.'

'Let go of all this hatred, Abbas; come with us to the States. You can help people from there, where you're safe. I'll arrange for your whole family to come.'

'Even if I wanted to'—Abbas stopped the car at lights, to let a group of children pass—'Israel would never let me and my family out. It would be easier for us to travel to Jupiter than to get out of Gaza.'

The light turned green and Abbas began to drive again.

'Where are we going?'

'We don't get many American tourists here in Gaza.' Abbas glanced over at me. 'I thought I'd show you around.'

'We're as Palestinian as you are.'

'You turned your back on us.' He looked in the rear-view

mirror. 'Both of you.'

'How dare you?' Yasmine had had enough of Abbas' self-righteousness. 'You know nothing about me, or what I have done for our people.'

I turned to Abbas. 'How did you even get involved with Hamas? You've never been religious.'

'During the Oslo Accords, our organisation joined forces with Hamas and the rest of the rejectionist front.'

'Why would you reject Oslo?' I asked. 'Don't you want peace?'

'Peace wasn't offered,' Abbas said. 'Israel wanted to rule us land, sea and air, create an open-air prison and keep their guards in place. Dr Habash could see that; he was a Christian, but it didn't matter: we were all Palestinian first.' Abbas gestured around him. 'Do you think we're liberated?'

'Well, no,' I said. 'But Hamas forced their hand—they were shooting missiles into Israel.'

'You're so naïve. You've bought into the Israeli propaganda. This blockade—this prison they've trapped us in—do you really think they did all this just to stop a few homemade missiles? They want to kill our hopes and dreams, destroy our humanity. The majority of us now live on donations—they've turned us into a nation of beggars. We were a hard-working, proud and resourceful people; now we have no trades for our men, no education for our children, no hope for a better future through our own hard work. They're doing worse than killing our bodies; they are breaking our spirits, taking our souls. Do I want my children and grandchildren to become beggars, or do I want them to starve? It is a Solomonic decision.'

I looked at Abbas. 'What you are suggesting is impossible. The whole world is watching.'

'Israel is breaking every human rights law conceivable and no one stops it. We are portrayed as ruthless, devious, bloodthirsty extremists. It's much easier to kill extremists, or just to turn a blind eye to their endless suffering.'

'So you believe that Israel is going to kill you all?'

'Its policies are calculated and systematic.'

'Then why did so many vote for Hamas—a terrorist organisation? If that is just playing into their game, why do it?'

'What do you think happened in 2005 when Israel told the world it had left Gaza? They gave us our own country? No, they removed their settlers so that they could strangle us in a different way. We didn't have a chance. Fatah didn't liberate us. Our economy fell apart. Israel never allowed Fatah to develop the infrastructure needed to succeed, but they allowed the Muslim Brotherhood, which became Hamas, to develop the proper infrastructure over years. When you can't feed your children, where do you go? Hamas provided us with food, schools, clinics and the means to better our lives. When Fatah couldn't deliver, the masses turned to the party that could. It's about survival. And my job is to represent the masses.'

'But Hamas' methods of sending missiles into Israel,' I said. 'Don't you see how counterproductive they are?'

'What would you do if you and your family were trapped in a prison, starving, freezing in a tent in the winter, with no clean water, no means to make money, and the world had turned its back on you? How else could we get the world's attention?'

'It's not the right kind of attention, Abbas. I wish you could see that.'

Abbas parked the car in front of a hospital. The windows on the south side were covered in plastic.

'The Israelis won't allow us to bring in the materials we need to rebuild. Don't kid yourself. The destruction meted out during Operation Cast Lead was anything but random. The Israelis wanted to make Gaza go back decades.'

Patients arrived in ambulances, taxis and carried in by relatives. Inside, we wove our way through people in various states of injury and illness, and their family members—all vying for attention. Abbas took Yasmine, Khaled and me to the paediatric ward.

Ten beds were squeezed into a room that should have held two. There wasn't a nurse in sight. The boy in the first bed had white bandages where his legs had once been. Bandages covered his arms and the entire left side of his face. All the other boys in the room were amputees as well.

Yasmine paled.

'This is Salih,' Abbas said. 'He's only five. All he did was go outside to get water. He was hit by a missile.'

'What's up, buddy?' Khaled said to the boy.

'Did you bring your book today? I can't wait to find out what happens to Gulliver.'

'Tomorrow, buddy.' Khaled saluted him and we left.

We walked from room to room.

The power went out. The lights turned off and the machines shut down. People just adjusted as if it wasn't a big deal. Abbas took us to the morgue next.

A man showed us baby after baby, the glare of a large battery-powered light picking out face after tiny face. 'They all died of blue-baby syndrome,' Abbas said. 'It's from nitrate poisoning.'

Yasmine's face was as white as my shirt. Where would Abbas take us next?

52

Abbas drove us as close as was safe to the walls that Israel had erected around Gaza.

It was clear from the pattern of destruction that they had methodically razed every building within a quarter of a mile of the border. Whole neighbourhoods were flattened. The further from this dead zone, the more buildings were still standing.

We visited Beach Camp, a warren of concrete huts and open sewers next to a sandy beach. An Israeli navy ship was firing at a fishing boat.

'What's going on?' I asked.

'Israel won't allow anyone to fix our sewage system, so it is spilling out and polluting the ocean. Our fishermen are restricted to the contaminated water in which to fish. Fishing once thrived here, but now we have to buy frozen fish on the black market or risk being blown out of the water.'

No one could escape Gaza.

We went to Jabaliyah, the place where Nora and Justice had planned on going. We drove through it on the way to the hotel. Over 100,000 people were crammed into a quarter of a square mile. Rubble, tents, bullet-riddled walls, dirty barefoot children everywhere. It was what I imagined hell looked like.

Abbas' car started to make a strange noise, but he didn't seem to notice.

'Israel doesn't need to make peace with us as long as the US continues to give its aid to Israel,' Abbas said. He parked the car in front of enormous piles of rubble, opened his glove compartment and showed us pictures of the Israeli settlements in Gaza with their deluxe houses, playgrounds and swimming pools. We had once helped to build homes much like these.

'That's how they lived before they were relocated,' Abbas said. 'US tax dollars helped build those settlements.' Abbas pointed out of the window to the demolished landscape. 'They blew everything up before they left.'

I imagined how many families could have been relocated here from the border areas that the Israelis had decimated. It would have cost them nothing.

Abbas started to drive, his attention on the cratered road. 'I know you'll forget about all this when you go back to your comfortable life in America tomorrow.'

'I'm not leaving tomorrow.' I turned to Khaled. 'Maybe you can come to the hotel and I'll explain my research to you.'

His eyes brightened. 'I'd love to.'

Abbas dropped Yasmine and me off at our palatial hotel. Deflated, we retired to our suite. Surrounded by the luxury we had so recently cherished, we were unable to even speak. Abbas was right: I was selfish. All I cared about was my work. I was buying my nephews convertible Mercedes while other children didn't have food or safe water. I thought sending money to my family was enough, but weren't these children my family too? How had my priorities got so screwed up? I'd made my peace by forgetting about my people. I knew they were suffering and I ignored them.

I stayed up until midnight so that I could call Menachem. It was seven in the morning in Boston. I explained Khaled's situation and he promised he would get Khaled a visa.

53

I met Khaled at the restaurant the next morning. I explained my work to him as we ate a hearty breakfast and watched the waves crash. He soaked up every word I said. He reminded me so much of myself.

'Would you come to study in America if I got you a visa?' I asked.

'Are you kidding?' His eyes sparkled with hope. 'That's my dream.' And then his shoulders sank. 'You'll never be able to get me out.'

'What would you do if I told you I could?' I asked.

'I'd become your slave,' he said enthusiastically.

'What if your father objects?' I didn't want to be negative, but I had to be realistic. 'You know he doesn't want you to leave Gaza.'

'If you can get me a visa . . .' He smiled. 'I can convince my father to allow me to go.'

'We'll continue later,' I said. 'I want to take your nieces and nephews to the zoo. It was highly recommended by the concierge.'

The rental car agency dropped off a van and we went to pick up the children. I was determined to show them a better life.

***

Majid spotted his friend Fadi in front of the zoo and called to him. He was talking to a group of children. When he saw me, he rushed right over.

'You must come and see our beautiful zoo,' he said. 'Since you were so generous to me yesterday morning, I'll let you all in for the low price of ten shekels a ticket. It's truly spectacular. We have two one-of-a-kind zebras. They are Gazan zebras.'

'Zebras aren't indigenous to Gaza,' I said.

Yasmine paid him.

'Please follow me.' Fadi waved his one arm. He stopped at an empty ticket counter, with his back to us, and said in a very serious voice, 'Go in. I'm working right now.' Then he peeked at us over his shoulder. 'But for an extra ten shekels I can show you around.' Majid laughed.

Yasmine handed him the money and Fadi smiled and bowed, gesturing to the turnstile. I watched him pay the ticket vendor from his other pocket and we walked inside.

A grassy field surrounded by a ring of cement and makeshift cages was filled with children. A couple of boys rode on two unusual zebras in the middle. They couldn't stop laughing. I'd never seen anything like it before.

'The two zebras died of starvation during the offensive.' Fadi spoke with authority as if he were the zookeeper himself. Khaled and Yasmine got in line with Abbas' grandchildren. They were giggling and pointing. All they wanted to do was ride the zebras. Fadi and I continued on to the lion's cage. 'Or perhaps an escaped lion ate one.' He gestured to a cage with a lion inside. 'For three weeks it was deadly dangerous for us to come here and feed the animals or help the ones who had been shot or bombed—so all but ten of the animals died.' He gestured grandly to large, empty cages. The nearest one had a damaged sign that read 'Camels'. He continued as we strolled back towards the zebra rides. 'To replace even one zebra would have cost us 100,000 shekels. We'd have to have it smuggled in through the tunnels. If you'd like to buy us two new ones, talk to me. I'm in charge of purchasing.'

'I'll take that under advisement,' I said.

A group of kids had gathered behind Fadi to see what he was doing.

'You know these aren't really zebras,' Fadi whispered to me. 'Don't tell the kids.'

'What are they?' I whispered back.

'I had two of my workers clip off the hair of two white donkeys and paint stripes on them with black hair dye.' He looked proud, as if he really was the brains behind this clever idea.

The fake zebras looked scrawny on their fragile legs, but the children didn't care. I felt like we'd stepped into a different world. Both the kids and the parents seemed so carefree. Kids were running from cage to cage laughing and excited. Others sat on their fathers' shoulders giggling and pointing.

Many of the cages were filled with domestic dogs and cats and the children gathered around them flapping their arms and throwing back their heads in laughter. I was happy to see that life could still be good, even in Gaza.

I'm so happy to see everyone having fun,' I told Khaled as he and the children joined us.

Khaled shook his head. 'You should have seen the burned carcass of the pregnant camel. Her mouth was open in pain. In her back was a foot-wide hole where a missile ripped through her.'

'Well, the zookeepers have done an excellent job restoring the place,' I said.

Yasmine turned, gesturing around her. 'The kids are having a great time.'

As we left the zoo, Khaled asked if we could make a couple of stops on the way home. The van would be very useful in an errand. Outside the zoo, several vendors had set up a neighbourhood market. One of them sold an array of starter plants in peat pots. I recognised most of the produce from the many gardens Yasmine had loved and coaxed into cavalcades of vegetables which we gave to neighbours and colleagues. Khaled pulled a ragged wallet from his backpack.

I put my hand over it. 'Your money is no good here, son. What do you need?'

'Some tomato, courgette, aubergine, cucumber, mint and sage plants, please.'

***

Once we were back in the car I asked for directions and Khaled told me that this is where his errand started. The plants weren't for his family.

We stopped in front of a building on the outskirts of the city. The walls bore gaping cavities in the stucco.

'During the invasion, the soldiers took over this family's house, wrecked their furniture, punched sniper holes in their walls.' Khaled opened the back of the van. 'They left behind bullet casings and stinking waste bags—the troops' portable toilets.'

What a good kid Abbas had raised. Even with all his anger, he must be a good father to have a son so kind. We entered what was left of the home. They had cleaned up the rubble, but left the graffiti. Some was in Hebrew, but much was in English: *Arabs need 2 die*, screamed one wall. *1 down, 999,999 to go* said another, and scrawled on an image of a gravestone were the words *Arabs 1948–2009*.

Five kids lived there alone, it seemed. Khaled and Yasmine placed the plants where the oldest, who seemed to be about twelve or thirteen, showed them, near the front door.

***

The van ride home was quiet. I had planned to invite Abbas' family to dinner at the hotel. I'd hoped to show them there is more to life than suffering, but somehow I just didn't feel like that was completely true at the moment. So I didn't interrupt the silence.

54

That night, Menachem called.

'I can't get him out,' he said. 'I even spoke with the Prime Minister.'

'Why not?' I felt like I had been punched in the stomach.

'His father works for Hamas,' Menachem said. 'Believe me. You'll never be able to get him out.'

***

The next morning Khaled was waiting for me in the restaurant. He was wearing a Boston Red Sox baseball cap and jeans. He could have been any teenager, anywhere, as he took the earplugs from his Walkman out of his ears.

'What are you listening to?' I asked.

'Eminem,' he said. 'I love rap. I hope you don't mind me coming over. I wanted to hear more about your research. I had a dream you were my advisor.'

Yasmine and I sat at the table with him. His eyes were filled with hope. I had to tell him. 'I have very bad news,' I said. 'I couldn't get you the visa. I'm so sorry.'

He deflated before me like a balloon. His eyes filled with tears and they spilled over onto his cheeks.

'Perhaps some time in the future, when things cool down . . .' I didn't believe it myself. He clearly didn't.

Yasmine slid to his side, stroking his hair. My impotence

paralysed me. How could I have filled him with false hope? Who did I think I was? That I was somehow better than my kinsfolk here? That I could magically solve their problems? All I had done so far was cause pain. I had to find a solution.

'Let's brainstorm,' I said. 'Maybe there's a way out. I mean, they sneak food and supplies into Gaza; maybe we could sneak you out.' As soon as the words were out of my mouth, I wished I could suck them back in.

Khaled wiped his eyes and looked up at me. 'You mean through the tunnels?'

'Do they sneak people out through them?' I said.

'My neighbour goes through them every week. He has a curable cancer and there's no chemotherapy in Gaza.'

'Why don't we look into that option?' I said. 'But first we need to speak to your father.'

Khaled shook his head. 'First let's find out if it's feasible and then, if it is, we'll ask him.'

I thought of how I'd waited until after the maths scholarship exam to tell Mama. If I had asked before, she wouldn't have let me go. 'That sounds reasonable,' I said.

'Can we go there now?' he asked. 'To the tunnels?'

Yasmine, Khaled and I got into our rented van and I drove us to Rafah.

***

The stores in Rafah were filled with smuggled goods at exorbitant prices—baby food, medicines, computers, bottles of water. In the storefront windows were pictures of tunnel martyrs clutching spades and drills. It looked very dangerous.

I looked at the prices. 'How do people afford these things?'

'They have no choice.' The storeowner shrugged. 'It's so expensive to smuggle anything in. They have to pay the Egyptians, and then there's the cost of the tunnel.'

'Let's go and see the tunnels ourselves,' Khaled said.

I agreed, but I had already made up my mind. All these dead men—I couldn't allow Khaled to risk his life.

We passed Nijma Square in the centre of Rafah. Tables of TV sets, fans, blenders, refrigerators and other electrical appliances were set up. Moving west towards the border were boxes of cigarettes, giant sacks of potato crisps. We passed the warehouse that sold the tools used to build the tunnels—shovels, rope, electrical cords, pickaxes, hammers, nuts, bolts and screws in all sizes—before we reached the entrances. People were selling wares out of wheelbarrows, calling out to us as we walked by.

Lurking under a complex arrangement of tents and jerry-built shacks along the border between Gaza and Egypt was Gaza's lifeline, a network of tunnels.

A man introduced me to his boss, who showed me the different kinds of tunnels. They varied in size, shape and purpose and were built in varying levels of sophistication. This only confirmed what I had already decided. There was no way I'd risk my nephew's life. We saw fragile ones with dirt shafts and narrow openings, and we saw wide wood-enforced passageways. Although the latter were less likely to collapse, they could still be bombed.

'Why does that entrance descend gradually to the tunnel?' Yasmine pointed.

'It's for livestock,' the tunneller said. 'It's easier on the cows and donkeys. Otherwise they'd have to be hauled out by a generator-operated pulley.'

Khaled laughed. 'I'll dress like a donkey and go through this one! My mother says I'm stubborn as a mule.'

When we didn't joke with him, he knew something was up. I told him that it was too dangerous; that I refused to allow him to try and sneak out through the tunnels. The light in his eyes went out.

'I can't put your life in jeopardy,' I said.

'What life?' he asked. 'I'm already dead.' He looked at my face, searching for some mercy. 'How do you think your life would've turned out had you not been allowed to study?'

I thought back to when I was expelled from the Hebrew

University. I remembered how dead I'd felt inside; how trapped.

'Listen, we can stay longer.' I was trying to sound cheery. 'I can tutor you.'

He walked up to the dreary wall before us where posters of martyrs were hung. He didn't say a word, only pressed his hand up against a picture of a young boy who was smiling and looked full of life. Perhaps a birthday portrait. All of us knew he was dead or his picture wouldn't be there. In a way, it was worse to see him as he was when he was alive. Then, he'd had hope.

'Just take me home.' Khaled turned sharply from the poster. It was startling to see how much he looked like the boy in the picture. 'Why does it matter? Sometimes I wish . . . I wish I was brave like them.'

'Like who?' Yasmine asked.

'The martyrs,' he said. 'The martyrs refuse to allow Israel to make their deaths as meaningless as their lives.'

'There are many peaceful ways to fight,' Yasmine said.

'Your father went to prison for helping a freedom fighter.' Khaled looked directly at me. He turned from the wall and we began to walk away as a group. He looked back and then set his face forward as we walked. 'I'm sure you were proud of him.'

'My father would be the first one to tell you that there are other ways to keep the cause alive,' I said. 'He'd tell you to focus on your studies and forget about politics.'

'I'm a prisoner in my own city. I can't do anything about it. What I need is freedom.'

'The world is always changing and only God knows what will happen,' Yasmine said.

'God doesn't exist,' Khaled grunted. 'The Israelis control our future.'

55

Khaled called the next morning.

'I was wondering if I could bring my family to your hotel for lunch. I wanted to celebrate,' he said. 'I think I found a way out of Gaza. I have an interview this afternoon. I thought it might be good for my family to see that there is still hope—I felt that when I was at the hotel.'

'Of course you can bring them,' I said. 'Nothing would please Yasmine and me more. Who do you have an interview with?'

'I want it to be a surprise,' he said. 'We can celebrate when I'm sure. Do you mind if I come over a little earlier? I wanted to hear more about your research. It might help my interview.'

'Come over now,' I said.

'Oh, and please don't tell my father. I don't want to upset him until it's official. He just thinks I'm going to a wedding.'

'I won't say a word,' I said. I could feel my whole body relax. Yasmine and I had been worried sick about him since we left the tunnels. Finally, something good was happening.

***

Abbas, his wife, Yasmine, Khaled, four of the grandchildren and I gathered around the largest table in the restaurant and watched the waves crash from the window. It was strange to see Abbas and his family in their worn-out clothes eating off china with silverware and crystal water goblets. Only Khaled fitted in.

He had completely transformed himself for the interview. He was dressed in a black suit with a crisp white shirt and tie. His hair was nicely cropped, his light beard gone and his body looked like it had been scrubbed. It truly did appear that a burden had been lifted from his shoulders. I prayed his interview would go well.

We ended the meal with almond cake and Arabic coffee.

'Let me see your cup,' I said to Khaled. I was going to read his future the way Mama always read ours. I looked into the bottom of the cup, but all the signs Mama had taught me showed that his future was black.

'Your future is bright,' I lied.

He smiled and suddenly I felt like there was hope for him. I was a man of science. I didn't believe in superstitions. Khaled looked over at Abbas with love in his eyes.

***

The videotape was dropped off in the middle of the night. Abbas and his wife rushed to our hotel because they didn't have a video player. We hovered around the TV, knowing that it was the worst news we could imagine, yet somehow all hoping without words that it would not be.

An image of Khaled appeared. He had a black and white kaffiyah wrapped around his neck. In one hand he held a machine-gun pointed up and in the other was a script. His hand was shaking.

Yasmine dropped hard into the closest chair, in shock. Mayada began to weep silently.

'I'm doing this not to enter paradise or to be surrounded by virgins. I'm doing this because the Israelis have left me no choice.'

Mayada and Yasmine now cried openly. Yasmine moved to the grieving mother's side, embracing her. They wept together.

'I'm doing this to advance the Palestinian cause. I'm doing this to further our resistance. I'd rather die with hope than live a life of imprisonment. I'd rather die fighting for a just cause than be trapped in hell on earth. This is my only way out. There is no freedom without a struggle. The Israelis must understand: if they imprison us, they will pay a price. I can only control how I die. Israel's crimes against my people are countless. Not only do they oppress us, but they have convinced the world that they are the victims. Israel has one of the strongest militaries in the world—we have a few measly rockets, and yet they've managed to convince the world that they need protection from us. The world not only believes their lies, it also supports them. They have forbidden me from using my mind, so I must use my body, the only weapon left to me.'

The video became fuzzy and I thought we had lost the picture, but in a few seconds it returned.

'To my beloved parents: I apologise for saying goodbye in this manner. I know how much you have suffered and I hope that you will be proud of me.'

He lowered his gun.

'Baba, please give Uncle Ahmed my notebook. It's in the bottom drawer of my dresser under my trousers.

'Until we meet again, I bid you farewell.' The video went dark.

'What have I done?' Abbas buried his face in his hands, sobbing. 'This is all my fault. Did I let him think that I wanted him to be a martyr?'

'Of course not,' I said. 'He knew how much you loved him. No one has any doubt that you would rather take a dagger to your heart than see him hurt.' I hugged Abbas. For the first time in fifty years, he hugged me back. Poor Abbas. He was blaming himself when I knew it was my fault. I had given Khaled hope in his hopelessness and it had made his life unbearable. I was so naïve to have thought that I could help him with my connections.

I had killed my brother's son.

56

When my mobile phone rang, I awoke with a gasp, my heart banging at the walls of my chest. The room was pitch-black except for the clock on my nightstand: 3:32am. I groped for the phone. The receiver slipped out of my hand onto the floor.

Someone else must have died.

Only a week had passed since Khaled's funeral. He had detonated the vest early. They said it was a malfunction, but we knew it was because he hadn't been able to bring himself to take innocent people with him. Of course, he'd still taken some—his whole, innocent family was suffering.

Now, any late-night phone call was reason for alarm.

'Hurry, answer it!' Yasmine's voice had an edge of panic. Neither of us had had a decent night's sleep since Khaled's death.

I grabbed the phone. Abbas was dead, I was sure. His death would break Mama's heart.

'Yes,' I said, a bit too loud. 'What is it?'

Yasmine turned on her lamp. She was sitting up, bug-eyed, a mirror of my fears.

'Is this Professor Ahmed Hamid?' a man asked in a polite voice. His accent was unfamiliar.

'Yes,' I said, fear in my voice. 'Who is this?'

'This is Alfred Edlund.'

My heart dropped. I knew his name from somewhere. Was he a friend of my son Mahmud's from Yale? This couldn't be good, not at this hour.

'Who is it?' Yasmine asked.

'Is Mahmud all right?' I held my breath.

Yasmine gasped and rocked back and forth.

'I don't understand,' the man said.

'This isn't about my son?'

'No. I'm the Secretary General of the Royal Swedish Academy of Sciences.'

I looked over at Yasmine and held up my hand. 'No one's hurt,' I whispered.

'Professor Hamid, are you there?'

'How did you find me?'

'Professor Sharon gave me your number.'

I sat up straight as the importance of this call sank in.

'I'm calling on behalf of the Royal Swedish Academy of Sciences.'

Menachem and I had been nominated for the Nobel Prize each of the last ten years. But who would call at this hour?

'I'd like to inform you—' He paused. '—on behalf of the Royal Swedish Academy, we're pleased to announce that you and Professor Sharon will be this year's recipients of the Nobel Prize in Physics.'

I had no words.

'Your teamwork in discovering how to measure the magnetic anisotropy in individual atoms was an extraordinary breakthrough. It led to the discovery of new kinds of structures and devices that will play a major role in the development of the new generation of electronics, computers and satellites.'

'Thank you,' I said. 'I'd be honoured, of course.' I could hear the flatness in my voice.

‘What’s going on?’ Yasmine gripped my arm. ‘Who are you talking to?’

‘We’ll present you with the Nobel Prize in Sweden at the Stockholm Concert Hall on December the 10th.’

‘I’m in Gaza right now,’ I said. ‘I’m quite honoured, but I won’t be able to attend.’ I couldn’t leave Gaza, not so soon after Khaled’s death.

‘Since we aren’t awarding the prizes until December, we can communicate about your options before then.’

‘What kind of call is this?’ Yasmine pulled on my arm. ‘Who is that?’

‘I’ve examined your lifetime’s research and I’m very impressed. You’ve greatly contributed to the advancement of the human race.’

‘Ahmed, tell me!’ Yasmine said. ‘I must know.’

I hung up.

‘I won a Nobel Prize.’ My voice lacked enthusiasm.

The sound of the phone ringing again startled me.

‘What’s going on? Who’s calling now?’ said Yasmine.

‘It’s about the prize,’ I said. The phone, I knew, would not stop ringing until I answered. I grabbed the receiver.

‘I still remember the day you told me you had a better way. And to think I almost ignored you.’ Menachem’s voice choked.

We had worked so hard for this. I didn’t want my personal pain to bring him down. He had been calling every day to check on me.

‘To think how much I used to hate—’

‘Do you have any regrets?’

‘Only that I didn’t see the truth from the start.’

As soon as I’d put the receiver down, the phone rang again.

‘Hello. Is Professor Hamid there?’ a man with a Spanish accent asked.

‘This is he,’ I said.

'This is Jorge Deleon calling from *El Mundo* newspaper in Madrid, Spain.'

'It's not even four in the morning.'

'I'm sorry, Professor Hamid. We have deadlines.'

The rest of the morning I fielded calls from European and Middle Eastern reporters.

I video-conferenced my family in the Triangle with equipment that had been smuggled in through the tunnels. Since I was twelve years old, I'd waited for the day that I would tell my father I had made something of my life. Now I had won the most prestigious award in the world. My voice carried over the network and was delivered through my family's speakers. Mama appeared in the window on my monitor.

'Get Baba,' I instructed her.

'What's wrong?' she asked. 'Is it bad news?'

'No—the opposite, Mama. Good news; the best.'

'Tell me now. I can't wait.'

'Please.'

Mama walked out of their kitchen and returned with Baba.

'I have an announcement.' I forced a smile.

Mama's hand was on her heart. Baba waited patiently.

'I just received word from Sweden. I've won the Nobel Prize in Physics this year jointly with Menachem.'

My parents were silent. They looked at each other and shrugged their shoulders.

'What's a Nobel Prize?' Baba finally asked.

'The Nobel Prize is awarded to those who have conferred the greatest benefit to humankind and have made the most important discoveries or inventions within the field of physics.' Normally I wouldn't have bragged about my award the way I was doing, but I wanted to make sure Baba understood that I had made something out of my life.

Baba looked at Mama. 'Ahmed has won a prize.' Then they both shrugged, as if I couldn't see them.

'There was this Swedish chemist in the late eighteen hundreds who invented dynamite,' I said. 'He was concerned over the ways in which science could impact humanity.'

'Did he know that they used dynamite to blow up our house?' Mama said. 'Is that the kind of impact he meant?'

How could I explain to Baba that I had managed to fulfil the promise I made to him all those years ago? I tried to further explain the award. 'He used his fortune to institute the Nobel Prizes. Since 1901, every year a committee selects the men and women who have realised the most outstanding achievements of various fields, physics being one of them. It's the most prestigious accolade that any physicist can receive.'

Baba smiled. Mama seemed unimpressed.

'I forgot to tell you, our horse is pregnant,' Mama said.

My mobile phones were ringing.

'You know what; wait until you watch it on video. Then you'll understand better. I'll be making a speech.'

57

'Thank you all for coming here today,' the presenter said. 'The Royal Swedish Academy is proud to award this year's Nobel Prize in Physics to Professor Menachem Sharon and Professor Ahmed Hamid for research they began over forty years ago.

'In the past, data storage was limited by size. Until we could determine the magnetic anisotropy of an individual atom, technology could get no smaller. Magnetic anisotropy is significant because it determines the ability of an atom to store information. Professor Sharon and Professor Hamid figured out how to compute the magnetic anisotropy of a single atom.

'In addition to enhanced storage capabilities and improved computer chips, their discovery could improve sensors, satellites and much more. They've opened the door for new kinds of structures and devices to be built from individual atoms. The atomic storage they developed for the individual atom allows us to store 50,000 full-length movies, or more than 1,000 trillion bits of data, in a device the size of an iPod.

'Professor Menachem Sharon and Professor Ahmed Hamid started with an idea whose applications were unknown at the time. It required vision and strength to take a leap of faith. It is my distinct honour to extend congratulations on behalf of the entire Academy to Professor Menachem Sharon and Professor

Ahmed Hamid. Through their joint efforts, they have made history.'

The applause was thunderous. A hush fell over the room as the packed crowd of the brightest minds in the world turned their attention to Menachem and me. Dressed in identical white ties and black tails, we walked onto the stage in perfect sync, each of our steps rehearsed the previous day. We stopped in front of His Majesty, the King of Sweden, and the rest of the royal family. Menachem stepped forward first. He extended his hand and His Majesty shook it and bestowed upon him a medal and a diploma. He stepped back and I stepped forward to receive my award.

The Royal Stockholm Philharmonic was playing as Menachem and I walked to the podium in the middle of the ornate hall. Menachem leaned forward and began to speak into the microphone.

'The greatest impetus for our work came from Professor Hamid. I first noticed his genius when he was my student in 1966. I'm embarrassed to say that, initially, I viewed his brilliance as a threat. And only by almost losing it all, was I forced to give him a chance. I remember the day he came to my office, a boy in rags wearing sandals made from rubber tyres. He told me he had a better way. I rejected him, but not for the merit of his idea: I couldn't imagine this Palestinian boy could offer me anything. He proved me wrong. He gave me the chance of a lifetime. It took us forty years, but Professor Hamid and I were able to accomplish more than we ever dreamed of by working together. He is also my closest friend. I hope we can be a lesson for Israel, the Palestinians, the US and the rest of the world.'

Menachem was crying. I, too, felt tears well up in my eyes.

Next, it was my turn. I stepped up to the microphone and began. 'First and foremost, I'd like to thank my father, who did more for me than anyone.' I looked out at the packed theatre and the many video cameras. 'He taught me what it means to make sacrifices. I am who I am because of him. I'd like to thank my mother, who raised me to persevere, and my first teacher, Teacher Mohammad, for believing in me. I'd like to thank Professor Sharon, my dear friend and colleague, for judging me on my ability and not my race or religion, for having the genius to see what others couldn't, and for introducing me to Professor Smart. I want to thank my family for bearing with me whilst I spent time learning, and my wife and sons for showing me what love is.' I paused. 'I tell my children, go with what you're passionate about. My childhood taught me that steady drops pierce rocks. I've learned that life isn't about what happens to you, but about how you choose to react to it. Education was my way out; and because of it I was able to rise above my circumstances. But now I realise that, in doing so, I left a lot of people behind. I have come to understand that when one person suffers, we all suffer. I've devoted my life until now to my family, my education and my research; tonight I hope to educate you about what is happening in Gaza, where I was when I received the call notifying me of this great honour.

'Education is the fundamental right of every child. Gaza, as it is now, is a breeding ground for future terrorists. Their hopes and dreams have been crushed. Education, the way out for the downtrodden, has been made virtually impossible. The Israelis who guard the borders have forbidden hundreds of children who have earned scholarships in the West to leave Gaza and attend those universities. They don't let school supplies, books, or building materials in. If I had lived there, I could not have accomplished what I did. We cannot permit this scholasticide to continue. No one can be at peace while others wallow in poverty and inequality. Where I once dreamed of manipulating atoms, I now dream of a world in which we rise above race and religion and all the other dividing factors and find a higher purpose. Like Martin Luther King Jr before me, I have the audacity to dream of peace.'

The audience rose to their feet and applauded. I held up a photograph of Khaled; cameras zoomed in for a close-up. 'I'd like to dedicate this award to my nephew Khaled, who chose death over a life devoid of dreams or hope. We have formed a foundation in his name that will provide school supplies, books and opportunities. Professors from MIT, Harvard, Yale and Columbia have signed on as partners to press Israel to allow deserving students to take their rightful places in schools around the globe and make their contribution, much as I have made mine. I urge you all to join us.'

Menachem stepped forward and stood shoulder to shoulder with me. He spoke into the microphone. 'I would like to pledge my half of the prize money, $500,000, to The Khaled Hamid Science Scholarship Fund for Palestinians.

'Cooperation between Palestinians and Israelis offers the only real hope for peace,' Menachem continued. 'History has proven that one people can't achieve security at the expense of another. A secular democratic state across all of historic Palestine, with equal rights for all citizens regardless of their religious beliefs, is the only way there will be real peace. One person, one vote. We need to stop fighting and start building.'

The thunder of the cheering crowd drowned out my response, but our embrace said it all.

58

Back at the village, I put my Nobel Prize medallion on the bookshelf in my parents' living room and looked out of the new window my parents had installed for a view of my favourite spot in all the world: the almond tree. She wasn't supposed to bloom for another month, and yet there she was in full blossom. Amal and Sa'dah, who had stood behind her to witness our suffering and protect us from hunger and the elements, remained strong and proud.

I was there to pick up my whole family for a trip to Gaza to visit Abbas.

Khaled's death had changed Abbas.

When I'd told him about my idea for the foundation, he'd cried. He told me he hoped one day his grandchildren could study in the United States. Now, he was being reunited with his family. We were starting to heal, together. It was still impossible to get any of them out, but not impossible to get us in for a week using my new-found notoriety and political clout. It was my parents' final dream in this life, and I would make it come true.

I went outside and sat on the bench next to the almond tree. It was a miracle, really, that this tree still stood. I remembered finding shelter in its branches when I was twelve years old, a boy full of dreams, completely innocent of what was to come. I thought of Nora, my beautiful wife, my Jewish angel with golden hair, and how I'd kissed her beneath these branches where she was now buried.

Through the kitchen window, I could see my sons, Mahmud and Amir, their wives and my grandchildren, sitting at the table with my parents, Yasmine, Fadi, Nadia and Hani. I could hear the deep voices of my sons, and the soft laughter of Yasmine, who, as my parents had anticipated, I had grown to love deeply.

'I'm ready,' I told Nora. I remembered the promise I'd made her; one that, at last, I was ready to fulfil.

I'd tell my story to the world.